# KEANE'S COMPANY

# KEANE'S COMPANY

## IAIN GALE

HERON
BOOKS

First published in Great Britain in 2013 by Heron Books
An imprint of Quercus

55 Baker Street
7th Floor, South Block
London W1U 8EW

A CIP catalogue record for this book is available
from the British Library

HB ISBN 978 1 78087 362 6
TPB ISBN 978 1 78206 091 8
EBOOK ISBN 978 1 78087 363 3

This book is a work of fiction. Names, characters,
places and events portrayed in it, while at times based on
historical figures and places, are the product
of the author's imagination.

10 9 8 7 6 5 4 3 2 1

Printed and bound in Great Britain by Clays Ltd, St Ives plc

Typeset by Ellipsis Digital Limited, Glasgow

For Anne and Harry Martin, Keane's compatriots

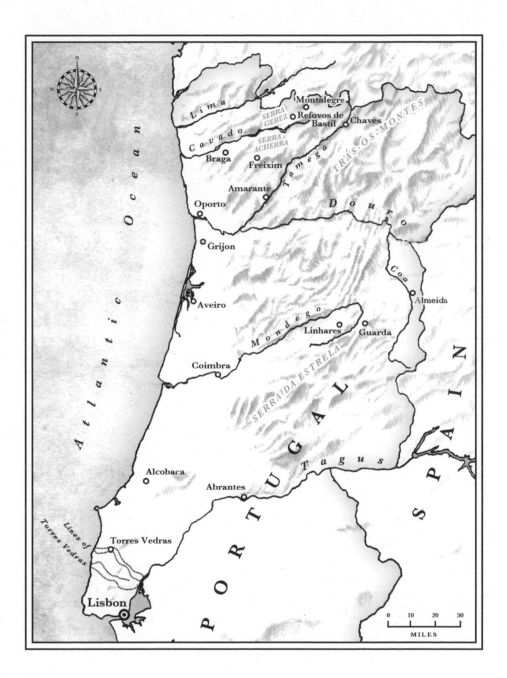

# PROLOGUE

Morning, and as he took a short step forward with his right foot on the dew-sodden grass, James Keane's sword caught the early sunlight and gleamed bright and sudden in the dawn. Moving just his right forefinger and his thumb, Keane made the tip of his blade trace a tiny circle in the air around the heart of the man who stood six yards opposite him. The man he had vowed to kill.

They were ready now, but neither man was inclined to make the first move and the razor-sharp edge of Keane's sword cut the air with a hiss as he took it away from the target and cut down to the left, suggesting a move he might make. As he did so he stared into his opponent's eyes and smiled. Keane came back en garde and stood, rocking gently on the balls of his feet. Then the referee called to them and at once both men moved towards each other until their blades were close enough to touch.

Keane shivered in his shirtsleeves, knowing that the very slightest movement of the wrist would make the blade move in a sweeping circle and, if he were not careful, open up his guard to a sudden riposte by his opponent.

He caught the other man's eyes again. Just for an instant. And realized almost too late what was about to happen. The other man, whose name was Simpson, lunged, and Keane, just managing to anticipate him, drew back a fraction to avoid the blade but at the same time extended his own arm so that it flicked up and caught the man on the face, cutting his cheek. The man yelled and stepped back and Keane smiled.

Somewhere he heard the referee speaking: 'A hit to Mister Keane.'

Keane, fired up now, stepped forward again and by instinct attacked around his opponent's blade. He knew that Simpson must be hurting now, fighting through the pain, and that he must act fast to capitalize. His blade turned the other and like a flash he was in, the point scoring a hit against the man's chest. Not deep enough to kill but hard enough to wound.

Again Simpson shrieked and stepped back and Keane recovered. He looked to his left for an instant. Saw his second, Tom Morris, smile at him and realized his mistake as Simpson double-stepped towards him and pushed his blade aside to cut through his shirt and into his chest, cutting open his left breast. Keane sprang back, conscious of the blood now flowing onto his white shirt. Damn, that was not the way he had planned it. He brought his sword up again to the en garde, confusing his opponent and hiding the pain. Both men were tiring now, but Keane had seen the weakness in his enemy. The slightly dropped right shoulder, the trailing blade.

He made ready to strike, but as he did so his mind filled with what had brought him here. An argument over a card game. Idiotic, really. Nothing to speak of.

But he did not regret it. Simpson had been a foolish oaf and to question his honour for a card game was a foolish way to lose one's life. Of course Keane cheated. Well, didn't everyone? But the fact was, this time he had not cheated. That was the point. Wasn't it?

He brought up his sword and again turned it through the air as if to strike to the right, and then, as Simpson brought his own blade across to parry left, Keane aimed for his arm. A flesh wound would suffice now. And then he would offer quarter and the man would accept and honour would be satisfied.

But as he did so Simpson came forward at a rush and before he could stop, the man was hard upon him. But more than that, he had run onto Keane's blade. Keane felt the cold honed steel sink deep into flesh then grate against bone and then through deeper elements, and he knew that it was done.

He stepped back, pulling his blade as he went, and watched as Simpson's body slumped to the ground.

Then Morris was at his shoulder.

'James. James. Quick. We must get away from here. Come. Now.'

And so, in what seemed an eternity, they turned and left as fast as they could go, slipping on the wet grass and making for the light though the clearing, towards the horses and away from the two men crouching over the body of the man who had been Lieutenant Greville Simpson.

# 1

At a thousand yards the figure of a single soldier appears as no more than a dot shimmering on the horizon; a regiment of men as a solid block of black. As they draw closer, though, it is possible to make out the detail. At six hundred yards you begin to see the individuals who make up the column bearing down on you. By four hundred yards arms become visible, and upright muskets tucked hard against shoulders. But on this fine May morning it was not until they were at two hundred yards that the sun caught the bayonets of the French. Standing in his position in the valley below a small Portuguese town, Keane knew to wait. And wait.

Keane looked at the advancing Frenchmen. A hundred yards. He could see their shakos now with the brass eagle plates and the tall, bobbing yellow plumes of the voltigeurs above blue uniforms and the white cross-belts. And behind them the mass of the column. Drums beating, colours flying, beneath a bronze eagle. He could hear their shouts too, half drowned by the insistent patter of the drums. He spoke again. Calmly, precisely. 'Take aim.'

One more look as they drew closer. Seventy-five yards. Until he was able, he fancied, to smell the bastards' garlic breath and look into their eyes before they died. Then, 'Fire.'

Eighty muzzles flashed into life, fizzing and cracking as hammer fell on flint and flame and smoke spouted from eighty barrels. Keane looked on and watched as the French were hurled back, men falling and jumping, plucked by the musket balls to dance like marionettes. He saw their second rank walk over the bodies of the first, trampling the fallen, dying voltigeurs as they dragged themselves through the dry grass, now stained red.

The commands were given again but they were not needed. Keane's men knew what to do now. This was their time. The wad was bitten, the ball spat down the barrel and rammed home. Then the carbines were at the shoulders again, and again they cracked out and through the clouds of white smoke that filled the field and choked the throat. He watched more Frenchmen fall, and as he looked on the column stopped. He had known it would. Ten years of war had taught him to expect nothing less of the British soldier. The French were changing now, moving from column into line, desperate to loose off a volley. But it was too late. Keane's men were already loaded. The third volley in less than a minute crashed out and the French officers died where they stood, even as they shouted at their men. And then it was over. Keane saw a colonel topple from his horse and then the bastards were turning. Another volley hit them as they went, and the eagle fell, to be gathered by a fresh pair of hands and hurried to safety in the rear. Keane's men gave a cheer. One of them, wiping the gunpowder from his mouth, turned to him, smiling. 'They're running, sir.'

'That they are, Thomas, but they'll come again before the day's out. Won't they, sarn't?'

'They will, sir, If I know they Frenchies. They'll be back just as soon as they can.'

Keane smiled. 'And we'll see them off again, shan't we, lads?'

Another cheer, and then a cough from behind him. Keane turned to see the figure of a senior officer, wearing the navy-blue frock coat favoured by many of the staff. He recognized him at once as Major Grant, of the 11th, a man already renowned for his bravery throughout the army, and wondered what business he could have here, in the firing line.

'Lieutenant Keane?'

'Sir?'

'You are relieved of your command. Forthwith.'

Keane looked at him and his heart sank. This was it, then. All that he had been dreading.

'Sir?'

'You're to come with me, Keane, at once. To the commanding general.'

'To General Hill, sir?"

'No, Keane, to General Wellesley. He commands now.'

Keane despaired. It was worse than he had thought. He had imagined that General Hill might have got to know that he had taken part in a duel, particularly as it had resulted in the death of his adversary, a brother officer. He did not regret it. Simpson had been a foolish oaf and it had been a stupid way to lose his life. Keane might have been cheating. Well, didn't everyone sometime? It was just unfortunate that Simpson had moved when he did. Keane had been aiming for his arm but the devil had moved. He wondered what had gone through the man's mind. Had wondered since it had happened. Whatever the cause, Simpson was dead, and he, it would seem, was in trouble.

He did wonder, though, how the devil Wellesley, newly arrived in Portugal, had come to learn of the matter with such speed, and why had he taken the trouble to take Keane out of the fight in such a manner for such a matter. And to send a staff officer to do it. He could only suppose that he must be used as some sort of example. As a warning from the new commander that, whatever General Craddock and General Hill might tolerate, he would not put up with such behaviour in his army.

Keane cursed himself for his stupidity. To have been called out in a duel and to accept had been expressly against the general's orders. And what was more, the offence that had provoked the duel – to be found cheating at cards – was almost as bad. Well, to have been accused of it. The conduct of officers was expected to be seen to be exemplary. Even if that were not always the case. Perhaps there was still a chance.

He thought fast. 'But sir. We are engaged with the enemy.'

'No, lieutenant, as a matter of fact, you are not. You have just seen them off. Very creditably, as it happens. But that is of no matter. The French are merely bidding us a good morning. They have sallied out from their lines to see what we are about and have been given a sound hiding. Your sergeant is quite able to see them off should they come again. Which they won't.'

He smiled at the sergeant who nodded, stony-faced, wondering what was going on, and why his officer had been ordered out of the line.

Keane too turned to his sergeant. 'Don't worry, Sarn't McIlroy. I'll be back soon. Captain Hannan is in command. Take orders from him until I return.'

He turned to catch up with Grant, who, although already a

few paces off, had overheard his comment. 'I'm afraid, Keane, your return may not be for some time. If ever.'

If ever? Keane blanched.

'Sir, may I enquire as to why I am being summoned by the general?'

'No, Keane, you may not. You will find out soon enough. Now where's your mount?'

In the saddle, cantering along the route that would take them back to the headquarters at Coimbra, Keane had more time to think.

All along the allied line the French were pulling back. It had not been a big attack. A brigade at most, sent far in advance against their own to the south of the coastal town of Aveiro. Grant was right. The French were simply trying their strength. Toying with them and seeing that theirs was not an attack in force, they would run back to their lines and let the British do the same. It had been a mistake, Keane knew, for Hill to have pushed forward before Wellesley's arrival, and what was more it had been, he thought – for all the fact that they had won the day – another example of wasted effort and wasted lives. He hoped that the new general would not make the same mistakes.

And he knew too, to his bitter satisfaction, that whatever his own fate he would not be the only officer to be disciplined that day. Hill had overstepped the mark.

Wellesley had a reputation for caution. The advance into Spain which would surely come would be made slowly and with care. But now it seemed that Keane was destined to take no part in it. He cursed again and dug his boots into the flanks of his horse.

They rode fast and in silence towards the rear of the brigade lines. And all the time Keane felt more apprehensive of what his fate might be.

He had arrived in Lisbon with the battalion in March, a full month ahead of Wellesley, and a high time they had had since then. The city's jails, it was said, had never been so full, and other buildings had been requisitioned. Sir Arthur Wellesley must surely have wondered at the state of his command. Some, like Keane, had shipped out fresh from home, but other battalions and squadrons had been there since before poor Sir John Moore's fighting retreat to Corunna last year. You could tell them apart from the new arrivals. Thinner, with their scarlet coats turned to a dirty brick red and their shoes in scraps, they were more inclined to question authority and more often disinclined to obey it.

It was a long ride back to Coimbra, made all the longer by Keane's trepidation. They stopped after twenty-five miles beside a stream, Grant allowing his horse some water. Keane wondered if now the colonel might give him some inkling as to the truth of his situation, but no sooner had he begun to speak than Grant pre-empted him. 'Mount up. We must make good time to be there by sunset.'

And so it was as the sun was sinking that at last the town came into view, its great citadel with the Bishop's palace and the churches rising high above the river Mondego. Almost Wellesley's first action had been to move the army here. After having divided into three divisional columns, he had marched out of Lisbon and made camp below the town, on the route that must take them from the capital to Soult's stronghold at Oporto.

As they rode up, the lines came quickly into view. The few proper tents, brought by fortunate officers, stood out amongst the crudely improvised shelters of the men. It was as if a town had sprung up overnight, thronged with thousands of men in coats of scarlet, blue and green and all their hangers-on, who now, even as the muskets blazed, went about their business in the dimming light, moving among the campfires with the focused and mindless purpose of a colony of ants.

The moon shone down from a cloudless sky and the evening was filled with the scent of citrus flowers and lavender, and other, baser smells: woodsmoke, sweat and gunpowder.

Keane brought down his hand heavily against his thigh, swatting a large black fly that had landed on his white breeches, then regretted it, for it had left a bloodstain and the talk in the mess was all that the army commander liked his officers well turned out. Ordinarily it would have worried Keane, but now he was acutely aware of the far greater mess he was in.

It was hard to believe that barely thirty days ago he had been in Cork, waiting to board the ship that would bring him here with 20,000 other men of the army and all their horses and followers.

Since their short halt on the journey Grant had said nothing, had not so much as reined in his horse. Now, as they dismounted and tied up, he was still silent. Keane knew that it was too late now to ask: all too soon he would discover his fate. As they walked up the final slope of the hill where Wellesley had made his temporary headquarters, Keane wondered what the general would be like. He had not been in Spain the previous year for the debacle that had resulted in Wellesley's being summoned home in disgrace for allowing the French army to escape. But then the general had won a famous victory at Vimiero and had been cleared by the official enquiry, and now he was back and in command of the army. It was strange, he thought, how such disaster could quickly be followed by triumph. But then, that was war for you. The slightest chance could make a hero of any blackguard and the slightest piece of bad luck reduce the finest of men to a ruined, bloody corpse. And Keane knew that, this time, for once fate had dealt him the poorer hand and it was his turn to suffer.

Wellesley, as was his custom, while having commandeered the Bishop's palace as his own, had also made a field head-quarters beneath the shade of a tree on a rise in the ground that afforded him a good view of the surrounding country. Around its base he had posted a mounted troop from the Blues, and it was to one of their officers that Grant touched his hat as they reached the foot of the small hill. The general was standing with a group of three or four officers around him at a table in the shade of the tree, with a map of the region spread out before him.

Grant approached him. 'Lieutenant Keane, sir.'

Wellesley said nothing but motioned to one of his staff and whispered something. Grant coughed, quietly. The General did not look up, but nodded sagely and slowly traced a line with his forefinger down the map.

They waited and watched as Wellesley scribbled his signature at the bottom of a sheet of parchment in his notebook, then tore it away and handed it to an aide. Only then did he look up, and when he did so it was straight into Keane's eyes.

Keane had never met Wellesley before. Yet here at once he knew the nature of the man. The thin beak of a nose, the tight lips set in a lean jaw, and above all, the eyes.

'Lieutenant Keane, is it?'

'Sir.'

'This is a bad business, Keane. Rotten bad.'

'Yes, sir.'

'What do you suppose that I should do with you?'

'I don't rightly know, sir. Not my place to say, sir. I suppose that I shall be cashiered – at best.'

Wellesley said nothing, but looked down at another piece of paper on his desk. 'You're from Ireland.' He paused, thoughtful for a moment. 'The Inniskillens. Ten years' service. Egypt, Alexandria, Malta, Maida.' He looked up, frowning, 'Quite a career to date, Keane. Yet you remain a lieutenant?'

'Yes, sir. I'm afraid so.'

'And now this. Accused of cheating in the mess and called out by a brother officer and then to have killed him. You know that I have forbidden all duelling.'

'Yes, sir.'

'And that gambling is a vice on which I frown. And moreover to be found a cheat. It's too bad. There's nothing else for it. What do you say, Grant?'

'Yes, sir. I agree. All in all, I'm quite convinced that Lieutenant Keane is the right man for the job, sir.'

Wellesley shook his head. 'God forgive me, but I've been persuaded by Major Grant to give you a reprieve. Against all my better judgement, I'm gazetting you captain. Effective as of now. On my staff.'

Keane was dumbfounded for a moment. Then he found his voice. 'Thank you, sir. What can I say?'

'Say nothing. As far as I can see you are a consummate rogue. Do not implicate yourself further or I may change my mind. Say nothing until you hear the real reason that I've called you here. I'm looking for someone with particular skills, Keane, and Major Grant here seems to be of the opinion that you might be the man.'

Keane said nothing but wondered what Grant might have seen in him. The general continued. 'How well do you ride?'

'Tolerably well, sir. I hunted at home.'

'Good. That's something. And you speak French.'

'I attended the Lycée in Paris as a boy. My mother's sister was resident there for a while and it was felt that I might benefit—'

'Any Spanish?'

'A little, sir. Yes, enough to get by.'

Wellesley nodded. 'And Grant tells me that you're considered something of an artist in the mess. Is he right?'

Keane smiled. 'He is kind, sir. I like to think that I can capture a likeness. Nothing more.'

'Can you capture the likeness of a place?'

Keane nodded, 'Yes, sir. I do draw landscapes. And any buildings that take my fancy. In fact I've just completed a drawing of—'

Wellesley smiled to silence him. 'Fine, that'll do. You are a good shot?'

'Since my youth, sir. I shot partridge at home on the farm.'

'And Frenchmen these last ten years. And you're fit? I can see by the look of you that there's little flesh on you.'

It was true, thought Keane, he was in good condition. He had never been unfit and ten years' soldiering had ensured that his body was nothing more than muscle, sinew and bone.

'I was brought up in Ireland by my mother, sir. My father being dead, I had to do his work on our farm. And that of others.'

Wellesley stared at him. 'And my sources tell me that you have a way with words too, Keane. That you are able to talk your way out of any situation.'

'I do hope so, sir.' He paused. 'Not this one, though.'

'No, not this one. No amount of lie and bluff will help you now. Were you cheating at cards, Keane?'

'On my honour, no, sir. Lieutenant Simpson was mistaken. It was he who slighted me and on my being challenged, sir, I had no alternative but to accept.'

'You are aware that Lieutenant Blackwood stands by the word of Lieutenant Simpson, who is, of course, no longer able to speak in his own defence.'

'I protest at Lieutenant Blackwood, sir. It was I who was insulted.'

'That was not what I asked you. Nor did I ask you to implicate Lieutenant Blackwood, whose father I have known since we were boys. I asked whether or not you were a cheat. But as it is universally accepted that you are a liar, then I imagine we shall never know the truth. You are a convincing liar, though, Keane. That much I can see to be true.'

He looked at Grant.

'It seems, Colquhoun, that you may indeed have been right.' He turned back. 'Welcome to the staff, Captain Keane.'

Keane smiled and bowed. 'Thank you, sir.'

'And now I am dismissing you from it.'

'Sir?'

'You heard me aright. From now on, Keane, you will be my eyes and ears. You will report to me or to Major Grant here, directly. You will also take orders when appropriate from Captain Scovell.'

As if on cue, like an actor in the wings another officer, who had been standing silently behind Wellesley, made his way forward and smiled at Keane. He was younger than Grant and less weather-beaten.

Wellesley went on, 'Captain Scovell here will be in command of several units similar to your own, yet not all of them, it would seem, will be possessed of your particular capabilities or qualifications.' He smiled at Grant and then looked back to Keane. 'We face an enemy of whom we must have the measure, or we shall fail. Marshal Soult is at Oporto with some twenty thousand men. Marshal Ney is in Galicia and Marshal Victor at Merida with yet more again.

'I need to know everything. Everything, Keane. I want you to get yourself behind the French lines and find out anything you can. Draw pictures of any fortifications, or indeed any buildings which might be of use to us. I want their plans, their troop numbers, ammunition stocks, morale. What the commander had for breakfast. And I don't care how you do it. And if in the course of your work you have any opportunity to disrupt their operations and delay or forestall them, then do it. Oh, and you shan't be going alone. You'll have a platoon. A troop, if you will. A company, perhaps. You are at liberty to choose who you will from the ordinary soldiers of the army.'

'From all regiments, sir?'

'All regiments and all arms, Keane. Infantry, cavalry, artillery. The choice is yours. But if you want my advice, don't look too high. Cutthroats, murderers, thieves: take your pick, the army's full of rogues. I dare say you'll understand them all very well. One in fifty of our brave fellows comes to the colours to escape the law. Major Grant? I'm finished with Captain Keane. Good day and good luck, captain.'

Keane gave a bow and, turning, walked away, feeling both elated and terrified. 'Captain Keane.' Grant was hard behind him. 'A word, Keane.'

'Sir?'

'This is a rum do. But the general has it in his head, so it can't be helped. If you want my opinion you've less chance than a man on the gallows. But get the right men behind you and you've more likelihood of not being killed quite so soon. You'd best start with the Lisbon jails. And you'll need to choose carefully.' He laughed.

'You'll need men with a variety of skills. A picklock would be useful to you, and a thief who can climb. At least one of them would have to be fluent in Spanish and another in French. They might need to look swarthy to pass for either. You might need a forger, and they'll all need to ride. We'll supply your mounts, and do try not to wear out the poor beasts, or lose them. Even though they're sure to be useless nags, all of them. We do not have a limitless purse for your activities, vital as they are.'

'You mean that I should recruit from the jails, sir?'

'I'm in deadly earnest. We've three of them full in Lisbon already and others filling up. Damned smart work by the provosts. Though I dare say they had their hands full. Filthy place. All drink and bad women. You won't be lacking in material. Take your officer though from where you will. You'll need an officer with you, Keane. To keep you sane.'

'What uniform do we wear, sir?'

'Well, only you can decide on that. If you want to avoid detection, of course, you should perhaps not wear any. But remember that if that is the case and you are caught you will be shot or hanged on the spot for a spy. I would advise that you keep some article of uniform somewhere about you for that purpose. You and all your men. I prefer to travel in full uniform, myself.'

'You go behind the lines, sir?'

This was something new to Keane. Scouting patrols he was aware of, and the fact that some officers had been selected to gather information on the enemy. A job that few would have wished for. But an officer attached to the staff riding into enemy territory to gather information? He had never heard the like.

'Frequently. It's most exhilarating. I know you'll rise to it, Keane. Best life in the world for a soldier. Whatever anyone may say. And now you had better go and find your colonel and tell him your good news. I dare say he'll be upset at losing you, Keane. You may direct him to me should he need to be convinced. See you in Spain, my boy. And you had better find yourself a billet for the night. You've a long journey ahead of you back to Lisbon. I would suggest you put into a mess. Try the artillery.'

Leaving Grant behind, Keane walked slowly back through the lines in search of a billet.

His head was still reeling from all that had happened. He had gone to the general expecting to be drummed out of the army and had been rewarded instead with sudden promotion. And then this. He was not sure what to make of it. Certainly it was better than being cashiered and disgraced or court-martialled for murder. And it was promotion, but to what must surely be one of the most detested jobs in the army. He supposed that he ought to be thankful for it, but he knew in his heart that his job was to remain in the firing line with his men. But it was, as Wellesley had said, a position that might have been made for him.

Keane knew that he could lie. And lie damn well. He'd become good at it while still a boy. In Ireland, when circumstances had reduced his family to penury and he had been forced to steal his neighbours' sheep to make ends meet. In truth his letter of commission – a complete surprise – had come, he thought, in the nick of time. It had been paid for by an anonymous friend of whose identity he remained unaware, and although his mother had begged him not to take it, not wanting to lose her son, Keane could not help but go. And so in the autumn of '98 he had become a soldier.

He had spent the last ten years as a company officer, learning to drill men in line and column. Teaching them to stand as he did and take the shot and the musket volleys before they loosed their own and sent the French to hell. Ten years of it. He thought back on the men he had known and lost. On the wounds and the times he had cheated death.

Well, he would do Wellesley's dirty work, and do it well. Providence had rewarded him in kind and now he knew he must make the most of this chance he had been given. And he knew too that, when the opportunity arose to rejoin his battalion, he would be sure to take it. The true glory of any war lay on the battlefield and Keane had made a promise to himself that if any glory and honour were to come out of this war, then he would surely have his share. That and whatever worldly riches he could take by any means. He was no common thief. But if any chance of booty presented itself, then Keane knew that he would take it. And one day, when all this was finished, he would return to County Down a rich man and damn those who had cursed him for a wastrel.

And he would keep his uniform, as Grant had advised, with its canary-yellow facings and with the castle of its home town on its brass buttons. Even with his stained breeches. He wondered when he would be able to pay for them to be cleaned.

From his daily pay of five shillings and threepence it would mean a sixpenny deduction, and that, after all other mess expenses, would leave him in lack of funds. Such was the lot of an impecunious officer. His new rank of captain would certainly double his pay. But when, he wondered, would he see any of that? They all knew that one of Wellesley's problems was with the payroll.

He would keep too the curved sword of the light company, his company, that clanked and rattled at his side. The ivory-hilted sword he had been given after the battle of Maida by a grateful commander and which had seen him through ever since, sending many a Frenchman to meet his maker.

What really angered him was that he knew he would miss his men. In particular his sergeant, George McIlroy, with whom he had been through so many close calls and who had taught him much of all he knew about soldiering. It had been McIlroy too who had thrust his bayonet high as the battalion had stood against the French dragoons on the beaches of Flanders nine years ago, parrying the sabre slash that would have ended Keane's young life.

With the French sent scuttling back to their own lines, the army was preparing to move. Wellesley intended to flush them out from the town and now that he had seen their strength, Keane knew, he would not delay.

In the meantime, those men who knew that at any time now they would be in the thick of the line of battle were doing their best to complete their tasks before the order came to move. While some shaved, others fed on stirabout or simply gathered up their meagre effects. Women, wives – common-law and otherwise – sat with their infants while other children ran about playing among the piled muskets. One of the women, up to her elbows in water at a tub, called to him as he passed: 'Hello, ducky. Need yer breeks washed? Take 'em off and give 'em here.'

Ignoring her, he walked on and with a heavy heart went in search of friends and a good bottle of wine.

The streets of Coimbra were not unlike those of Lisbon. Beautiful yet vile. Most of the townspeople had retired inside for the night, although here and there at the cafes men sat playing dice and backgammon. While the rank and file had been confined to the camp down in the valley, the better class of British officers had, as was their custom, chosen to make their temporary homes in the houses of the town. He had been told by Grant that the finer houses were on the upper part of the hill and so he climbed now in search of a mess that might offer him some hospitality. The artillery had been a good suggestion. He had never found their hospitality wanting and there was even a chance that an old friend might be here.

At length, close to eight o'clock, at the end of a cobbled street near to the palace, he found a merchant's house, simple and with a single balcony. Outside, an artilleryman armed with a musket stood guard. Keen nodded to him and entered, hoping for a welcome.

What he found was beyond anything he could have wished for.

For there, sitting on a chair in the entrance hall outside the mess room proper, he found the man whom he could call his oldest friend in the army. Wanting for money like himself and thus still a lowly lieutenant, Tom Morris of the Royal Horse Artillery was nevertheless a legend on the battle-field. The man who had killed twelve French alone at

Alexandria and who at Maida had single-handedly rallied the 78th. At present, though, he was content to be sitting outside the mess sipping a glass of madeira and playing with his dog, a terrier named Hercules.

Seeing Keane, he leaped from his chair. 'James? What news? They say you were called to see Wellesley?'

'Yes.'

'Well then, what news? Why did he ask for you? They say you're appointed to the staff.'

Keane nodded. 'Yes, that's right. And removed from it.'

'Removed? How "removed"? How's that?'

'I'm to be given a command.'

'James, what luck! What are you to have? A company? Is it with the 27th? Not the Devil's Own, the 88th?'

Keane shook his head.

'With whom, then? It is promotion?'

'Yes, I am to be promoted captain.' He paused. 'I'm to be an exploring officer.'

Morris frowned. 'Oh. I see. How then can you have a command?'

'I'm to have a platoon. Or rather, a troop. We are to be mounted. We operate behind the enemy.'

Morris shook his head. 'I am sorry for you, old friend. That's not real soldiering.'

'Yes, I know. I had wondered whether I might still be welcome in any mess, or indeed quite to what part of our military family I now belong.'

'Don't talk such rot, James. Did Wellesley know of the duel? And Simpson?'

'Oh yes. He gave me no respite on that count. D'you know Blackwood's father is an old friend of his?'

'I say, that's bad luck. But he still promoted you.'

'Yes. I'm still attempting to fathom it out. It is not what I would have wished, Tom, but it is what I must do, it seems, if I am to survive in this army. I thought I would be cashiered, on account of Simpson's death. But this. Promotion, for God's sake. With a captaincy.' He laughed. 'Now you must call me 'sir'. Come on, let's celebrate. But no fuss.'

Together they entered the mess, which contained a dozen officers. Finding a soldier-servant, Keane managed to get a bottle of the local wine left behind by the French. Morris walked across to one of the drums, which had been laid in the mess as was the custom, and before Keane could stop him was thumping on it with his fist, silencing the room.

'Lieutenant Keane has expressed his desire to buy a drink for every officer present on the occasion of his captaincy.'

There was chorus of hurrahs. Several of the officers, two from his own regiment, clapped him on the back. Another, though, in the dark-blue uniform of an officer of the Light Dragoons, approached him more slowly.

'Well done, Keane. Well, well. This is a surprise. When I heard you had been called for, I presumed the worst: that the commander meant to ask for your sword.'

'No, Blackwood. I'm promoted. I didn't expect your congrat-ulations.'

'Sorry, did I offer them? My mistake. Tell me, Keane, to what regiment you might be gazetted captain? The Guards?'

'No. As a matter of fact, I am to be close to the general. An exploring officer.'

Blackwood laughed and repeated the words, slowly. 'Exploring officer. Well, that's better than I could have wished. Of course I expected nothing more from you, Keane. It seems fitting that you should end up playing the spy. It is not a gentleman's work. But then you are not—'

Morris spoke. 'I'll thank you to hold your tongue, Blackwood.'

'Why should I, Mr Morris? We all know his position. It is only he himself, it seems, who does not. Besides, lieutenant, I have no quarrel with you.'

Keane snarled, 'But you do have a quarrel with me. Hold your tongue, Blackwood.'

'Or what will you do? You have already refused my challenge. You kill my friend but you would not dare to call me out, now that you are become Wellesley's lapdog.'

'You'll regret that, Blackwood. In another place.'

'Perhaps I shall find you first, sir. But I'll take your drink, Captain Keane. Very generous of you. I know how much it must mean to one with such a meagre purse.'

Morris put a hand on Keane's shoulder and led him away. 'Let it go, James. He's not worth it. His time will come. Such an officer is the first to fall when the French are his enemy. Either from their fire, or more likely a bullet in the back.'

Keane smiled. 'You're right. He's not worth it. Thank you, Tom. As always you cool my temper. Although I think you have done yourself no favours here with Blackwood and his cronies.'

'It's of no matter. Besides, I'd have done the same for anyone. But in your case and with him, it was a real pleasure, James.'

He paused. 'A toast. Captain Keane.'

Both men drained their glasses and then Morris spoke again. 'I can't help but admit, though, that without your company in the mess I shall feel a little awkward.'

Keane looked him in the eyes. 'Come with me, then.'

'What? Why?'

'Come with me. I'm at liberty to recruit whosoever I will. I need a lieutenant and I can't think of anyone I'd rather have. I know it might not be the most honourable of roles, but I can guarantee any amount of diversions. Accept?'

Morris shrugged. 'I don't know. I hadn't thought.'

'You accept?'

'Yes, of course. If you need me, of course I'll come with you. I'll have to talk to my colonel. But if it's at Wellesley's orders—'

There was a sudden commotion from the other side of the room. They looked across and saw Blackwood among his friends. He had gone red in the face and was spitting on the floor where he had already regurgitated the contents of his glass.

He pointed at Keane. 'Keane, this is your doing. Trying to poison me. You saw it, all of you. He tried to poison me.' He spat more wine onto the floor. And opening his eyes, found himself staring at the highly polished boots of the adjutant of the 23rd Light Dragoons, Blackwood's own regiment. Blackwood straightened up and wiped his mouth as the adjutant spoke.

'Lieutenant Blackwood, what are you doing, sir? You are a disgrace to the mess.'

Keane and Morris turned away, stifling their laughter as Blackwood tried to speak. 'He tried to poison me, sir.' Blackwood pointed at Keane.

'Who? That officer? How could he? Don't be absurd.'

Keane, looking appropriately concerned, shook his head. The mess steward stepped forward, close to Keane. He spoke with a Scots accent, 'Must have been a bad barrel, sir. Sometimes gets that way. In the heat, major. Shall I pour another glass for the lieutenant, sir?'

The adjutant shook his head. 'No, I think he's had enough.

Mr Blackwood, you will excuse yourself. Attend me at regimental orders.'

As Blackwood hurried from the room on the heels of the adjutant, Keane noticed an area on the right sleeve of the mess steward's coat where the scarlet had not yet faded to brick red. Three chevrons.

Keane looked at him. He was a huge man, with brown eyes and a mop of dark hair set above a face that looked as if it might have collided with an artillery limber. 'Don't I know you?'

'Couldn't say, sir.'

'I do know you. Sergeant Ross of the 42nd. You saved the colours at Alexandria. What the devil are you doing here? And where are your stripes?'

'Broken to the ranks, sir. Thieving. Though I was only taking back what was rightfully mine. My French medal, sir. Got in Egypt. Private MacGregor claimed he won it at cards, sir. But it wasn't won. He thieved it. So I just took it back. He never knew. Would have been fine an' all, if his missus hadn't taken a fancy to me. I won in the end, though. Put him in the frame, sir. In the hulks now, he is. That'll teach him.'

'I hope it was worth it, Ross. Whatever your revenge was.'

'Worth every minute, sir. Though I can't deny I do regret losing my stripes.'

Keane swirled the wine around in his glass and took a sip. 'What was it exactly that you put in Lieutenant Blackwood's wine?'

'Just some vinegar, sir. Well, that and perhaps a pinch of baking soda. Old trick. Couldn't let him leave with the upper hand over you, sir. Not in my nature. Old Egypt and all that.'

'Thank you, Ross. I hope you don't suffer for it.'

'No matter, sir. Worth it just to see him choke.'

Keane smiled at him. 'What would you say if I offered you your stripes back?'

'I'd ask you kindly, sir, not to tease an old soldier.'

'No, Ross. Really. I can do it. On the highest authority. You're wasted here and I can use a man like you. What do you say? Will you come with me and Mister Morris here? Though I'm not sure where we're going.'

Ross grinned. 'For my stripes back, sir, I'd follow you to Bonaparte himself, right through the gates of bloody hell.'

Keane laughed. 'That's settled, then. Though I don't think we'll be going that far, sarn't. Will we, Mister Morris?'

Morris smiled and shook his head. But in his own mind, Keane was not quite so sure.

# 2

They had not quite come to the gates of hell, thought Keane, but it was surely damn close. It was hard to believe that a few centuries ago the part of Lisbon known as the Alfama had been the district of noblemen's houses. Now it was a place that few foreigners frequented and certainly few officers. To call it unsalubrious was a gross understatement. Rather than any civilized western city, it reminded Keane of the bazaars of Alexandria. And now there was no beat of drum or staff adorned with a gaudy colour to accompany their mission. It was here they had come as a recruiting party. For sheer stench and ugliness this place beat any of the dives and taverns of Belfast or Londonderry where Keane had gone in search of new blood as a young officer. The three of them, Keane, Morris and Ross, were alone in the squalor, the heat and the noise. They walked close together up the steep, stepped streets of the quarter; the sweat was pouring off them, soaking the red serge of their coats, dripping down their backs and irritating the lice who had as always made a home on their unwashed bodies. Keane scratched at his left shoulder, then as quickly stopped, hoping that no one had been watching. It was not, he thought, so very dignified for an officer to attend to such irritations in front of his men. He would just put up with it. Sword clanking against his left thigh, he pushed on through the narrow streets, the others following close behind. As they passed, local women, standing alone and in groups on the balconies above their heads, called down to them.

Keane had a reasonable command of Spanish, gained for the most part from talking to veterans, and he was sharp to pick up a language. Always had been. But this guttural back-streets Portuguese patois was almost beyond him. Once or twice he made out a few words. And they were exactly what he had expected. Well, he thought, who could blame them for calling down wished-for obscenities upon three such well-turned-out young men as they? Even Sergeant Ross, he conceded, must have his admirers. On another day, in other, more salubrious surroundings, he might have taken up their offers. But here, where he might be assured of catching the pox, he preferred to hurry on. Yet even as he had the thought, he chanced to glance upwards just at the moment when a particularly pretty dark-skinned girl raised her skirts up to her naked waist above his head, affording him more than a passing glimpse of tanned flesh through the iron bars of the balcony.

Keane turned and called behind him to Morris. 'D'you see that, Tom? Pretty sight, ain't it? They're giving us a hearty welcome. Pity we've no time to return their civility.'

Morris laughed, looking up. 'Very pretty, James. But I swear that even you would pause before entering one of these houses. You'd be on mercury in a day.'

As they passed the last house on the street and turned the corner an older woman, proprietress of one of the establish-ments, Keane guessed, spat at them and began to remonstrate with her girls for not being bold enough to capture their custom. The next street was much the same, but the girls here, what few there were of them, were quieter still and they found themselves alone, save for two dogs, one of whom barked at them before turning tail. It was hardly a glorious progress. Not one of his finer moments of soldiering.

But such things were part of the day-to-day drudgery of an officer in His Majesty's army. It was not the stuff of great stories. But it was necessary if they were to do the commander's bidding. And if they did that, then, he thought, their actions might somehow lead on to paths of glory.

He trod in something putrid and stinking on the cobbles and swore. Back home in England, Keane thought, there would be enthusiasts of the new 'Romantic' school who would have termed this place 'picturesque'. Seen from a distance it would have made the perfect subject for young ladies to capture in watercolours. Up close, though, its streets were as filthy as any he had ever seen. And in ten years of soldiering he reckoned that he had passed through some choice places. The towns of Flanders, and further afield, in the Levant, Alexandria, and the Mediterranean hothouses of Valetta and Maida. He had known them all and had grown familiar with their rat-infested vennels and the teeming backstreets, when as the youngest lieutenant he had been charged with leading his men in search of deserters or the fugitive enemy.

This place was no different from those others.

Together they continued through the quarter's maze of backstreets, following the little urchin boy to whom Keane had promised a few escudos to guide them to the jail where the bad *ingléses* were being held. Keane led the way, with Morris behind him and Sergeant Ross bringing up the rear. The boy walked quickly through the streets, at such a pace they had to trot to keep up with him. Gradually, Keane perceived they were passing into a yet more unsalubrious part of the quarter. Washing was strung across the streets above them, and where elsewhere the gutters had held brackish water, here they were filled with what looked and smelt like raw sewage. In fact, the smell was appalling. On top of the ordure lay a heavy odour of filth, amplified by cooking. While Keane had been known to enjoy the flavours of the country, and when hungry would be content with much that would have been thrown in the dogs' slopbowl at home, this new smell spoke clearly of a cuisine with which he was in not in any way acquainted; nor did he have any desire to be. Glancing at Morris, he smiled at a look which suggested that he was of the same opinion.

'God, James, where the devil are you taking us?'

Keane laughed. 'Don't ask me, Tom. I'm just following the lad.'

At length they came to a large house, rising three floors, with barred and shuttered windows. The boy looked at Keane, speaking in Portuguese. 'This the place, senhor. This the place for bad *inglêses*. This is where they die.' He drew his finger across his throat and then quickly held out his hand for his reward. Keane thanked him in Spanish and gave him the agreed sum. At once the boy turned and ran off back along the way they had come, disappearing into the shadows beneath the fluttering chemises.

Ross muttered, 'We're buggered now, sir, beggin' your pardon, if we can't find our way back.'

'We'll be all right, sarn't. You'll see.'

But in truth it was more brag than certainty. Keane surveyed the house before them.

To his great relief there was a British sentry posted at the door, who, suddenly noticing the officers, made a desultory attempt at a 'present arms' as Keane and the others walked up and passed through the narrow archway. Instantly it seemed as if all the air had been sucked out of the place, and the changed intensity of a new and richer stench hit them full on.

Morris pressed a handkerchief to his mouth and Ross coughed. 'Christ, sir, that's ripe.'

A redcoat, his tunic unbuttoned and without the black neck-stock that was regulation dress, was sitting at an old oak table that passed for a desk. He did not look up, but on hearing the men enter simply muttered. 'Yes?'

Keane spoke. 'Sergeant of the guard?'

The man looked up and, seeing two officers, rose swiftly from his chair and smiled. 'Yes, sir. That's me, sir.'

Keane smiled at him. A smile that told the man that Keane recognized him for what he was. One of those soldiers who somehow always managed to play the system. To manage it so that they found themselves sitting pretty in some job that, although it was a necessity, was sure to keep them out of harm's way. Not that this place was pretty. But to that sort it was preferable to any battlefield. Keane had seen enough of the sergeant's kind, and he hated them.

Still smiling, he drew out a paper from his pocket. 'I believe that you have a man here, sarn't. Name of Silver.'

The sergeant raised an eyebrow and nodded. 'Yes, sir. I dare say you might be right, there. Lots of men in here, sir. No end of men in here and more coming in all the time. They're a right terrible lot, our soldiers, sir, ain't they? Won't be told. Always the same, your honour. Wherever we go. India, Malta, Egypt.'

Keane, refusing to be drawn into agreement of any kind with the man's attempts to ingratiate, moved on. 'You're a well-travelled man, sergeant.'

'I've seen some service, sir. But now this is my lot and I'm glad of it.'

He raised his right hand and Keane and the others saw that it was missing an index finger. So that was his trick. It was common enough. Maim yourself, or get someone to do it for you, and then no more front-line duty for you. You'd find your-self posted home, or better still in the sergeant's boots, sitting in a foreign jail creaming money from the poor sods inside and waiting till the army had a nice victory and you could share in the bounty. Keane nodded and smiled again, looking the sergeant straight in the eyes. The man stared through him and continued. He was a hard one, right enough.

'On account of the fact that I cannot do nothing no more with my musket, your honour. My finger having been taken away by a ball at the battle of Corunna, where I was proud to fight in company with the late Sir John Moore, God bless his soul.'

Keane nodded. 'Yes, the general is a sad loss. But now we have a new commander and those of us still able to do so will do our duty in the field. I'm sure that you will serve His Majesty in your new role just as well as you did in the thick of battle.'

The sergeant, understanding Keane's words, shrugged and pointed into the gloom. 'Silver's down that way, if you really want him, sir. But if you ask me you'd best let him be. We're all better off leaving him to rot here.'

'That will be for the general and for me to decide, sarn't. Thank you.' Keane pushed past the man and walked down the stinking corridor. He turned to Morris. 'In the company of Sir

John; would you believe it. God help us, Tom. It's men like that who run this army, you know. And that worries me. It really does. Sarn't Ross, see if you can find this Silver fellow. The sooner we leave this place the better for us all.'

'Sir.'

Ross set off down the passageway ahead of Keane, peering as he went into the doors that led off but seeing no sign of life within. At length, with Keane on his heels, he came upon a doorway into a room that was larger than the others. The old schoolroom of the place, he guessed. Inside there sat around a score of men in various uniforms: green, blue and brown, but mostly the ubiquitous red coat of King George's army.

Ross yelled at them. 'Silver. Is there a Horatio Silver in here?'

No one spoke. Then one voice piped up. 'He's over there, whoever wants him. At the back.'

Ross walked into the room and skidded on the slimy stone floor. Steadying himself, he looked at where the voice had come from and, finding the man pointing, followed the direction of his arm. At the back of the room, slumped against the wall, lay a man. He was tall and even in this poor light Ross could see that he was painfully thin. He walked over to him.

'You Silver?'

The man looked up. 'What if I am? Who wants to know?'

'Who wants to know, sergeant, if you please, Silver. You may be in jail but you're still in the army, lad.' He gave him a kick. 'Get up. Officer present.'

'I can't see no officer.'

'I don't care what you can see and what you can't. Get up.'

Silver looked up at Ross and saw that it was no use arguing with such a man. Not, at least, until he was on his feet. Placing one hand on the floor to steady himself, he pushed himself up to his full height. He stood a good three inches taller than Ross, who was himself over six foot.

'So who wants me, then . . . *sergeant*?'

Silver spat out the last word and then, for dramatic emphasis, knowing that all eyes in the room were on him, turned away and spat into the corner of the cell onto the back of another recumbent soldier.

'I bloody do, Silver. Though from the look of you I surely wish I did not.'

Silver took a step back and Ross recognized at once what he meant to do. As the prisoner's right fist flew towards him, he parried it with his left arm and followed up with a punch which connected with Silver's solar plexus, the fist striking rib as it went into the man's emaciated body. Silver doubled up and swore.

Ross drew back. 'That'll teach you not to hit a sergeant.' He looked around the silent room, seeing the men were restless that someone should have hit one of their brethren.

'Yes? Who else wants to go on a charge? Oh, I forgot, you're all criminals anyway. Well, you'll just have to rot in here. It's this bugger we want. Though why, I can't think.'

He rubbed at his fist and then bent down and grabbed the still doubled-over Silver by his shirt, pulling him up. 'Like I said, Silver. Officer present. Stand to attention.' He gave him another tap with his fist.

Keane, who had been watching from the door, now walked into the room, followed by Morris.

'Thank you, sarn't, for that lesson in good manners. Well, Mister Silver, you've been recommended to me. It's your lucky day.'

'Sir?'

'We've come to save you, man. You're free.'

Walking back through the streets, Keane did not speak to Silver but let him walk along with Ross. The sergeant, not yet trusting him, had attached a noose to his neck just in case he should attempt to escape.

Morris glanced at it. 'Is that really necessary, James?'

Keane nodded. 'Until we rescued him, Mister Silver had an appointment to meet his Maker. He was awaiting execution for killing a Portuguese civilian in a bar. I'll bet he can't believe his luck. But you know as well as I, Tom, that given the chance the man would run now and we'd never see him again, and a fine start that'd be.'

'And what's to stop him running when we take off the rope?'

'Nothing, I suppose, except the promise of a new life with us and booty.'

'Booty?'

'How do you suppose I'm going to keep these rogues with us unless I tell them some yarn about booty and untold wealth?'

'Yes, of course, I see. Booty. Who was it recommended Silver to you?'

'Grant, through Scovell. Says he's just the ticket. Told me himself before we left.'

'What d'you know of him?'

'Only what I've been told. His name is Horatio Silver and he claims to be aged thirty. He was in the 69th, till he got caught. He's a thief, is our Mister Silver. Aptly named, don't you think? According to Scovell he was one of the best burglars in London. Till he was caught there too and sent to the navy. It was either that or the gallows.'

'The navy? James, are you quite sure he's for us?'

Keane nodded his head. 'Certain. He's just the sort. But I've got to trust him first. And he me.'

'Trust you?'

'Of course. He must be wondering why the devil we've come to rescue him. Two officers and a sergeant. He'll know that something's up and he won't be happy about it. His sort have no respect for authority. And it's up to me to make him love us.'

Morris shook his head. 'Can you do it?'

'I don't know. We'll just have to see what comes up, shan't we? We know that he isn't all bad.'

'We do?'

'According to Major Grant, he claims to have fought at Trafalgar and to have helped carry Admiral Nelson down below. If that's really so, then he's not beyond salvation. Not that I'm on any mission to save souls.'

Morris laughed. 'Hardly, James, I'll say. A salvationist? Not you.'

'No, but what I do want is to bring out whatever sense of duty he once had to whatever it is he respects and whatever he craves. Gold, women. I'll find it. And then I'll have him.'

They were in the street of balconies again and the girls, goaded and beaten by their mistress, were louder now, determined not to let the soldiers get away this time.

Silver laughed. 'Thank you, sir. Thank you for bringing me here. Never thought I'd see it again, I didn't.'

Keane was wondering what he might mean when there was a shout from one of the upper windows. A young girl's voice. Silver stopped in his tracks, jerking the rope round his neck so that it pulled taut in Ross's grasp. Keane looked up and saw a pretty girl, all black eyes and brown skin. One of the ones he'd noticed in particular before. She was shrieking and pointing directly at Silver.

'Silver. Silver. No. No!'

Silver laughed. 'She thinks you're taking me for the drop, sir. Daft doxy.' He shouted back to her, 'No, no, Gabriella. They've saved me. I'm to be freed.' Then, quickly and before Ross or the others could stop him, he had slipped the noose from his neck with a skill that only such as he could have and was running to the house. With a great spring, he leapt up and grabbed hold of a small lower balcony which protruded from the filthy facade, swinging himself up onto it. In a second he had done the same again and was up above their heads standing on the higher balcony with the sobbing girl in his arms, smothering her with kisses.

Keane turned to Ross. 'Sarn't. What the devil's this? How did he manage that?'

'I've no idea, sir. That rope was as tight as any I ever made. I just don't know.'

'Well, bloody well get him back down here or there be hell to pay from the general. And from me.'

As Ross ran across the street and into the building, Keane turned and looked up at Silver. 'Silver, you can't get away. Don't think that you can. Anyway, you're a dead man if you leave us. We're your only hope. Don't be stupid, man.'

Silver laughed. 'No, sir. I'm not that stupid. I'm not gonna run. I just wanted to see my little girl again. My Gabriella. That's all, ain't it, Gabby? Never thought I would, sir. See her again. I'll come with you, sir.'

Ross had arrived at the balcony now and was squaring up

to Silver who simply shook his head. Keane shouted up. 'Wait, sarn't. Do you mean it, Silver? Who is she?'

'My girl, sir. We . . . we're married, sir. *Casado*.'

At this the girl, who up till now had merely been holding onto Silver, pulled back with a look of surprise. '*Casado?*'

'*Sim*, Gabriella. *Casado. Um matrimônio*.'

The dismay turned to a grin, and squealing with delight she hugged him again.

Keane frowned. 'She's your wife?'

Silver hesitated, but for no more than a moment. 'Yes, sir. That's right, my wife she is. Well, near as dammit, your honour. Common-law wife, you might say.'

Keane shook his head and then smiled and looked up. 'Well, you had better bring her along with us, then, Silver. Get her out of this hellhole.'

He turned to Ross, who was looking on, incredulous. 'Sarn't Ross. You can leave them. They're coming down.'

Ross shrugged and, backing down, left Silver and Gabriella, who followed him from the balcony until all three were standing before Keane. A small crowd had gathered around them in the street and the madam of the establishment was making it clear that she had not the slightest intention of allowing her newest and prettiest acquisition to escape. Silver walked over to her and spoke in Spanish. Her hand moved to her side and Keane saw the flash of light on a small blade. Moving quickly, he grabbed hold of the woman's hand, making the knife drop to the ground. The madam struggled, shouting all the time at Keane. Gabriella was shouting too now, and Silver. Keane glimpsed two men emerging from the doorway of a neighbouring house. They were Portuguese; one wore a kerchief tied on his head, the other a bicorne hat. Both were carrying sabres. He called to Ross, who turned and levelled his carbine at them, bayonet already fixed. Morris followed, drawing his own sword. The men stopped in their tracks.

Without relaxing his grip on the old woman's arm, Keane turned to Silver.

Quietly, and keeping his composure, he instructed: 'Ask her how much she wants. For the girl. How much she needs for the girl, your wife, to come with us.'

Silver lowered his voice, and telling Gabriella to be quiet turned to the woman with some words of Portuguese. She spat on the ground and laughed and then spoke quickly to him.

'She says she wants five guineas, sir.'

'Five guineas? That's rich.'

Silver looked forlorn. 'Gabriella's her best girl, sir.' He seemed proud of the fact.

Keane stared at the woman and tightened his grip on her arm. The two Portuguese were looking restless.

Morris called out, 'James. What should we do?'

'Nothing. Wait.'

Keane turned to Silver. 'Well, she'd better bloody well be worth it, Silver. And I expect to be repaid. In full.'

Without letting go of the woman's arm he reached into his pocket with his free hand and drew out a purse which he handed to Silver. 'The money's in there. Take out just enough. No more. I know what's there, to the penny.'

Silver opened the purse and took out five coins, which he gave to the woman. Keane let go of her arm and she turned the coins over then bit each one in turn. At last, satisfied, she nodded and smiled through broken teeth. Then she smiled at Silver and the girl and muttered some words of Portuguese that Keane did not understand.

'Blimey, sir, she's given us her bloody blessing, the old witch.'

Silver turned back to her and spoke in English. 'And a plague on you too, you old whore. May all your girls get laid up and may your best customers die of the clap.'

The woman smiled at him and nodded, not understanding.

'The purse, Silver. I'll have my purse back now, if you please.'

Silver handed it back. 'Oh yes, sir. Sorry. And thank you. Truly, thank you.'

'I meant what I said. I mean to be repaid.'

'Don't you worry, sir. I'll repay you. In money and in kind.'

Keane drew together the strings of the purse and replaced it in his pocket. It was a good deal lighter now.

Five guineas, he thought, a high price for a tart. Charged for by the night she might have been more than he had ever paid to one of her kind, even in Pall Mall to the best of Mother Hayes's doxies. Five precious guineas from his savings. All that he had to show for a life of soldiering. But he knew that it had been worth it. For now he had Silver in his hand. It was as simple as that, and he thanked providence for putting the whore in their path.

'And, Silver, I think you might now give your bride a decent wedding, don't you?'

'Yes, sir, of course, sir. Like I meant to all along.'

'Yes. Of course.' He paused. 'Your Portuguese is remarkably good. How is that?'

'My father, sir, his mother was from Spain, sir. Still speak a bit of the lingo. My real family name's Da Silva, sir. My dad changed it on account of we English was always fighting the dagoes, sir, and it wasn't too good for a family in London. But my old nan, my dad's mother, sir. She taught me the lingo when I was a nipper. And I ain't never forgotten it, sir.'

'It'll be damned useful to us, where we're going.'

'Where are we going, sir?'

'You'll find out soon enough, Silver. Come on, let's get out of this place. I can smell the corruption.'

Keane had decided to stay in Lisbon for one night before starting back to Coimbra, where he had been told by Grant that he might expect to find the others of his force.

But before that, and before they would be able to find shelter for the night, he had one more task. Scovell had mentioned to Grant that it would be of vital importance to have one native Portuguese member of their party and that he thought that he might have found the man. Also, Scovell had added that it was his opinion that the man he had in mind was not guilty, hinting that there might also be another reason for his release. Here in Lisbon, in another part of the city, it seemed that just such a man was being held by the authorities.

Jesus Heredia had been a regular soldier in the Portuguese cavalry. According to the charge, Heredia had stolen a large sum of money from the valise of a member of the British general staff. The victim's identity had not been given. He was to be tried. But it was known that he would be found guilty and then sentenced to death.

Such instances had become common and the Portuguese as much as the British were determined that they should not sour any good relationship that might exist between the two armies. Heredia would die. But Scovell had proposed that he be given another chance. Keane knew that the Portuguese would not surrender him easily. But this must surely be an easier task than rescuing Silver from the gallows and a murderous whore.

Leaving Ross to make sure that Silver stayed true to his word, Keane, taking Morris for support, walked the short distance to the headquarters of the Portuguese army in Lisbon.

Colonel Luis Maria Fonseca was not accustomed to having his afternoon siesta disturbed. Particularly when it involved leaving the arms of his favourite whore. He gazed at the aide standing at the foot of the bed and growled, 'Who is this man? What does he want? Tell him to go away. I'm busy.'

The girl giggled.

The aide coughed.

'I'm sorry, Colonel. The man is a British officer. He carries a note from the commanding general. He asks for you by name.'

Fonseca swore, and heaving his bulk from the edge of the bed pulled on his breeches and then stood up. He pointed and the aide hurried over with his coat, which he then buttoned closely around the Colonel's corpulent frame. Pulling on his boots, Fonseca walked slowly to the door and, with a last touch of his moustache, opened it.

Keane saw a man in his late forties whose grossly overweight body had been shoehorned into a uniform that might have fitted him once. His face was ruddy, as if from exertion, and his balding head was heavy with beads of sweat. As an example of Portuguese soldiery he left much to be desired.

The aide spoke. 'Captain Keane, sir.'

Fonseca nodded. 'Captain Keane. What can I do for you? Please be quick, I am a very busy man. I understand you have a message for me. From your general?'

'Yes, sir. That's right. We have an interest in one of your prisoners.'

'One of the prisoners, eh? Which one?'

'Sergente Heredia, sir. Jesus Heredia. We have orders to return him to the allied army at Coimbra.'

Fonseca bristled. 'I'm afraid that is going to be impossible, captain. Heredia is going on trial tomorrow. It is very important for my army. And for yours, I think. He will undoubtedly hang. It's quite impossible. I am afraid that you have had a wasted journey.'

Keane reached into his pocket. 'I have a letter, sir, from the commanding general, Sir Arthur Wellesley.'

Fonseca looked at the letter. Then he pointed at it and looked at the aide, who took it from Keane. 'It is from the general, sir.'

'Well, man, what does it say?'

The aide hesitated. 'It says that you must give up Heredia into the captain's care.'

Fonseca frowned and snatched the paper from the aide. 'Let me see.' He scanned it. 'It seems, captain, that your general must want my prisoner very badly. I wonder why? He is no more than a thief. What use can he be to you?'

'I have no idea. I am merely a messenger, colonel, carrying out orders. Now, if you please, I need to get on my way.'

Fonseca returned the paper to the aide, who in turn gave it back to Keane.

The colonel said nothing, then walked across to the window and looked outside. Turning, he retraced his steps and looked at Keane.

'Very well. Captain Hernandez, take these officers down to Heredia. You may discharge the prisoner into their care. But make sure that you get them to sign for him. I am taking no responsibility for this affair. God knows what my general will say when he learns what has happened. Good day, captain.

And to you, captain.' Then, turning away, Fonseca returned to his bed.

Sergente Jesus Heredia was sitting at a table in the room which for the last week had been his home, eating his dinner. He savoured each spoonful of mutton broth as if it had been a course from a banquet prepared by the king's own kitchen. For he knew that very soon now a meal he took at this table would be his last.

He wore the uniform of a senior NCO in the Portuguese Dragoons. It was a shame; he had always hoped that he might have been destined for higher office. He had even thought that one day he would be commissioned. It should have been so. His family was a high caste. Gentlemen. It had not been his father's fault that they had lost everything. But at least Heredia had made something of his life. Until now.

He thought about the circumstances that had led him to this place. How he had welcomed the appointment to act as escort to General Bacellar and his excitement at being attached to the British at General Beresford's headquarters. What, he wondered, had driven him to open the British colonel's valise? He had suspected that something was not quite right about the man for some time. It was not merely his manner or his words but the fact that he could not be accounted for at certain times of the day. When the other staff officers were to be found about their duties, time after time Colonel Pritchard was not. He had wondered about mentioning the fact to another British officer, but realized that he would be dismissed disdainfully for daring to cast the slightest doubt on one of their number. And then one day, during one of Pritchard's absences, the opportunity presented itself for him to act and Heredia at last found himself brave enough to go into the colonel's valise. It had been lying on the officer's camp bed in the headquarters building at Coimbra. It had been the work of a second to slip the strap from the buckle. Then Heredia had reached in and taken out a sheaf of papers, and what he had found there had made him gasp.

On a map of the area Pritchard had drawn with meticulous care the positions of all the British and Portuguese corps, divisions and brigades. That was fine, just as it should be. But what puzzled Heredia and then sent a chill through him was that beside each of the blocks the names of the units were written in French. Their exact strengths were given and the commanders' names. There was only one conclusion to be drawn. He had rummaged through the other papers and found nothing until his eye had been caught by a sealed envelope, unmarked. Taking his life in his hands, he had broken the seal and found inside a pass. It was green edged and written in French, and at the top it bore the embossed stamp of the golden eagle of the Empire. There had been no doubt in his mind then. Heredia was in the process of replacing the papers in the pocket of the valise when the door to the room had opened.

Pritchard had looked at him and smiled. Then he nodded and withdrew from his belt a pistol which he cocked and pointed directly at Heredia. The *sergente* had waited for the flash, the bullet and death. But Pritchard had not fired. Neither had he said anything. Instead he had crossed the room, the gun still pointed at Heredia's head, and had reached inside a purse that lay on the campaign chest. He had taken out a sheaf of banknotes; Heredia had no idea how much money, and then in one movement had thrown them towards him.

Then he had spoken. Had shouted for the guard. Had shrieked that he was being robbed. And that was that.

Nothing that Heredia could say or might have said had made any difference to his plight. Indeed, it had only made things worse to have suggested that a British colonel might be a French spy. No one had questioned the officer's word. How could they? He was a gentleman, wasn't he? Instead, Heredia was taken in disgrace to his own lines. There he had been interrogated. His story, though, was useless. He was a poor man. The money obviously had been the attraction. His excuse was pathetic. And then the decision had been taken to hand him over to the British. A gesture between the two armies. He was being used as a pawn, a sacrifice to cement their alliance. This was war. Life was cheap and the honour of the two armies must be seen to be respected.

He laughed to himself. Honour? If only they knew the truth; could bear to know it. The fact that a British staff officer was giving information to the enemy. But he would take that secret to his grave. It was too late now. He took another sip from the spoon and imagined he was in a grand restaurant in the centre of the city. It was then that the door opened and the jailer entered, accompanied by General Fonseca's aide Hernandez and two British officers.

Heredia did not rise.

Hernandez barked at him, 'Officers present. Stand up, sergente.'

He sloped to his feet and only then put the spoon down on the table. What was this now, he wondered. More questions. Another game. When would they give up and let him die?

One of the British officers, the one in the bright-red coat rather than the blue, spoke. 'Sergente Heredia, we have come to take you to Coimbra.'

Heredia laughed.

'What? Am I now to be permitted to die among my own people? You want to hang me yourselves?'

'No, on the contrary, we are come to save you from the noose, sergente. We have need of you.'

Heredia looked at the aide with a questioning expression. 'Are they lying?'

Hernandez shook his head and shrugged. 'Why should they lie? It's true. You're free to go. By order of their commanding general. God alone knows why.'

Heredia sat down in the chair and buried his head in his hands on the table. Someone somewhere had answered his prayers. He shook his head, lifted it and looked into the eyes of the redcoat officer.

Keane gazed back. Saw the tears and the strain. 'Come on, sergente. We have much to do. Are you ready?'

Heredia nodded.

'Where is your kit?'

'Kit? I have no kit. I have nothing. But now, I have everything. Thank you, captain. How will I ever repay you?'

Keane smiled. 'I'm sure you'll find a way.'

# 3

The road back to Coimbra was long. Longer, it seemed to Keane, than it had been on the journey down. The air was balmy and hot for late April, with a sweetness that rose from the aromatic plants growing at the roadside. Aside from the jingle of the harnesses and the clip-clopping of the hooves, there was no noise save for that of the martins circling and swooping above them and the sound of a brook a hundred feet below, running westwards at the foot of the drop on the left of the uneven, heavily rutted road. The way was crowded with soldiers – blue-coated Portuguese reinforcements moving northwards, up the line to join the army for the great offensive that they all knew must soon come. The dust cloud rising up from the road announced their presence more readily even than the cacophony of a column on the march, and had any French scouts been on patrol this far west they would have been in little doubt as to what was happening. But Keane knew that the French would not reconnoitre here. They were still close to the Spanish border, probing all the time of course, but hope-fully unaware of the British manoeuvrings.

Had he but been taken into the confidence of his newest

recruit, however, he might have thought differently. For Jesus Heredia knew that the French did not need to send their spies this far west. They had all the information they needed, supplied by a man in Coimbra. But Heredia said nothing and rode along in apparent contentment at the rear of their little column, happy to follow where his new captain took him. At least as far as Coimbra and the prospect of finding Colonel Pritchard.

Keane for his part had been pleased with Heredia's readiness to join them. He had explained the reason for his release and the man had seemed to warm to his new incarnation as a spy for the British. For the second time Keane surprised himself. He had not been prepared for this new role as a saviour of the fallen and he found it curiously satisfying to give these men a second chance and a new life. Once again he pondered Heredia's guilt and resolved to speak to him about the whole affair when a moment presented itself.

Perhaps, he mused, this was what fate had intended for him. He had always seen his prospects as either dying in glory at the head of his own company – or perhaps his own battalion, or if the gods of war were kindly, to live into old age as a general. He was not a godly man. Not in the way that his mother had been godly. He believed as all soldiers did in some greater power which guarded and preserved on the battlefield. But that was really superstition. Luck. In truth, he preferred not to think on it. But whatever power it was that watched over the warrior, it was surely with him now, he thought, as he led his men to the front of the dusty column.

They made a strange party. They travelled in pairs as cavalry did when on the march, Keane at the front of the group and Morris beside him. Behind them rode Silver and the girl, with

Ross and Heredia bringing up the rear. He had wondered how they would all fare in the saddle.

His new command was in essence to be mounted, and using the money given him for that purpose by Scovell he had managed to purchase three further horses in the Lisbon market. A mount for Gabriella had been an unexpected expense, but he had settled on a horse rather than a mule in the belief that the animal would be of more use to them. He had taken much the same attitude to the girl herself and congratulated himself on his instinctive decision to take her along. It was just the sort of unorthodox move that he thought would now be expected of him. Besides, who knew when a woman might help them in their subterfuge? And he was sure that one of her profession was doughty enough to deal with most of what their travels might throw at them. She could ride, too, from the look of her. He had half expected her to travel side-saddle, like all ladies of his acquaintance. But he had forgotten her station and had not been too surprised when Gabriella had hitched up her skirts, tucked them into her belt and sat astride the saddle.

Keane himself was a competent horseman, confident and sure-footed, having learnt to ride on the family farm in Ireland at an earlier age than he could recall. Of course, after his father had died, the family had never been able to afford very fine mounts, but Keane knew that any Irish horse was better than those to be had in England. And certainly, he thought as he shifted in the saddle, any of the horses with which he had grown up on the farm would have been an improvement on the nag with which he had been saddled by George Scovell.

The army had a problem with its mounts. Half the cavalry was similarly ill-served, and in their company only Tom Morris, who had brought his own mare from the horse artillery, was well mounted. Keane glanced round at him now and took in his natural ease in the saddle, as if he was somehow fixed in place, sure that nothing the horse might do would shake him. Turning, Keane tried to look back at the others. Sergeant Ross seemed less than happy, tugging and cursing, while the old sailor, Silver, was swaying from side to side as if on a ship. Looking at the two of them, he wondered if they would ever learn how to fight from horseback as well as on foot, using sabres, carbines and pistols.

A little distance behind them, at least Heredia was riding along with confidence, as might be expected from a caval-ryman. Keane wondered about him and whether he had been wise to take him into their brethren. But Scovell had been keen, although like Silver, and indeed all of them, Heredia was yet to prove his worth.

They pressed on, pushing the horses as hard as they could. Keane knew that time was of the essence and that he could not spend more than two days in the hundred-mile journey. They passed through Torres Vedras, Roliça and Caldas da Rainha and by the time that dusk was falling had reached Alcobaça, close to the coast. Keane halted the party and saw that the horses were flecked with sweat and the riders themselves in no fit state to go further.

'Sarn't Ross, we'll stop here.' He swung himself out of the saddle and, leading the horse across to a little inn, tethered it to a post. 'Sarn't Ross, Silver, take the horses round to the rear. Find the landlord and get them fed and watered. Then come and do the same for yourselves. All of you.'

Together, he and Morris entered. The barroom was filled with cigar smoke and the smell of wine. Four of the six tables were occupied, all by men, some in Portuguese uniform. Keane and Morris removed their headgear and nodded to the men before sitting down at one of the free tables and calling for wine and food. It came quickly, delivered by an unsmiling woman, in the form of a stone carafe of local rosé, a loaf of brown bread and a single cured sausage. The other inhabitants eyed the newcomers with interest, eager to see what they made of the offering, but as soon as Keane and Morris began to eat, they turned away. Nothing was said.

At length the door opened and the others entered, Ross reporting to Keane. 'Horses are stabled out the rear, sir. Seems a good enough place. Landlord says we can have rooms – two of them.'

Keane smiled. 'Just two rooms, eh? Well then, sarn't, I'm very much afraid that means that you and Heredia will be sleeping down here.'

Ross smiled. 'Yes, sir. I guessed as much. All the better then, nice and warm by the fire. Permission to get fed, sir.'

'Off you go, Sarn't Ross. General Wellesley's paying.'

The four of them sat at the other free table and it was not long before they were joined, at Silver's insistence, by two of the locals.

Morris talked of home. He spoke of a girl and of his mother and all the time Keane, ever the watchful officer, kept one ear trained on the level of conversation at the other table, gauging the atmosphere. For a few minutes Morris's chat drove his thoughts back to Ireland, and looking across at Silver with his arm around Gabriella he thought what strange things life and war could be. A life where one moment you were awaiting death and the next sitting with friends and your future wife enjoying a drink by a fireside. Morris was a good friend, but always seemed to Keane to have an air of innocence about him. He wondered if he had grown too cynical. He knew that his eyes had been opened by all that he had seen over the last few years. Man's inhumanity to man. And he half wished that it might not be so. But the thought went as quickly as it had come and Keane knew that deep down he was a better man for it. He knew exactly what he wanted from life and was determined to get it or die in the attempt. Love? That was for fools and idealists like dear Tom. Money? That was essential if you were to get anywhere, be anyone. Fame? That was something to be hoped for. To be talked of in the mess in hushed and reverent tones. Glory? Now that was the prize, he thought. That was what kept him here. He wondered what glory lay in his new appointment. None, he thought, but that which I can make myself. He spoke.

'Tom, why do you do this? Soldiering, I mean.'

'James, what a curious question. Why do you? Why does anyone? Because we are soldiers. That's just it, isn't it? It's what we do.'

'But why do you do it?'

Morris looked at him. 'Is this the wine talking, James? I swear you've become quite the philosopher these last few days. What's got into you?'

Keane smiled and shook his head. 'Nothing, merely a notion. Here, let me refill your glass.'

He was pouring the wine when he heard Silver's voice raised at the other table. He cursed himself for not keeping an ear on the conversation and turned to see what was going on.

One of the local men was talking hotly to Gabriella with Silver pushing in between them. Keane watched. He knew that for him to go in now and try to sort out the situation would be too heavy-handed and that it could easily bring the spark of tension to a flame and an ugly scene. He caught some of the words: 'Whore', 'English', 'French', 'filth'.

It wasn't hard to guess what was being said, and he knew that Silver was restraining himself from taking a swing at the villager, who had now been joined by his companion at the table and a third man. As he watched, Heredia walked forward and spoke quietly to the first man, shaking his head. For a moment Keane's hand was on his sword. Surely, he thought, a Portuguese cavalryman taking issue with a villager would not help things. But to his astonishment the man backed down. Within seconds he was smiling and then he and Silver were clapping each other on the back and drinking together. Keane let his hilt go and turned to Morris.

'Well, did you see that?' Heredia had been watching all the while, gauging the moment at which to intervene, and he had timed it perfectly. Whatever he had said to the villager, it had clearly had the right effect. 'That man is turning out to be a most surprising soldier, Tom. I shall have to keep my eye on him.'

He took a long drink and spoke again. 'When we reach Coimbra it would be best if we made our bivouac away from the army, don't you think? I'm sure that we shall attract more than our fair share of comment in the coming weeks. No point in encouraging it before its time.'

Morris nodded. 'As you think, James. Ours is a curious form of soldiering, isn't it? Do you suppose Bonaparte has anyone like us?'

'No, I shouldn't think he has. Although he must have spies of a sort. I suppose that's part of what we're meant to do. Find them.'

'How shall we do that?'

'To tell the truth, Tom, I have no idea. But I'm sure that we shall manage it.'

The night was uneventful, save for Morris's loud snoring, which kept Keane from sleep. In a period of this enforced wakefulness he lay still in the small hours, and his thoughts again turned to Silver. He became impatient to reach the camp.

They rose at dawn and once Keane had paid the landlord they saddled up and rode fast by way of Leiria and Pombal, reaching Coimbra as the sun was lowering in the afternoon sky.

As Keane had proposed to Morris, they made camp away from the inquisitive eyes in that temporary city that was the army's lines. Remembering a knoll on the road to the north, he led them there and left Morris in charge. The others found what little shelter they could and unrolled their blankets, while Keane set out on a mission that would wait no longer.

He presumed at least that acquiring the next of his recruits would not necessitate such a challenging expedition as that they had just undertaken. No brothels or gouty colonels. Merely a stroll and a conversation with an old friend.

The main camp of Wellesley's army lay a short distance from the town, on rising ground to the west. As Keane approached he was able to gain a better appreciation of the site: a good four acres of grey and white and red shelters. It was a shanty town, no less. The men had made do with what few materials they had to hand, but with precious few tents most of them had simply a blanket on the ground, and with an abundance of rain on every second day even the dry earth of Portugal had turned to mud. The more ingenious had rigged two blankets together over their muskets as a makeshift tent. Others still had contrived to hang their red coats over sticks. It looked to Keane's eyes as if all the gypsies in the world had arrived in Portugal. For apart from the soldiers, the camp followers – the army's tail – were here in abundance and the place thronged with women, children and animals of all sorts. To the uninitiated it might have presented an unfathomable puzzle, but it did not take long for Keane's seasoned eye to find the lines of his old regiment, the 27th Inniskilling Fusiliers. Their colours were crossed in a stand outside the colonel's tent, the King's colour of the Union Jack set at diagonals to the other, the regimental colour of yellow silk; both torn and ragged but still as splendid and heart-stopping as the day he had joined, thought Keane.

He walked past the sentry at the tent entrance and coughed. A voice from within asked him simply to come in.

Colonel Willoughby was some years older than Keane and his curly hair was already showing signs of greying at the temples. As Keane entered his terrier rose from its position by the colonel's feet and trotted happily towards Keane, recognizing an old friend.

The colonel too was pleased to see him. 'James, how good to see you. You've not come to rejoin us?'

'No, sir, I'm afraid I have not. I've come to plunder the ranks, if I may.'

Willoughby nodded. 'Yes, I had heard that you were after recruits. Wondered how long it would take you to do that. I've heard that you're to form a new corps.'

'Hardly a corps, sir. Merely a company, if that. But yes, I am in need of men.'

'Now let me see, who can I think you have come for? I know. Milligan, the rogue who stole the chickens. He'd suit you very well. Or maybe Flynn. Yes, it'll be Flynn you want, I'll wager. He's not been flogged for a month.'

Keane shook his head 'No, sir. It's neither of them, I'm afraid. It's Martin I want. Will Martin.'

The colonel shook his head. 'Will Martin. No, James, I'm afraid I can't allow that. The boy's too good to lose.'

'I know, sir. That's why I want him. He's bright, he can shoot straight. He's good with a horse. And he's got his wits about him.'

Willoughby nodded. 'Yes. It's a shame that he ain't got the funds to go with them, to purchase his rightful rank. But that's our loss. His background's quite sound, you know.'

'Yes, I know where his family farms. His father has ten thousand acres, near Bangor. Good land. That's why I want him too, sir. Not just for us but to give him a fresh chance. With me he might have the chance for advancement he won't find in the ranks.'

Willoughby smiled. 'You're right, James, of course. It was good fortune for you and it will most certainly be his best chance. The only way he'll make officer with us is if he joins the forlorn hope, and we all know what chance he'll have there, storming a breach against enemy fire. Take him, with my blessing. He's an eye for the ladies, though, James. Damn near cost him his life already. That run-in in Lisbon.'

'Yes, he's rather too much governed by his heart.'

'His heart be damned. It's his fondness for a tumble that's his undoing. Needs to keep it buttoned up, eh?'

'Quite right, sir. I'll need to watch him.'

'Take care of the lad, James. His father asked me to look out for him. I would never have allowed him to go in the forlorn hope. You know that.'

'I'll bear it in mind, sir.'

He found Martin where the colonel had directed him. The boy was sitting on a barrel throwing dice with two comrades on a blanket laid out on the dust. As Keane approached Martin saw him and stood to attention. The other two followed suit. He recognized one of them as Sean Macguire, a notorious gambler and cheat with whom he had had some dealings in the past, accounting for twenty-five of the scars that the man carried on his back. Macguire looked sheepish.

'It's all right, lads. I'll not trouble you long. It's Will here I'm after.'

Martin frowned. 'Me, sir?'

'Don't worry, Martin. I'm not here to punish you. I'm here to make you an offer. How would you like to join my company?'

'What, leave the 27th sir?'

Keane nodded. 'Yes. I'm forming a new company, directly answerable to the commanding general. Scouts, you might say. I thought you might fit with it well.'

Martin shrugged. 'Don't know, sir. I'm not inclined to leave the regiment. It's home to me now, sir. Like family.'

'Yes, I realize that. And I know it's hard. But you know me, Will. And I'm in command. So you'll be among friends. It might offer you the chance of advancement and fortune.'

At this Martin brightened. 'Really, sir? Advancement?'

'Well, more than you're likely to get here, with these ne'er-do-wells.'

The others forced a laugh but Macguire looked cynical.

There was a noise from behind them and Keane turned and

locked eyes with another friendly face. 'Mister Keane, sir. Good
to have you back. You here to stay, sir?'

Keane shook his head. 'Sorry, Sarn't McIlroy. I'm afraid that
much as I would like to, I have not returned. Fact is I've come
to steal one of your men.'

'Oh, you can take Macguire, sir. Any time you want. Welcome
to him. And that one too.'

'It's not them I've come for, sarn't, and you know it. It's Will
here.'

The sergeant shook his head. 'That's a shame, sir. A real
shame. I had high hopes for him.'

'And so do I, sarn't. That's why I'm taking him.'

'What exactly are you doing, sir? Can I ask?'

'You can ask, sarn't, but I don't think I can tell you. Let's
just say I'm doing something for the general. Something very
important, and Will here is going to be a part of that.' He
thought for a moment. 'As a matter of fact, I wonder if you
might consider joining us. All I can tell you is that we will be
operating close to the enemy and that we will be entirely independent of regimental command. What do you say?'

McIlroy shook his head and smiled. 'Sorry, sir. I don't think
that's the life for me. Too tied to the regiment here, sir. I'm a
soldier through and through, Mister Keane. It's not for me to
creep about. I'm best facing the enemy in a fight. Like you,
sir. With the men in the line.'

Keane nodded and realized for an awful moment that McIlroy
might indeed have hit a truth. That he was himself a fighting
soldier, a man of battles, better facing the enemy. He wondered
whether he was doing the right thing but decided that he was
now in too deep to go back.

Martin piped up. 'I'll come with you, sir. 'Course I will. I can't do better than that and though I shall miss my friends here, I must think of my prospects.'

'Good lad, Will. I knew you wouldn't let me down.'

'No, nor never I will, sir.'

Morning broke over Coimbra with a clap of thunder. The heat of the past days had finally come to its end and as Keane awoke the heavens opened.

Ross, who, used to it from his time in the mess, had happily turned to the duties of Keane's soldier-servant, opened the tent flap. 'I've made some tea, sir. Mister Morris is about and the others too. He's gone off to find someone, he said. But we were wondering what you want us to do, sir.'

Keane cursed himself for sleeping after the others were up. It was not like him. 'Wake me earlier tomorrow, Ross, if you would.'

The sergeant nodded. 'Yes, sir. And you've had a message, sir. You're needed at General Wellesley's headquarters. Soon as you like, sir.'

Keane smiled. 'You can stand the men easy then, sarn't. Just tell them to make sure everything's in order. They might practise their skills at arms or their riding. You might do so too if you've a mind to it.'

Ross laughed. 'You'll have seen then that I'm not one of nature's horsemen, sir. Some work to do there. I'll just fetch that tea and a pail of hot water.'

Keane shaved fast and gulped down the tea as he did so. There was no time to waste, and much as he knew he must not keep the general waiting, there was also another matter to which he knew he must first attend.

*

The Royal Dragoons were encamped some distance away from the infantry, as befitted their status, and the difference was evident from the moment Keane saw their bivouac. In fact, he heard it before he saw it. The air was filled with the sound of whinnying horses and not least with the unmistakable smell of them, made all the more pungent by the damp. The rain had stopped now and throughout the dragoons' lines grooms and troopers were busy rubbing down their mounts. But it was not just the horses or the smell that struck him, but the way in which through the haze of smoke from the campfires the whole place shone as the watery sun glanced off the leather straps and highly polished brass harness hung from specially constructed frames. To Keane's mind, though, all was just too perfect. There was no mistaking the work of a martinet in command here and he had been dreading his encounter with their colonel ever since Grant had suggested that one of his number might be a man in their ranks who was currently under a sentence of flogging.

Sam Gilpin had impersonated an officer. Of that there was no doubt, nor of the gravity of his crime. But even Keane felt that a battalion punishment – a proper public flogging – for such a crime seemed overzealous. However, Colonel the Honourable Sidney Hackett had never been renowned for his clemency in such matters. Keane, with Morris at his side for moral support, advanced towards the officers' tents with some trepidation. At least, he thought, he had the authority of Grant and ultimately Wellesley to back him up. But to be honest, at this moment he felt that he would rather have been assaulting an enemy position than about to encounter a brother officer.

Reaching the tents, he sought out the adjutant, a major

whom he knew by sight, but could not find him. There was no alternative but to enter unannounced. As he had done at Willoughby's tent, Keane coughed, but this time there was no cheery response. A voice from within snarled, 'Yes. What?'

Sidney Hackett was sitting in his shirtsleeves smoking a cheroot. 'Who the devil are you?'

'Captain Keane, sir. Late of the the Inniskillens.'

'And you want?"

'I want a man, sir. One of your men, sir. That is, I have orders from the commanding general to request the transfer of a man from your battalion.' Nothing like getting to the point, he thought. Play the trump card first.

'You have, have you? Let's see them, then.'

Keane reached into his pocket and withdrew the letter that Grant had given him for use in such a situation. He gave it to Hackett and recalled its wording.

*You will give Captain Keane every possible assistance in his request.* It was signed Arthur Wellesley.

Hackett looked at the paper, turned it over and examined the reverse, and for a moment Keane thought that he might be about to crumple it and throw it to the floor. But he seemed to have second thoughts and handed it back.

'Well, captain, that seems to be in order. Who is it you want?'

'Private Gilpin, sir. Sam Gilpin.'

Hackett laughed and shook his head. 'Gilpin? What could you possibly want with Gilpin? He's nothing but a rogue, as useless a piece of shit as ever took the King's shilling. You are quite sure that you actually want him? Are you quite certain, captain?'

'Yes, sir. It's Gilpin that I want.'

Hackett called, 'Sarn't Bates. In here, now.'

The tent flap opened and a sergeant of horse entered, a rough-looking fellow with a scar on his left cheek. 'Sir?'

'The captain here wants Gilpin. Isn't he on a charge?'

'Yes, sir. 300 lashes, sir. Lack of respect due to an officer.'

'Oh yes, remind me of it.'

'He, er . . . he impersonated you, sir.'

'So he did. Yes. That was it. Insolent blackguard. Knew I had reason to hate him. Well, I'm very much afraid you shan't have your Mister Gilpin, captain.' Hackett took a long drag on the cheroot. 'He's mine for now. At least until he's undergone his punishment.'

'And then, sir?'

'Oh, then you can have him, captain.'

Bates sniggered.

Keane asked, 'Might I ask what his punishment is, sir?'

'What was it, sarn't?'

'Three hundred lashes, sir.'

Keane frowned.

Morris spoke up. 'Three hundred lashes? Good God. I mean, I'm sorry, sir, but three hundred lashes. That will surely kill him.'

Hackett smiled and took a drag of his cigar. 'Uh . . . yes, I suppose that it probably will. What say you, Sarn't Bates?'

'Oh yes, sir. I've known men to die under the lash at a hundred. Three hundred will do for him, sir. Sure enough.'

Keane shook his head. 'Then I'm afraid, sir, that I shall have to appeal to the commanding general. I've no use for a dead man.'

Hackett's face turned purple and for an instant he was speechless. Then, 'No, captain? Well, nor have I for a man who treats his betters with such contempt as you would reserve for a dog.'

Keane turned on him. 'And that's how you treat him, sir. Whip him till he's dead.'

Hackett looked down at the desk and picked up a piece of paper. 'Captain Keane, I think both you and I know that this interview is at an end.'

Keane knew when it was pointless to continue. Hackett had military law on his side, whatever Wellesley might have said and whatever the value of the piece of paper in his pocket. This time there was no escape.

He nodded to the colonel and he and Morris took their leave, hearing as the tent flap dropped the laughter of the colonel and his sergeant behind them.

Morris turned to him. 'James. We must do something. That is absurd. Killing a man by flogging for such an offence.'

'Yes, I agree, but we are not in the right and for once I wonder whether the general will be able to do anything.' He thought for a moment. 'That's it, Tom. Wellesley must know full well that even he can't do anything about this. Always did. Don't you see? He's set us a test. We'll have to get Gilpin ourselves.'

Gilpin was being held in the dragoons' camp, in a small enclosure close to the horses. Morris, who had left Keane and taken a stroll through the lines, reported back that there were only two guards, although from the look of it Gilpin was tied with rope to a wooden beam.

It had been Silver who had suggested that they might use Gabriella. Not in any sordid way, but just as a decoy, to distract the guard. Then Heredia would go for him from behind. Anyone glimpsing his uniform would blame it on the Portuguese. He would knock the man unconscious, nothing more, and then the two of them would be in. Slash the rope with Heredia's sabre and hurry him off into the night. It was as sound a plan as any and just as likely to fail.

Of course, Keane himself could not be seen to be involved and so, reluctantly, he sent them off into the night with words of warning. 'If you are caught I cannot possibly be associated with you. I'm sorry, but it would jeopardize the whole operation.'

They left quickly, with no scabbards or bags to rattle or encumber them, Heredia's sabre tucked into his belt, wrapped in a scarf. Keane waited for them to go and then, unbuckling his own sword belt, followed on.

He tracked them at a distance of some twenty yards, taking cover at every opportunity, ducking between tents and wagons as he went. At length they came close to the dragoons' encampment and the enclosure where Gilpin was being held. He watched as Heredia seemed to melt into the shadows and Gabriella alone walked forward. Keane saw her smile at the sentry and watched as he returned it. She was talking to the man now, using her broken English as best she could to tell him, Keane guessed, how fine he looked, and asking when he would be free. There was little time before someone would spot her. And as he watched a shadow appeared from behind the sentry and in an instant the man was on the ground, unconscious. The enclosure gate was secured only with a wooden catch, which was quickly slipped, and then Heredia was inside. With a single slash of his sabre he cut the rope securing Gilpin and then all three of them were out and running back towards the camp.

Keane pushed himself into the shadows as they came past

and then, emerging slowly, returned himself to their encampment, as if on no more than a stroll.

In the event he arrived back before them, as he knew he would, for they had taken a circuitous route around the camp to throw off the scent any dragoons who might have followed them.

Keane was in mid conversation with Morris when they came, and there was no sign of any pursuit. Gabriella was first, her body heaving, her face glowing red in the firelight. And then, behind her, pushed forward by Heredia, came a bewildered Sam Gilpin.

Keane looked at him carefully. Square set, with powerful shoulders, Gilpin looked the very picture of a heavy cavalryman. A man who, wielding one of the straight-edged swords its owners had christened 'the butcher's cleaver', would bring down his full strength in the swing and cut a man clean in two. But this evening Sam Gilpin was far from being a master of the battlefield. In the firelight, he looked around at them all with frightened, ferret eyes.

Keane spoke. 'Don't worry, Gilpin. You're quite safe now.'

Catching his breath at last, Gilpin saw the gold braid on Keane's coat and managed to speak. 'Thank you, sir. But what's going on? Why am I here? Who are you, sir?'

'You're safe, Gilpin. My name is James Keane. Captain Keane. I'm your new officer and these are your comrades.'

The man looked even more puzzled and stared at the others. 'You ain't dragoons, sir. You ain't even cavalry. What are you?'

Keane ignored the question. 'Tell me, Gilpin, where are you from? Originally, I mean. Your home.'

'Somerset, sir. I worked on a farm before I took the shilling. As a wheelwright.'

'I see. And your age?'

'Twenty-six, sir. So I believe.'

'Now tell me. What did you think you were doing, mimicking your colonel?'

Gilpin looked worried again. 'Oh, it weren't nothing, sir. Just a bit of harmless fun really. Colonel took it real bad, though.'

'I'll say he did. A bit of harmless fun? Good God. You're a cool 'un, Gilpin. I'll say that for you. It almost cost you your life, man.'

Gilpin nodded. 'Yes, sir. I think I went a bit far.'

'You could say that. Well, thank God we've saved you. And where I come from mimicry is a skill to be used to advantage. That's what we're about. Apart from your talent, what else can you do? You were recommended to me from high up.'

'I was?' Gilpin smiled. 'Thank you, sir. I can speak French, sir. Not half bad, and I can manage a bit of the Spanish too.'

Keane thought for a moment and then turned to Silver. 'Try him.'

Silver nodded and spoke to the man quickly in Spanish. From what Keane could make out it was a complex series of sentences involving the weather, the price of grain and not least the virtue of Gilpin's sister.

He was surprised to hear what seemed to be a perfect reply. He turned to Silver. 'Well?'

'Very good, sir. He speaks a form of Galician. He's clever, sir. Even dropped in one or two of them local words when I quizzed him about his sister.' He smiled.

'That's good, Gilpin. That's very good.'

Then, sensing an opportunity, Keane himself passed quickly into French and again Gilpin took him up, this time in a guttural accent that Keane thought quite convincing. He nodded. 'Yes, we can certainly use you.'

'Use me, sir? How? For what?' Gilpin looked puzzled. 'Anyway, I don't yet know why you saved me.'

'I'm forming a new company and you come highly recommended.'

He looked amazed. 'Recommended, sir? Me?'

'You, Gilpin. That is why we saved you from being flayed alive. We saved you so that you can be of more use to General Wellesley's army.'

'I'm very touched, sir. But what am I to be doing?'

'What you do best, Gilpin. Making use of your talents. But this time you're going to use them to beat Boney.'

Keane was pleased. He had accomplished what he had set out to do and had come away with the bones of a command the like of which the army had never seen. Felons, Wellesley had said, and that was for the most part what Keane had got. Save for Martin, of course, and Gabriella.

He was sitting on a tree stump considering the achievement when Ross found him.

'Evening, sarn't. I think we've done quite well with our little band, don't you?'

Ross nodded. 'Very well, sir. Not bad at all.' He paused. 'But in my own opinion, there is one more man we should have. If you don't mind my saying so, sir.'

Keane looked up. 'Not at all, sarn't. You really think so?'

'I do, sir. One man.'

'May I ask his name?'

'Garland, sir. George Garland.'

'And who is he, this Garland?'

'Private. 4th Foot, sir. And I reckon he's about the best prize-fighter I ever seen. Best we've got in this army most likely. He's never lost yet in the ring. Not once. I heard that before he joined the colours the Marquess of Queensberry hisself was after him. Proper handy lad is Garland, sir. He'd be good in any fight. Might be useful to us, sir.'

Keane thought for a moment. It was true. He might have assembled a fine group of liars and thieves, but what was certainly missing was a proper Ajax.

'And where is Garland now, sarn't?'

'That's just it, sir. That's what made me think of it. Saving these lads from the gallows. That's where he's bound for too, sir. Killed a man. Portuguese bloke. Only took one blow, sir. A brawl in an inn, it was. Only last week. Doesn't know his own strength, see, sir. Specially after strong drink. That's what always does for him.'

'He's under arrest?'

'No, sir. Not as yet. He's in hiding, sir.'

'But you know where he is?'

'I might know someone who does, sir.'

'You're a sly one, Ross. You know that you could be in as much trouble as him?'

'Really, sir, why would that be?'

'Aiding a wanted man. You could swing for it with him.'

'But I won't, sir, will I?'

'Can we get him?'

Ross nodded. 'I think we can, sir.'

'You're certain it's Garland we need?'

'I'd put my shirt on it, sir. Can't think of anyone I'd rather be in a fight with, when the fists start flying. Garland is the equal of five Frenchies. More, even.'

Keane nodded and walked across to where Morris was feeding scraps to his terrier, with whom he had now been reunited by his soldier-servant.

'Tom, it would seem that we have a problem. Sarn't Ross is of the opinion that we might be lacking a strong-arm man.'

'Yes. I think that might put us at a disadvantage.'

'He has a man in mind. Fellow named Garland. A prize-fighter.'

Morris nodded and grinned as the terrier, Hercules, jumped a foot to take a piece of sausage from his hand. 'I'll say. Ain't you seen him box, James? Surely you must have. Beat that giant of a man from my mob in less than two rounds last spring. What a man. Well done, Ross. Where is he?'

Keane spoke. 'That's just it. As I said, we have a problem. It would seem that our friend Garland has got himself into a spot of bother on account of his killing one of our Portuguese comrades.'

Morris shook his head. 'Not again, surely?' He produced another scrap and teased the terrier. 'Please, James, don't tell me we have to ride back to Lisbon and make another trip to that bloody hellhole.'

Keane went on, 'No, I'm not springing any more convicts. This one hasn't been taken yet.'

'A fugitive?'

Keane nodded.

Morris whistled. 'You're certain of your powers, James? You have the authority?'

'From Wellesley himself, Tom. You know that.'

'Then we must act at once. Find the man before others do.'

Keane called to Ross. 'Sarn't Ross, can you find him for us?'

'Yes, sir. Just give me the nod.'

'You have it, man.'

They did not ask how Ross had managed to find the fugitive, but find him he did and within an hour the two of them were back at their bivouac. The smell was unmistakable and revolting. Garland had been hiding where no one would think of looking for him, and they did not need to ask where that had been.

'You weren't followed?'

'No, sir. Where I've been not a soul would have followed us.'

Keane looked at Garland. Ross had not exaggerated. The man was huge, with hands the size of shovels. He stood before him, his clothes sodden and stinking, looking terrified out of his wits.

Ross spoke. 'I managed to convince him, sir, that you were all right. I mean that we weren't going to hand him over to the provosts. I don't think he's quite sure, though.'

Keane walked towards Garland, who seeing the officer's uniform shrank back into the shadows.

Keane spoke quietly. 'Private Garland. Captain Keane. Don't worry, man.' The look on the huge man's face suggested that of a puppy being chided by its master, and that was exactly how it seemed to Keane. There was a childlike innocence about Garland which seemed utterly out of keeping with his frame. 'We're all friends here, Garland. We know what you did but we want to help you. Did Sergeant Ross explain?'

'Yes, sir. He said you wasn't going to turn me in.'

'More than that, Garland, we want your help.'

'My help, sir?'

'Yes. We need you. You're a valuable man, Garland. Didn't you know that?'

'You mean my fighting, sir. My boxing. You want me to fight?'

'We certainly do, but not in the ring. We need you to fight the French, with us. Will you come with us, Garland?'

The man thought for a moment and then looked across at Ross who smiled and nodded. 'Yes, sir. I'll come with you.'

'Good. That's settled. Now, have you had anything to eat? No, perhaps first we should get you some fresh clothes. Though God knows where we'll find any to fit you.'

So Garland stripped off the sodden, stinking clothes and Gabriella took them away, wondering if she could ever remove the stench. They found him a shirt of Ross's and a pair of Gilpin's grey overall trousers that they fastened with string and a stable belt. Then they gave him what was left of the day's food, and as he ate Keane sat down and spoke to him.

'So man, tell me what happened. You were in a fight and you hit a Portuguese? You killed him?'

'Didn't mean to, sir. I just hit him.'

'Why?'

'He was laughing at me, sir. Called me stupid. Can't take that, sir. Never have been able to.'

'You just hit him the once?'

'Yes, sir, I swear. Just the once. My right hand. Like this.'

Keane grabbed Garland's arm to stop him and sensed the strength in the man. 'No need to show us, Garland. We believe you. Don't we, Tom?'

'Of course. Most unjust. You're better off with us, Garland.'

'Captain Morris is right, Garland. You're invisible now. You're one of us. One of the forgotten men of this war. Tomorrow no one will remember you and you'll be a different person.'

Garland looked at him. 'Sir?'

'You're safe. You're with us now.'

'Thank you, sir.' He paused and then remembered what he should say. 'I'm in your debt.'

Morris smiled, and the two officers got up and left Garland to finish his supper. Then, walking away a short distance, Keane poured a little wine into his friend's cup.

'Not the first time I've heard that in the last few days, James.'

'But I heartily pray that it might be the last. I'm done with saving lost souls, Tom.'

Arthur Wellesley stared from the window of the salon in the Bishop's palace of Coimbra down at the town and the teeming river, then, turning to face the room, spoke. 'Well done, Keane. Colonel Grant tells me you've found the makings of a proper company.'

'Yes sir, I believe I have. Although I'm not sure how proper.'

'But they'll do the job, Keane? Won't they?'

'Yes, sir. They will do the job.'

'Well, now's your chance to find out how good a judge of men you are. I want you to take them out into the hills. I need to know the positions of the French. Accurate as you can. Marshal Soult is in Oporto. That is well known, as is the savagery with which he took that place. And that may be of use to us. But there are other armies out there: Ney, Victor, Joseph and Sebastianni. I have had only garbled reports, Keane. I want facts.'

'Yes, sir.'

Wellesley continued. 'And I want to find the Spanish, Keane. Not General Cuesta and his blasted army; I know where he is, or was until his last defeat. I mean the *guerrilleros*.' He hissed the word. 'The irregulars, Keane. The people's army in the hills. I want you to make contact with them. Major Grant here has done so already on his own. He's seen them in action. But we need to know more of them. I want a full account of their nature, their character and their morale. And I want to know how far I can rely on them. Everything there is to know. And I need to know now. You will move east as quickly as you can. Speed is the key to all this. To be one move ahead of the enemy. You understand?'

'Sir.'

'Cross the border into Spain. Major Grant and Captain Scovell will furnish you with all the details. You do understand, Keane?'

'Yes, sir. Completely.'

'Very well. And I do need you to return. Don't go getting yourself killed, Captain Keane. That would be both tiresome and unnecessary. Don't take any undue risks. Major Grant will see you out. Good luck.'

Outside in the anteroom, Grant spoke quickly to Keane and flashed his finger fast across the map laid out on the table.

'Go here, James, by way of the Serra da Estrela, to Guarda. Then cross into Spain and head for Ciudad Rodrigo. By then you will be in the high sierra. The real mountains. It's my guess from what I know that Marshal Victor will be below you – but that's what we want to know for certain. Go down off the mountains through the pass, but only as far as you dare. I'm sure that you'll manage it.'

Scovell took over. 'Your contacts are three guerrilla leaders: Morillo, Merino and Cuevillas. They are none of them partic-ularly attractive characters. Morillo is an embittered ex-regular from the Spanish navy. He styles himself colonel but was never a soldier. His entire family was slaughtered by the French early on in the war. He has every reason to hate them. Cuevillas was a originally a smuggler by trade. His real name is Ignacio Alonso. Merino was a semi-literate parish priest with a particular penchant for cruelty. They're a bad bunch by all accounts, Keane. Not much to choose between them. The very best of luck.'

Scovell left the room and Grant smiled at Keane.

You've done well so far, James. Damned well. The general is impressed. With everything.' He raised an eyebrow. 'Answer me one thing, though. How the devil did you manage to get Gilpin away from his flogging?'

'Gilpin, sir? Hadn't you heard? He escaped before we could get to him. His guard was overcome.'

'Yes. Colonel Hackett's furious. The word in the mess, though, is how he was overcome. Something about him being distracted by a señorita and then being coshed. You wouldn't know anything about it, I suppose?'

'Me, sir? Why would you think such a thing, sir? How could I know anything about such a business, Major Grant? I only wish I knew where he was. Sore loss to us, that one. He'd have been an asset, I'm sure. Talented lad.'

'So I believe, Keane. And there was someone else. Big chap. Prizefighter. Wanted for murder. Name of Garland. Went missing four days back. No one's seen him since. I don't suppose . . . You wouldn't by any chance . . . ?'

Keane shook his head. 'I'm afraid I've never heard of him, sir.'

Grant smiled and nodded. 'Very well. We'll say no more about it.' He paused. 'You know, Keane, I've learnt a few things in the past year. You have a natural talent for playing the spy. You simply need to keep your eyes and ears open and listen to everyone and everything. Always be prepared to take advice. From whatever quarter it might come. Expect the unexpected. Use whatever local knowledge you can find. But do not trust everyone. One important thing above all others. Learn to make yourself invisible. You must be able to slip through the enemy like water through a grate. All of you. Make a study of it, Keane, and you will be repaid.

'Now, get on your way. And mind what Wellesley said. No risks. You're too valuable a man to us to lose you now. And that goes for all of you. You'd better get some rest. You've a long day in the morning. And, James, best to post some sentries. Wouldn't want anyone, that Garland fellow maybe, to surprise you.'

# 4

The height of the sun above their heads in the burning blue sky told Keane that it must be close to midday as the little party trotted up the dusty road, sending up clouds of fine sand beneath the horses' hooves. As always, the pace of their troop was uneven, with the inexperienced horsemen slowing them down. Silver and Ross were as unsure as ever. Garland too looked unsteady, even though they had given him the tallest of the horses. But Gilpin rode with the arrogance of a trained cavalryman and Will Martin had evidently been educated in horsemanship and seemed perfectly at ease, as if out for a morning hack.

To their right rose the mountains of the Serra da Estrela, their peaks cloud-shrouded against the blue of the sky. He knew from the pitifully poor map given him by Grant that they must by now be nearing the town of Guarda, not far from the border between Portugal and Spain.

Noticing the way in which the sides of the road were marked by gaps in the grass-line, Keane pulled out a leather-bound notebook and wrote: 'Hills some fifty miles north-east of Coimbra. Road unsuitable for heavy vehicles. Light guns may pass and all manner of troops, but nothing more as sides inclined to give way under pressure. Sheer drop.' He tucked the book away again and gazed down into the ravine.

They had been travelling for fully three hours but Keane did not plan to stop just yet. He wanted to probe deeper into the mountains and then to cross the border into Spain where he was sure the guerrillas would be. And he was working on the assumption that the further into the mountains he could get, the higher the rank of the guerrilla capitan he might find.

Tom Morris rode up alongside him. 'Should we not rest for a while? The horses, I mean.' He patted his horse. 'Poor Tilda's sweating like a good 'un.'

Keane looked at the foam-flecked flanks of Morris's beloved Matilda and nodded. He glanced back at the rest of the troop and saw their weary faces and drooping shoulders. Ten minutes, he reasoned, would make no real difference and they would ride on refreshed.

'Yes, I think perhaps we should. And, to be honest, I could do with a drink myself.' He half turned over his shoulder. 'Dismount. Ten minutes.'

The men and Gabriella swung their legs from their mounts and jumped down onto the path, stretching, swearing and rubbing the sweat from their necks.

'We'll take a rest here. Not long, Sarn't Ross. Ten minutes. No more.'

They sat down on the south side of the road a good distance away from the uneven edge, on sun-baked rocks that sent the heat through their clothes. As they opened their canteens, Keane took a swig from his own, careful not to have too much, and reached for the leather valise strapped to his saddle, taking

out a rolled map. He was spreading it on the flank of his horse
as Morris came up.

'So, James, where exactly would you say we are?'

Keane traced his finger along the road that had been marked
on the map by the engineer surveying officer with a thin red
line.

'We've come this way. About fifty miles, and we have another
fifty to go before we reach the border with Spain.' He took a
pencil from his pocket and looking up for a moment to the
west wrote on the map, drawing in a contour of hills where
previously there had been none. 'Have you noticed, Tom? Map's
all wrong. Keeps happening. Makes you wonder if they ever
actually carried out the survey.' He went on. 'As I was saying,
we reach the border, here, just above Guarda, at a place called
Almeida. Fortress of a place. Then we leave the road and head
for the river. The Coa.

'Scovell's instructions were to ride deep into the mountains
. . . here. Well, we shan't make it there before nightfall. We'll
stop here.' He jabbed at the map. 'At Linhares, if we can. If it's
actually where it's shown on this damn thing.'

'What chance of a French patrol, d'you think?'

'Little, I imagine. We're too far south for Soult and further
north than Victor, if Grant's intelligence is to be believed.
Besides, these are the mountains. You'd be a very foolhardy
Frenchman to venture in here. This is guerrilla territory.'

'I wonder what they're like, these guerrillas.'

'Pretty ferocious, apparently. They give no quarter and have
been led to expect none. That at least is what Grant said. Good
fighters, though. Said he'd rarely seen the like. Glad they were
on our side. I suppose that we shall have to make sure they
know who we are.'

'They'll know us from our uniforms, surely?'

Keane laughed. 'I wouldn't take a wager on it. You can't be certain of anything here, Tom. You know that. Besides, Sarn't Ross, Gilpin, Silver, Garland and I might be in red but you are all in blue, hadn't you noticed? And Heredia too, with that ludicrous helmet. Worse than a French dragoon's.'

'My own ain't much better. But won't these heathens know a British officer when they see one?'

'Oh, they're not heathens. Far from it, actually. They owe allegiance only to God and their leaders. That's why they're so incensed at the French. They consider the French to be godless.'

'At least that's one thing we have in common. We're all Christians.'

Keane laughed. 'Not exactly. They're Roman Catholics, Tom. In their eyes we're heretics too. Don't forget it wasn't so long ago that we forswore the Pope and killed our king. Cut off his head, just as the French did with King Louis. As far as the Spaniards are concerned, we're almost as bad as Boney.'

'Well, God save us all from them then. I've said it before but this is a strange country, James. It's like going back in time five hundred years. At home we are creating a new world. Travelling faster, making everything at double the speed and for twice the money. My cousin is thinking of buying a mill. A mill, James. He says it's going to make him a fortune. Ten thousand a year. I sometimes wonder why I'm here and not at home getting fat while my workers do the same for me. Do you ever wonder why you're here?'

Keane shook his head. 'No. I can't say that I do. It just feels like home to me. The army. I couldn't stomach commerce.'

82 KEANE'S COMPANYKEANE'S COMPANY

'But ten thousand a year, James. Just think of it. And here we are living in the Middle Ages.'

'I'd sooner take my chances on the ramparts with the forlorn hope, Tom, than be in trade. You know that.' He got to his feet. 'Right. I think we had better be on our way.'

The ten minutes had run its course and Keane gave the order to mount up. They all moved fast, amid a chorus of groans that were shouted down by Ross, and on Keane's command the little party trotted on.

Wellesley had ordered them not only to return with intelligence of the guerrillas, but also if Keane thought it prudent and in their interest to do so, to leave a man behind, an officer who might instil some sort of organization, should it be lacking.

This was the greater part of his task, he knew, and he had not yet had the heart to mention it to Tom Morris, to whose lot it would undoubtedly fall to be that officer.

In Keane's opinion such a move was doomed to failure. The guerrillas, he reckoned, would be insulted and the officer placed in a dreadful predicament. Of course, it was not in fact Wellesley's idea but that of a Spaniard, the Duque del Infantado. Well named, thought Keane; only an child would have imagined that British discipline would have any effect among the guerrilla fighters. He imagined that they must be something like the American riflemen who had done so much damage and inflicted such casualties in the Revolutionary War. A fat lot of use an English officer would have been to them. They did not even obey the doctrines that Baron Steuben had instilled into the regular continental troops. But Keane knew from the regimental veterans' stories of that affair that the American irregulars had been just as much to blame for the British defeat as their drilled and polished 'properly trained' brothers. And he imagined that the same role would fall to the guerrillas if they were ever to rid Spain of the French.

The road became steeper now as it rose into the high sierra, and looking down into the valley Keane noticed how the fields gave way to acres of trees. On the hillsides huge granite boulders seemed to have grown into strange shapes, some resembling human forms. Gabriella was whispering something to Silver.

Keane asked, 'What was that?'

'She doesn't like it, she says, sir. It's the Serra da Estrela. The mountains for the stars. Her mother told her about it. It's a wild place. Beautiful but a place of spirits. Full of strange folk, she says. Gives her the shivers.'

'Tell her that there are no spirits here. Only the ones waiting for us in a bottle wherever we stop to rest.'

But Gabriella seemed to be having none of it and clung to the neck of her horse as they climbed ever higher into the hills.

The huge granite rocks were everywhere about them now, carved by the whipping sierra wind into strange, outlandish forms. Again Keane heard Gabriella talking to Silver. She spoke in almost a whimper now, betraying what sounded to him like genuine fear.

For her sake alone, if not for the rest of them, Keane was relieved when they came in sight of the town of Linhares, just as the light was beginning to fade. They reined in and looked up from the road at the town, bathed in the evening sunshine.

The ancient medieval town rose up before them, its simple

houses clustered around a hill surmounted by a castle. It was a superb strategic position. Keane could see instantly what had driven the original settlers to build here, and the soldier in him worked out instantly how the place might be defended in its present state.

The buildings seemed to Keane to have been carved from the very rock of the mountains, the orange pantiles added merely as an afterthought. The place was dominated by the twin towers of a pre-medieval castle and the remnants of the defensive walls still guarded the entrances.

Garland spoke. 'Christ, sir. Is that where we're going? That place?'

'That's where I intend for us to rest for the night, yes, Garland. Why?'

'Don't like the look of it, sir. Bit funny, if you know what I mean.'

'No, what do you mean?'

'Well, sir, sort of sets you off all a shiver, doesn't it? You'd expect some old knight in armour to come rising up out of it. Like a spirit, sir. Or a hobgoblin, wouldn't you, sir?'

Keane laughed. 'No, as a matter of fact I wouldn't. And nor should you. You've been reading too many of Mrs Radcliffe's stories, Garland.'

'Mrs who, sir?'

'Radcliffe. Never mind. Well, that's where we're going. There's no alternative apart from the rocks. So don't trouble yourself. Now, let's see if someone can find us a bed.'

They wound their way down the little road and entered the town under a medieval arch cut into the defensive wall and topped with battlements. Once inside Keane felt enclosed and as if they might indeed have stepped back in time three hundred years. Nothing here had changed, it seemed, for centuries, and for an instant he heard Garland's words. But only for an instant. Emerging into a narrow street, they walked their horses on over the worn cobblestones until they found themselves in a square with a bell tower and an inn, outside which hung a sign painted with a wine bottle. The place was deserted. Two doors creaked open on their hinges and in response to the clip-clop of the horses' hooves, swallows flew from under the eaves of a house, making them all start. They were jumpy and with good reason. This place, for all he had said, had a strange air about it. Keane gave the command to dismount and, with his hand resting on his sword hilt and Silver, Heredia and Morris close behind him, pushed open the door of the inn.

The place was deserted, save for an elderly man sitting at a table in the far corner of the room and a girl, mopping away at the floor. As they entered, the man looked at them with a frown.

Keane spoke in Spanish. 'We're English. English soldiers, señor. We are looking for a bed.'

The man looked at them again and then waved at the girl to leave.

'English? You are not French?' he asked.

'No, sir. Not French. Look at our red coats. English.'

The man pointed to Heredia. 'He is Spanish.' Then at Morris's blue coat. 'French. He is French.'

Before they could stop him the man had moved his hand from beneath the table and stood up, producing as he did so an ancient blunderbuss which he aimed at Morris.

Keane spoke: 'No!' and his hand went to his sword.

At the same moment Morris walked towards the man, and as he did so removed his helmet.

'No, I am English.'

The man looked uncertain for a moment and kept the gun levelled at Morris, his finger hovering over the trigger. He spoke, haltingly: 'English?'

Morris nodded and stood there. Heredia spoke, in Spanish, and the man stared at him quizzically. Silver joined in, in his own self-taught, half-remembered dialect and to Keane's surprise the man began to smile. He lowered the gun and shouted to the girl, who walked quickly across to the counter.

'Carlotta, wine for the gentlemen.' He turned to Morris. 'English. Yes, we can give you a bed. How many are you?'

Morris replied, 'Eight and one woman.'

The man looked surprised. 'A woman?'

Keane spoke: 'The wife of one of my men.'

The innkeeper, who had now laid down the ancient weapon, looked at Keane. 'You are a long way from your army, no?'

'Yes. We come ahead of them. You know where our army is?'

'Of course. Does anyone not know?'

As Keane sent Ross to summon the others, the girl returned with a tray and two bottles of wine, along with nine glasses.

The innkeeper spoke to Keane. 'Your army is coming here?'

'No, not the whole army. Not here, exactly.' He tried a different tack. 'We are here looking for the French.'

'The landlord smiled and then looked grim. 'Why come to look for the French? We do not want them to find us. We have heard too much about what they have done. Pray God, señor, that they never find this place.'

Keane nodded and turned to find Silver behind him. 'What the deuce did you say to him?'

'I just told him that we were all English, apart from Heredia who was our guide. I also told him that I was married to a Portuguese girl, that her family had been killed by the French and that I personally wanted to cut the bollocks off the next French officer I met. Was that right, sir?'

'Quite right, Silver. Well done.' Heredia was standing close by. 'And you, Heredia. Well done you too.' Heredia managed a smile, but something told Keane that he resented Silver's clever quip, and he detected just a whiff of rivalry.

Keane took a sip of wine and Morris did the same, turning to the landlord who had poured himself a large glass and offered some to the others. Keane nodded and the girl poured. Morris spoke: 'It's a beautiful village.'

The landlord smiled. 'Yes, it is. Very old. The Romans came here. The castle is very old. My family have lived here for many hundreds of years. Pray God, they will do so hundreds more. We do not want war here, señor. We want peace. Why do you bring war?'

Keane shook his head. 'Not us, señor, but the French. We are here to save your people from war.'

The man shook his head. 'Then, señor, you are too late. The war is here now and I know that it will not leave my country until many thousands of people have died.'

Keane grasped the moment. 'What do you know of the guerrillas? There's a man called Morillo.'

The landlord looked at him.

'You are looking for Coronel Morillo? You must be a fool.'

'Why? You know him?'

The man was quick to respond. 'No. No, I have never met him. But I have heard about him. Many things. I don't think you want to know him, señor.'

'He's a patriot, isn't he? He fights for Spain. For all of you, against the French.'

'From what I have heard, señor, Pablo Morillo fights for no one but himself. But yes, he hates the French.'

'I've heard that he gives no quarter.'

The man waved his hand and rose to his feet. 'Please, please. Don't talk of him, señor. Lest he should come here. We do not need him here. Or the French.'

Or us, thought Keane. You don't need us, do you? You just want to be left alone. But you're right. It is too late. War has come to this place and now you have only one hope of salvation. And that is us. 'I'm sorry, I didn't mean to alarm you. If you know anyone who can direct us to Morillo, I should be in your debt. I can pay for information.'

The man sat down again. 'Carlotta, more wine. I do remember something now. There is a story about where he is meant to have his camp. Although he changes it all the time. My niece here overheard a conversation between two officers, Spanish officers, just three nights ago, didn't you, Carlotta?'

The girl nodded.

'There were Spanish cavalry here?' Keane asked.

'Yes, sir. Do not think you are the only ones to come here. She might tell you what you want to know. For a price.'

Yes, thought Keane, I'm sure she will. And he wondered just how she had 'overheard' the Spanish officers speak; in what circumstances, and what she had charged them for the pleasure of her company. She came over now to their table.

'Carlotta, this English officer would like you to tell him what you heard from the two gentlemen. About Coronel Morillo's camp. He'll pay you.'

She looked at Keane. 'How much? It's dangerous to talk.'

The man spoke. 'Shall we say five guineas?'

Keane shook his head. 'I'm sorry, señor. Five guineas, and I don't even know if it will be true.'

'It's worth five guineas, isn't it?'

The girl looked at him with brown saucer eyes and opened her mouth just a fraction so he could see the white of her teeth.

Keane smiled. 'Five guineas, and for that you can send her up to my room later.'

The man pretended to look shocked. 'My niece? Señor.'

'She might be your daughter for all I know. Do we have a bargain?'

The girl nodded and flashed a smile at Keane, who brought out his purse and laid the money on the table. The girl picked up one of the coins and bit it to test it, then laid it back down. The man scooped the money into his palm as she spoke. 'Morillo's camp is just on the other side of the hills, to the east, and across the plain of the Coa. Then it is a climb into the mountains. By horse it will take you four, maybe five hours. Go just as far as Trancoso, then turn east, further into the mountains.'

'How will I find him?'

'Oh, don't worry about that. He is sure to find you, señor.'

She flashed another smile and then turned and walked away. Keane thanked the landlord then went to join his men, and began to turn his thoughts to a warm bed.

When Keane awoke at dawn, the innkeeper's niece, if that indeed was what she was, was long gone. He felt as he always did in such circumstances. Saddened, yet reassured once again that there was more to life than the business of death in which he was more usually engaged. He felt no remorse. No more at least than she might have done, and no regret. It had been a deal. Part of a deal, and she had carried out her part of the bargain admirably. And then she had gone. Pulling on his clothes, Keane tried to remember a time when he had not felt like this about women, and could not. To him such encounters were merely a part of soldiering.

He buckled on his sword belt and opened the shutters to the light.

They saddled their mounts as the sun was crowning the peaks of the Serra da Estrela and moved off through the little town as noiselessly as they could. At the old defensive gate a sheepdog stood and barked at them like some ancient sentry, but that was the only sign of life they saw. Taking the high road towards Caloric, they gradually dropped down into the valley of the Mondego. The country now was quite different. The stark grey granite had gone, to be replaced by lush fields and pastures where sheep grazed in their hundreds. Along the banks of the river's tributaries stood watermills and to Keane the land seemed untouched by time. He was reminded of the landlord's words and wondered how much longer this paradise would exist. The French armies lived off the land, taking what they needed and laying waste to anything they did not. Soon, perhaps, he thought, all this will be gone. For all we know we may be the last travellers to see this land as it is. As it has been for hundreds of years and may never be again.

Following the road, they began to climb again on the route that would take them deep into the mountains. The earth was hard and dry and the horses' hooves crunched on the stones. Reaching a junction in the road they saw below them a valley.

Keane pulled up and dismounted. Opening his valise and taking out Grant's map, he unrolled it and smiled at Morris. 'That's the Coa, Tom. And over there' – he pointed eastwards. 'Over there, that's Almeida and then Spain.'

'And the French, James.'

'Aye, and the French. But that's not where we're going.' He turned to the north. 'That's our road, there. North, across the river and into the hills.'

'To the guerrillas.'

'Yes. God knows what we'll find, if the girl's to be believed. I can't help but think that we've had it too easy these last few days. I know it's been hard going. But I have a feeling that we're about to get a rude awakening, Tom. Make sure you're ready for it.'

It was down in the valley where the girl had sent them, on the banks of the Coa, that Keane first became aware that they were being watched. He was conscious of movement in the undergrowth quite a way off in the hills away to their left. Nothing visible. Just a general feeling of unease and an imagined, unwanted presence. It could have been anything, he supposed. A deer, a goat, or a flock of sheep. But somehow he knew it was a man. Or men. They went on another few miles, with no one saying a word. Only Silver carried on humming one of his monotonous shanties. But even he was quieter now, such was the growing sense among them all that they were being tracked.

They were in a defile now, narrow with steep sides and the stream running along to their right. Following a bend in the road, they found the way blocked. A fall of rocks had come down the hillside and now extended from the rise on the left to the drop on the right.

Keane stopped in his tracks. But it was not the vertiginous view that unsettled him. For now he could see that behind the rocky barrier ahead of them stood a man.

He stood with his arms folded, staring at them. He was of medium height with a shock of dark-brown hair which fell forward onto his tanned forehead in two long curls and in his right hand he held a cigar. He had piercing black eyes which were fixed on Keane, and above the curiously feminine bow of his lips was the suggestion of a moustache. He wore a black bicorne hat trimmed with a cockade in the Spanish colours, placed fore and aft as Wellesley did, and the blue uniform of an officer in the Spanish army, heavily encrusted with gold braid. On his breast he bore the star of the Order of Charles III.

The man nodded formally at Keane. 'Coronel Pablo Morillo at your service, captain.'

Keane nodded in return and slipped down from his horse, ordering the others to do likewise.

'Good day, colonel. James Keane, captain attached to the staff of Lord Wellesley. I'm obliged to you, sir.'

'I have been following your progress with interest for some time, Captain Keane. And here you are at last. So tell me, what is it that brings you to our camp, at the risk of your life? I am sorry, but some of my men cannot tell an English soldier from a French one. You might have been killed.'

Keane smiled. 'Yes, that would have been awkward. I'm here at the request of the commander-in-chief of the British expedition to Portugal, colonel. He desires information and in return will assist you in ridding your land of the French.'

Morillo smiled. 'That is most generous of General Wellesley. Tell me, how does he intend to help me? With your little command? Seven men and a girl? Or is he planning to send a brigade to me? Men who know of no other way of fighting a war than to stand in line and be shot at by the enemy. They would not be of very much use in the sort of war I wage in these mountains.'

'Believe me, colonel, General Wellesley will assist you in whatever way you wish, up to a point.'

Morillo paused and seemed to Keane to be staring at him in an effort to understand him.

'And what does he want from me, captain? How will I help him? Undoubtedly he wants to know our strength. Well, that is rather hard to say, captain. You see, some days I can count on a thousand men following me. On others it might be merely threescore. That is the nature of our war.'

Keane continued. 'I am also instructed, colonel, to offer advice as to how best to organize this army, and if I see fit to leave behind one of my own officers to facilitate this.'

Morillo said nothing for a moment but Keane could see that he had rushed it; had even perhaps overstepped the mark and offended the Spaniard.

At last the colonel spoke. 'Captain, I have been a proud soldier all my life. Since I was thirteen. I joined the army of Spain in 1791. I fought against your navy at Trafalgar as a marine, and after the battle of Bailen I was promoted to officer. It was the greatest moment of my life. I serve the king of Spain and the people of Spain. I have known war and I have gained from war all that I have. It is as much as a humble shepherd boy could have hoped for. I do not need your advice and I do not need your men.'

'Colonel, please accept my apologies. I did not intend to offend you. I am sure that your men are great fighters. We are on the same side. We both fight the French.'

Morillo shrugged. 'True. At present that is true. But what will happen when we drive them out? Will you go too?'

'Of course, we are not invaders.'

'No? For three centuries your people and mine have been at war and now you are here as our friends. Why? Because your government sends you.'

'Times change, colonel. We have no argument with you. I am only a soldier. I obey my orders. We are both fighting Napoleon.'

'Yes, but you want what you have always wanted. You English.' He put the slim cheroot that he was holding in his right hand to his lips, and, pursing them, took a long drag, blowing the smoke high in the air where it curled in circles.

Keane said nothing. He knew that there was more than a grain of truth in what Morillo had said. He was canny enough, an Irishman's sensibilities aware that the English did nothing without a clear motive. Spain was a mess. The king had fled, and if they did manage to drive out the French the country might dissolve into anarchy. He knew that when that happened, the government in London wanted to be there to pick up the pieces of the shattered country and what was left of its empire. This was the final act, as Morillo had said, of a tragedy that had played out over three centuries ever since Drake had defeated the Armada.

Morillo spoke again. 'What will your general give us in return?'

Keane had known that this would come eventually.

'We can offer you muskets and ammunition. Supplies too, if you need them.'

Morillo thought for a while. 'Very well. But I will need to see the muskets or something in good faith.'

Keane reached into his valise and drew out a sealed leather bag that he had kept for just this occasion. He tossed it to Morillo. 'In there, colonel, you will find ten guineas. That is my general's pledge to you of his aid. I trust that will be sufficient proof.'

Morillo took the bag and, breaking the seal, pulled it open. He smiled at Keane and nodded.

As they had been talking, Keane had become conscious of a noise from beyond the landslide. The sound of men's voices. He presumed that they belonged to Morillo's guerrillas and wondered how many there might be on this day: threescore or a thousand? At that moment the noise became increasingly loud and the silence which had followed their conversation was filled by a great shout, a cheer almost, followed by a terrible scream. It was the sound of a man in pain, but it was almost animal in its despair.

Keane started. 'Christ, what the devil was that?'

Morillo took another long drag on his cigar. 'The prisoner, I would guess.'

'Prisoner?'

'Oh, I didn't tell you, captain? My men caught a French courier this morning.'

'What are they doing to him?'

Morillo smiled. 'They are making him talk. And they are killing him. Slowly.'

Keane paused. 'They can't do that. It's against the articles of war.'

'No? Watch them, captain. Actually, perhaps I will do just that. You might like to join me. If you have the stomach for it.'

He turned and walked away from the landslide and Keane could see now that what had previously seemed to be an impenetrable barrier had in fact been carefully constructed so that a slim passage just wide enough for a man on a horse to slip through had been cut into the rocks. Morillo went quickly through the gap and looked behind him to see if Keane was following. The last thing that Keane wanted to do was to watch a man being tortured to death. But he knew it was vital that he make a show of his own machismo and at the same time atone for his earlier blunder. He followed, but turned as he did so and motioned to all the others except Morris to remain behind, and also to cock their weapons. Morris drew his sword.

Hurrying after Morillo between the rocks, Keane found himself in a circle of perhaps a hundred men. He followed the colonel to the front and what he saw stopped him dead.

The banditti were ranged around the unfortunate Frenchman, who had been stripped naked and roped to a St Andrew's cross which was set against a boulder. From his green and gold uniform, which lay on another rock, Keane could see that the man had been an officer of dragoons. Still was, in fact. For the Frenchman was not yet dead. He groaned and tried to writhe against his bonds. Keane could see now that his naked body was flecked with blood and covered in cuts.

In front of him another man, one of the guerrillas, stood with a knife in his hand and Keane noticed that both it and the man's arms and body were spattered with gore. The man placed his hand under the Frenchman's head and brought it up to stare into his eyes, then moving quickly he flashed out the knife and made a cut in the man's upper arm. The Frenchman screamed and the blood flowed. The guerrilla let the man's head sag again and turned, grinning, to face his appreciative audience. Then he walked up to the man again and, moving to his left side, stood for a moment contemplating his handiwork. The knife flashed again, and again the victim screamed as its razor-sharp blade took a slice from his ribs. This time the executioner held up the flap of skin for all to see. Keane realized that, having merely played with the Frenchman, the executioner was now starting to flay his victim alive.

Making sure that no one was watching, that all eyes were focused on the appalling obscenity playing out before him, Keane reached into his belt and drew out a pistol. Placing it behind his back, he drew back the lever until it clicked into place. Then, as the executioner raised his knife for a third time, he brought the gun round and aimed it carefully at the Frenchman's head. He pulled the trigger, and the shot shattered the expectant silence. The bullet entered the Frenchman's head at the temple, killing him instantly. Then, having passed through his head, it smashed into a tree on the opposite side of the road.

For a moment there was silence and then a hundred pairs of eyes turned on Keane, who had replaced the pistol in his belt and drawn its pair, which was cocked and ready. He needn't have bothered. A glance to his right and left told him that his six men were now to the rear of the circle, with their own carbines cocked and pointed towards the crowd.

Morris whispered to him. 'Didn't think that we wouldn't follow you, James, did you?' He caught sight of the mangled corpse. 'Good God. What's that?'

'All that's left of a French officer after these tyros have had their way with him. Not a pretty sight, is it?'

The executioner lowered his knife with a muttered oath, then, raising it quickly, plunged it into the dead man's heart. Then he looked straight at Keane with emotionless, steel-grey eyes.

Morillo spoke to Keane. 'Why did you do that?'

'To put him out of his misery, in the same way that I would kill a wounded dog.'

'You don't know anything. Nothing. He was a beast. A rapist. A killer of children.'

'He was a man, colonel. That's all I know. And now he's a dead man.'

The executioner began to move towards Keane, but then saw the raised guns and stopped. Morillo threw his cigar to the ground and stamped on it. 'You're a fool, captain. That was not necessary.'

'In my eyes it was absolutely necessary. What you did was inhuman.'

'No. What he did was inhuman. What his countrymen do every day to my people is inhuman. Clearly you have no idea, captain. Besides, we needed the information and we got it from him. Information, I think, for your general.'

He smiled, happy that he had shifted the blame for the torture to Keane and the British. Keane shook his head. 'Had I known what you intended to do I would have done it myself.'

'What?' Morillo laughed. 'You would have had your sergeant beat him to a pulp with his fists? Is that any different?'

'Yes. Of course it is. And you know it. It's not the sort of systematic cruelty that I've just been privy to. Killing a man by degrees. Humiliating him as he dies for the cruel pleasure of others. I'm all in favour of using force where necessary, colonel. But that? That was just wrong. It was immoral.'

Morillo shrugged. 'It's life, Captain Keane. One more life is taken. One more Frenchman is dead.'

The executioner, still wiping the blood from his hands, walked towards them, expressionless but clearly furious. He was a huge man whose massive, bloody hands seemed to Keane to be incapable of having performed the horribly precise butcher's job he had just carried out on the Frenchman.

He shrugged at Morillo. 'What did this fool think he was doing? The Frenchman should have suffered. After what he did.'

Morillo gestured to Keane. 'You haven't met our new friend, have you, Ramon? Let me present Captain Keane of the British army. Ramon Sanchez. My ablest lieutenant.'

Sanchez smiled and then, looking at Keane, resumed the same blank expression. 'Why did you do that? Why have you come here, captain? What do you want from us?'

'We need your help. Information. We need to find out how much you know about the French.'

The man laughed. 'I know enough about them. But I know more now than I did half an hour ago. Thanks to that piece of dead meat over there.'

'What did he tell you?'

'Why should I tell you?'

'We are on the same side, aren't we?'

'Are we?' Sanchez looked at Morillo, who nodded. 'He told me that the French generals are on the move. That they're going to combine their forces.'

This was it. This was what they had come for. 'You're certain of that?'

'That was what he said, captain. And I don't doubt it to be true. The idiot thought that if he told us we might spare his life. At least he thought we might stop the pain.'

'Do you know where they intend to move?'

'Yes. He was most obliging.'

He was evading the question. Playing games in revenge for Keane's ruining his sport. It was going to take longer than Keane had imagined and there was no alternative but to play along.

Morillo smiled at him, as if realizing that Keane now understood the game they were playing. 'You will stay with us tonight?'

'That is most kind, coronel. But I think we had better get on our way. My general will be awaiting my report.'

'But you have no report to make, yet. At least then let me offer you a drink and some refreshment for your journey.'

There was no alternative but to accept.

The body of the dead Frenchman had not been touched and since none of the guerrillas looked as if they were inclined to deal with it in the near future, Keane was relieved when Morillo led him away to another part of the camp where, in the shade of a makeshift shelter, Morillo offered him a glass of the heavy local wine and some olives.

'My men will look after yours. Who is the girl? A Portuguese?'

'Yes, she's the wife of one of my men.'

'She's very pretty.'

'Yes. And of course he's devoted to her and very protective.'

Not for the first time Keane felt slightly threatened by Morillo and his men. They might have declared themselves to be allies of the British, but in Keane's mind they seemed in reality no better than a band of brigands, willing to slit the throat of any man who might have a purse of gold and probably more than willing to take something or someone they had an eye for. He decided to make a point.

'She's a feisty one too. A good fighter.'

Morillo nodded. 'Yes, I can believe it. We have similar women in our *partidas*. They are the worst when we capture a Frenchman.'

'Tell me about the *partidas*, coronel. How many of you are there?'

Morillo laughed. 'It's hard to know. I never have an exact headcount. Men come and go. We do not have the same discipline as your army. I don't flog my men.'

Another evasive answer. Never an exact headcount. Keane's mind was racing. He tried again.

'Your command seems very extensive. What area do you cover? Is that how it works? By district?'

Morillo shrugged. 'Yes, captain. We are each in command of men in an area of the country. That way we can move onto another's command if the enemy invade our own. We know every road, every hill, every river and all the places where we can catch the enemy best. That is how we fight. You won't find us where you expect to.'

'How are we to find you, then?'

'When you want us all you have to do is to ride into the mountains. We will find you, captain. Of that you can be sure.'

He smiled and took a long drink.

Keane drank slowly. He had half wondered whether Morillo, for all his talk of comradeship, might not have drugged their drinks. But he put the thought from his mind. The wine was a strong local red and the olives bigger than any he had ever eaten. The idea that Morillo did not know how many men were in his camp had fired his imagination and he thought of Gilpin, with his Spanish and his gift for mimicry. Making his excuses and leaving Ross and Morris to drink with Morillo, Keane walked to the horses where the others had been standing. He found Gilpin talking to Silver.

'Gilpin, I've a plan.'

'Sir?'

'You are to disguise yourself as one of the guerrillas and remain here.'

'Sir?'

'Just what I say. Take a disguise and use all your skills. Then in two days' time, if you have overhead enough, ride out of the camp and find us.'

Gilpin blanched. 'But sir. How am I to find you?'

Keane had thought of this. 'In three days' time we will be back at Coimbra. Make for there. I will give you one of my maps. They're poor, but good enough for you.' Keane reached into his saddlebag and drew out a duplicate map of the area, giving it to Gilpin. 'We will see you there. You may count on it. You had better get to it soon. Slip into the shadows. They have no idea how many we are, let alone how many of their own men they have here, and they're all getting tipsy on that local filth. Will you do it? Can you?'

Gilpin nodded. 'I'll do my best, sir.'

'That you will, Gilpin. Of that I'm sure.'

Gilpin said no more, but removing his red coat and placing it carefully in one of the saddlebags, he drew out from the same one of the simple Spanish costumes they had packed for just such an event, and in a moment he was gone.

Keane hoped that he had done the right thing and not sentenced the man to a certain and horrible death.

Having once again refused Morillo's offer of remaining in the camp, they left, without Gilpin, shortly before nightfall, and retraced their steps back towards civilization while the guerrillas continued to drink and sing.

They slept that night in the open. The night was warm and the sky clear, and the sound of the cicadas echoed across the hills. Keane stood on his own, a little way away from the camp-fire. He was content. Morillo had at last him given the infor-mation he needed: the placings and movements of the French armies and their strengths. And what was more, he had learnt much about the guerrillas. He congratulated himself too on having formed a relationship with Morillo. He stared at the stars. He had always enjoyed sleeping outdoors; had grown accustomed to it as a boy and become hardened by the army. These nights in Portugal were kinder but he was always conscious that the same sky looked down on Ireland. He was aware of a presence behind him and thought it must be Morris, but on turning he found Gabriella.

'Can't sleep?'

'No. Not after today. Too much has happened.'

'Are you sorry you came with us?'

'How could I be? I have him.' She pointed to Silver, sleeping soundly with his head on a rolled blanket close to the dying embers of the fire. 'And I am free of a life that I never wished for myself.'

'I won't ask how you came to be there.'

'The usual story. My parents died. There was no money. That's all. What else does a girl have apart from her body?'

'You have your mind. You can work.'

'That was work. You think it wasn't?'

'I didn't say that. Nor did I mean it.' Keane looked back up at the stars and then down at the landscape, bathed as it was in moonlight.

'It's beautiful here.'

'I thought it frightened you.'

'Not tonight. Not any longer. Nothing could be more frightening than that man. It is beautiful. And it has a beautiful name. "Serra da Estrela". The mountains of the stars.'

'It seems right tonight, with so many up there above us.'

'You are a stargazer, Captain Keane. I'm surprised. I took you for a soldier.'

'Soldiers can be many things, Gabriella. At this moment I happen to be a stargazer.'

'Where are we going now, captain? Deeper into the mountains?'

'No, we're going home now. At least back to Coimbra. Back to the general. I have a report to give him.'

'And then?'

'And then he will attack.'

'And then we will have a battle and many men will die.' She looked again at Silver. 'Perhaps he will die?'

'I don't know. Who knows? We're all soldiers. We know that whether we live or die is only a question of luck.'

'Luck? Everything is luck, isn't it?'

'You think so?'

'Not quite everything. It was lucky for me that you were there. But then it was you, captain, who thought to let me come with you. That was not luck.'

She smiled at him and for a moment he wondered if there might be anything more to it. He would stall it, now.

'Silver needs you. We all need you.'

'I hope that I will be able to prove you right, captain. I am a soldier too now. I will fight for my country. And for Spain too, to rid this land of the French.'

'I think we had both better get some sleep. We have a long journey in the morning.'

She began to walk back to where Silver lay but then she turned and, retracing her steps, walked up to Keane and gave him a kiss on the cheek.

Nothing more. Just that one friend would give to another. And then she turned again and went back to her sleeping husband.

# 5

The morning had come upon them cold and unforgiving and Keane was out of sorts. Having had the previous two nights to consider the events in Morillo's camp, he was less happy with the situation than he had been initially. The encounter had not gone as well as it might have done. His early euphoria he now put down to their having got away with their lives from a place of such hideous sights as none had ever before witnessed. Furthermore, while he had gained the information that Wellesley sought, he had not come away feeling that they had found a wholly dependable ally. The guerrillas, he now could see, were out for what they could get, and only after that for what might benefit Spain. As for their attitude towards the English, he felt that Morillo and his men considered them little better than the French.

He wondered too about his decision to persuade Gilpin to infiltrate the camp. In truth, he did not give much for the man's chances of survival over a week among such desperadoes.

But now they were distant from the guerrilla camp. They had ridden hard for two days away from the 'mountains of the stars', so hard indeed that he thought his poor nag might have given up the ghost. But she had survived. They all had, and Keane had never been so glad to come in sight of the first red-coated sentries as they neared the British camp at Coimbra.

Now, rested, refreshed and changed, he entered the ante-room of the Bishop's palace, in the centre of the hillside town and found Wellesley standing beside the huge carved fireplace. The general was in conversation with Grant but on Keane's arrival turned to greet him with a smile.

'Keane. Major Grant here was only just talking of you. You found the guerrillas.'

'Yes, sir. At least, we found one of them and his men. Colonel Morillo.'

'Ah yes. Major Grant has been describing him to me from your account. A rogue, you said?'

'You might say so, sir. Though I do believe he is a good fighter. He seems to command respect and admiration among his men.'

'Who are, you would say, also good fighters?'

'I'm afraid that I did not have the opportunity to witness them in action, sir. But if looks speak, then yes, they look as if they would give the French a run for their money. In a pitched battle, though, I would not trust them an inch not to cut and run the moment the first ball was flying towards them.'

Wellesley laughed. 'That's much as I expected. But the war they fight is very different in its tactics to that in which you and I are engaged.'

'Apparently so, sir. It is what they call the "guerrilla".'

Grant interjected. 'The word guerrilla itself seems to have many meanings, sir. Derived from the Spanish for "war", it may be used to describe the guerrilla band, which they also refer to as the *partida*. It can also be used as a term for the operations themselves and moreover a piquet of men standing guard.'

Wellesley nodded indulgently. 'Much obliged, major. Pray continue, captain.'

Keane went on. 'I left one of my own men behind, sir, in disguise, to gather further information. I expect him to return here today and have left instructions for him to be conducted to us here, should he appear while I am with you.'

Wellesley smiled. 'You have done well, Keane. Let's hope that your desperadoes do not see through his disguise and that your man makes it through.'

Keane continued. 'What is certain, sir, is that Boney's men will have faced nothing like this lot before. These men are quick on their feet, sir. Damn quick. Like mountain goats, or deer. They know every road there is to know in the hills and every trick by which to confuse their pursuers. They have the ability to close roads with the aid of nature and thus sever communications. And what's more, they will fade into the hills before you can see them.'

Wellesley nodded. 'A formidable ally, then, captain. And a formidable adversary for the French. And will they fight for us?'

Keane shook his head. 'Not for us, sir. That they'll never do, in my opinion. But they will, I think, fight with us. If we give them what they want.'

Wellesley laughed. 'Why, I wonder, does that not much surprise me? They told you a good deal, I gather. That was well done, Keane. I would have thought that Morillo would be especially guarded with his information. Major Grant has acquainted me with the basic facts.'

There was a knock at the door and an aide, a captain of Foot Guards, entered. 'Sir, there is a man here. A Spaniard. He claims to have an appointment with you and Captain Keane. What should I do, sir?'

Keane laughed. 'Gilpin. It's Gilpin, sir. I'm sorry – the man I left with Morillo. It must be Gilpin and he has duped your aide.'

Wellesley frowned at the young officer. 'Well, Featherstonhaugh, is he English or Spanish?'

'A Spaniard, sir. At least he looks like a Spaniard and sounds like one.'

'And smells like one too, I'll wager,' said Grant. Keane smiled and turned to Wellesley. 'It is Gilpin, sir. I'm sure of it.'

Wellesley waved his hand at the aide. 'Admit him, Featherstonhaugh, for heaven's sake.'

The aide vanished and in his place entered a small man, clad in breeches and salopettes, a white shirt, and an embroidered waistcoat. About his head he wore a coloured handkerchief and there was heavy stubble on his chin. But Keane knew his eyes at once and ran towards him. 'Gilpin! Sam Gilpin. Well done.' He clapped him on the back and instantly the figure snapped to attention. Wellesley stood back. 'Well, I'll be damned. He is an Englishman.'

Grant spoke. 'Got the smell off, though, hasn't he?'

Keane smiled. 'So what did you find out, anything more?'

Gilpin, seeing the map spread out on the large oak table that dominated the room, walked towards it, as he did so untying the handkerchief from his head. 'If you don't mind, sir, I could show you on this map.'

Wellesley walked towards the table. 'Show me, then, man. Here.'

Gilpin walked up to the map and pointed. 'According to the information they obtained from the captured Frenchman, sir, General Silvera's Portuguese have been driven from here, the bridge at Amarante, north-east of Oporto. The enemy, favoured by a dense fog, attacked General Silveira on the 2nd and defeated him, taking eight pieces of cannon.'

Wellesley frowned. 'Silvera's been pushed back, eh?'

Gilpin went on. 'There is more, sir. And better news. Morillo reports that there is a spirit abroad among the French army in Oporto that almost amounts to mutiny.'

Wellesley looked at him. 'Mutiny? Go on.'

'It was all I could do, sir, to listen in. I did my best, sir. I have an ear for a tongue and can carry it off quite well, if you understand me. I made out that I was from Madrid and had not any idea of events. They were ready to tell me. It would appear that among the French in Oporto the hospitals are over-crowded with the sick, and that among the rank and file the feeling is of a profound dislike for the command and indeed for war as a whole. Morillo believes that, far from attacking us, the French – well, Marshal Soult at least – may now have plans to evacuate Portugal, sir. Marshal Soult, they say, is desperate. He is even now employed in the destruction of his stores and magazines, in Oporto. He may leave, they believe, by marching to the Tagus or by going here' – he pointed – 'across these mountains they call the Tras os Montes.'

Wellesley pondered the information for a few moments and then, stretching his hands across the map, pointed in turn to Oporto and Amarante.

'If you and your man here are correct, Captain Keane, then we have but one option. We must leave aside any notion of attacking Marshal Ney along with Victor and Lapisse. We will take the army in two divisions and march directly upon Soult on the Douro. One wing will move here to Aveira, the other to Vouga. General Beresford with his Portuguese will take a flying column and move upon Lamego to turn Marshal Soult's left flank.'

He raised his head and looked at Keane. 'Thank you, Keane. That was very clear and well interpreted. Excellent information.' He turned to Gilpin. 'And thank you, Private . . . ?'

'Gilpin, sir.'

'Thank you, Gilpin. Keane, see that he gets something. A drink and some clean clothes might be a start.'

Keane nodded and smiled but as he murmured his thanks to the general, he thought of the way in which the information had been obtained by the guerrillas from the Frenchman and felt a wave of nausea.

But Wellesley was not yet finished. 'Before you go, tell me more of the guerrillas, Keane. I would know everything.'

'In their hearts they detest the French, sir. That was evident from the atrocity they committed on the French officer from whom the information was obtained.'

'Yes, Major Grant related the account to me. Go on.'

'But they have at the same time no great love for us.'

Wellesley looked thoughtful. 'But you do think that we can use them?'

'Yes, I'm convinced of that. More than that, though, sir. We need them. They can become our eyes and ears. We simply have to learn how to treat with them, and to turn a blind eye to the methods they use to defend their homeland.'

'Is there anything you need, Keane? Any material?'

The obvious answer here was money. Keane needed funds. He had used all that Grant had provided and a good deal of his own in the operation. But he did not ask for it. He thought that, not for the first time, Wellesley was now testing him. 'New maps, sir. The maps are quite useless, sir. I tried to correct the course of the roads and to draw in hills where none were shown. I also did this, from memory.' Reaching into his leather valise, he gave Wellesley a piece of paper. The general took it and looked at it hard. 'This is a drawing of their camp? The guerrillas?'

'Yes, sir. As I say, it was done from memory, but it is as accurate as I can make it.'

'Why, it's good, Keane. Damn good. It gives one a true sense of what they're about.' He showed it to Grant. 'Wouldn't you say so, Colquhoun? Very good. Most evocative.'

'As you say, sir. Captain Keane has a good eye and a fine hand with a pencil. Quite as good as Mister Sandby.'

'We shall need more of these. This is exactly the kind of thing I had in mind when I commissioned you, Keane. Well done.'

Keane and Gilpin left the anteroom accompanied by Grant, who spoke after having first closed the door behind them, leaving Wellesley poring over his map.

'James, you seem a little incommoded. Out of sorts.'

'Not out of sorts, sir. I am merely a little out of pocket.'

'How so?'

'The general asked me what I lacked but I was loath to say "money", sir. Yet that is the truth of it. I had to use Captain Scovell's funds to buy off Silver's doxy from her madam, and then my own to bribe the executioner to swear that Gilpin here had been killed. I then used the emergency fund to persuade Morillo of our good intentions.'

'Good, that was its purpose.'

'But now I'm out of pocket, personally. To the tune of five guineas.'

'Well, I'm sure that it will all sort itself out somehow, Keane.'

'Sir, I trust you are not implying that the army will not reimburse me? How am I then expected to survive?'

Grant looked at him. 'I'm sorry, James, but the army's no better off than you at present. We await His Majesty's payroll with anticipation. Until that arrives from England we are none of us in funds and Wellesley is out of favour with his command. If you want my opinion, James, what we need is a victory or two.'

Keane walked disconsolately with Gilpin back to the bivouac which they had made at the same place as before, a short distance from the camp. He had posted Martin as a lookout, aware that there might still be a bounty to be had for apprehending Garland, and the boy saluted as he approached.

He found Silver sitting on a rock. He was carving a shape from a piece of wood and as Keane looked at it more closely he saw that it was a model of a ship of the line.

'That's wonderful, Silver, quite beautiful. To have that skill. Where did you come by it?'

Silver looked up at him and for a moment stopped his whittling. 'Always had it, sir. Well, near as always. Had it since I was a little nipper. In the Royal Navy, I was, you see, sir. Since I was a boy of ten. Press gang got me in Pompey. That's Portsmouth, sir. Eight years at sea, I was. Plenty of time to carve then, sir. When I wasn't running powder. Monkey, I was. Then I advanced. Able seaman. I fought at Trafalgar, me, sir. On the Admiral's flagship, sir. The *Victory*. She was a lovely ship, sir.'

'Really, Silver? You were at Trafalgar?'

He thought wryly of Morillo's talk of the battle.

'Really, sir. I'll swear it on my mother's grave. And what's more, I helped carry the admiral himself down below decks. I saw it all there, sir. Saw Mister Hardy give him a last embrace. We was all in tears, sir. All of us. He was a great man, sir. Lord Nelson.'

'You saw Lord Nelson die?'

'That I did, sir. Close as you are now to me, he was, and he says, Silver, he says. You go back out there and get the man who done this thing.'

'He asked you to find his killer?'

'The very same, sir. And to kill him. Couldn't do that, of course. No one knew who had shot him, sir. Could have been a Frenchie or one of the dagoes up in the top masts of a Spanish ship.'

Keane smiled at the thought that the very man might have been Morillo himself, for all he knew. He hadn't of course told Silver the guerrilla leader's history, nor now did he intend to.

Silver looked at his handiwork and went back to carving the warship.

Ross came up. 'Gilpin's told me what he heard, sir. We're bound to move soon, ain't we, sir?'

'Yes, Ross. It is in the general's plan. We're to march north against Marshal Soult.'

'What do we do then, sir? I mean us lot and you. When the army gets to grips with the Frenchies. Where do we go?'

'We, Ross, I hope, will be at the very front of the army. Scouting the way ahead and ensuring that the general's plans do not go awry. Where exactly we fit into his plans, though, I have yet to be informed.'

*

The three days that followed were spent resting and re-equipping the men. Morris, Ross and Keane between them managed to scrounge supplies from various sources, including their own old regimental stores, and by Sunday, 8 May, were ready to move again. Keane was settling down to an afternoon's game of loo with Morris when a runner arrived, a lieutenant of the Horse Guards.

'Captain Keane? Order from Major Grant, sir. You're wanted at headquarters.' He looked down at Keane's hand – five cards of the same suit: ace, king, jack, ten, and six of hearts.

'I'm sorry, sir. But you're wanted immediately.'

'After this hand, lieutenant.'

'Not in my orders, sir. Major Grant was most insistent.'

Keane threw down the cards and stood up. 'Damn it all, lieutenant. Take a look, Tom, when I'm gone, and see how much I'd have had you for. Damn it. A guinea at least.'

Grant looked stern and Keane wondered what might have had happened since his last visit.

'There's news, James.'

'Sir? Nothing bad?'

'Good and bad, if you like. We've found the French. Two days ago, Wellesley sent General Hill, with Mackenzie's and Tilson's brigades, north along the coast ahead of the main column to engage what we presumed to be a cavalry screen. We found them in greater strength than we imagined.'

'General Mackenzie? That's my old mob.'

'Yes, the 27th. They engaged the French just south of Grijon, from what we gather. The French broke and retired back to Oporto.'

'That's good, isn't it?'

'Normally it would be, yes. But as it stands we've lost surprise. There's worse, though. I have a report that Marshal Soult has broken the only remaining bridge across the Douro.'

'Meaning, sir?'

'Meaning, James, that we now have no means of attacking the city. We have to find a way across the river. Tomorrow we will march north. The entire army. By the time we reach Oporto we will need to have found that means.'

'I take it from your tone, sir, and from the very fact that I am here, that you intend that I should find that means?'

'Those are Wellesley's orders.'

Keane was just digesting the magnitude of his task when there was a commotion from the corridor, and as he watched a group of people swept into the anteroom. Civilians, mostly, they were led by a woman. She was short and plump and dressed in a bright canary-yellow silk dress and matching bonnet, and in her hand she clutched a yellow parasol which she was waving animatedly. What was more, she was English.

She spoke in a loud, bellowing voice, almost shouting at the bewildered aide de camp of hussars who had brought her into the room.

'No, no, no. That's simply not good enough, young man. We have travelled from Lisbon to see my son on the eve of battle and you say that he's not here. Where's the general? Where is Arthur – Arthur Wellesley?'

Grant moved quickly as she advanced across the room. 'Madam. May I be of assistance? Major Grant, ma'am. I'm on the general's staff.'

She stopped. 'Major Grant. It's General Wellesley I want. Where is he? He has sent my son off on campaign to fight the

French before we have had a chance to bid him adieu and farewell. It's too bad. It really is.'

As she spoke, Keane noticed the others who had come into the room with her. Behind her stood a middle-aged man in a top coat and a tall hat, whom Keane presumed must be her husband, and behind him a girl.

She was, he guessed, about twenty years old, with black hair that hung in curling tresses around her shoulders. Her skin was a milky white and barely covered by the fashionable décolletage of her gown, which almost matched that of her mother. As Keane watched her she looked up and for an instant their eyes met. Keane felt like a schoolboy caught out in class and quickly looked away. But he knew it to be too late. A look had been exchanged and nothing could change that. He knew that he must have her.

He was aware of the others in the room and the conversation. Grant was speaking now, trying to calm things. 'May I ask your name, madam?'

'Blackwood, Lady Sarah Blackwood. And this is my husband, Sir William. We are old friends of the general.'

'Ah yes, your son is in the dragoons, is he not? A fine officer.'

She relaxed for a moment. 'You are kind, Major Grant. Yes, he is a good boy. But you see, we have travelled from Lisbon to see him only to be informed that he is gone.'

'I'm very much afraid that will be the case, Lady Blackwood. His regiment is with General Hill. They are on the left flank of the army, at Aveiro. I can show you on the map, if you will?'

She walked with him to the table and pretended to understand. 'Have they been in fighting yet? Have they killed any Frenchmen?'

Grant nodded. 'Yes, indeed, they have. They have beaten back the French as far as Oporto.'

She turned, a look of horror on her face. 'William, d'you hear, he's been in action. John.'

Blackwood spoke. 'Have you any more news, major? Have the lists been posted?'

'No, Sir William. There are no casualty lists as yet. But General Hill's force did not take heavy losses. I'm sure your son will be well.'

Lady Blackwood spoke again, quicker now and her voice an octave higher, it seemed to Keane. 'But he might be wounded. Or worse. Oh no. Oh dear. I do believe I feel a little faint.'

She began to tremble and Keane reached for a chair, which he placed beside her before helping her to sit down.

'Thank you, thank you, young man. I don't know what came over me. I do feel queer.'

Grant signalled to the aide-de-camp. 'A glass of wine for Lady Blackwood. Or eau de vie, if we have it.'

Sir William spoke. 'Was it a large engagement, major?'

'No, Sir William. Merely a skirmish. But it served its purpose. Marshal Soult is wrong-footed.'

Blackwood shrugged. 'Good. That is good. But either way, it would appear that we are too late to see our son.'

'It would appear so, sir. I'm very much afraid you've had a wasted journey.'

The wine was brought and as Lady Blackwood was drinking it, the colour returning to her cheeks, the door opened and Wellesley entered.

'What the devil's going on out here? I can't hear myself think. Grant, who are these people? What is all this noise?'

He saw Blackwood and smiled. 'Why, William, my dear fellow,

and Sarah. What a pleasant surprise. And this must be Kitty. How lovely. How delightful to see you all. What brings you here? If it's John you're after, I'm afraid you've come on a wasted errand. He is on campaign in the north.'

Blackwood spoke. 'Yes, that's just it, Arthur. We have just been told as much by Major Grant here. He has been most kind. As has your aide here, Captain . . . ?'

'Keane, sir. James Keane.'

Wellesley smiled again. 'And he's no aide of mine, Sir William. He has a command of his own. A highly important command. Don't you, Keane?'

'Yes, sir.' Keane was reeling. Blackwood. How could it be that the beautiful creature who stood before him was the sister of the man who had very nearly had him cashiered?

Lady Blackwood spoke. 'Do you know our son, Captain Keane? John Blackwood, Light Dragoons?'

Wellesley answered for him. 'Yes, Sarah, John and Captain Keane are old friends. Isn't that right, Keane?'

'Absolutely, sir. Firm, old friends.'

Blackwood's sister looked at Keane and smiled. If she only knew the truth of our relationship, he thought, she would not look at me in that way.

Lady Blackwood rose to her feet. 'Kitty, my dear, have you met Captain Keane? You know he is a friend of John's.' She turned to Keane. 'I'm surprised, Captain Keane, that we have not heard talk of you, or met you previously. John brings his friends to us from time to time. Even that poor Mister Simpson. The one who died, William, you remember? Captain Keane, you must come and visit us at our house in Lisbon. Mustn't he, Kitty?'

Kitty Blackwood smiled and looked at the floor.

mother happy, shall we? And you might find yourself with a chance to meet the family again.'

He smiled. 'I want news, Keane, of everything. Not merely of Captain Blackwood, but of General Hill's exploits and his casualties. And chiefly I want news of Oporto.'

Walking back to the bivouac, Keane wondered again at the cruel fortune that had made him lose his heart to the sister of the man who had vowed to hound him from the army.

But as he walked he thought more clearly, and alongside the vision of the girl's pretty smile and pale flesh, a fresh thought came into his mind. He imagined the look on Blackwood's face when he heard that his baby sister had been bedded by James Keane. And he smiled, amused now by the irony which had led him to the resolution that sometime, somehow, Kitty Blackwood would be his.

The camp was full of the rumour that they would soon be on the move and Keane had it from the lips of every sutler and washerwoman.

Tom Morris was ebullient. 'Isn't it wonderful news, James? We're on the attack. Wellesley is moving the whole army north. We're to take Oporto.'

'Yes, I am aware of that, old friend. I do admire your keenness, Tom. You're obviously determined to be at them.'

'Of course, James, aren't you?'

'Oh yes, and I'm thankful that we have been accorded the privilege of being the first to do so.'

'We have?'

'We have indeed, Tom. We are to be the advance party. First into Oporto. And let us hope that fortune is with us.'

They were disturbed by a shout from the direction of the

tents. Silver's voice and then another. Martin's too. Both men turned and began to walk fast towards their encampment, but they saw all they needed to before they were twenty yards away.

Silver and another man were on the ground, fighting tooth and nail, while Martin was exchanging blows with a redcoat, knocking over cooking pans and sending arms and possessions flying. Garland too was busy, but he had just picked a man up by the neck and had him hanging in mid air.

Keane yelled, 'What the devil's going on? Sarn't Ross!'

He looked for Ross and found him. The big Scot was being held back by two redcoats while another punched him in the face and stomach. Keane ran across and tried to pull the man off. The soldier turned, and seeing an officer left Ross and ran, followed by his two comrades who let Ross fall to the ground. Keane turned back to the others. Heredia had joined in now and was trading blows with a large man in shirtsleeves.

Keane turned to Morris. 'Who the deuce are these men and what are they doing?' He ran across to Martin, who had pinned his adversary to the ground and was sitting on his back aiming rabbit punches into his kidneys, with great effect. 'Will, who are they?'

Martin stopped for a moment but increased the pressure on the man's neck. 'Sorry, sir. It all started when Silver got into a fight with one of them. The fellow just wandered up to him and made some comment about how they were going to fight the French but all we were good for was riding around "observing".'

Keane understood now. Word had finally got to the rank and file that these men were different. Special, chosen if you like. This was the army at its ugliest. Expressing its disdain for those who did not conform. Those who might be seen as cowards for not standing in line on a battlefield and waiting for the next cannonball to strike.

'So you thought you should join in, did you?'

'Yes, sir. That's about the way of it.'

'You did well then, Will. I won't have my men called cowards.'

He watched as Silver, who had just doubled over a man with an uppercut, followed up with a well-aimed boot to the groin. The man fell to the ground groaning. Keane turned back to Martin, who again stopped raining punches on his now near-unconscious victim. 'What regiment are they, d'you know?'

'88th, sir. The Connaughts.'

'Irishmen? They should know better. You had better kick their arses out of our camp. They've had their fun.'

Martin shook the man to what was left of his senses and dragged him to his feet. Keane shouted across to Silver. 'That's enough now. Let them go. They'll know better next time.'

Silver smiled back at him through bloodied teeth. 'Sorry, sir. Couldn't take that from no one, sir.'

'Quite right too. Well done. Now get this place tidied up, and yourselves. We move tomorrow.'

In the morning and under a misty Spanish sun, as Keane had said, the army at last was on the move. In a long, meandering column of men and animals, it snaked its way through the dust of Portugal, carrying hope to the conquered and death to the French. Somewhere a village church bell pealed eight times, slow and sonorous, and above the cacophony of horses, harness, marching feet and wagons, the smells and sounds of a peaceful Portuguese May morning invaded Keane's senses, as from his position at the head of the long column he turned in the saddle to look back. He marvelled at the operation, knowing as he did what it took to get such an army on the march. The sheer size of the undertaking.

It was an awe-inspiring sight. Ross caught his mood. 'It is a thing, sir, isn't it? You just wonder how Boney's lot can stand up to that. If I was them I'd be running back to Paris already.'

Keane smiled. He had grown to like the Scotsman more and more over the past few weeks and was glad at his choice for a sergeant.

'You're right, sarn't. It's enough to make any enemy quake. But remember, those are Boney's soldiers you're talking about. They fight for their emperor and for their eagles and they go into battle with the sound of drums and trumpets.'

'And you know why that is, sir, don't you?'

'Tell me, sarn't'.

'Why, it's to drown out the noise of the dying. That's their real drums and fifes, sir. Screams as we give them volley fire and canister at fifty.'

There was no music from the column as they marched. No bands nor even any singing. Just the noise of men and animals on the move, the tramp of thousands of feet and hooves and the rattle of equipment, creating its own martial music which to Keane's ears was as good as any marching tune. A song, he knew, would cheer the spirits and improve the tempo of the march, but this was no time for songs. While there had been no specific orders from the command to march in silence, the officers knew that the French were close, just the other side of the river, and that a thousand men in full cry was the last thing that was wanted.

And this too was when any army was at its most vulnerable, open to attack from the flanks. But from Keane's intelligence there were no hostile troops this side of the Douro. He had done his job well and was content in the knowledge that the column would not be threatened.

The British soldier, he knew, could move in formation better than most, but there was still a horror of ambush in any army on the march. The sudden gut-wrenching sensation of being fired on from the hills.

Still looking behind him, he knew that not far away beyond the immediate vanguard of which he and his men formed the foremost part, rode Wellesley and Grant and Scovell.

And somewhere up ahead of them, with the flying column, was Blackwood. Keane's thoughts turned momentarily to Kitty and then back to the matter in hand. They had been on the road for two hours and it was time now for them to detach themselves from the army, time to perform the new role assigned to them by the commander.

He turned to Ross again. 'Sarn't Ross, let's get the men on now. We need to be away from here. We're meant to be ahead of the army, remember. Tom?

Morris trotted up. 'James?'

'We need to make some ground. Order them into a trot, I think.'

Keane spurred on his own horse and quickly the men followed suit, with their various levels of competence.

They pulled away from the troops immediately behind them, a company of rifles, and rounded a bend in the road which brought them into a defile. Another fine place for an ambush, he thought for a moment, before they were through and urging their horses on at a gallop now along the dusty road. As they grew closer to Oporto it was plain to see that the French had been there. To their right and left cottages lay in ruins, their stone walls broken down and their pantiled roofs smashed. Keane saw what had once been pretty kitchen gardens now no more than wasteland. The houses had been burned and looted, and the meagre possessions of their inhabitants that had been left by the French lay strewn upon the ground. What had once been a verdant country was now laid waste and he knew that worse was to come.

Five miles more and they came to the crest of a hill. Keane reined in and looked down.

The great city of Oporto rose on the opposite bank of the Douro, silhouetted against the hills. Smoke coursed lazily up from its chimneys and from this distance at least there was little sign of activity. Where, wondered Keane, was Soult's great army this morning? Packing its bags to leave? He had expected a further scene of devastation. Burning buildings, perhaps worse. But Portugal's second city looked from here outwardly no different from Lisbon.

And it was breathtaking. The river was as clear as day, curving away past the walls and houses. Beyond, he could make out the tower of Clerigos and the spire of the Sé cathedral. That was their objective. The centre of the city. Take that, and the French would not be able to hold. It would be hard going; as tough as it got. Street fighting was a sanguine affair. But the regiments in that long column would not be deterred by that. The Rifles and the Light Bobs, he knew, would be best for the job, although for the first assault he knew that Wellesley would have selected one of the old battalions.

He wondered what was going on down there. How the towns-people lived now from day to day under French occupation. Whatever was left of them. He had heard from the many fugi-tives who had filtered into the British camp the stories of what had happened when the French had taken their city back in March.

Eight thousand dead. That was the figure he had been given by Morillo and heard repeated by Grant. Men, women and children. Women had been raped in their own houses before their husbands and families. Keane had experienced at first hand the horror of the wrath of the Spanish guerrillas and was sure that soon it would infect the entire population. He wondered about Morillo's suggestion that there was little difference between the French and themselves, and felt pity for the two nations. If they could push the French from Portugal perhaps they might begin to help Spain. It did not matter to him that they had been engaged in war with the Spanish for three hundred years. They were people, just people, the sort of peasants he might pass by on any road at home in Ireland. No matter what Morillo said or what their priests declared, they were all united by a common bond of humanity.

They rode on and began to enter a more built-up area. Narrow streets of new houses. A suburb created to house the population from the expanding city. Villa Nova.

Tom Morris rode to his side. 'Curious place, James, ain't it? Just stuck here on a cliff.'

Keane was aware of eyes looking at them from behind half-closed shutters. The people who had remained in the new village were surveying this army and he felt the fear that must fill their hearts, knowing as they did that the British were moving into their part of the extended city before the French had left the old town. There was to be a battle. That was clear, and as if in response one of the doors opened and he watched as a mother and father ushered their children away down the street, trailing a little handcart filled with their belongings. Here was the sadness of war. A family dispossessed, who perhaps had only recently welcomed the new chance they had been given to escape the squalor of the city and find a house in the new village. Better to leave, though, than find yourself caught in the crossfire between two armies.

They continued to walk their horses through the streets and at length emerged at a tall building. The old monastery of La Serra dominated the hill on the south bank of the river and Keane could see instantly that it would make a fine headquarters from which the commander-in-chief might spy out the enemy position.

He took out his glass from its leather case on his saddle and surveyed the town. Oporto lay opposite and below them with the mouth of the Douro to the west. That was the direction from which Wellesley had told him Soult expected them to attack. So, as the general had explained, if that was what was expected, then they would offer the enemy something quite different.

He moved the lens to scan the bank and watched a group of French soldiers idling on the quayside as their comrades bathed in the river.

Whatever the state of morale within Oporto, it was clear that Marshal Soult had not issued orders to be on the alert. The French were enjoying their time in the ruined city and their guard was down. If they could manage it properly the enemy would be taken completely by surprise. The only question was, how?

# 6

Keane continued to move the eyeglass along the opposite bank of the river, scouring it for some form of crossing. He knew, though, that it would be in vain.

Grant had told him that there was no bridge and so it must be. But still he could not resist harbouring the hope of some solution. He knew that the main crossing, some yards further upstream just below them, had collapsed during the capture of the city as the populace had crossed it fleeing their attackers. Looking down at the river he imagined the scene: the water a boiling froth of humanity; men, women, children and animals washed away in the current and lost under the waters.

After that, to ensure that their prize would be secure, the French had destroyed the other bridge that had sat just below where he was now standing at Villa Nova. Nowhere, so the map – whatever its merits – had assured him, was there a place where the river was shallow enough to effect a crossing, even on horseback. In any case such a venture would be doomed to failure. Somehow, he thought, they must remain hidden and yet cross over the river. He took the glass from his eye and closed it with a snap. He gazed at the river, hoping that somehow it would provide inspiration. As he watched, a vessel emerged from around the bend which swept past the cliff below the town. A wine barge, one of the low-slung kind with a huge red sail that carried the barrels of port to and from the bodegas.

Keane smiled and nodded his head with such conviction that Morris stared at him. 'James?'

He turned to Morris. 'That's it, Tom. That's what we need. It's the only way to do it.'

'James?'

'The only way to allow the army to cross. On barges. The only way, Tom. An amphibious landing. We must find a sufficient number of barges and get them across to this side of the river. No one else can manage it. It's up to us. Either that, or Wellesley will be kicking his heels here till kingdom come. For he'll not get across any other way.'

'I thought that we were here principally to reconnoitre. That we were to return to the general with information.'

'You know as well as I do that our orders were to find a means to get into the city.'

'And to impart that means to Wellesley, yes.'

'And if possible to manage it ourselves.'

'I don't recollect your having told me that part of the orders.'

'No, search your memory, my friend. For that's what we're going to do. My orders are to find the weak spot in the enemy defences, to find a means of crossing the river and otherwise to do as we see fit. We must somehow get hold of barges and bring them across to this side of the river.'

Morris smiled. He knew his friend well enough to see that he already had something in mind. 'You have a plan, James?'

Keane returned the glass to his eye and scanned the town.

'We'll get across the river somehow. Enter the town. Then I'll have a plan. Then we'll know what's what. Then we'll see what we can find.'

He again snapped shut the glass and turned to Ross.

'Sarn't Ross, tell the men to cover their uniforms and we'll leave the horses here with Garland, Gabriella and Captain Morris. Tom, you can report to the advance party of the army if they arrive before we return. Captain Scovell's sure to be with them. Garland, take care of my gun, will you. Guard her with your life.'

Garland nodded. 'Yes, sir. With my life.'

Keane turned back to the men. 'The rest of you, try to make yourselves look as much like the natives as possible. Leave your shakos here too. See if you can find a hat, or tie a kerchief round your head. And we had better split up to get down to the bank. In pairs. Make sure you're with a good Spanish-speaker.'

Heredia stared at Keane and shrugged. 'Of course, sir. But this is madness. What hope have we got against a whole French garrison? Six men?'

'You'd be surprised, Heredia. In fact, we have more chance as a small number than all of our men. Surprise is everything.'

They unstrapped their saddlebags and pulled out the clothes that Keane had selected for just this purpose. Ross pulled on a bright-green coat over his regimentals and immediately earned a laugh from Silver.

'Shut your mouth, private. You heard what the officer said. Get dressed.' Silver was already clad in a dark-brown overcoat that reached to his knees. 'See, you're no better.'

Keane removed his own bicorne hat, placing it carefully in

the leather bag he had attached to his saddle beforehand. He replaced it on his head with a broad-brimmed round black hat of the type worn commonly in the Peninsula.

Morris laughed at him. '*Buenos días*, Señor James.'

'Very funny, Tom. How do I look?'

'As a matter of fact, not at all bad. Quite splendid, actually. I'd take you for a don myself if I didn't know better. All you need now is a cheroot.'

'Perhaps I'll find one in the town, eh? And a great deal more besides. We'll liberate some of that French booty, shall we?'

The men nodded approvingly. He surveyed them and smiled. 'Very good. Yes, that's very, very good. You look like a proper bunch of cutthroats.' Which, he thought to himself, is exactly what you are. 'Right. Get in your pairs and keep it quiet. No English at all. Is that clear?'

They all nodded.

'Nor no French, neither,' piped up Gilpin.

'No. No French either, he's right,' said Keane. 'Too risky. I'll see you down by the riverbank.'

He walked closer to the parapet and pointed down into the bushes below them. They followed his gaze. 'You see there? That curve in the river. Find the big building on the opposite bank. The seminary. Got it? Now trace a line down from it to the river. See now? There. Where the curve comes round. Where those trees are. We won't be seen there, not from the other side. I'll see you all down there, in those trees. In half an hour, or near as dammit. And remember. What we do now is vital to the general's plan. These next few hours will tell whether we win a victory here or end in disaster.'

With Ross at his side, Keane climbed over the walls that

masked the garden of the convent and made his way gingerly
down the hillside, through the heavy undergrowth and the
rows of carefully tended vines, trying all the while to look
every inch the Portuguese and fearing every moment that he
could not look anything but a British officer. Even Ross, he
thought, looked more convincing. He seemed to have a
peasant's gait. From his earlier observations, there seemed
to be no French on this side of the river. At least, they saw
no one and no other creatures save a goat and a half-wild
cur of a dog that snarled at them and then ran off. Through
the vines they went, snagging their clothes on the stalks,
until they emerged on another terrace which in turn gave
way to a steeper incline down to the river. A deep gully led
down to the water and Keane slithered down the wet grass,
grabbing at the few branches and saplings for support as he
went and trying not to make too much of a commotion. Then
they were in the trees that hung low over the edge of the
river.

He could see the water stretching out ahead of them and
was beginning to wonder how clever his plan really was and
whether any of them might find a boat, when there was a
sudden movement ahead of them. Both men froze. Ross said
nothing. Keane looked at him and, placing a finger to his
mouth, peered through the trees.

He could hear voices now. Quite distinctly. A horrible thought
came suddenly to his mind. Christ, it was a French patrol.
Their intelligence had been wrong. Soult had left a brigade, a
division perhaps, here on the east bank. In a few moments he
and his men would be discovered and killed, and Wellesley,
unapprised of the reality and riding in the van of the army,
would blunder into the French waiting for them. He listened

more closely, waiting to hear the English that would tell him the patrol had already caught one of his men.

But then he listened again and he realized that the voices he could hear were speaking not in French but in Spanish or Portuguese.

Peering more closely, Keane began to make out the outline of a man. He wore a black coat and a black hat with an upturned brim like a sail, and he appeared to be reprimanding another man standing beside him. Keane struggled to make out the words in Spanish but heard only 'Holy Mother' and 'disgrace'. The man in black must be a priest, he thought, addressing one of his flock perhaps. In a few moments, he knew, the others would be with him. He decided to act on the moment. Walking forward with apparent confidence, Keane pushed through the trees and emerged close to the two men. In fact, as he could now see, there were others of them a little way off. They were dressed in Portuguese clothes, no uniforms, and his hunch appeared to have been correct, for the man in black was wearing clerical garb.

Hearing him, the men spun round and he saw that both were armed with short knives. Keane coughed and spoke in Spanish. 'Señor. I'm sorry. I mean, father. Good day.'

The priest looked puzzled. 'Good heavens. Where have you come from? I thought the farm was deserted. Did they go to Lisbon?'

'Yes. That's right. But I'm looking after it.'

'Are you, indeed? And who might you be?'

Keane remembered the alias that Grant had suggested he adopt if caught. 'Marandes. Don Pascal Marandes, father.' He bowed.

The priest stared at him. 'Do I know you?'

'I don't think we've ever met before.'

The priest looked suspicious. 'Where are you from?'

'I told you, father. I live here. I'm one of the cousins.'

The priest looked at the group of five men to his right and slightly to his rear, who had been staring at them throughout the conversation. He nodded to them and instantly the man closest to them drew from his belt a pistol and pointed it directly at Keane.

'Now, Don Pascal Marandes, tell me who you really are. There are no cousins and the owners of that farm died a week ago at the hands of the French. Horribly. Only a son survived. So who are you? Perhaps you are French spies, come to bring more misery to my people?'

Keane raised his hand, keeping it away from his belt where the sword hung at his side. 'I'm sorry, father. No, no, we're not French. Please allow me.' He drew open the coat and indicated that he wished to unfasten the jacket beneath. The priest nodded and Keane undid the buttons to reveal the faded scarlet tunic of the 27th Foot.

The priest smiled. 'So. Not French, but you are soldiers all the same. British.'

Keane nodded and decided that he must take a gamble. 'We are here in advance of the army.'

'Then you're British spies.'

'I am an exploring officer, father. Sent by our general to explore the ground.'

'And how do you find it, the ground, that is? How did you find it, Captain . . . ?'

'Keane, father. I find it hard and I am wondering how we might find a passage across to the other side.' He looked at the man with the pistol, which was still pointed at his heart.

'Is it possible to dispense with that? It's making me a little nervous.'

The priest turned and waved down the pistol. Keane relaxed.

'Captain Keane, I am most pleased to see you. My name is Father Ignacio Sanchez. That is my convent, up there.' He pointed up the hill. 'I am the Prior. The Monasterio de la Serra. We have been waiting for you to come, sure in the knowledge that the British would not abandon us. You intend to take the city back from the French?'

'Yes, that is, we shall if we can find a way across.'

'Tell me how we can help.'

'There are barges on the river still?'

'Yes, the French thought they had taken all of them, but we are clever.'

'Good. That's how we'll do it. Can you help?'

Sanchez turned to the closest of the men and spoke fast, then pointed towards the river. He turned back to Keane as the men began to hurry down to the river. 'You are a clever man, captain. I think it is the only way across'.

He pointed after the peasants. 'Go with them. There is a boat here. It will take you and your men. How many are you?' He nodded to where Keane's men were concealed in the trees.

'There are six of us to cross immediately, father. But we need more. Have you more barges?'

Almost on cue the men began to come in through the trees. They looked surprised to see Keane in conversation with a priest.

Father Sanchez smiled and nodded, unshaken by the sudden appearance of the men. He kept talking. 'The boat will carry you across. One of my men here will take you. On the other side you will find four barges. Manuel will show you. Good luck. And be sure to kill as many of the French as you can, my son. Send them all to Hell.'

Keane smiled. 'You hate them, don't you?'

The priest shook his head and crossed himself. 'They are without God. Their emperor is a new Satan. He has forsworn Christ and wants the Lord's world for himself. And he will do anything to get it. He orders his men to do murder, captain. Do you know how many they killed when they took the city?'

Keane shook his head.

'Eight thousand, captain. Men, women and children. Slaughtered in cold blood. Women raped before their husbands' eyes before they were killed. Children butchered before their mothers. That is what these men do. Yes, I hate them. And so should you.'

Keane nodded. 'We'll do what we can, father.'

Hurrying away after the peasants towards the rest of his command, Keane tried to work out whether it could succeed. Four barges for the entire army. That might be enough for four companies, half a battalion at most. They would have to repeat the process dozens of times. Still, for the present it was the only chance they had.

The men ordered by the priest to take them across pulled on the oars and began to row the little boat across the river. Keane looked from the prow at the city on the opposite bank. Silent and forbidding, it rose and fell above them with the rhythm of the oars in the water. To their left, in the west, lay the river gate with the outskirts of the city above it: another great rampart of stone. Their objective, though, lay dead ahead. From the water's edge a sandy cliff rose from the riverbank to a grassy hillside. Above it stood the walls of the seminary that was their goal.

Keane looked for a way up, a change in the colour of the undergrowth that might betray a hidden path. But he saw none. He supposed that the men at the oars might be able to direct them and his eye fell back to the riverbank and the towpath that snaked along it. Then he froze. For there, making its way along the bank, was a French patrol. A dozen men in blue coats and shakos marching sluggishly at the foot of the cliff. He whispered the discovery to the others.

All of them lay as low as they could manage in the bottom of the boat and Keane signalled to the oarsmen to rest their oars in the rowlocks, lest the French should hear. But the soldiers, who Keane presumed must exemplify the general feeling of torpor among the garrison, did not bother to give it a second glance. When it was clear that the French had not seen them he looked up cautiously and watched the patrol disappear around the curve in the wall, the men talking among themselves.

'All right, you can breathe again. But keep your eyes peeled. We don't know how often they come past. And remember, not the slightest sound.'

Slowly the oarsmen took up the rhythm again and the boat resumed its passage across the broad river.

Keane could see the opposite bank more clearly now through the dappled sunshine and fancied that he could make out the shape of boats on the shallow beach below. A few more strokes and the little skiff hit the sand. Keane motioned to the men and they all scrambled out and quickly up onto the ledge of the shore. Sure enough his eyes had not been wrong. There just below them, cleverly hidden among some overhanging branches, rolling on the wash, lay four long flat-bottomed barges, their sails furled along the lowered masts.

He signalled to the oarsmen who nodded in unison and climbed out of the boat and onto the bank. 'Right. There's our prize. We need to get those back to the other side. They're big enough to take a company across, and judging from the condition of that patrol, that might be all we're going to need to take this place.'

But hardly had the words left his mouth when he heard voices. French voices. Keane and the others stopped where they were. The oarsmen had heard them too and looked alarmed. Keane motioned his men back against the wall and beneath the bushes at the water's edge. It was not a second too soon. Around the side of the wall came another French patrol. Six men this time, in grubby blue-and-white uniforms, all with shouldered muskets, their bayonets fixed. They were talking among themselves, laughing. One of them stopped and pointed to the little party of oarsmen who alone had remained in view, unable to find cover. The sergeant, a large man with a moustache, shouted at them in coarse Spanish and led his men towards them.

'You. Who are you? What are you doing here? You're not meant to be here. There's a curfew.'

The lead oarsman shrugged and muttered something to another. The Frenchman, closer now, yelled at him and struck him with the butt of his musket on the arm. The man howled in pain and grabbed at his arm. The others did not move. The sergeant turned to the soldier beside him and switched back to French. 'Corporal, put these men under arrest. Then shoot them.'

The corporal smiled and motioned his men forward. They walked slowly, muskets levelled now, and pushed the oarsmen, at point of bayonet, away from the river and back towards the wall. Keane saw the corporal raise his own musket and knew that his next movement would be to cock the hammer. Once that was done, when the gun went off, whether or not the oarsmen died, all hope of secrecy would be lost. Quickly, Keane looked across at Sergeant Ross. Catching his eye, he nodded and the Scotsman turned and signalled to the others. Then, before any of the French had time to realize what was happening, Keane and the others burst from their cover.

Ross was the first upon them. He went in head first, bent almost double and careering with his full force into a scrawny Frenchman, sending him sprawling to the ground. Picking up the man's musket, he hovered over him for a moment and then, with one dreadful thrust, skewered him with his own bayonet before moving on to the next.

Keane himself took on the French sergeant, who looked at him in alarm and opened his mouth to shout a warning. It was the last thing he ever did. Before the words had time to leave his mouth Keane slid the great curved blade of the Egyptian scimitar into the man's side and, drawing out the bloodied silver streak, watched as he slumped to the ground.

Keane looked to his left and saw that Ross was smashing the second Frenchman's head against the wall. Ahead of him Silver had slit another's throat from ear to ear. Heredia was drawing tight the knotted leather rope he used to garrotte his victims and within less than two minutes it was all over, as Gilpin slid his sword, wiped clean of the last Frenchman's blood, back into its scabbard. Keane, the adrenalin still pumping through him, nodded to them. He recovered himself, impressed by this first outing in battle for his new command. This was teamwork at its best. Every man his own master, yet conscious of his comrade's position.

'Good. Right, drag these bastards into the bushes. No, strip them first. We can use the uniforms.'

Silver shook his head. 'Sir, I'm sorry. Going native is one thing. But I'm damned if I'm going to dress up like a bloody Frenchie.'

Ross turned on him. 'That's enough. You'll do as the officer says, Silver. Now get to it.'

Keane watched as reluctantly Silver began to peel off one of the dead men's uniforms.

'You'd better make it quick, before they're missed.'

It did not take long to dispose of the bodies and despite a few more protests the men managed to dress themselves in the resented uniforms, discarding their civilian clothes and piling them in the boat. They kept their own grey overall trousers, though, and were careful too, as Keane had instructed, to keep their own tunics rolled up in a blanket and strapped on top of the French packs.

Keane tugged at the cuffs of the dead sergeant's tunic, which was too short on his long, athletic frame, and pulled the straps tighter on trousers that hung slack on his slim waist.

Once dressed, they dragged the half-naked corpses under cover of the trees and disguised them with foliage. The oarsmen, to their credit, had stayed with the British, helping them with the dead, and now stood ready for Keane's orders.

'Right, let's get these barges across the river. We'll tie them onto the boat and pray that no one spots them.'

There was a coil of rope in one of the barges and Keane used his sword to cut it into four equal lengths. They tied one of the barges to the stern of the rowing boat and then the others in turn to each other. Keane turned to Heredia. 'Can you explain to them what I want to do?'

Heredia nodded and Keane turned to the lead oarsman, his words being relayed by the cavalryman.

'We need to row out into the middle of the river. Don't worry about being seen. I want the French to think that you're just a convoy of wine or stores. And you'll have one of my men in French uniform in each of the barges. If they shout at that man he will shout back in French and tell them you're heading for the harbour. It's my guess they'll be too concerned with their own welfare to challenge you. Once you're in mid stream just gently push the boat back towards the other shore. I'm sure you know what to do. The trick will be making it look as if you're not heading for the bank but simply drifting slightly across. Have you got that?'

The man nodded and muttered a respectful, '*Si*, Señor.'

Keane turned to Ross. 'Right, sarn't. You stay here. Silver, how's your French?'

'Good enough, sir. Better than my Spanish, Gabriella says.'

'Heredia?

'I can speak their filthy language, if you need me to.'

'Gilpin?'

'I'll pass for a Frenchie, sir.'

'Right. That's good. Silver, you come with me and Martin in the barges, one per boat. Heredia, you stay here with Sarn't Ross. If you are challenged you do the talking. Martin, if we are hailed from the town, stay buttoned up. Let Silver or me do the talking if it comes to it.'

The four of them clambered into the barges and each of them sat down in the stern while the oarsmen got back into the little boat. Then, on a given signal from Keane, the lead oarsman took up the strain and slowly, edging its way out from beneath the overhanging boughs, the little convoy set off into the river.

Out on the water, Keane instantly felt uncomfortably exposed. Should the French spot them and see through their disguise, they would be entirely at their mercy. He reasoned with himself, though, that in their new uniforms and given the plan he had formulated to navigate the river, they stood a good chance of getting across. He hoped too that Ross and Heredia would be safe on the opposite bank. The Portuguese had a volatile temper and he hoped that if they did encounter a French patrol Heredia would not allow his desire for revenge to get the better of him. Ross, he thought, would keep him in check, and he was a better choice to have left behind than the edgy Silver.

The train of boats continued into the centre of the river, meandering on a lazy course. Keane glanced up at the rampart above them, but, despite the feeling that they might be being observed, he saw no one. They were almost at the other bank now, edging their way closer, the oarsmen desperately pulling with all their might. It was more difficult here, though, and suddenly the current began to pull. There was a shout from the boat as one of the oarsmen lost an oar and then the second-to-last barge, hit by a sudden swell, careered into the one in front with a loud crash. Keane, who was on the first barge, turned and saw that the prow of the fourth barge had made a hole in the stern of the third, just above the waterline but not enough to be a danger. The most worrying thing, though, was the noise. Now, he thought, the French are sure to come to the ramparts and find out what the din was about.

He called to the other three. 'Lie down. Lie down in the boats.' Then he motioned to the oarsmen to do the same, but the men were already running for their lives and wading through the shallows and onto the bank. Keane ducked down into his barge, and just in time. From above on the opposite bank he heard the sound of distant voices and then the unmistakable clap of musketry as the French on the ramparts saw the running Portuguese oarsmen and opened fire. There was a shout as one of the men was hit. Keane clung to the unclad hull of the barge, tasting the foul water in his mouth, mixed with the spillage of rancid port and all manner of other filth. He retched and it was all he could do not to vomit. But he lay still and prayed that the others would do the same. The voices continued from the city bank. Clearly the French had seen the barges and were aware that something was wrong. But they must be equally aware, he thought, that there was nothing they could do about it. The firing had ceased and Keane heard a French voice shout something, but could not make out what. He wondered whether any of them had been spotted. The vile stench of the sodden boards filled his senses and he wondered how long they would have to wait before taking a look. A voice from above put him right.

'Captain Keane, they have gone. You can come out now.'

Looking up, he saw Sanchez.

'I almost took you for a Frenchman. You are quite convincing.'

Keane stood up, managed to climb out of the barge and began to brush down the French uniform. 'You flatter me, father. One of your men was hit?'

'Yes, but I do not think it will be bad. The French cannot hit anything. They were lucky this time. And so were you.'

'We have to get back to the other bank.'

'Captain Keane, I know you to be brave, but are you quite mad? Why not wait here for your army? You have the boats now.'

'Yes, but I also have men on the opposite bank and I cannot leave them. And I promised my general that I would find a way into the city for him and the army.'

Sanchez laughed. 'You English, you are so very honourable. Just like us. But it surprises us. We would not expect the French to behave like this.'

'And there's another thing. Surely the French will try to send a boat across to take back the barges. They must know that they will give Wellesley a way across.'

Sanchez spoke again. 'I have that in hand. We will move them further upstream to where the French will not find them and if they row their boat across here my men will be sure to give them a warm reception.'

Morris walked over to them. 'James, you stink like an alehouse. And what the deuce are you meant to look like?'

Keane grinned. 'A French sergeant, I believe. I know, scruffy bit of kit, isn't it?' He scratched at the collar of the faded blue coat. 'Damned itchy too. The fellow must have been crawling with lice. The sooner I get out of this the better. But first we need to get inside that monastery.'

'You're going back?'

'I left Ross and Heredia on the riverbank. God knows what's happened to them. And we need to get a foothold in the city. Anything. We might have the barges, but when our boys go ashore over there, they'll need someone on the inside if they're to survive. You had better stay here, Tom. Wellesley will want a full account of our affairs. And where's my gun?'

'Garland has it still. I'll find him.'

As they spoke, Father Sanchez busied himself with moving the barges. He had brought up more men now, and attaching

a length of rope to each vessel teams of twelve men were dragging the boats, walking along the towpath that ran along the
river. The French had not yet reappeared on the opposite
rampart and Keane prayed that the barges would make it round
the small spit of land that would hide them from view.

He turned to Morris who had returned. 'When the general
arrives, Tom, tell him his barges are there and that it might
be expedient to make the assault from that position as it will
mean that our lads are out of sight of the enemy. Oh, thank
you.' He reached out and took the gun from Morris, then
placed his finger on the trigger very gently and felt its weight
in his hand. The perfect symmetry, the balance, the sweetness of it.

'She's a lovely piece, Tom. Best I ever had. I knew she'd come
in useful one day.'

'You'd never have had the use of her in the field.'

'You're right. But this ain't the field, is it? Now she'll have
her day. Just as soon as we get back over the river.'

He looked across to the spot where he had left Ross and
Heredia but could not see them. He could only assume that
they had gone into hiding. Either that or they had already
been taken by the French. Either way, he would find out when
they returned across the river.

Three of the barges were hidden now, and as the fourth
slipped around the bend Keane looked back up at the walls.
There was still no sign of the French. Perhaps, he thought,
they had presumed that the British were already on the opposite bank and did not dare come over to retrieve the barges.
Or perhaps they had simply forgotten about the entire affair
and dismissed it as nothing of importance. The question of
how he and his men were to return to the city had troubled

him but he thought that he might now have come up with a plan.

He walked across to Sanchez. 'Father, I may need to borrow one of your men again.'

'Captain?'

'I need someone, maybe two men, to row us back. I intend to hide myself and my men in the bottom of your boat, under a cover. We can deal with any French when we arrive.'

Sanchez nodded. 'Yes, to cross in full view, even in those uniforms, would be folly. Take two men.' He signalled. 'And good luck, captain. God be with you all. Where are you headed?'

'I had thought we might cross in the same place and make our way eastwards towards the seminary.'

The huge building stood several hundred yards away from the city. With its high white walls and central bell tower, it would, Keane had decided, make an excellent strongpoint for them to take and hold. It would also be the perfect beachhead from which the army might assault the city, when it came. It was directly opposite the bend where Sanchez had hidden the barges and would allow them to see exactly what was unfolding at the point at which he had told Morris to suggest to Wellesley that the troops should cross.

Sanchez nodded. 'Yes. It is entirely empty. It is not finished and the houses there were abandoned by the bishop and all the priests fled when the French attacked the city.' He looked disdainful. 'They left their people to the mercies of the enemy. What sort of man does that? Bishop or not?' He realized that he was speaking his thoughts aloud and stopped. 'It would make a good place to defend, though, captain, if that is what you have in mind.'

Keane nodded. 'You're a natural soldier, father.'

Sanchez smiled. 'Yes, I somehow suspect that I will have to be just that before we rid our country of these heathens.'

Keane motioned to Martin, Gilpin and Silver to make their way down to the boat, at one end of which he could now see Sanchez had placed a large oilcloth of the kind used on the river to cover stores in transit. Once in the water up to their knees, Keane and the others climbed in and, squashing in against each other, managed to fit themselves snugly into the bottom of the boat. Two of Sanchez's men draped the cover over them and they lay beneath it in the darkness, smothered and ready to start off across the water. Keane felt the boat rock as the oarsmen pushed off.

Within a few minutes that seemed to Keane like an eternity, they were well away from the shore and in mid-river. There was no noise now save for the heavy breathing of the men round him and the splashing of the oars as they moved through the water. And something else. A deep thudding, booming noise that Keane finally realized was his own beating heart.

With every stroke of the oars Keane was convinced that shots would come ripping through the oilskin and tear into their bodies. The men seemed to share his anxiety, so hard now was their breathing, and the stink of their foul breath mingled with the sweat of fear. But no shots came and it was with relief and disbelief that they suddenly came to a shuddering halt as the boat drifted against the riverbank. He heard voices from above the oilskin and winced against the bright daylight as the cover was peeled back, to reveal Sanchez's men. 'Señor,' said one and Keane rose up and with the others stepped ashore at the spot where they had left Heredia and Silver a short while before. No sooner were Keane and the others ashore than the two men emerged from the sandy cleft in which they had hidden themselves. Ross smiled. 'Glad to see you, sir. We wondered if the Frenchies would come back for us. They don't seem to have missed the patrol yet. But if you ask me, it won't be long, sir.'

'Yes, Ross. We need to move from here.'

'Where to, sir?'

Keane pointed. Above them, half a mile higher than the city's lowest levels as it sprawled up the hillside, stood the seminary.

'Up there, sarn't. We're going to take that building there and we're going to hold it until the army crosses over to take back the city.'

A zigzag road, fringed with strong-smelling plants, had been cut into the hillside, and it was up this road that Keane now led his men. Sanchez had been right. The monastery was indeed unfinished. A great brick-built building, only partly limewashed, it stood on the brink of a cliff. Reaching the garden wall they found it pierced by a great wrought-iron gate decorated with the bishop's coat of arms.

Keane led the small party round the wall, constantly alert, looking in all directions to find a French presence. But there was none. They came round the north side of the building and found the gates standing wide open. Keane was hardly able to believe his luck. The French, it seemed, had neglected to occupy the place. More than that, they had not even destroyed it, or made it indefensible. He called behind him.

'We're in luck. Quick as you can. Get in, and don't stop looking for them. They might be inside.'

The men threw themselves through the gates and once they were all safely inside, Keane himself, joined by Heredia, pushed the gates shut and dropped the wooden crossbars into their brackets.

'Sarn't Ross, secure this side and the courtyard. I'll take Martin inside. Silver, you and Heredia search the balconies and the rooms up there.'

They fanned out and began to make their way through the silent buildings. There was some evidence of recent habitation. A table with a half-empty bottle of wine and two plates littered with crumbs testified to the speed with which the clergy had taken their leave. Keane thought of Sanchez's contempt for the bishop and his entourage. Ross had ordered Gilpin and Heredia upstairs and he could hear them above now as they pushed open every door and the muffled shouts of 'clear' that rang through the buildings. It took them and the others barely twenty minutes to check the entire place and it occurred to Keane that they were turning into a good team, working well together here, as they had before in the brawl at the camp and in the fight with the French.

Ross reported to him. 'All clear, sir. Not a soul. Just what the monks left behind. We snaffled a few bottles, sir. No food, though. We'll go hungry.'

'Well, that's too bad, sarn't. We have rations enough in our packs for one night. We'll barricade the doors, every one of them. As before, sarn't, same drill but this time find whatever you can in every room. Tables, chairs, beds, anything. And stack them all against the doors.' He had noticed as they entered the place that there were a great many windows. 'I want only every tenth window left open; others to be shuttered and barred. We're going to turn this place into a fortress.'

For the next two hours they worked without stopping, dragging whatever they could find into place. Apart from the main gates there were three other access points that Keane spotted as being vulnerable. These they concentrated on, wedging settles

and tables under door handles and double banking other pieces
of furniture. The windows were next. Those on the ground floor
they blocked completely, in the same manner as they had the
doors. On the upper storeys they closed and barred most, but
made sure that just enough were kept open to enable the six of
them to have a clear field of fire from all sides of the buildings.

Keane walked from room to room, watching them and
helping out with moving the heavier pieces of furniture. A
huge ornate four-poster bed they dismantled and used as a
barricade across the courtyard.

'Second line of defence,' he told them. 'If they break in we'll
fall back behind here. It's not much but it's better than nothing.
Let's hope it doesn't come to that, though.'

As they manoeuvred the great oak limbs of the bed into
position, pushing them so that they locked into the wheels of
an overturned wagon, Keane spotted half a dozen sacks of
grain lying in a corner of a storeroom on the west side. He
called to Heredia and together they heaved the sacks into the
courtyard to create a stronger structure around the bed where
they could absorb the impact of enemy musket balls. At last
he nodded his head. 'That'll do. Well done. We've done all we
can. Sarn't Ross, check the ammunition. All of you, make sure
you tear off ten and have them ready.'

He walked over to one of two staircases that ran along the
wall and up to the overhanging balconies, and climbed again
to the first floor. They had left open one of the big windows
in the front facade of the monastery, and Keane leant his arms
on the ledge and gazed out in the direction of Oporto.

Soon the French will come, he thought. All we have to do
is sit and wait for our boys to get over here and pray that the
enemy don't get to us before they do.

Soon the French will take a look over here and one of them will remember about the abandoned monastery on the hill. And then someone will notice that the gates have been shut. And then they'll come. And we'll be ready for them.

# 7

Keane stood at the window and looked down at the river passing below. In the past hour he had paced the floor of the monastery restlessly, hoping that at any moment their infantry might be seen climbing up the cliff towards the city. He had placed all five men around the place at different vantage points. Silver, keen-eyed as ever, he had put up in the bell tower as befitted a man who had once climbed the top mizzen of one of His Majesty's men-o'-war. But as yet no sighting had been reported.

Keane himself had at first remained at the front of the monastery, on the west side, still watching the town lest the French should sally out to the attack. But latterly he had moved back to the south and to the window they had left open overlooking the cliff. Now he scanned the landscape. Where was the vanguard of the army? What the devil was taking Wellesley so long to cover the remaining distance from Coimbra?

Keane tried to recall which units would arrive in the van. The light cavalry would be first. Blackwood's mob. Then the light infantry, at running pace, the Rifles to the fore.

He stared again and half fancied that he could see dust in the distance on the road leading into Villa Nova. Hoping against hope, he reached into his pocket, withdrawing the glass. Then putting it to his eye he focused the lens and his heart leapt. It *was* dust. A great cloud that could mean only one thing. They were here. The army was here and not a shot fired yet. Well, near as dammit here, some of them at least. He twisted the glass again trying to get a clearer view, and saw blue coats, and for an instant his stomach felt hollow. Were they French? Had one of the other enemy armies beaten their intelligence and marched across the mountains to intercept Wellesley before he could them? He twisted the glass again and saw more dust and more blue coats. Or were they black? Running out of the room he found the entrance to the bell tower and leapt up the stairs in search of Silver.

'Can you see them? There. Over there.' He pointed across the river at the dust cloud. 'There, man, what's that? Tell me. Here, use this.'

Keane thrust the eyeglass at Silver who looked at it appreciatively and held it up to his eye. 'Oh my, that is good, sir. Admiral Nelson had one of these just like that, he did, sir. Wonderful thing, ain't it?'

'Yes, man, but what can you see? Tell me. Are they our redcoats or the French in blue?'

Silver squinted into the glass and after a short pause lowered it.

Keane was impatient. 'Well, who are they? Are they ours?'

'Oh, they're ours, sir. I'm sure of it. Dead sure. That's our column, come to take the town.'

Keane rattled down the staircase and ran back into the room at the front of the monastery. Oporto lay bathed in sunshine. He scanned the rampart that overlooked the river and saw no sign of French interest. Whatever the dust cloud was, the enemy hadn't seen it yet. But as he looked back to the north, what Keane now spotted made his heart go cold. A column of blue-coated soldiers was making its way on the road that led from the city towards the monastery. He tried to count them. Saw the officer in front on his horse. That would mean company strength at least. They must have noticed the closed gates and be coming to investigate. He ran down into the courtyard and found Ross peering through one of the two windows they had left open on that level, facing west.

'I can see them, sir. The buggers.'

'We almost made it. Silver's spotted the army. They're here.'

'Beggin' your pardon, sir, but they're not here, are they? I mean, they're on the other bank. They've still got to get their-selves across.'

'Yes, sarn't. You're quite right. We must hold here until they cross.'

The French column was still a fair distance away. Keane urgently reviewed his situation with the eye of an old hand. Six of them against perhaps eighty men. The odds looked grim. But he had been up against worse. On a burning Egyptian afternoon eight years ago in Alexandria, with the sun hot enough to boil your brains. One company of the 27th had stood in square against three thousand bloody Mamelukes. Firepower had won the day then. Firepower, bravery and good British grit had done for the Arab horsemen. And it would be the same today. The only answer was to channel all their fire into an enfilade that would rake the head of the column as it came into range and then to keep the fire up and force the French back. A second attack might be too much for them. But surprise could kill perhaps twenty of the enemy before they reached the gates. That would shorten the odds. And by that time, who knew, the redcoats might be scaling the cliff.

He turned to Ross and the others. 'Take off these bloody rags. Put your own coats back on. If we're going to die, we die in red coats. Sorry, Heredia, I was forgetting your uniform. We'll fight them in our own uniforms. And we'll show them how we bloody well fight.'

Quickly, they unrolled the blankets tied to the tops of the French packs and retrieved their coats. Then, throwing off the hated French tunics, they replaced them with their own.

Gilpin sighed and grinned. 'That's better, sir. I feel myself again. Fits proper. Well, it's never fitted proper, but it's better than them rags.'

Keane brushed off his own scarlet tunic and adjusted the fringe of gold bullion, his badge of rank, that hung on the left shoulder. 'You're right, Gilpin, that does feel better.'

His coat was of course a better fit than those of the men, having been handmade for him some years before by a regimental tailor in London. It was patched now and more than a little worn. But ten years of campaigning had kept him fit and it still fitted Keane like a glove. Some of the cleverly replaced squares of cloth of a slightly different shade of red were proud mementoes of wounds received, which brought with them brought vivid memories of other desperate moments such as this. He prayed that this would not be his last.

He watched as Gilpin began to fasten about his neck the thick black leather stock worn by the other ranks of infantry, and had a thought. 'Gilpin, there's no need to wear a stock any more. We have no need of that here and it's hot enough without making it any worse. And that goes for the rest of you.'

Gilpin smiled. 'Thank you, sir. Much appreciated.' He threw the hated stock into a corner, where it was soon joined by those of the other men.

Keane turned to Ross. 'Sarn't, we're going to shut all the windows here on the ground floor and place ourselves only at the front face of the upper storey. D'you understand?'

They all nodded. 'Sir.'

'Let's get to it, all of you. And keep it quiet.'

Ross ordered Heredia up to the tower with orders to tell Silver their plan of action and to bring him down. And then he began to count, for a third time, the rounds still remaining in his cartridge bag.

With the utmost care, Keane gently pushed the remaining shutter into place on the left-hand window of the ground floor and dropped the crossbar to secure it, trying, lest the French might see it, to make it look to all the world as if the shutter were somehow swinging in the breeze. He repeated the process on the other window, as the others closed the shutters on those sides unobserved by the French.

'Right, that's the whole place all secure. We'll go up and then, if they breach the gate, we come down these stairs and fall in behind the barricade.'

The men nodded their understanding and then all six of them, with Keane in the lead, raced up the two staircases to the first floor. There were three of them to a window, he thought. That should be sufficient to keep up a constant fire. So while one of them fired, the second would be reloading. The third, ready loaded, would step in immediately after the first firing, and then the third and so on. He looked out of the opening, careful not to be seen, and saw that the French were closing. They were at about five hundred yards now and he could see the men at the front. Two moustachioed sergeants with long-service stripes strode out in front on either side of the commander, a lean youth who looked as if he might at any moment fall from the saddle and whose tall black shako sported an even taller white plume.

Keane whispered to Martin. 'See if you can take the officer. You're as good as any of those smart boys in green jackets. Here, use this.'

Keane picked up the rifle and handed it to him.

'Thank you, sir.'

Martin took the gun and ran his hand over the polished walnut stock and up the length of the barrel. It was a beautiful gun. Elegant and well balanced. Keane saw the light in the boy's eyes.

'Remind you of home?'

'Funny, it does a bit, sir. All those days on the farm – shooting partridge. Pigeon too.'

Martin went silent for a moment and Keane could sense his thoughts drifting.

'Well, see if you can shoot that bloody French partridge for me' – he pointed to the officer – 'when he comes into range.'

He handed Martin a box of cartridges, ready made, and turned to Garland, their third man. 'You know the drill, Gilpin.'

'Think so, sir. It's just so as we can keep up a regular fire at them, isn't it?'

'That's it. Rake them with fire so they don't know what's hit them. They'll never guess how many of us there are in here. That's the trick.'

They could hear the chatter of the men in the column now and the steady tramp of their feet. There were fewer than he had reckoned. Barely sixty of them.

Gilpin spoke in a whisper. 'They're not doing anything, sir. They've posted no skirmishers. They can't know we're here.'

He was right. The French seemed utterly unaware of their presence. They would have just one chance and they had to make the most of it. 'And that's just how I want it. Make ready, first man. That's you, Martin.'

Keane watched as Martin knelt at the window embrasure, resting the rifle firmly on the sill, careful not to let too much protrude lest it should be spotted. The boy pushed his cheek hard into the stock of the gun and felt the balance as the foot-plate nestled into his shoulder. Keane admired the ease he had with a gun, how it became a part of him, an extension of his hand. He counted himself lucky to have plucked Martin from the ranks of the Inniskillens before the Rifles had a chance to spot his talent. The French were closer to them now. Two hundred yards. Too far for a musket to shoot with any accuracy, but not too far for a Baker rifle, in the right hands.

He whispered to Martin. 'Not yet. Hold your fire until you're close enough for all of us.'

The boy waited, the rifle steady in his hands against the wood of the sill. Their breathing was slow and shallow now as they watched the French walk towards the waiting guns. At a hundred and fifty yards Martin cast a glance with one eye. Keane shook his head. A few moments later, though, he whispered, 'Now.'

He looked out at the French and saw the officer turn in his saddle and call out something to his men. And at that instant, as his mouth opened in command, Martin squeezed the trigger. In an instant the captain on the horse froze in the saddle and then, as the dark red-black stain spread over his chest, he crumpled like a doll over the back of the animal, legs and arms splayed wildly in the puppetry of death. The noise of the shot echoed round the room, and through the dense white smoke Keane was aware of the French column coming to a halt. There was no panic. Just shock, and the noise of the sergeants and lieutenants giving commands. And then it began.

Gilpin was at the window as Martin reloaded. A shot. A cry. Gilpin ducking back inside and then Keane. He pointed Martin's carbine into the densely packed column. No point in aiming with these things, he thought, and pulled the trigger. More shouts, and as he pulled back and let Martin go forward he was aware of more men falling, killed from the window to their right. Good, thus far it was going as he had planned. Here was commotion on the ground before them and, he was pleased to see, bodies lying in the dust. They took their turns at the window a second time, a third and a fourth, pouring a relentless fire down on the French. Through the drifting smoke Keane tried to count the dead and wounded. He saw five, eight, a dozen or more bodies, some still, some writhing. Two men were limping back towards the city and the dead officer's horse galloped ahead of them, maddened by the gunfire.

But there were still men standing down there, firing up now at the windows, blindly. A shot ricocheted off one of the walls and struck Gilpin on the forearm.

He yelled and swore.

Keane turned and saw the blood pouring down his arm. 'You're hit.'

Gilpin bit his lip and tore a strip from his shirt to bind the wound.

'Nothing, sir. Had worse. Just a graze.'

They carried on firing, but the French were running now.

Martin, still kneeling, cheered. 'They've had enough, sir, look at them go.'

Keane yelled so that the others could hear. 'Cease firing. Hold your fire.'

There were two more shots from the other window and then silence. He heard Silver give a cheer and then he was out of the room and across the corridor.

'Well done, all of you. How many did we get?'

'I shot one of the sergeants, sir. Clean through the head.'

Heredia was smiling. 'We hurt them, captain. Look at the blood.'

Keane looked from the window and watched the French go. They left the corpses behind them, all save the young officer, who they carried between them as quickly as they could away from the monastery. They counted sixteen dead and Keane guessed they might have put a good ten others *hors de combat*.

Ross was smiling, grimly. 'That was deadly work, sir. Proper deadly. My barrel's red hot.'

'Piss in it, sarge,' Silver offered. 'That's what we used to do on the ships. Hot work on them.'

'When I want your advice, Silver, I'll ask for it.'

'They'll cool down soon enough,' said Keane. 'And just in time to welcome those buggers back, I would guess. Now they know we're here, we'll have no rest. But we must hold, boys. Our lads won't be long in coming.'

He ordered Gilpin to keep a watch on the city and walked back to the west side of the upper storey. Reaching the window, he looked out again across the Douro and this time his patience was rewarded. For there on the opposite bank he could at last make out ranks of men in red coats. There were at least a battalion of them with another coming up to the rear. Clearly, he thought, Wellesley is doing all he can to keep as much of his force as possible hidden in the dead ground behind the big hill to the east of Villa Nova. The French would not spy them from the city. But from his vantage point here, up in the monastery, they were as clear as day, and Keane had never seen a more welcome sight.

He called down to the others. 'They're here, boys. The army's come up.'

The men rushed up the stairs and pushed towards the window.

Silver whooped and slapped the window frame. 'Christ, sir. In the nick of time, an' all. Just as I was thinking we'd never make it out of this bloody place. Sorry, sir.'

There was a shout from above, from Gilpin up in the tower. 'They're coming again, sir. The Frenchies are coming again.'

They all ran to the west window and saw that sure enough a French column was making its way out of the east end of the city. This time, though, even at this distance it was possible to see that there was no officer on a horse at their head. There were skirmishers in front now and behind a column which as it left the confines of the buildings fanned out into a dense line of blue figures, their muskets carried at the high port of the *marche d'attaque*.

Keane swore. 'That's bad. They want to take this place and to pay us back for killing their comrades. Either way, we're in a spot. Sarn't Ross, how much ammunition do we have?'

Ross looked in his cartridge bag. 'Two strips of ten, sir. Twenty rounds.'

'You others?'

'Fifteen, sir.'

'Twenty, sir.'

'Eighteen.'

'Seventeen, sir.'

'And I have . . . ' He reached into his own bag. 'I have nineteen rounds. That's just over a hundred rounds. We'll have to make them count.'

Keane was well aware of the poor killing-power of the cavalry carbines with which they had been issued. He would even have preferred to have the old Brown Bess muskets of the infantry. He knew that, either way, if they fired down as they had done before into a dense mass of the enemy, their bullets, propelled at God knew what angles from the barrels, would stand a good chance of hitting someone. If the French opened out and if the skirmishers stayed as they were then many rounds would be lost, for it was almost impossible to aim accurately. Martin would have to do his stuff and take out the skirmishers before they came into range. Then the rest of them would join in with the carbines. That was how they would play this one. But it was going to need careful timing.

Martin said, 'Am I still to use your rifle, sir?'

Keane smiled. 'I can't think of a better use for it.' He wondered how quickly Wellesley would get his men across on the barges. Soon, he reckoned. There was no point in delaying and risking the French destroying them with cannonfire. He hoped for their sakes that he was right.

'Same positions as before. But we'll do it differently. Volley fire this time. Hold your fire until you hear my command. Martin can deal with the skirmishers and then we'll let the rest of them come on until they're in range and give it to them just as hot as we did before. And remember, make every shot count.'

Again they stood at the windows and watched the French

come on at them across the dusty white earth. The skirmishers moved quickly, zigzagging across in front of the main body, moving in pairs, expecting that at any moment they might be picked off. The French who had survived the first assault would have gabbled to those in the city something at least about how their captain was shot clean through the heart, and whoever was in charge would have guessed that at least one of the men in the palace must be armed with a rifle. That explained their tactics now. And also why their officer came on on foot.

What they would not know, though, Keane thought, was the size of the force that opposed them. Sixteen men dead was no little butcher's bill for such a short engagement. The French officers might be reckoning on perhaps as many as forty men firing at them from the windows. The force they had now sent seemed to confirm his supposition, for as he watched another French column began to move out of the town. Two companies with skirmishers and at a greater strength than before. He wondered how far the redcoats had got with their barges. Now, though, was not the time to find out. Gilpin was no longer in the tower, having come down to join them, so there was no way of knowing. They would just have to stand their ground and hope for the best.

The skirmishers were nearing them now. At a hundred and fifty yards Keane said, 'Right, Martin, now's your time. Steady. Get as many as you can.'

The boy took aim at the man nearest to him and squeezed the trigger of the rifle. The Frenchman toppled backwards and Martin reloaded fast and was on another of them as they scuttled for the meagre cover of the rocks. Another shot and the man crumpled forward, a thick black stain spreading beneath him. Martin reloaded. The skirmishers were pressing on now although the four-deep line to their rear had stopped. The officer gave the order to load and the French reached into their cartouche bags and inserted their cartridges. Still Martin continued. The skirmishers were firing back now, taking it in turns in their pairs to find cover and get in a shot. It did not do them any good. Within a minute Martin had accounted for another two of them.

Keane muttered, 'Good, Martin, very good. Keep it steady.'

He watched as the skirmishers, still moving forward, began to move faster. He'll have to finish them now, he thought, or they'll be at the windows. Martin fired and another went down. And then another. The main body of the French were loaded now and Keane saw the reserve company gaining on them. The French officer barked another command and the men came on, again at the *marche d'attaque*, with fixed bayonets.

Keane called out, 'Ready.'

Martin was still going at it. Keane stopped him. He had put paid to some ten of the skirmishers and the remaining few, perhaps five of them, had gone to ground in the lee of the wall beneath the monastery windows.

'Hold your fire now. Keep some of the ammunition. We'll need it later. You've done well, Martin.'

He yelled again so that those across at the other window could hear. 'Present.'

From below he could hear the French officer barking a command. The halt. They were preparing to fire. But he would get in the first volley before they had a chance.

Again he shouted, 'Fire.'

The five carbines, including his own, crashed out and tore into the ranks below. Five of the Frenchmen fell. The officer shouted again and the French made ready their weapons while

Keane and the others reloaded as fast as they could. Four rounds a minute, his men could manage in the Inniskillens. He wondered how fast this lot would be. Before the French could fire the carbines loosed off again and another five men fell. The officer was shouting now, trying desperately to push his men forward, to do the undoable. But the French were shaken. There was a crash of musketry and a few rounds smashed into the stonework and the wood around the window.

Keane yelled, 'Everyone all right?'

'Sir.'

They had all reloaded again and on his word of command the carbine muzzles flashed. This time only three of the French went down, but Martin was as good as ever and with a clean shot he felled the red-faced officer in mid command.

The French stood for an instant and stared. It was time enough. One more volley, he thought, before your friends arrive to help.

'Fire.'

Five guns opened up and three more Frenchmen died. And that was enough. Twenty-six of their eighty men dead and wounded, and along with them their officer. They had no stomach left for a fight. The others turned and fled back towards their advancing comrades.

Keane wiped the sweat from his forehead but did not put down his gun. This was no time to rest. The reserve company were closing fast and he was unsure of where the remainder of the skirmishers had got to. And that was a real worry now, as he could not see them retreating with the others.

'Not bad. Two attacks beaten off. Gilpin, quickly up in the tower. Tell me what you can see. Are the army crossing?'

He turned to the others. 'The rest of you, with me. We'll

give them a few shots and then get down to the barricade. You all have swords?'

'Sir.'

They had been issued with light cavalry sabres, curved and not unlike his own Mameluke sword. Swords would befit their new mounted role and Keane had made sure that when they swapped clothes they should not take the Frenchmen's weapons, but retain their own. The French muskets he thought worse even than British army issue. While Keane and Morris had given them some tuition in swordplay, he was not sure how they would get on in a melee.

They had worked well against the patrol, but that had been dirty fighting. Now would be the first real test for the men in a proper hand-to-hand engagement. Sabre against bayonet.

There was a shout from Gilpin, who came careering down the steps from the tower.

'They're crossing, sir. The army. Using all four of our boats, and the Frenchies ain't seen them yet. Leastwise, they ain't firing at them.'

'Good. Now at least we have a chance. Come on.'

Keane ordered them back to the windows and they watched in rapt anticipation as the French second column moved forward. They had turned back the retreating skirmishers and now they were in front of the front rank. As they neared the field of corpses that now lay before the walls, the French began to slow down. Keane heard the officers and sergeants shout at the men and watched as they whirled around at the front exhorting them to attack the closed gates.

'Fire on my command. Ready.'

The guns came up. Martin's too, this time.

'Present. Fire.'

Again the carbines and the rifle spat fire from their muzzles and more of the Frenchmen fell. Martin had not been idle, and the French officer lay sprawled in a twisted heap in front of his men, his brains and half his head spread across the dust. The French sergeants, though, had taken over along with another junior officer, who was pushing forward from the rear.

'One more round,' shouted Keane. 'Then down to the barricade.'

He watched them. Made certain they were steady. 'Present. Ready. Fire.'

They did not wait for the smoke to clear to survey their handiwork but led by Keane clattered down the steps and into the courtyard. By the time they reached it the French were already hammering at the gate.

Keane stopped. 'Stand where you are, men, and when they break through the gate fire and reload.'

He had placed the barricade deliberately at the rear of the courtyard, leaving a good hundred yards between it and the gate. That would allow more than enough time for them to manage another two shots before the French closed with them.

The gate was moving now as if some great titanic force were pushing against it from without, the heavy crossbar bending in its brackets.

'Steady,' called Keane, his voice strong and steadfast. 'Steady. Wait for them.'

There was a commotion from behind him and then hammering on the windows to the south. Christ, he thought. It's those damned skirmishers. The ones who had managed to get away in the lee of the wall. They've been smashing at the windows. In a matter of minutes, they'll break through and come round behind us.

He shouted to Martin. 'Will, get over to those windows. See if you can find a hole in them and shoot anyone you see outside. We've got to stop the French from getting in through them. The rest of you stay with me. They'll be in through the gate soon enough. Hold steady.'

Martin ran across to the south wall and stopped at the first window. It was being pushed through, splintering with every blow of musket butt and bayonet, and the timbers were hanging ragged on the shutters. He looked for the best place to fire his rifle and found a splintered hole in the upper part of the shutter. The main gates were moving more openly now, the crossbar straining as the French leant all their weight against it.

Keane saw Martin. 'Shoot the buggers, Will. Keep them out, for God's sake.'

This was it. In a moment they would be inside. Two more volleys, and then it would be the clash of steel and steel. But he knew it was a fight they could not hope to win. At best they would take down more of the French with them before they were overwhelmed by numbers. And then their foothold would be gone and the men in red who would struggle up the slope would find the place alive with French muskets. All for the sake of a few blessed minutes.

He cursed. Why had Wellesley taken so long?

Martin shouted something from the window. But Keane couldn't hear above the din, the noise of which seemed to swell and ebb like a wave crashing against the rocks.

'Shoot them, Martin. Shoot.'

Martin shouted again and this time he heard the words, above the sound of splintering wood as the front gates gave way. 'I said, they're red, sir. They're redcoats. It's our men, sir.'

With those words the gates opened and the French swarmed in. Keane, his head fuddled with Martin's words, came back to his senses. 'Fire.'

The five guns opened up and all hit their mark. The gate was wide enough to accommodate only seven Frenchmen standing abreast and so the dead stopped the attack in its tracks. But within a few seconds the French were climbing over the bodies of their dead and dying comrades.

But it had been long enough for Keane's men to reload and as the French moved forward another volley hit them full on. Keane had not relaxed but had leapt across to join Martin, and, ripping open the shutters, had seen the British outside trying to get in. And with them, distinctive in his blue artilleryman's tunic, came Tom Morris. Now the redcoats were climbing through the open window: a sergeant followed by four men, and as they did so Keane was aware that the French were closing on the barricade. He pushed the sergeant across to it.

'Quick. Hurry, man.' The redcoats ran to help the others and as he struggled to open a second window and a third, Keane could hear the sound of bayonets clashing.

More redcoats were pouring in through the windows now and there was another commotion from outside the walls. Keane guessed that the remainder of the force that had been the first to scale the cliff after the crossing had taken the French in the flank at the gate.

He turned and ran to the barricade. All of his men were still on their feet, fighting for their lives with sabres parrying away the thrusts of the French bayonets. He drew his own scimitar and plunged in, aware of Martin making a neat thrust and skewering a French sergeant in the ribcage.

'Hot work, Martin.'

The boy grinned and turned to fight another of the French as Keane saw Morris take on a big man in a blue coat and tall black shako, topped with a green plume. One of the voltigeurs that had escaped Martin's rifle. The man did not thrust immediately but waited, trying to anticipate Morris's move, and amid the melee around the barricade for an instant theirs became a personal fight, one on one. Morris, experienced swordsman that he was, would not make a move but feinted, trying to draw the man on. Finally, he decided that his next feint would be the real thrust. Sure enough he sidestepped and made a lunge at the Frenchman's left. The man, tricked by so many feints, parried to the right and Morris's blade sank home in the Frenchman's side. The man shrieked and clutched at the cut, trying to staunch the blood and push back the huge flap of flesh, but now his guard was down, and with another blow to the man's chin Morris finished him off.

Keane had but a second to marvel at the elegance of his friend's swordplay before he himself was in the thick of it again and turned to face another Frenchman whom he had sensed, with an instinct honed in battle, was closing on him. This time the man thrust with his musket, pushing the long steel shaft of the bayonet fast towards Keane's chest. But Keane was quick, quicker than the Frenchman, and in turning he used the base of his sword – the strongest part – to deflect the bayonet. Then, bending his arm hard over the top of the useless musket, he hacked at the Frenchman's left arm, cutting it to the bone. The man screamed and dropped his musket to grab at his mangled limb. Keane left him as useless and turned on another of them. The courtyard looked like a sea of blue uniforms, punctuated by red, but with every second the scarlet tide seemed to be growing.

As the British came on, appearing apparently from nowhere to the bewildered French, the blue-coated ranks began to fall back.

Keane yelled, 'That's it. We've got them. They're retreating. Come on, boys.'

Together, Keane's men and the newly arrived British swarmed across the barricade and pushed against the French. Keane watched as a huge corporal from the reinforcements plunged his bayonet into a Frenchman with such force that he was lifted off his feet, screaming and grasping at the shaft.

Martin and Silver were cutting in all directions with their sabres, fighting like demons as the French raised their arms to protect themselves against cuts which severed wrists and fingers.

They were almost at the gate now and the French had turned to run through the opening. Three of them still stood facing the defenders, two with muskets and bayonets levelled. Keane saw Martin make a deft sabre cut at one who, parrying with his musket, was then wrong-footed and suffered for his mistake by taking the full force of a sabre blow to his neck, which gouted spurts of bright-red blood. The second man looked uncertain. Then he threw down his musket and raised his hands. Heredia was closest to him. But rather than accept the man's surrender, he walked up to him and having stood staring into his eyes for more than a few moments, raised his sabre and made a hard and deft cut across the man's chest. The Frenchman, taken by surprise, looked on as the blood flowed freely through the slash in his blue-and-white tunic and then fell to the ground without so much as a groan.

Keane shouted to the Portuguese, 'He was surrendering. That man was surrendering.'

Heredia looked at him and smiled. 'I don't know what that means, sir.'

The last Frenchman, seeing the fate of his comrades, turned and ran and made it through the gap in the doors. Together, Keane, Martin and Ross ran after him and found themselves in the doorway. Outside was carnage. Apart from the corpses they had left before the walls with their earlier gunfire, more French dead lay piled before the gate. And with them no few bodies of men in red coats.

Keane tried to see who they were, but was not certain. Buff facings. They might be the Third Foot, the Buffs, but could just as easily be the 73rd.

Directly before them a small knot of men were fighting. Three French and two of the redcoats, one of them an officer. Keane ran to help, his bloodied blade above his head. As he closed with them one of the Frenchmen, himself an officer, saw the threat, and disengaging from his duel with the British officer turned to face him. Keane cut into him with an upper stroke which cleft his chin and sliced into his face.

He pulled back and watched in horror as the reality of what he had done unfolded. The officer was barely more than a boy and his eyes seared into Keane's with a helplessness as his face disintegrated in a mess of blood and ruined flesh.

The redcoat officer grabbed at his forearm which, Keane now saw, had been cut by the Frenchman. It looked superficial, a glancing blow, and Keane turned back to the fight. But the French had gone, leaving their dead behind them.

Martin turned to him. 'We should get after them, sir. Chase them from the town.'

'They're not finished yet, Martin. They've just started. There's hundreds more where they came from. Thousands. They'll be back. Don't worry.'

He turned back and found the officer with the wounded arm. He was young, very young; younger even, he thought, than the Frenchman he had just sent to meet his Maker. In fact, as a corporal tied up his flesh wound he looked up and smiled at Keane. Barely sixteen, he guessed, and still in shock from his first engagement. The eyes were wide, the veins high in the temples where a wisp of fair hair fell down in a ringlet. Yet the boy was keen for advancement, had pushed himself into volunteering for the forlorn hope that had been the first across the river in the first barge. Keane wondered what his story was. Passed over by a father? Family ruined by debt and drink? He fitted all the criteria that the army demanded on such occasions as these when the forlorn hope charged into the breach. He was brave, he was foolish and he was expendable.

The boy gabbled excitedly, trying to keep his voice down, high-pitched as it was. 'Thank you, sir. We didn't know who held this place and then my sergeant saw your coats. Thank God we have prevailed. Have you seen him, sir? My sergeant, I mean. Sergeant Copeland. I hope to God he's not fallen. Sorry, sir.' He came to attention. 'James Watkins, the Buffs.'

Keane nodded to him and smiled as he cleaned the blood from his sword on the blue coat of a dead Frenchman and returned it to its scabbard, the boy watching avidly. 'Keane, Inniskillens, as was. You came with good timing, Mister Watkins. And you did well to do so.' He saw Ross. 'Sarn't Ross, any losses?'

'Gilpin is hurt, sir, not bad though, and Heredia's a cut to his face, but it's only a scratch, whatever he says.'

'Thank God for that. Sarn't Ross, this is Lieutenant Watkins of the Buffs. Come to relieve us.' He laughed. 'But in truth, I don't think we'll be free of the French for long. The last thing they want is for us to hold a strongpoint on this bank of the river.' He turned to Watkins. 'How many are you, lieutenant?'

'Just twenty-five, sir; at least we were. We've lost a few men, though.'

'And how many more are coming over?'

'Another three boats, sir, all of them with twenty-five men apiece.'

'That gives us a round hundred, if you count in my men. Better odds than we've had, eh, sarn't?'

'Yes, sir, a damn sight better.'

Keane walked across to the south towards the cliff face up which the Buffs had made their way and to his relief saw two boats midstream and another making its way back across the river. The lieutenant was as good as his word. On the hillside he could make out the figures of redcoats making their way, unopposed now, towards the seminary.

Looking across to the opposite bank he made out plenty of activity as the army came to battle. The fields behind the river were a mass of black dots, men moving like so many ants in response to orders. It was a fine sight and he knew that it would be enough, if they could hold onto this foothold they had gained.

There was a puff of smoke on the opposite bank, followed by another and then another. British cannon, opening up on the town. He noticed that Watkins was on his right. Watkins pointed at the smoke. 'Look, General Wellesley has placed three batteries on that hill, sir. Eighteen nine-pounders, at the height of the convent.'

They watched as the guns continued to fire and saw the black specks that were cannonballs flying high above the Douro before disappearing into the city. The boom of the guns obscured the sound of impact. The gunners were using round-shot first, to gauge the range. Soon though, he thought, they would use the howitzers to hurl shell and hollow case shot fitted with a slow-burning fuse. Hollow iron balls filled with gunpowder and designed to explode when the timed fuse burned down, causing death and destruction and with the ability to set buildings afire. He felt sorry for the people of Oporto. Raped by the French and now bombarded by the British. But it was the price they must pay for freedom, and he suspected that they were aware of what would happen.

He was astonished that no French guns had yet opened up in counterbattery fire or indeed on the barges ferrying the redcoats across the river. The second barge was nearing their bank, about to beach.

'Those are your men down there?'

'Yes, sir. That's my company commander. Captain Lawrence.' Watkins continued, still pointing. Following the ensign's finger Keane saw a third boat leave the opposite bank. 'And that boat there, sir. That's Major Danvers. The adjutant. He's a fine man, sir. A great leader. You might know him.'

Keane ignored his embarrassing enthusiasm and watched as the boats slipped across the river, and still no noise could be heard from the French in the town. The first vessel slid from their view as she neared the shore.

'Do you know if the general is intending to cross elsewhere?'

The boy nodded. 'We were told when we were picked for the assault. I know that General Wellesley has sent General Murray with the German brigade, the 14th Dragoons and a battery three miles upstream. He believes that it will be possible for him to attempt a crossing there. There was no word, though, when I left, as to whether he has succeeded.'

'It's of no real matter to us. What we need is more infantry and guns over here. We'll have to manage that somehow.'

He pondered the situation. These barges could hold only penny parcels of men. It would take the entire day to move an army. And the French would start to bombard them ere long. 'We'll just have to make do with what we have for the present. Put yourself in order, lieutenant, and gather your men in the courtyard. We need to waste no time in repairing the damage done.'

Watkins hurried away and Keane remained for a moment looking down on the little boats. They had done well, but as he had told the ensign, they would have to do better. The only way would be somehow to get down to the city and find bigger boats. They would need to mobilize the townspeople. But how to do that, he wondered, if the French had them penned up in the seminary?

Ross came up, grinning. 'Look, sir, they're pouring across. Why don't the bloody Frenchies shoot? They must have seen us by now. If we keep this up the whole army will be across and not a shot fired.'

Keane shook his head. 'It's beyond me.'

But he knew that time was running out and cussed under his breath for their both having tempted fate. This was too good to last: a frontal assault by boat in broad daylight against a position which overlooked the attack. Any moment now the French would see them, and then it would all be up.

# 8

Still standing on the cliff top, gazing down at the Douro, Keane realized with a start that he was wasting precious time. He turned to Ross. 'Sarn't Ross, we must fix the windows. Come on.'

Together they ran back into the seminary to find Watkins already posting his men. Keane shouted to him. 'Mister Watkins, place half a dozen of your men under Sarn't Ross here. We need to use everything we can find to barricade the windows. Get them to rip out the floorboards, anything. We have to secure this place. Get the rest of your men down to the first-floor windows. We have to stop the French getting in. If they make any breach they'll have us. I want to know if anyone sees a gun coming up. And if you see any gunners tell Martin, he's the best marksman.'

Within moments the sound of tearing wood and hammering filled the place. Everywhere men were pulling at panelling, boards, anything that looked as if it might move. They used the same nails and the butts of their muskets to hammer home the pieces of barricade. Keane walked from one window to another, inspecting their handiwork, testing its strength, making them do it again.

The front gate he had left open, waiting for the two remaining boatloads of infantry. He was inspecting the fabric of the gates when there was a noise from the hill and around the corner of the wall appeared a dozen redcoats, led by a red-faced captain.

'Captain Lawrence?'

'Indeed.'

'James Keane, the Inniskillens. We were expecting you. Your ensign did well.'

'Where are the French, Keane?'

'We pushed them back into the city. But I don't think we'll have long to wait for their return. You have twenty-five men?'

'Twenty-five, and a few others besides.'

Tom Morris clasped him by the shoulder. 'James, at last. We thought you dead.'

'Not so soon, Tom.'

Morris clapped him on the shoulder. 'Truly, it is good to see you. And the others?'

'Fine, unscathed for the most part. Garland is with you?'

Morris nodded. 'But not the girl. This can be no place for a woman.'

'You're right on that account. I tell you, the French morale may be low, if we are to believe Morillo, Tom, but they still fight like dogs when cornered.'

There was shout from the tower, where Keane had posted Silver.

'Sir, they're coming again.'

Keane turned and saw that a column of men were leaving the town. They marched in threes with a colonel at their head, in proper order, and behind them came a team of horses pulling an ammunition limber and a gun.

'That's bad. I knew it would only be a matter of time.'

Keane turned to Lawrence. 'Captain Lawrence, I presume you have no objection to my taking command?'

Lawrence smiled. 'I have no objection. I would imagine our commissions are of a similar time.'

Keane hesitated. Protocol demanded he should admit that his was only a brevet rank. That he was in effect a mere lieutenant until confirmed by Horse Guards. But now was not the time to invoke protocol. He would play on Lawrence's good nature.

'Thank you, captain. Very well, I should be obliged if you would take your men and split them in two divisions. Post a dozen, with your best sergeant, up there.'

He pointed to the two windows above them, which they had kept open as before. 'Use them to shoot down into the French. The others we'll keep down here under your own command. Be ready for the French when they break in.'

'You think they'll get in?'

'Oh, I'm certain they're going to get in. We're going to let them in.'

'We're what?'

'We'll fire down on them and then when they think we're beat we open the doors and let them have a full volley and then another one. How are you for ammunition?'

'Fine. We've enough.'

'Good. We'll share it out between us all. How many men have you, all told?'

'Steady on. That ammunition is recorded for us. Signed for from the stores. And I'm afraid I haven't had a headcount.'

'Well, let's get one. And don't worry about the damned stores. I'll account for the ammunition. Give me a headcount first and then we'll divide up the cartridges. Then we'll know what we're dealing with and we can measure the odds.'

Lawrence stared at him, incredulous. 'You actually plan to open the gates?'

'Yes. And I plan to kill the French. Now do as I ask. We need that headcount.'

'Very well, Keane, but it's folly, if you ask me.'

The men had done a good job of repairing the main gate of the seminary. The locks proper had been blown off and the crossbar had snapped in the last struggle. But they had made a new crossbar by tying together several iron railings from the fence around the kitchen garden and this they had fastened between the brackets, both of which were still intact. It was almost impregnable.

The French column was growing closer by the moment and Keane could see that once again they had sent out skirmishers. A cloud of them this time, deployed far in advance. The cannon had turned out of the column and pulled away to the right onto a piece of rising ground. Here the drivers were unfastening the limber while the gunners set about preparing their piece. Keane hoped that they would not use shell or case shot. Roundshot would be bad enough coming in on a high trajectory like a mortar. He wondered how clever their officer was. The column itself seemed stronger than before. These men, he noticed, were all in dark-blue coats without the white waistcoats of their earlier attackers. Light infantry. These were men who had been trained to fight fast, to get through difficult country and, importantly, to take buildings.

Just then there was another massive crash from the left bank of the river and Keane and the others watched as a salvo of black cannonballs flew into the air from the guns on a hill above the river. The first seemed for a moment to be coming directly towards them but then it appeared to slew away and head towards the French.

It exploded in the air, close to the right flank in the centre of the French column. A short fuse, thought Keane, as he watched the red-hot metal rain down upon their heads, cutting shakos, bone and flesh like a heated knife going through butter. The French screamed as half a dozen men went down in a mess of gore, and the column stopped. Their officers turned and then another ball came in. Keane thanked God the British artillery on the heights by the seminary on the opposite bank had found their range. As he had known they would, the fore-most files of the French dissolved in a panic-stricken mob and milled around the mutilated bodies lying in the carnage on the approach road.

Morris was at his side.

'How many men do you suppose we might have on this bank in the next hour, James? I mean, how many can come across?'

'Oh, I don't know, five or maybe six hundred men. Enough to persuade them to retreat.'

'Enough, providing we can hold on here.'

They watched them come. Marching in column along the approach road they had used before, officers and skirmishers to the front. Keane yelled at Ross. 'How many would you say this time, sarn't?'

'A good four hundred, sir. At least.'

There was a shout behind him as Gilpin came running into the garden. 'They're coming up the other two roads from the west, sir. Captain Morris reckons there could be as many as a thousand of them.'

Ross appeared with a man, a soldier dressed only in a shirt and overalls, and dripping wet. 'A runner, sir, from the commander-in-chief.'

The man was drenched from head to foot. Keane looked at him. 'You swam the river?'

'Yes, sir.'

'Well done, man. Have you a message?'

'Yes, sir, the general says to hold on. The 66th and 48th are on their way, sir.'

Keane nodded and smiled. 'Thank you. That's good news. Well done. There is no need for you to return. Best stay here with us. Get dried off and then get yourself a musket.'

He looked at Ross. 'Good news, then, sarn't. Two battalions on the way to our relief.'

Ross grinned. 'Believe that and you'll believe anything, sir. I'm sure they're on their way right enough. But when are they going to get here, sir? In those boats? Not before Christmas.'

Keane knew him to be right, but they had to believe, at least.

He called to the men still outside the gates. 'Right, get inside. Tom, that means you too.'

Morris had been standing on a piece of rising ground observing the French gunners through a field glass. 'It's bad, James, but not as bad as it might be. A six-pounder. Why didn't they bring up a howitzer? The fools.'

'Don't chastise them too much. That's what we want, isn't it? And it'll be bad enough, won't it? You had better get inside. All of you inside, now, and shut the gates.'

Captain Lawrence appeared. 'Captain Keane?'

'Captain Lawrence?'

'What are you doing?'

'I'm sorry? What am I doing?'

'You are closing the gates, sir.'

'Indeed I am. Have you not see what is outside and coming in our direction?'

'Of course I have, sir, but have you not seen what is below us on the cliff and also coming our way?'

'If you are alluding, sir, to the men of your regiment who are making their way up the hill, then yes, I have seen them. But if we do not close the gates now then we will most certainly not be here to greet them.'

'You cannot shut them out. They will be taken by the French, or killed. By God, man, the odds are four to one against them; more. That's my commanding officer down there, Keane.'

'That's as maybe, but if I keep the gates open then I risk losing the monastery. And that I cannot do.'

'But you're condemning them to death, man. All of them.'

Keane looked at him and then looked down towards the men toiling up the track on the cliff. He turned away and yelled at Ross, who was closing the left gate, the right already being in place. 'Sarn't Ross, hold off there a moment.'

Keane ran to the gate and out onto the road. The French skirmishers were only a few yards away and took careful aim at the English officer. Keane ducked as two bullets thwacked into the white walls behind him, sending chips and shards of stone and plaster up into the air. There were more shots now and he ran, half doubled over, along the south side of the wall. He was suddenly aware that another man was with him: Silver.

'What the devil are you doing here? Get back inside.'

Silver ignored him. 'What are you doing, sir? Where are we going?'

'I need to see if the others are here. The third boat. I can't shut the gates on them.'

Silver shouted over the bullets. 'Look, sir, down there.'

Peering down the cliff into the bushes, Keane saw the top of a black shako and then a bicorne and a dozen red coats. He cupped his hands and shouted. 'Hallo on the cliff! Come on. Get up here. The French are at the gate.'

The men looked up and doubled their pace as best they could. Keane turned and dashed back towards the gate. The French were there now, the skirmishers first, while to their left the column, an entire company with a mounted colonel, was deploying into three-deep line. They would have to get inside before the French opened fire or all would be lost.

He drew his sword and plunged upon one of the voltigeurs who had reversed his musket and was using it as a club, trying to smash the already bloodied and broken hands of a young redcoat who was holding the gate. Keane raised his sword and brought it down on the Frenchman's arm, almost severing it above the elbow. The man spun round and collapsed to the ground. Silver was in the thick of it too now, thrusting and parrying against the skirmishers' bayonets.

Then the British reinforcements reached them. Immediately Keane heard an officer's voice giving orders. 'Form up there. Form line.'

A tall officer, presumably the major of whom Watkins had spoken, stood in their midst, sword drawn. He caught Keane's eye and nodded before turning back to his men, who had done as ordered. 'Present. Prepare to fire. Fire.' A volley rang out into the mauled French ranks, killing one of the officers.

'Thank you, Captain . . . '

'Keane, sir.'

'Thank you, Captain Keane. Major Danvers, the Buffs. Had we not better get inside this place before the Frenchies send more of their friends?'

'Aren't there more of you?'

'More? There's the whole damned army, sir. But not here. Not now.'

Keane glanced towards the French column. They were readying their weapons now, reaching into their cartridge bags to bite open the cartridges. As he watched two of them fell, shot from the windows of the seminary. There was still time. Just.

He sliced up with his blade into a skirmisher's chin and felt a bayonet cut into the red cloth of his tunic, searing his forearm. Keane pulled himself away towards the gate and shouted, 'Pull back. The Buffs, with me. Inside the gate.'

Keane swung his sword down on the head of another Frenchman, severing it across the scalp. He shouted a command at no one in particular. 'Inside. Get inside.'

The major was locked in a fight with a voltigeur. As tall as Keane himself, he used his body weight to crash into the Frenchman and then before the man could recover, drew back his infantry sword and plunged it into his side. The close-quarter tactics of an old-school fighter, thought Keane. Dirty and effective. He yelled at the major, 'Fall back. With me. Get inside, sir. There are too many of them.'

Then, standing shoulder to shoulder with him, Keane held off the few remaining French skirmishers while behind him the major's men pushed through the gate into the seminary. The French line beyond was at the 'present', their muskets raised and ready to fire, now. More of them had fallen, were falling, shot from the walls, but Keane knew what was coming next and that neither of them would survive it.

He turned to the major. 'Come on, sir. It's our turn now.'

Together they squeezed through the gate. Keane yelled to Ross. 'Shut it, sarn't. Shut the gate, man.'

A lone voltigeur poked his musket through the gap, trying in vain to force it open, and was shot in the face for his trouble by one of the Buffs.

Ross and seven men pushed the gate shut and as they did a volley rang out from the French lined up outside the wall. A bullet entered through the gap and struck one of the redcoats in the forehead, killing him. Other bullets struck the walls and the gate, splintering wood and stone. Meanwhile from the upper storeys the defenders continued their fire.

Keane turned to the major. 'What the devil are the French trying to do? Anyone knows that you can't take a position with musketry. This is madness.'

The major, doubling over to regain his breath, straightened up. 'I'm in your debt, Captain Keane. Reckon you saved my life.'

'It was a close thing, sir.'

Lawrence walked over to them. 'Well done, Keane. Welcome, sir. We're in a bit of a hodgepodge here, as you can see.'

'So I do see, Lawrence. What's our state?'

'Sarn't Copeland's just now calling the roll, sir. We've lost six, sir, all told, but there's another five as won't fight again today.'

Danvers turned to Keane. 'What's your strength, Keane?'

'I have seven men, sir, and myself.'

'Seven men? You took this place with seven men?'

'We took it and have held it with seven men, sir, yes.'

'Good God. Seven men.' Shaking his head, the major paused. 'Well, we shall have to do as well as that, shan't we, Lawrence? Now I am here I shall assume command.'

There was another volley from outside the walls and a shriek from above as a redcoat fell from the tower. The major continued. 'You're quite right, of course, Keane. It is ludicrous to attack a fortified position in this way.'

'They do of course have a field piece, sir.'

'Yes, by God, so they have, damn them. By God, I vouch we shall feel that soon enough.'

Keane smiled. 'Sir, if I may suggest, perhaps we should regroup. We could distribute the remaining ammunition and so on.'

'Are you telling me my duties, captain?'

'No, sir, not at all. I was merely suggesting.'

'Well, do not "suggest" any further.'

He turned to Lawrence. 'Captain Lawrence, where is that state report? And I want to know exactly how many rounds we have.'

Lawrence went off in search of his sergeant and still the firefight continued outside the walls. And then suddenly both Keane and the major turned as they heard a strange noise. A great rush. The seminary shook as a six-pound cannonball smashed into the fabric of the bell tower.

'Great heavens,' exclaimed the major, holding his hat as shards of plaster fell about them.

Keane brushed the dust from his coat. 'Well, sir, now we know they've got the range. Not bad shooting for a first attempt.'

It would take time for the single gun to reload. Time that they must now put to good use. Keane ran to the foot of the tower and yelled up. 'All of you get down from there. Now.'

He wondered whether the French gunners would now do what he would have done. Move their target from the tower down to the windows of the upper storeys. He didn't have long to wait to find out. There was another boom from the cannon and a ball came flying at them, but this time it hit the wall close to the left-hand window and continued into the building. The screams from the room rocked the air. Keane ran up the steps and pushed through the redcoats crowding the corridor towards the room.

The cannonball had taken away half of the window and part of the wall, and with it most of the men who had been crowded around it. Two redcoats lay mangled on the floor while another, a headless corpse, was kneeling where it had been when the ball had struck. Of his own men there was no sign and Keane feared the worst, but just then Ross and Heredia appeared at the door.

Ross spoke. 'Knew they'd do that, sir. They was just finding their range. I told those boys to come away, but they wouldn't.' He looked with horror at the headless corpse. 'Christ almighty.'

Keane slapped him on the shoulder. 'Well done, sarn't. Might have been you. Come on.'

He guided them down the stairs, but not before noticing that the French line, whose purpose had been to entrap the men at the windows, allowing the gun to target them, were pulling back.

He walked over to Danvers. 'You've lost three more men, major. Up there. Oh, and the French are retiring.'

'What? Why?'

'They mean to come on in force. It's my guess they're waiting for reinforcements. Then we'll be in trouble.'

One of the redcoats called from the south side of the building. 'Sir, Major Danvers, sir. There's more men coming up the hill. More of our men.'

Together, Keane and the major went over to the south and peering through a crack in one of the shutters saw a cloud of red-coated men moving up the hill. Battalion strength, at least.

Danvers smiled. 'The rest of the battalion. Well, another company at least. Three more boatloads. That'll show them.'

Morris, who had been standing listening, turned quietly to Keane. 'Between you and me, James, I think it will take more than another three boatloads to make the French quit Oporto.'

'Allow the man his moment, Tom. Ours will come.'

The major moved to the front of the seminary and barked an order. 'Open the gates. Allow our men inside.'

Keane hurried across to him. 'Is that quite wise, sir? At this moment the French are not far away; they might easily rush the gates before we had a chance. We could signal to the men on the cliff our situation. They could wait and take the French in the flank as they pull back. As the gates are now shut they have no alternative, unless they want us to pick them off. We've learnt our lesson from the cannon. Surely it would be better to get our men under cover. Their gun is sure to open up again.'

Danvers laughed and shook his head. 'Don't be so foolish, Keane. The Frenchies won't dare try their luck with us again.' He called to his sergeant. 'Open the gates, man. Do it.'

The great gates swung open slowly and through the widening gap they saw the wall of blue that was the French. Danvers called out again. 'Form up. Form up. Form line. We must give our fellows covering fire.'

It was as if Keane was watching it happen in a dream, slow and unreal. The French had clearly been dumbfounded at first as they had watched the British open the gates. But now he saw their officer turn and wave them on, and then, slowly, the blue lines began to march forward, their bayonet-shining muskets levelled in the attack position, straight towards the open gates.

Keane tried again. 'Major Danvers, sir. This is not the way. There are too many of them and they are too close.'

'Don't tell me, captain, what is the right way and the wrong way to fight a battle. Go and mind your own men, sir, and leave me to defend this place like a soldier.'

Keane walked away cursing, leaving Danvers to form two ranks of his depleted company. He found his men together, near the barricade. The French were nearing the open gates now and he wondered how long it would be until the new arrivals reached them.

Ross had seen what was happening. 'Christ, sir, the Frogs'll be inside before his lads have time to loose off even one volley. We've got to stop them.'

Keane nodded. 'Get up in the windows. I don't care about the gun. Don't bunch together. Get every man you can who Danvers hasn't got down there playing toy soldiers. Come on.'

Desperately, Keane grabbed two lightly wounded redcoats and with Morris and Martin behind him ran headlong as fast as he could up the steps. He placed them in the left-hand window.'

'Shoot down on the French. Stop them in their tracks.'

He looked across the fields towards the French gun where it sat on the hill and saw that the gunners were re-laying. Soon another round would come hurtling into the palace. He realized, though, that it was not a howitzer and thus could not hurl the projectiles which would set the palace afire. But the French must also know that and it would be merely a matter of time, surely, before such a cannon would be brought to bear on them.

Looking down from the shattered window, from the room still littered with dead and dismembered bodies, he saw that the French line had almost reached the gates and still Danvers' redcoats had not fired a shot. The French stopped now, as he had known they would. He heard the sharp shout of their officers making their commands heard above the din. Danvers, of course, was doing exactly the same but Keane knew that the muskets at his disposal were barely a third of the French. When the volleys were exchanged at such a range, Danvers' men would be decimated. There was one chance.

'Quickly,' he yelled. 'Fire at whoever you can. Martin, you shoot the officer. The rest of you shoot at the sergeants.' He raised his own musket and tried as best he could to take aim. 'Fire.'

There was a crash as their guns rang out, together with those of Ross and his men from the other window. And below them the bluecoats fell. Ten of them, plucked from the ranks. The French looked up, brought in their surprise to a temporary halt by the men in the windows. And at the same time Danvers' men opened up, catching the French before they had a chance. But Martin's rifle bullet had struck home and the officer had been dead before he had been able to give the command. Another nine Frenchmen went down, and at that moment screaming round the corner came the men from the boats.

They crashed into the right flank of the French line, driving home their attack with the bayonet and pushing the French off their feet like skittles in a shy.

The far end of the French line, officerless, turned and ran, while the others attempted to defend themselves as best they could.

Danvers, standing in the courtyard below, yelled 'Charge,' and his men joined in the melee. It did not last long.

Keane and the others rattled down the steps and watched as the French who had not yet been shot or bayoneted raised their arms in surrender.

Danvers placed them in the charge of three of his men and turned to Keane. 'You see, captain, that is how to fight a battle. And how to win.'

Keane fumed but said nothing. He knew that any retort would be pointless. Silver came up to him. 'Sir, you know and I know that wasn't him that did that. That was us, sir. We saved him and all his men. If them Frenchies hadn't been taken by us from above they'd have got in the first volley and that would have been that.'

Keane smiled. 'You may well be right, Silver, but Major Danvers is the senior officer and we must accept his word.'

There was a sudden whooshing noise that sucked the air from around them and instinctively Keane and the others ducked. The cannonball smashed into the front of the building, shaking it to its foundations and knocking a hole in the wall. It caused no casualties, but it was clear to Keane that, even in the elation of victory, the redcoats were shaken.

As the French prisoners were led away to the rear of the buildings, Keane began to wonder what their next plan of action might be. He wondered how much longer it was going to go on, this game of cat and mouse, played out with human lives. He wondered too who might have led the relief column up the cliff and to whom he might now be answerable. He hoped that it might be someone superior in rank and intellect to Danvers. A colonel at least.

The gate was clear now, save for the dead and wounded, and as Danvers' men dragged their fallen comrades into the monastery, the redcoats who had made the flank attack at last came through the gate. They were led by two officers. One, a captain, wore a stovepipe shako and on his shoulders carried the green wings of the battalion's light company. The other, though, was different. He wore a bicorne hat on his head and on his chest a lanyard of gold bullion and the Garter star. He saw Keane and instantly gravitated towards him. Not a colonel, then, but a general.

Keane snapped smartly to attention and nodded a greeting. 'Sir.'

The general smiled and returned the salute. 'General James Paget. And you would be?'

'Keane, sir. Captain James Keane, late of the 27th, now attached to the Corps of Guides.'

'Ah, yes. Keane. You're the intelligencer, are you not? Sir Arthur has told me of you. And Major Grant also speaks highly of you.' He saw Morris. 'And this must be your lieutenant.'

'Captain Morris, general.'

Paget nodded and Danvers, who had just noticed the new arrival, now came hurrying over to join them. He was in a state of some consternation.

'General Paget, sir, good day. Major Danvers of the 3rd, sir. I command here. And this is my second in command, Captain Lawrence.'

Paget smiled and nodded. 'Yes, major, and a quite splendid job you've made of it. But I'm afraid it's not over yet. The French do not as yet seem to have any notion of leaving the city, although I am told by Sir Arthur that is Marshal Soult's intent. We have two companies on this side of the river and another on its way. The general has plans to make a further crossing downstream, closer to the city, but for that he will need more boats. Until then it would seem that we are on our own. Whatever they may throw at us.'

Keane spoke up. 'Sir, it would seem prudent, were it possible, to send a detachment of men somehow into the city to make contact with the populace and perhaps obtain some means of ferrying over the greater part of the army.'

Paget nodded and at that moment another round came crashing into the monastery. This time it overshot the walls and landed with some force in the centre of the courtyard, throwing up cobblestones as lethal shrapnel. Two of Danvers' men were hit, one in the neck. Blood began to spurt from the wound as the man fell to the cobbles.

The general pointed to him. 'Someone help that man.'

He turned back to Keane. 'Indeed, captain, were it possible. Do you suppose that it might be?'

'A small party of men, sir, perhaps in disguise or otherwise rendered inconspicuous, might do so.'

'You are suggesting, I presume, Captain Keane, that you and your men might constitute that party?'

'That was in my plan, sir.'

'You are willing then to have a go?'

'More than willing, sir. I think we can do it.'

Paget shrugged. 'Then by all means, Keane. You have my blessing on the enterprise. You're better doing that than standing here penned up and waiting for the French. In truth I wish I could go with you.'

Keane assembled the men in the courtyard. As he did so, another French round screamed in overhead, higher now. Nevertheless they all ducked as it took away part of the tower. The stones crashed into the yard and Keane spoke above the noise. 'I have some good news for you. We're getting out of here.' There was a cheer. 'The bad news is that we're going into the city. And more bad news is that we're going to get dressed up as Frenchmen again.'

Someone swore. Ross's eyes flashed across them, but missed the culprit.

Keane went on. 'We'll leave through a window on the south side and come round the wall beneath the line of the cliff. From there it should be plain sailing until we reach the city.'

Silver moaned. 'Do we have to wear these clothes again, sir? I can't be doin' with it.'

Ross growled. 'You'll be done with it when I'm done with you, Silver. We're wearing them and that's that.'

Keane smiled. 'Yes, I'm afraid we do have to wear them. At least until we're safely in the city and we've done what we need to do.'

Martin spoke. 'And what is that, sir?'

'We're after more boats, Martin. We need to find boats big enough to get more of our men across. Many, many more. The whole army if they can manage it. And for that we'll need some of the locals. Such men as Father Sanchez have no love for the French and they're sure to help us. Most of you have Spanish, some of you can speak French. What we have to do is let the local people know who we are without making ourselves known to the French.'

Heredia shook his head. 'Sir, do you really think that we will manage it? Of course I can pass as both a Portuguese and a Frenchman. But what of the others?' He indicated them with his hand as if to emphasize the hopelessness of their situation. 'I think it's madness.'

It was much as Keane had come to expect from the trooper and he brushed it off.

Silver spoke up. 'You're talking out of your arse as usual, Heredia. You know it's the only way.'

The trooper turned on Silver, and Ross stepped forward, but Keane was quick to speak. 'You might think that but it is not open to discussion, Heredia. Just remember where I found you and what your fate might have been. Now get yourselves changed. We've no time to lose. And make sure you put on the French clothes over your own. When we meet the good people of Oporto we'll have to get these bloody blues off before they have time to shoot us.'

The French uniform was as itchy and twice as uncomfortable as it had been before. It had never been a good fit, but now, over Keane's red coat, it was almost intolerable. He presumed that the others must feel the same and told himself it would not be for long. Nevertheless, as they crawled through the grass beneath the line of the cliff top Keane wondered for a moment whether Heredia might not in fact have been right. Perhaps this was madness. Still, it was as mad to remain in the seminary and be blown to pieces by French cannon before the army got across.

He wondered when the French would open up with shell.

Not long. And then the buildings of the seminary would be set ablaze and the redcoats would die in that burning hell.

And then he heard it. On their right. The earth beneath them shook and a familiar, repetitive noise clattered out. He knew what it was. Drums. The sound of French columns advancing into battle. Keane rolled across to the bank and, raising himself up on his elbows, peered over and through the parched grass on top. Three columns of French light infantry, headed by mounted officers and drummer boys in their imperial green and gold, were advancing upon the seminary, two from the road they had used before and the other from a road to the north. And with them came two more guns, and this time Keane could make out the short, stubby barrels of howitzers.

He squinted and tried to reckon the numbers of the infantry and decided that they must be three full battalions, each with a colonel riding at its head. Twelve hundred men and a full battery of guns against – how many had they left in the seminary? Perhaps five boatloads of the Buffs. Barely a hundred and fifty men. The odds were worse than ten to one and he began to sweat, horribly aware that apart from the penny parcels still coming ashore from the barges, his mission was the only way in which the French might abandon their assault on the seminary and reprieve Paget and his garrison.

Ross was with him now. 'By God, sir. Will you look at that? All them Frenchies just to take that little place? And it's not as if it would be of any use to anyone, is it, sir?'

'But it must be taken, sarn't, if the French are to prevent us retaining a bridgehead on this side of the river. If Wellesley is right, if Marshal Soult intends to escape, then he will not want his rear harassed by the likes of us. That is why he must take this place. And that is why we must stop him.'

As he spoke the battery of British guns opposite them on the hill at Villa Nova opened up again, hurling roundshot into the advancing French columns. Keane watched as the first of the balls, perfectly placed by the gunners, landed before the flank of the lead column and then bounced up and into it, scything its way in a welter of gore through the files. He felt for them. He himself knew what it was to be in that mess of mangled flesh and part of him could not help but feel the sympathy for his enemy, French or not, that only a soldier knows. The French continued to march forward, walking on and across the broken bodies of the dead and dying, and all the time the drums at the head of the column pattered out their familiar tattoo.

Spellbound, they gazed at the columns for a moment longer. Keane spoke. 'I'll wager you're happy we didn't stay in there now, sarn't.'

'Aye, sir, damn happy. I don't envy them one bit.'

The two of them slid back down and rejoined the men on the track that skirted the cliff top. Slowly and silently they made their way along the tiny path. Keane had ordered them to stow their canteens, lest they should clatter and give them away. Their muskets too were without their flints. They had taken muskets rather than carbines, and any muskets, French or English, were unpredictable tools at the best of times: the slightest knock might send a spark from a flint or cock the hammer. It sounded unlikely, but he had seen it happen. A hammer snagged on an overhanging branch and the man in front killed on the march.

Not that any of that mattered now, with all the din the French were making and the boom of their own guns. They were closer to the town now, only some five hundred yards away from the first house. Keane tapped Ross on the shoulder and signalled him to halt.

'We'll stay out here. No point in going in before we have to.' He pointed ahead towards a road that led away from the river, beyond which they could see the spires and towers of the city proper. 'We'll make for a point over there. That road must lead down to the river. If we move in through there and pass ourselves off as French, we can make ourselves known to the townspeople and try our luck in finding those boats.'

On Keane's command the men rose slowly and assembled on the road, trying to look for all the world like a French patrol returning from the river. They shouldered their muskets in the French manner at high port and with Keane, as sergeant, leading them forward, began to march into the city. Any keen-eyed observer would have noticed telltale signs about them. The fact that their sergeant carried at his side a curved sword with an elaborate mother-of-pearl hilt, the glimpse of scarlet tunic beneath the tails of Gilpin's coat and the red stripe on Morris's grey artillery overall trousers were the most obvious giveaways. But from a distance and to the untutored eye they looked the part, and even if they had not, as they entered the town it became evident that no one would be looking. The place was in an uproar, with soldiers running in all directions and commands being shouted. The French were attempting to restore some order to their semi-mutinous troops and Keane knew that they had done the right thing in coming here. The most important thing, he thought, is not to get caught up in the French chaos. At all costs they must avoid being ordered to join a unit. He turned to Ross. 'In a moment I'm going to slip away down a side street. All of you, follow me.'

Keane timed his moment well, waiting until they were

halfway along one of the narrow streets and could not see any
French officers. Then he ducked left and into a side alley. The
others followed and they stood leaning against the walls,
waiting for his orders.

'We'll carry on along here and then double back left and
head down towards the river. There are some big houses there.
We're sure to find someone to help us.'

Heredia spoke. 'Are you sure, sir? I mean that this is the
right thing to do?'

Silver rounded on him. 'Course it is. The captain's as good
as his word. Has he got it wrong before?' He paused and smiled.
'Perhaps you're just scared.'

Heredia moved towards him and Ross held him back. Keane
spoke. 'We're all scared, Silver. You too, I suspect. Thank you
for your faith in me. That's what we're going to do. Follow
me.'

They advanced along the narrow passageway, encountering
no one as they went. Twice they saw bodies of French hurrying
past the far end, but none bothered to glance in their direction. At last they emerged into a wide street dominated by a
single huge house with a high garden wall. Keane heard French
voices from the garden and looked back down the passageway,
but their line of retreat had been cut off by a group of French
soldiers moving fast towards them.

He turned to Morris. 'Come on.'

Putting on his best air of confidence, he led them into the
street and past the walled house. They were going downhill
now, heading towards the river as they passed the gate, and
knowing that he could not look behind Keane walked on,
praying that they would not be stopped. Still the voices spoke
in the garden, rising in tone in what he guessed must be an

argument. He led them left into a street that curved down the hill, past tall houses with tiled walls and ornate wrought-iron balconies that spoke of the wealth of their departed owners.

Reaching the bottom of the street they emerged into another wide boulevard facing the cathedral. Looking to their left they saw the river and the place where until recently the bridge had stood, now destroyed by the French.

'Down there,' said Keane. 'If there are boats to be had they'll be down there, at the harbour.'

He led them across the road. The French were everywhere now, but somehow with so many he felt more secure. Surely there was less likelihood of their being challenged here?

Two well-ordered companies advanced past them up the street, heading north and led by a colonel on a horse. One of the sergeants cast a quizzical glance at Keane, who smiled back through gritted teeth, his hand hovering over his sword hilt. But the sergeant turned and marched on.

He was turning to Ross when someone spoke to him, in French.

'The sooner we get out of this pisshole the better, that's what I say, eh?'

Keane smiled and nodded. 'Yes, of course. Let's hope it's soon.'

The man, a fellow sergeant, looked at him. 'What mob are you from?'

Keane thought fast. He remembered that the shako plate of the hat he was wearing said 108. 'Hundred and eighth. God knows where the rest of us are. We were down by the river.'

'You too? Your lot were ordered up with the rest of us. We've got to take the seminary. Bloody British are in there. They killed Colonel Hesdin, you know. Jules Hesdin of the 45th. He was a good man. They should suffer, but my lads are in no mood for a fight. How about yours?'

'No. Mine too. Just want to get out of here. We'd better find our own lot.'

'I'm telling you, they're up there on the hill. That's where you'll find them.'

'Thanks, I'll take your advice. But first I'm going back to where we last saw them. Good luck.' He turned to the men. 'Come on.'

The sergeant nodded but Keane had the impression that he was staring after them as they made their way down the hill towards the river. Had he guessed? Had he seen through his accent? Perhaps he suspected they were deserters and was thinking of challenging them. Keane waited for the shout. But none came, and after a few dozen yards he turned and the sergeant had gone.

Morris looked at him. 'That was a little too close, I think, James. Well done.'

Keane shook his head. 'I can't help thinking that our luck is bound to run out.'

The street, as Keane had predicted, gave out onto the river, and as they went so they passed more French hurrying against them, up the hill. A corporal shouted out to them. 'Where are you going? We're all ordered to the seminary. You're going the wrong way.'

'Orders,' said Keane and smiled, but he knew what this might mean.

Sure enough, as they reached the city's harbour area the Frenchmen gave way to groups of local civilians. Realizing that this would be their only chance, Keane made for a group of seven men who stood out from the rest, being as close in appearance to guerrillas that Keane could see. And, what was more important, two of them were holding billhooks and oars. They had boats.

They were standing on the quay, watching the French leave, as Keane and the others approached. One of them, a tall man in his early thirties wearing a black cloak and a tall black hat, fixed Keane directly with his eyes and smiled at this French officer. Then he pushed back his cloak to reveal a pistol tucked into his belt. Keane stopped. His men levelled their muskets and as they did so the Portuguese drew swords and knives. Two of them had pistols. Now, thought Keane, was the time.

Keane raised his hands and then with a swift movement plucked at the buttons of his tunic and pulled it apart to reveal the red coat beneath. The man in black stared hard still, but his expression now had changed from defiance to puzzlement. His hand though remained hovering over the pistol.

Keane spoke, in Spanish. 'My name is James Keane, sir. I am a captain in King George's army.'

'Then why are you dressed as a French pig?'

'We have come from the monastery.' He wondered if he should continue, but realized that now there was no going back. 'We hold it against the French. But we need boats for the rest of the army. If we cannot get the rest of the army across, the French will push us out and we will lose.'

The man thought for a moment.

'A captain, you say?'

'Yes, sir. And these are my men.'

Keane signalled to them and reluctantly they lowered their muskets and undid their tunics to reveal the scarlet beneath.

The Portuguese hesitated again but after a pause, turned and nodded to his men to put away their weapons.

'I believe you, Captain Keane.'

'Thank you. I take it the French have gone from this part of the town?'

'All except you, Captain Keane.' He laughed. 'Alonzo del Vaga. Tell me what boats you need. We have many. The French were guarding them, but now . . . they are at your disposal, captain.'

# 9

Within half an hour the river was filled with boats of all sorts, ferrying the army across. Keane, who had sent Gilpin back with the news of the boats, watched, as the first to come, the 29th and the Foot Guards, crossing lower than the monastery, on the site of the old bridge, ferried over on the larger port barges and on the boats used to take livestock down the river. They swarmed up the steep streets into the heart of the city, moving from district to district and house to house, mercilessly mopping up pockets of French resistance as they went.

It had not taken long for Soult to realize that he was beaten, and faced with the threat of an overwhelming flank attack, he had called off the assault on the monastery and ordered a general retreat along the road to Valongo.

Then it had been a bloody business, the British cannon maintaining a relentless fire on the retreating French columns. Keane and his men, their job done, had taken a welcome rest and watched it from the window of an empty mansion, dining on the sausage, wine and bread they had found in the pantry. But as soon as the entire army was across, Keane had known that he would have to find the general and make his report and, inevitably, invite another assignment.

He had known exhaustion before, of course, but never, he thought, like this. Dragging himself away from his men, he made his way through the streets, which were filled with the aftermath of battle. Dead Frenchmen lay against the walls, contorted like grotesque puppets, dragged there to clear the way for the army. Victory was never a pretty sight, he thought. He passed the hospital where, Morris had told him that the victorious redcoats had found close on two hundred French wounded. According to a friend of Tom's in the Blues, it had taken all the power of the provosts and their officers to prevent some of the men, the worse for drink, and for that matter the good people of Oporto themselves, from butchering the French in their beds.

At length, arriving at Wellesley's new headquarters in the Palacio das Carrancas, in the centre of the city, Keane began to wonder what the general had in mind for him. He stood in the courtyard of the Palazzo and wondered for a few moments quite where he should go.

The courtyard was filled with staff officers and aides and he scoured it in vain for a friendly face. At length he saw Scovell and hastened across to him. 'Captain Scovell.'

'Keane. Good God, we thought you might be dead. The general has been asking for you. Where the devil have you been?'

'In the seminary, sir, and lately in the lower town. At the port.'

'At the port, indeed, were you? Follow me.'

Together they hurried through the buzzing crowd, and ascending a large gloomy stair, entered the anteroom, similar to that of Sir Arthur's headquarters in Coimbra. Inside another long table, formerly used for formal dinner by the Bishop, was now occupied by a dozen red-coated staff officers, all of them writing furiously.

Scovell spoke to one of them. 'Captain Gordon, this officer must see Sir Arthur.' Before the sentence was finished, though, the door opened, and Wellesley entered. The room was instantly silent. He addressed them.

'Well, what is it?' Then he saw Keane and smiled. 'Captain Keane. The very man. Come in, come in. Scovell, you may join us.' As they entered the main salon, Wellesley turned back to the room, silencing once more the chatter that had begun on his exit. 'Where is General Sherbroke?' he asked an aide-de-camp. 'Find him at once and send him here.'

Then he entered the salon, followed by Keane and Scovell, who closed the door behind them. The room was large and airy, with a window which opened onto a view of the Douro. Keane was pleased to see that standing beside the window was Grant. The major smiled at him and nodded.

Wellesley spoke. 'Well, Keane. You did well. The seminary was the key to our victory. And now I'll take you into my confidence, as most of the army will know it soon enough and you long before them even if I do not tell you.'

'Sir?'

'We have won the battle for Oporto, Keane, that you know. The French can count four hundred men killed or wounded, and almost as many again taken prisoner. Add to that the fifteen hundred men they abandoned in the city's hospitals, and some seventy guns, and you have a fair tally. Our losses amount to something over one hundred and twenty killed, wounded or missing.'

'A victory, sir.'

'A victory, Keane. A palpable victory.'

Scovell spoke up. 'Yes, sir, and it might have been a famous victory indeed had General Murray, having crossed the Douro at Avintes, made any attempt whatsoever to intercept the French on their retreat.'

Wellesley turned on him. 'Captain Scovell, as I have already indicated, the matter is not open for discussion.'

Scovell nodded and fell silent. Wellesley went on. 'In short, Keane, Marshal Soult is beat and I intend to invade Spain.'

Keane baulked and before he could prevent himself said, 'Sir, is that wise?'

Wellesley rounded on him, fixing him with fierce blue eyes. 'You are surely not questioning my judgement, captain?'

Keane shook his head. 'I'm sorry, sir. No, of course not. I do apologize. It was not my place . . . but the French . . . '

Wellesley interrupted. 'I know the French outnumber us. What do you know that I do not?'

'I know just as I told you, sir. They have three armies.'

'Indeed, under Marshal Soult, Marshal Victor and Marshal Ney. Soult will say he is not yet beaten. And indeed our masters in St James's might agree. But I intend to push Soult from Portugal and to take the battle to the French.

'We might have taken Oporto but Soult saved the majority of his army and he will regroup. Of that I have no doubt. What is absolutely vital – absolutely, mark you – is that those three armies, Soult, Ney and Victor, must not be allowed to combine.' He paused and looked thoughtful. 'I need you to go back into the mountains, Keane. I need you to go back into them, and I need you to find Colonel Morillo once again.'

'Sir?'

Wellesley turned to Grant. 'If you would be so kind, Major Grant.'

Grant walked closer to them. 'Captain Keane, good to see you again, in one piece. The facts are these. Five days ago, so Captain Scovell has informed us, Colonel Morillo liberated the port of Vigo from the French. This in itself is a very good thing. But the truth of the matter is that in pushing the French from the town and sacking their baggage train he helped himself to no less than 150,000 gold francs.'

Keane whistled beneath his breath. 'That's about £60,000, sir, give or take a penny?'

Grant nodded. 'Yes. Give or take a few sous, yes. Not bad for a day's work. So Morillo is also a very, very rich man.'

Wellesley interrupted him. 'He's also more influential than ever before. Morillo has a new commission since last you encountered him. Go on, Major Grant.'

Grant cleared his throat and extinguished the cigar on which he had been puffing. 'Colonel Morillo has now been commissioned by the Seville Assembly to raise the Galician peasants and prevent Soult from making supply dumps in Galicia.'

'He's in Galicia? That's far in the north, sir.'

'Exactly, Keane, he's moved his force and with it extended his area of influence. But one thing that has not changed is his success. Morillo is in the ascendant, Keane, and as much as we need to harness his power, we also need to be sure that it does not escalate beyond our control. He is a powerful man and commands great respect. If we are not careful he will become nothing less than a local warlord, a land-based buccaneer out for all that he can get regardless of who profits by it. We know that he hates the French, but as you told me yourself, he also has no love for the British. With power from the government in exile and the Galician people behind him, he will be invincible.

'You know Morillo, Keane. And he knows you?'

'Yes, sir. As you know.'

'There is therefore no one else in this army who is capable of meeting Morillo face to face.'

'You want me to kill him, sir?' Keane felt the colour drain from his face and wondered whether it had been evident to either Wellesley or Grant. Wellesley shook his head.

'No, Keane, we don't want you to kill Morillo. He's much more valuable to us alive. Providing he can be persuaded to cooperate. That is where you come in. We need to control him. I need him and his men, Keane. You must tell him that this time he cannot have threescore follow him, he must have a thousand. Ten thousand, if he can find them. You may promise him an honorary commission in the British army if you must. It will never be confirmed, of course. That might appeal. I know that you can do it. Only you, Keane.'

Keane thought for a moment. 'I will find Morillo, sir. Or rather, I can make certain that he will find me.'

Wellesley spoke. 'Major Grant has perhaps not made things plain. Colonel Morillo is now more powerful than General Cuesta and more valuable to me. He was always the better commander. That was clear. But what we need to know is whether he will be able to hold off the threat from Marshal Ney. His Galicians are really no more than peasants, but from what you have told us he has a core of real fighters and might very quickly mould the Galician levies into a real fighting force. It may in fact be a great deal better than the professional Spanish army fielded by Cuesta. Do you fully comprehend what I am saying to you, Keane?'

'Yes, sir, it's quite clear.'

'As it is now my intention to invade Spain and attack Marshal Victor in the east, I will be compelled to take General Cuesta with me.' He shook his head. Grant laughed. 'That is my problem. Morillo must hold off Ney if we are to have any hope against Victor. If we cannot defeat the two of them piecemeal, then we are lost. We might even lose Portugal, or at the very least to be forced into another Corunna.'

Keane looked down at the map that was spread on the table and noticed that the other end was laid for dinner, with food – a half chicken – on the plate. Wellesley saw his glance.

'Marshal Soult's dinner, Keane. He was considerate enough to leave it for me.'

Keane grinned and looked back at the map. 'Do we have any idea where he may be, sir?'

'We believe, or at least, that is, Captain Scovell here has informed us that he believes Morillo to be somewhere here' – he pointed to the map, to an area marked in different shades of light brown – 'between the river Lima and the Sierra Gerez. Centred on Montalegre, but in the hills. Major Grant will provide you and your men with the necessary resources, the fodder and animals to get there and back. And you must be quick, Keane, just as quick as you can. I need that assurance from Morillo. Now, rejoin your command.'

Grant stopped him. 'There is one other thing, sir, which you have neglected to mention to Captain Keane.'

Keane wondered what on earth it might be.

Grant continued. 'James, you recall Cuevillas, the smuggler?'

'The other guerrilla leader, sir. Yes, I did not find him.'

'We have heard that he is resentful of Morillo's newfound

power and wealth. And that he might be in the area attempting to wrest at least some control from Morillo.'

'That could be a problem, sir.'

'Indeed, Keane, it is somewhat more than a problem. I'm not sure who has the worse reputation.'

'You forget, sir, that I have seen Morillo's ways with a prisoner at first hand.'

'But you have not yet seen Cuevillas at work, have you, Keane?'

'No, sir, and nor do I believe that I want to.'

Wellesley smiled. 'But meet him you will, Keane. Return to your men now.'

Keane turned to go but, nearing the door, stopped and turned back. 'Sir, I have one question. How did our men do in the seminary? General Paget?'

'General Paget was hit. Shot in the arm. But he lives.'

'And the others?'

'Oh, Major Danvers is commended in dispatches and Captain Lawrence with him.'

Keane smiled at the news. It was always the same. A name and influence would talk you into glory, whatever the truth.

'But what of the ensign? Watkins.'

'Ah yes, Grant, have we heard any news of Colonel Watkins's son?'

'Oh, yes, sir, poor fellow. I'm afraid that a roundshot took off his head. Damned bad luck. The battle was as near as won.'

The sun was high in the summer sky as they came to the river. The Tamega flowed down to the south from its source high in the hills of the Tras os Montes and here it ran below the town of Amarante, which stood perched on the hillside on the opposite bank. They had ridden east out of Oporto after barely a day's rest since the fight and had come thirty miles in the first day. Now, having slept overnight in an abandoned barn, they were making good time. And time was of the essence, Grant had told Keane.

Keane understood that Wellesley was consolidating his command, making sure that when they caught Soult they would be ready for a fight. He was going to advance from Oporto in two days' time, moving towards the Spanish border and Orense by way of Braga. Beresford's division would be sent ahead on a right-flanking march up through Chaves. Keane's role was to take a central route and in doing so, go high into the hills between the two wings of the allied army and find the guerrillas. It was possible that Beresford would find the French first. But whatever happened, when they were found Wellesley had to ensure that he had as many men as he could muster. And of course there was the problem of Morillo's wealth, and that of Cuevillas.

As usual, Keane and Morris rode at the head of the column, with the others behind and Silver and Gabriella bringing up the rear. She was humming a tune, a local melody with a pleasant, lilting line, not dissimilar to the sort of thing the soldiers sang, and the music floated on the air, transforming the landscape and momentarily banishing thoughts of war.

Ross and Garland rode side by side and were engaged in conversation that cut through the clatter of hooves on the dusty road and the jangle of harness.

'See, what I don't understand, sergeant,' said Garland, his great brow furrowed in puzzlement, 'is why we're being sent back into them mountains again to find another Spaniard. That's just what we did before, ain't it?'

'Garland, you're a good lad and there's not many I'd say

that about, but when the good Lord blessed us all with brains he must have missed your share. What do you mean, why are we going there again? How many times do I have to tell you? We just obey orders. In this case you are part of Captain Keane's command and you should be glad of it. We have been sent on a mission to make contact with the Spanish bandits, otherwise known as soldiers. Not the same ones as we met before, thank God, and let's hope these heathens are a bit more God-fearing. But they'll still be papists. Who knows what we can expect? That's what we do, Garland. We're here for exploring and Captain Keane is our exploring officer.'

'I know that, sergeant. All I'm saying is, I don't really see why we have to do it again.'

'I give up. Don't think, Garland, it'll hurt your head. Just ride with the rest of us and fight the bloody French. There's a good lad. Besides, them ain't the same hills. Them is different hills.'

'All look the same to me, sergeant.'

Morris turned to Keane. 'James, do you suppose we'll find Morillo again?'

'I'm rather hoping we will. The general wants an assurance from him before he attacks Marshal Soult again.'

'And what of this other commander? What was his name again?'

'Cuevillas, but his real name is Ignacio Alonso. He's a smuggler. Was, rather. Now, I gather, he's a patriot too.'

Morris laughed. 'Do you suppose we'll find him?'

'I suppose that he will find us. That is the way of it with these people. You remember Morillo. Eyes and ears everywhere and men who can hide four yards from you without detection. Don't worry, we won't be alone for long.'

'How much did you say Morillo had taken?'

'About 150,000 francs.'

Morris whistled and shook his head. 'That's £60,000. If I were he I'd give up fighting and settle at home.'

'This is his home, Tom. And look at it. Raped and laid waste by Boney's armies. What choice does he have but to rid it of the French?'

'Yes, I suppose that you and I are fortunate, James. At least we have a place to call home. A country, I mean, that is at liberty and not under the heel of a tyrant.'

'We can be thankful for that.' He thought about what Morris had said, of how lucky they were to have somewhere to call home, and realized again how untrue that was for him. He had no home. There was no house in England waiting for him to come back. No parkland, farms and settled income. If Tom succeeded out here, he thought, if he should make something of himself, then there was surely the chance that he would return to a hero's welcome from his family and end his life a contented man.

Keane had no hope of that sort and no one. His mind drifted to Blackwood's sister and he flirted with the idea, but only for a moment until lust overtook it. She was incentive enough for him to get through the next few weeks and back to Lisbon. But he wondered in retrospect whether he wanted her for the woman she was or whether in truth he wanted to bed her to satisfy himself against her brother. Either way, it did not matter. He was determined to have her, and if he was not killed, maimed or emasculated in the coming fight he was going to do his damnedest to ensure that would happen.

He turned back to Morris. 'Did you ever meet Blackwood's sister?'

'No, can't say I did. Did you?'

'Yes, as a matter of fact I did.'

'What of it, James? Dont tell me you're enamoured?'

'She's a fine woman, Tom.'

'I know you when you talk like that, James, and this time it is madness. You cannot think that you would lure her into your bed? The sister of the man who as you well know has sworn to avenge himself on you for the death of his friend.'

'It would add a little spice to the relationship, don't you think?'

'I think you must be mad, James, even to contemplate such an action. And to use her in such a way.'

'Women are there to be used, Tom. It is in their nature. Why should we not enjoy ourselves a little, her and me? What harm could it do?'

'You know damn well what harm it could do. And not just to you, James. You would be involving another, and a woman at that, in a matter that concerns you and Blackwood. No one else.'

'But she is a damn fine woman. As fine as ever I saw. She would make someone a fine wife.'

Morris shook his head. 'I can scarcely believe what you are saying. I will not talk to you further on the matter, James, and I advise you to put it out of your head.'

Keane shrugged, but he didn't put it out of his head and as they rode on the idea of Kitty Blackwood became more firmly embedded in his mind. She was someone, something that he knew he must have, and when Keane had set his heart on something there was no going back. He was damned too if he was to be deterred by Morris's sense of propriety.

They rode on another two hours and entered the rugged

country of the Tras os Montes. This was a place of defiles and passes, perfect for an ambush. More so even than Morillo's old country. Keane wondered when Morillo or Cuevillas would find them. Undoubtedly either Spaniard, having tracked them, would take some relish in surprise, in emphasizing the fact that had they been his enemies he could kill them as easily as if he were on a pigeon shoot.

Ross rode up alongside him, as clumsy as ever in the saddle, but at the same time trying as always – and failing – to look every inch the cavalryman.

'Gives me the creeps, sir, this country. I can't help thinking it's us as might get ambushed in these hills.'

'The guerrillas are our friends, sarn't. They're hardly likely to kill us.'

'It's just the feeling of being so helpless. Can't stomach it, sir.'

'You're a Highlander, Ross. You should be used to this sort of terrain.'

'I'm no Highlander. Thought you knew that, sir. I'm from Glasgow and before that my mother was Irish. You of all people know that, sir.'

'I was merely jesting with you. There is a propensity in our army to pass off any Scot as a wild Highlander. It is part of the idea of Romance. Have you heard of that, sarn't?'

'Can't say I have, sir. All I know is that I'm as much a Highlander as Martin is, or Garland there. I only joined the regiment for the King's shilling and for the kilt. Gets the lassies, sir.'

'That's what I meant, sarn't. Romance. You do understand.'

'If it's to do with making the lassies turn their heads, then yes I do understand, sir. But I'm still no Highlander and I still feel out of sorts in these hills.'

As they neared the river, Keane held up his hand. 'Halt. We'll stop here. Ten minutes. Water the horses. Then we're going north.' He pointed to the left and towards the mountains. 'That's our road.'

They dismounted and led the horses towards the riverbank. A bridge ran across to Amarante, but the men walked the horses down the shallow slope beside it, letting them go into the river. Keane and Morris watched them and each took out a flask and drank a short mouthful of water. Gabriella and Silver were splashing each other with water like two children, while Ross had taken off his tunic and rolled up his sleeves to bathe his face and arms.

Morris plugged the top back into his water bottle. 'They're a good lot, James, don't you think? You chose well.'

'We chose well, Tom.'

'I feel that somehow we've given them all a new life.'

'I would like to think so. I'm not so sure about a couple of them. Heredia worries me. But yes, I do think we have done some good.'

That wasn't something he often felt. It wasn't something any soldier was ever likely to say. Doing good was hardly part of their craft. But as he watched Silver and his woman at ease in the sunshine and the others laughing as the horses frolicked in the water, he had a sense that something was right. He caught himself and shouted to them. 'Remount. We're moving on.'

Turning to the north, away from the town and the river, they took a narrower road which almost as soon as they turned onto it began to climb.

Keane had studied the map before they left and had seen that the road they were now on, although marked by the engineers, appeared to peter out after some distance. He had hoped that this was not the case and could see that beyond where it stopped three towns in the hills were marked which must surely be connected by road. After ten miles they came to the first of these. Keane signalled to halt, but still in the saddle he unbuttoned his valise and withdrew the map. Taking out a pencil, he carefully marked in the continuation of the road and confirmed the town's existence. The place was quiet, but seeing a man look out from his doorway, Keane called across in Spanish. 'Señor, what is the name of this place?'

The man looked startled and for a moment did not speak. Heredia called out in Portuguese the same question. The man replied. Heredia turned to Keane. 'He says it's called Freixim, sir.'

'Thank you, Heredia.'

Keane marked it down and they carried on through the town and past the terrified man.

From the village they climbed again and began to toil up a steep incline. According to the map they must now, thought Keane, be on the very top of the Sierra Cabrera. But still the road climbed up. Then, just as they seemed to be reaching into the very clouds, it levelled out again and they found themselves passing through the mountains in a narrow gorge.

Almost immediately, Keane began to share Ross's sense of apprehension. He reassured himself that the guerrillas were on their side, but the soldier within him kept his eyes scanning the tops of the cliffs that rose up a good fifty feet on either side of them.

Martin called out from the rear of the column. 'Did you see that, sir? Over there on the left. Something shiny, sir. Metal. Might be a musket.'

Keane looked to his left and saw nothing, but then, as they went on deeper into the gorge, something caught his eye. A flash of the sun reflected on silver. He froze and then called out. 'Halt. Draw carbines.'

They reined in, but hardly had they done so when a shot rang out. It echoed off the sides of the gorge, almost deafening them. All as one, save Gabriella, pulled the carbines from their holsters on the saddles. Keane looked around them. Surely this could not be the French? They could not possibly have negotiated this road, he reasoned. Not with wagons, and this was no place for artillery, either. He scoured the cliffs but in his heart he knew what and who it was that was observing them and had them at its mercy. Then to confirm his suspicions a voice rang out – in Spanish.

'Don't worry, Englishmen. We are friends. Don't shoot at us and we will not kill you.'

Above them on all sides the tops of the cliffs were filled with scores of men. Some wore the uniform of Spain; others, most of them, civilian clothes. All were armed, most with muskets. Keane tried to identify where the voice had come from and then saw its owner. The man descended the gorge quickly and nimbly, jumping from rock to rock like an animal. He was followed by his men, and by the time he reached them at the bottom he had fifty on his heels. He walked up to Keane and smiled. 'They call me Cuevillas. You are looking for me?'

'Yes, Captain Cuevillas. My name is Keane. Captain James Keane. I come from our general, General Wellesley.'

Cuevillas looked at the men standing behind Keane. 'Your general does not send me many of you. Are there more?'

'No, captain. We are not here to fight with you. We are

guides. We gather intelligence. That is our purpose in seeking you, captain.'

Cuevillas nodded. 'Yes, I knew that. I just thought that perhaps you might bring men, or money. That is what we need. Not giving intelligence.

# 10

Cuevillas led them up a track which even Keane had to admit he would not have detected. It climbed to the top of the gorge and there on a flat plateau lay the camp. It was remarkably similar to Morillo's and it seemed to Keane that the guerrillas, like the British army, had brought their entire families with them on campaign. A pig dangled from a tree, roasting slowly over a fire. He surveyed the group and saw the same mixture of partly uniformed ex-soldiers and peasants. There were priests too: two young men, minor clergy, in black cassocks, one of whom was playing a game of tig with one of the children.

It seemed a slightly more civilized set-up than Morillo's, and even without properly making the man's acquaintance Keane felt that he might be beginning to warm to Cuevillas when, looking directly to his left, he saw that they had a prisoner.

The man sported a flamboyant moustache, and long braided pigtails hung from the sides of his hair. He was dressed in the gaudy uniform of a French hussar: a sky-blue dolman and breeches with a red-and-white barrel sash and tassled Hungarian boots. His arms were bound tightly at the wrists and it was evident that he had been beaten, for his left eye was half shut and there was blood streaked across his forehead.

'You have a prisoner, Captain Cuevillas.'

Cuevillas laughed and pointed to the hussar. 'Him? Yes. We ran into him at Miserela only yesterday. He was hiding beneath the bridge. He carries papers to Marshal Soult. Interesting papers. Perhaps you would like to look at them later, captain?'

'Thank you, I shall, but tell me, where are you taking him?'

Keane knew the reply before it was uttered.

'Take him? We don't take him anywhere. We are going to kill him, captain. When the moment takes us. When we grow bored of his pleasant company.'

Keane was not surprised, after all. For all its bucolic appearance, Cuevillas's camp and its inhabitants were equipped with the same morals as Morillo. But this time he was damned if he was going to let them do to this man what Morillo and his men had done to their prisoner. Or even get close to it. He decided to play for time.

'May I talk to your prisoner, captain? Interrogate him?'

'I don't see why not. You can try. We haven't begun to do that yet. Not properly.' Keane looked at the Frenchman and saw the blood on his face. Morris whispered to him. 'Not properly, James. You and I know what that means.'

Cuevillas continued. 'We have his papers. I've seen them. I don't think he will tell us much more. But we will give him the chance, captain, when the time comes. We have our methods.'

'Let's see if my methods work better than yours, shall we? And might I also now take a look at the papers?'

'Of course, captain. But I don't think you'll see anything that I have not.'

Cuevillas snapped his fingers and one of the guerrillas, whom Keane presumed must be his chief of staff – a ruddy-faced man wearing a tall hat and a handkerchief beneath it – appeared with a valise, from which he drew out the Frenchman's letters.

Keane took them and turned them over in his hand. There was a letter of introduction for the officer and the usual letters that he might have expected to find in a similar valise from Wellesley to any one of his command. A letter from Soult to other generals in the field. A letter addressed to Marshal Ney and another to the emperor himself, in Paris. This last sent a frisson down Keane's spine. He marvelled that this was the nearest he might ever get to Napoleon.

But, as Cuevillas had said, there was in none of them anything different from the intelligence they already had. Soult had merely confirmed to Ney that he had been driven out of Oporto and that he would make contact with him in Galicia and mount a joint offensive against Wellesley. At least, he supposed, it confirmed what they had suspected.

He handed the papers back to Cuevillas, thanked him and then, with Morris at his side, walked across to the French hussar. The man, while still looking downcast, seemed a little less terrified to be confronted by two English officers. Here, perhaps, was his last chance of salvation.

Keane spoke to him in French. 'What is your name?'

'Fabier. Philippe Fabier, captain, 1st Hussars.'

'Yes, I noticed your sabretache. A fine regiment. We fought you at Alexandria.'

'You were there?'

'Yes.'

The hussar managed a faint smile. 'Me also.'

'My name is Keane, captain. Captain James Keane. You know, Captain Fabier, what these men intend to do to you?'

The hussar nodded and shrugged. 'Yes, of course. We are all warned about what will happen if we are captured in the hills. I know.'

He looked away and Keane could sense the terror and despair in him.

'Perhaps, captain, there might be a means by which I can save you from that fate.'

'Sir?

'Perhaps if you were to tell me what you know then they might let you go.'

'I don't think so. They want me for sport. For amusement.'

'But I am a British officer. Give me what I need to know and I give you my word that I will persuade them.'

'How can you do that? Why should I believe you?'

'What other options do you have?'

Fabier thought for a moment. 'I could say nothing.'

'You could, and then I would walk away and leave you to them.'

He gestured to the guerrillas, who were drinking from several leather flagons and taking turns to throw rocks at a crow that they had roped to a log and which had already lost one of its legs and half a wing.

'How will you persuade them?'

'I have my ways. I have options. Which is something you do not.'

Fabier thought but said nothing for a while. 'I swore to my general that I would say nothing, even under torture.'

'That was a foolish oath to take.'

'I took it to the emperor and to France. I was not so foolish.'

'I swore an oath to King George when I took his shilling twenty years ago. But I'd break it if I thought it would save me from what they will do to you.'

The hussar looked away again, trying to contemplate it.

Keane seized his moment. 'You know I did see, not too long ago, what they did to one of your countrymen. First they cut him all over his body. They were flaying him alive and no doubt about to castrate him when I shot him through the head.'

'You did that?'

'It's no more than I would do for any man. Whatever nation he comes from and whatever master he serves. And I would do the same for you. But perhaps I can save you from that . . . horror.'

The hussar did not speak again. He seemed to go limp, as if all the fight had gone from him. He said nothing and then he looked up at Keane. 'Very well. What do you want to know?'

'What can you tell me?'

'Marshal Soult is leaving Portugal.'

'Don't play games with me, captain. Tell me something I do not already know.'

'He is leaving Portugal and Marshal Victor has abandoned his position at Alcantara.'

This, thought Keane, was good. This was something new.

The man seemed relieved that he had managed to blurt out the secrets. And now there was no stopping him. 'And there's something more.'

'Yes?'

'Marshal Soult is leaving behind his baggage train. He is destroying everything: supplies, ammunition, weapons. Everything. His men may even kill some of the horses.'

Keane nodded. 'It's understandable. You would not want any supplies to fall into enemy hands. Our hands.'

The hussar smiled. 'Yes, captain, but also within that train is a great deal of money.'

'Exactly how much? Do you know?'

'Fifty thousand.'

'Francs?'

'No, crowns.'

Keane paused, so great was the amount in question. It came to around £40,000*.

Not betraying his amazement at this revelation, Keane continued to question the hussar. 'And that he will take with him, no doubt.'

The hussar shook his head and smiled. 'No, captain, that is it. It is in silver coin. He cannot possibly carry it across the mountains on a cart. It would have to be divided up and taken on horseback. And that also is impossible.'

Keane frowned and stared into the man's eyes. 'Why are you telling me this?'

'Because you promised to save me.'

'I said that I would try. No promises, captain. But why tell me this information? Why me? Do you suppose I will try to grab it myself?'

The hussar shrugged again. 'I do not know what you will do, captain. All I know is that I tell you because, yes, of course, I do not want French gold to fall into British hands, but even more I do not want it to fall into the hands of the *guerrilleros*. Can you for a moment imagine what effect that money would have on these bandits? Can you imagine men like that so rich?'

* About £1.7m today.

Keane thought of Morillo's recently acquired fortune and wondered that the French should be carrying so much money with them, when Wellesley's army was waiting for the payroll. 'Yes,' he said. 'I can.'

Cuevillas crossed over to them. 'Well,' he smiled. 'Did you get anything from the man with your methods?'

'Yes, as a matter of fact I did. It would appear that Marshal Soult is abandoning his supplies and equipment along the route. Specifically, he is leaving a quantity of arms at a particular place, and Captain Fabier has given his word to lead me there.'

Cuevillas spat on the ground. 'His word? What is the word of a Frenchman worth? Don't tell me that you believe him?'

'Yes, I do.'

'But you will not take him?'

'Of course. What else do you expect me to do?'

'I expect you to hand him back to me. He is my prisoner.'

'No. He is now my prisoner. I have given my word to spare his life, in exchange for his leading us to the weapons. And my word, unlike what you believe to be true of that of the French, is my honour. I will not return him to you, captain.'

Cuevillas fumed and stared at Keane. 'You have no right to do this. He is my prisoner.'

'I have every right, captain. I am an officer in the British army and I am attached to General Wellesley's staff. My orders come direct from General Wellesley. If you go against me and attempt to take him back by force of arms, then whatever happens you will have General Wellesley and the British army to answer to.' He paused until he judged the moment right. 'Oh, and I'll take his papers too, if you would.' He held out his hand.

Cuevillas continued to stare at him but said nothing. Keane did not move and all the time the hussar officer stood slightly behind him, in absolute silence.

Eventually Cuevillas walked closer to Keane, until their faces were so close that Keane could smell the rank stench of his breath. Then he spoke. 'Very well. Take your lousy piece of French shit. You're welcome to him.'

Cuevillas pushed the hard leather valise towards Keane with a quick, unexpected action that caught him off guard and made contact with his diaphragm as Cuevillas had intended, with the impact of a punch. The pain seared through him but Keane did not move. He continued staring unblinking into the Spaniard's eyes, took the valise from him and smiled.

Cuevillas, beaten, backed away, still staring into Keane's eyes. Then, turning towards Fabier, he spat hard in the hussar's face, and going towards his men who had been watching the events, he announced what was to happen. There were loud protests from the guerrillas but he held up his hand and quietened them. Then he turned and walked back to Keane.

'Captain Keane, I suggest that you get on your way. I have agreed to your terms, but my men have not and I doubt whether they would. Go now and take him with you. Go and find your guns.' Again he turned back to the men.

Keane found Morris, who had been standing nearby, listening. 'Tom, I think we had better take his advice. Have the men mount up. We'll ride out of the gorge past the guerrillas. It opens out soon and descends the mountains. Just bluff it out.'

They remounted, and slowly, with Gabriella and the hussar tucked between two files, rode past the guerrillas and through the gorge. Keane did not look back and neither did the others, but at any moment he expected to hear a shot and feel a bullet in his back. None came, though, and at length he breathed again. They rode for another hour and although there was no sound to suggest that they might be being followed, Keane kept going. Night would be upon them soon and he did not want to be anywhere near Cuevillas and his guerrillas when it came.

Morris turned to him, talking as they rode. 'James, do you realise that we have just managed utterly to fail in our mission. We have alienated Cuevillas's guerrillas and all for the sake of saving the life of a Frenchman. Is that right?'

'It's certainly not an auspicious start, is it, but we still have to find Morillo. He's the man Wellesley wants. Cuevillas is second-line stuff. Morillo is the prize. He's the one whose head we have to turn.'

'All the same, James, I do think we might have enlisted Cuevillas's help, rather than arouse his enmity.'

A commotion from behind them brought their conversation to a halt. Gabriella had began to gabble in Portuguese and Silver was trying to calm her. Heredia rode up to Keane and Morris.

'She says that we're mad, sir. That the banditti, Cuevillas's men, will come and kill us in our sleep. That we should have left the French bastard there to be disembowelled. That he is no better than' – he paused, trying to find the words – 'than pig shit.' He smiled and rode back into line.

Keane turned and looked back at her. Silver was having a hard time of it and the hussar was trying to ignore her. Keane spoke to Morris. 'Yes, I knew she'd be worried. But this hussar is definitely worth more than pig shit.'

'Meaning?'

'Once we get across these mountains, I'm sending three men

back towards Oporto to meet up with Wellesley's force. He'll
need to know what we learned from Cuevillas about Victor
and Soult. Everything.'

'Three?'

'Safer. We need the intelligence to get through.'

'While we go and find Morillo. I see.'

Keane shook his head and smiled. 'Not exactly, Tom.'

'I thought that our orders were to return with the information and to ensure that Morillo will help against Ney.'

'I intend to go on. You can join me if you wish, or go back.'

Morris stared at him. 'I'm not sure that I understand you,
James. Where exactly are you going? What do you intend to
do?'

'I'm going with Captain Fabier, to find that treasure. The
50,000 crowns.'

'Good God, are you serious? I thought that story about the
weapons was just a tale to rescue Fabier. Surely, James, this
goes directly against our orders, against Wellesley's orders,
doesn't it?'

'Perfectly. We need it.'

'We do?'

'The army needs it. Think about it, Tom. Wellesley is crying
out for the payroll. And the French are leaving hundreds of
thousands of crowns lying around the Portuguese countryside.
It's simple enough to work out what we have to do. The army
is desperately in need of pay and supplies. Money like that
could be the answer to all of the problems.'

'I suppose you do have a point, James. But how do we know
that he was telling the truth, not simply spinning a line to
try to persuade us to rescue him from the guerrillas? And
even if it is true, how on earth are we meant to take silver

coin with four men? Silver coin? How on earth will you get
it?'

'I don't know yet. But I intend to try to get whatever I can.
We might hide it somewhere and take what we can carry back
to the army. I don't know.'

'And no doubt you'll manage to take some for yourself too.'

Keane shrugged. 'There's no point in leaving silver and gold
to rot in these mountains when they can be put to good use.
Whether that use be for the army or for ourselves. The booty
of war, Tom. Fair shares.'

'I'm not sure which is your stronger motive, James. Finding
the money for Wellesley or lining your own pockets. You know
that I am not entirely at ease with this kind of soldiering. It
is not what I know and what I have learnt to do. In fact it is
hardly like soldiering at all.'

Keane's tone was abrupt. 'I have said already, Tom, that if
it does not suit your character then you'd best rejoin your regiment. But that would be a pity.'

'Old friend, do not think that it is your company that is at
fault. It is merely that I find this life unfamiliar and unset-
tling. Of course I shall carry on with you. For the present, at
least. And devil take the money. Wellesley will get his share.'

Keane smiled. 'Do you not know me that well, Tom? How
could I be anything less than wholly patriotic? You will you
come with us?'

Morris laughed. 'Can you think of one reason why I should
not? Who will you send back?'

'Sarn't Ross can go, with Heredia and Gabriella. I'll keep
Silver, Gilpin and Martin. And Garland. We might be in need
of some brawn and muscle.'

*

Together they rode on and Keane wondered whether he had done the right thing. Certainly he knew the money to be invaluable to the army, but in splitting his force had he not committed the cardinal sin of all wars? He wondered too whether Fabier might have been inventing the truth. Had Soult really left so much money in coin just because he was unable to take his wagons across the mountains? It seemed unlikely. But there again, in war everything was unlikely and anything possible.

He also knew that Morris was right about one thing. That taking treasure, even from the French, was not a part of their orders. But surely, he reasoned, when such an opportunity presented itself and with the army in such a plight, who could possibly decide not to try, at least, to take what had become the spoils of war?

He could not help but wonder, too, what a difference such a sum might make to his own life. At last, he thought, he would be able to attain the lifestyle that had been denied him all these years. Certainly he had been better off in the army than he would have been had he remained at home after the farm had failed. But the years of jibes from fellow officers, the pointing fingers and whispers in the mess when his bills had not been paid: all of these things weighed on his mind and he longed to be rid of them, longed more than anything now to be the gentleman he knew himself to be. The money might make that happen. Would make it happen. And then, he thought for a moment, even the accursed Blackwood would no longer have cause to doubt him, and what might have been merely a dalliance with the lovely Kitty might even become something more affirmed.

He caught himself and swore and tore himself away from such thoughts, returning to the matter in hand.

They were nearing the end of the gorge and before them through the tiny space of the defile he could see the expanse of the country spreading away into the distance like a vast tableau.

Directly below them lay a village, and as they began to descend Keane could make out the church and a small square which seemed to have been etched into the very hillside, with the houses all around it set at curious angles. Beyond it the mountain range continued to their right, while on the left the plain stretched away towards a river and more mountains beyond. It was as if they were descending into a basin and he suspected that they would have to climb out of it again before they found Morillo.

He half turned his head and called to Ross. 'Sarn't Ross, we'll find billets here tonight.' Morris was beside him. 'You see that road that cuts across the plain, over there to the left. That's the road to Braga. Tomorrow we'll send the others off down there to find Wellesley. We'll take that road.' He pointed to a narrow road that ran away from the village and off to the north, skirting the high country and then eventually climbing back into the mountains. 'I'll wager that's where we'll find Morillo. And if I'm not mistaken, it's also where the good Captain Fabier will lead us to Marshal Soult's treasure.'

The village was no more than that, but to his surprise Keane found that they were welcomed by the villagers. He had not expected here such jubilation as they had experienced after Oporto, for it had never been the case in any of the more remote places they had passed through in this hard, mountainous country. As they rode in along the filthy narrow street, seeing the red uniforms people came slowly from the houses.

A man came up to Keane and grasped him by the hand, muttering his thanks. A pretty teenage girl did the same to Morris, smiling and pressing a small white flower into his hand. Keane looked at him. 'We would appear to have done something right, Tom. Soult must be moving faster than we had thought. They seem to think we've won the war already.'

They found shelter at a little inn where the landlord plied them with the local wine and ham at his own expense, and later Keane asked him if he knew where Colonel Morillo might be found. But the man shrugged and said merely that he was somewhere in the mountains, and poured Keane another glass of wine.

They slept well that night, and in the morning when Keane walked in to rouse Morris, he found him lying in his bed entangled with the lithe brown form of the village girl. Keane said nothing, but later, as they mounted up to rejoin the road, he saw her kiss Morris on the cheek and watched as his friend placed a small bunch of the little white flowers in his valise.

He looked at them, the men he had led here, some of whom were now about to leave, and enjoyed a brief moment of self satisfaction. They had worked well thus far and had the makings of a good team. Even Morris, he thought, whom at first he had wondered might not be cut out for this life and be better suited to the line of battle, seemed to be becoming accustomed to their work.

Leaving behind the village, which they had learned bore the name of Refovos de Bastil, they rode across the plain for some five miles until they reached a fork in the road. Keane called them to a halt and had them dismount.

'I'm dividing the command. Sarn't Ross, you will take Gilpin.

Ride west, along there.' He pointed down the road that snaked away to the left across the plain.

Ross looked at him, raising an eyebrow. 'If you'll pardon me, sir, is it wise to split ourselves?'

Keane stared back. 'Sarn't Ross, much as I value your wisdom and agree that in other circumstances it might be unwise, this time I would ask that you accept my order.' He pointed again. 'That leads to Braga. It's about thirty miles. But don't stop if you can help it. I don't think you'll find any French, or any guerrillas, come to that. Keep going as fast as you can and you'll encounter General Wellesley and the army. Find Major Grant and tell him that we have gone to find Colonel Morillo. Tell him that Marshal Victor has abandoned Amarante and that Soult is leaving his baggage train as he goes. Tell him that Cuevillas is in the Sierra Cabrera with maybe four hundred guerrillas. And give him these papers.'

He unslung the hussar's leather valise from his own saddle and handed it to Ross, who attached it to his own then turned back to Keane. 'Should we not take Captain Fabier himself, sir?'

'No, Ross, I don't think there's any need for that yet. He might be of use to us. Besides, it would only complicate matters. Just say that we were given his papers by Cuevillas. You had better let Major Grant know that Captain Cuevillas does not seem overkeen to work with us. Tell him that we cannot fully depend upon him and his men. Oh, and you had better take the girl.' He motioned to Gabriella to join them and Silver explained to her what was happening. She shook her head and Silver spoke again, and then, after kissing him, she led her horse across to Ross.

Keane waited with Morris, Martin, Silver, Garland, Heredia

and the hussar and watched with hope and concern the small party of riders as they made their way westwards towards the distant hills to the east of Braga. He prayed that they would get through quickly and then he turned his horse and led them away to the north, towards the mountains.

Keane knew that Ross would be less than happy to be sent back, but there was nothing else for it. But he could not see the smile that played across the features of one member of the sergeant's party.

Heredia's heart had lifted. They were riding back to Wellesley and now here was his chance to find a man at the very heart of the allied army. A man whom, given the opportunity, he somehow intended to kill. Heredia had thought initially that, having been released, he might make good an escape from his benefactors, although he did have a sense of gratitude. But it had not taken long for the reality of his new situation to dawn upon him. He had not, of course, told Keane anything of the truth of the situation within the staff. The man might have released him for special duties, but why should he have been any readier to believe him than any of the others with whom he had already pleaded? Indeed, for all Heredia knew, to repeat his allegations of treason against a British officer might have jeopardized his new situation. And the natural urge to escape had soon subsided as his overpowering sense of self-preservation was outweighed by the need for revenge. And now it seemed as if that need might be satisfied. There was too though, a sense, since he had joined Keane, of being a part of something and, for the first time in his life, Heredia actually felt welcomed by his comrades. It was a pleasant sensation and whatever the outcome of his quest, something within him hoped that it would last.

*

After a few miles Keane and his party arrived at a river. Keane drew out his map and spoke to Morris. 'This is the Cavado. It runs out to the sea from the mountains. It's the marker between the plain and the hills.'

They crossed at the town of Pontenova and made north-east along the road. The mountains rose directly ahead of them now like an insurmountable barrier with their high peaks disappearing into the clouds. Silver spoke. 'Please don't tell me, sir, that we're heading into that lot.'

'I'm afraid that's exactly where we're heading, Silver. Right to the top.'

At Saltador, the last village marked on Keane's map, they began to climb and once again they found themselves on a winding mountain road with a river running below to their left.

Slowly, as they rode on, Keane began to notice something curious about the road. It was littered with items of clothing. A French shako lay at the roadside. He reined in his horse and dismounted, walking over to pick it up. Morris rode across to him. 'French?'

Keane nodded. 'Yes, 43rd infantry of the line.' He examined the red felt binding which ran around the rim of the crown and the red feather above the brass eagle. 'Belonged to a Grenadier. I think we've found Soult's army, Tom. What's left of them.'

They rode on, and as they went, the amount of abandoned clothing increased. There were packs now and knapsacks. Some of them appeared to have been torn open by other passing fugitives and their contents fluttered across the road in a sad parade of forgotten owners. Letters and clay pipes lay scattered around. It looked, thought Keane, not unlike the aftermath of a battle, with the field strewn with the possessions of the dead. The only things missing were the bodies.

But a few hundred yards further along the road, he was proved wrong.

The corpse lay at the side of the road contorted in the agony of death. It was that of a Frenchman, an infantryman, and its form, otherwise emaciated, had a bloated stomach and staring, sightless eyes. It showed the signs of dysentery.

'Disease,' said Morris. 'If that takes hold in the army then Soult won't just be leaving Portugal behind him.'

Keane knew the cost of disease. He had seen it in Egypt. An entire brigade wiped out by typhus. Napoleon's own army had succumbed to the plague out there and he had run back to France, leaving his men to rot at Jaffa.

Disease could do more to an army than any amount of roundshot and ball. Keane shuddered and fancied for a moment that he might be breaking into a fever himself, but he was sure it was only the suggestion of the dead Frenchman. They rode on and every so often passed another corpse. The stench of death haunted their route and Keane wondered how long it might be before they found any clues as to the whereabouts of the abandoned train. He did not imagine for a moment they would find it wholly without a guard. You simply did not leave such a vast amount of money in the middle of a road in an enemy country. Or perhaps that was just what you did. It was such a curiously unimaginable situation that he found it hard to understand how any commander could do such a thing. But in despair he supposed you might do anything. And clearly Soult was in that position now. The litter on the road told him that. Particularly now, for as they advanced past the corpses and detritus, they began to see more abandoned weapons. This was surely an army no longer.

Their little group stuck closer together now. A retreating army was a dangerous thing and they had to be ready for a surprise attack. He called over to Morris. 'Tom, we need to keep our wits about us. There's no telling what these French will be up to. They've lost all their discipline. That's clear. Just keep your eyes open.'

But there was no sign of any renegade French, nor indeed of any more guerrillas.

Fabier, who had given his parole as an officer not to escape and knew that in fact to do so would be to court death at the hands of the guerrillas, was riding behind Keane and Morris and just in front of Silver. Now, after a long silence, he spoke. 'It is sad, is it not. That these brave men, my countrymen, should die in such a way. They came here to fight for their emperor and to die if they must on the field of glory. But look at them now. Condemned by a useless general to die at the roadside like beasts.'

'You are not overly impressed by your Marshal Soult?'

'He is not the emperor. He has no love for his men. He uses them like pieces on a chessboard and if he has to lose them he loses them, no matter how. The emperor would not do that. He cares for us all. And we would willingly die for him.'

Keane was impressed. 'You really believe that? You believe that he cares about every one of you?'

'Yes. I know it. And when he finds out what Soult has done, the Marshal will have hell to pay.'

Keane laughed. 'If I thought for a moment that General Wellesley cared for all of us, I would cease to have faith in him. Surely a general has greater things to concern himself with than the welfare of his men? Funny how we are so different, isn't it?'

They rode on for another two hours and took the road that stretched high up towards the north. A river flowed alongside the highway. It was called the Cavado, according to Keane's map, which by now he was attempting to re-draw at every possible opportunity.

They climbed steadily, looking around themselves all the time, fearful of the joint threat of the French and guerrillas. On and up they went, and as they did so night began to fall. It came on fast at this time of year and soon they were barely able to see in front of their horses' hooves.

Morris turned to Keane. 'James, this is the very wildest place to which you have brought us yet. Do you suppose we shall find shelter or do you propose that we should rest on the road?'

'I think that we shall have no alternative but to do the latter. We might as well stop here as anywhere.'

And so they halted for the night on the side of the mountain. Ahead of them a wagon lay on its traces, where it had been left by the retreating French. They smashed some wooden planks from its chassis and Silver lit a fire. There was no point in trying to hide their presence, and the cold had set in. It was better, thought Keane, to die fighting even in an ambush than to perish horribly from cold on a hillside in the dark. They wrapped themselves in their blankets as best they could and settled for the night, one man taking a watch every four hours.

Keane woke with a start at dawn to find Garland asleep at his post. In normal circumstances this would have been a hanging offence or at least worth a damned good flogging, but these were not normal circumstances and Keane let the matter pass. He stood over Garland for a moment and then gave him a nudge with his foot, and the big man jolted into consciousness.

'Sir, sorry, sir. That is, good morning, sir.' Garland rose to his feet and picked up his carbine.

'Good morning, Private Garland. You'll be relieved to know that I took your watch for you. No enemies attacked us. You'll be pleased to hear that we were not surprised and no one was killed. All of which is no thanks to you. Don't do it again, Garland.'

'Sir. Thank you, sir.'

Keane looked about them, taking in the terrain. They had stopped perhaps halfway up the mountainside, making camp a little to the right of the road which meandered around the contour. To their left was a cliff, dropping away some hundred feet to a plateau and then beyond that falling away again to the river, a silver line of water hundreds of feet below them. The litter of Soult's army lay across the countryside but here at least there were no bodies. He walked across to the wrecked wagon from which they had taken last night's firewood and saw that it was full of baskets that had once contained food.

They were all awake now. Morris asked, 'Where on earth are we, James? Not Spain already, surely?'

'No, the Spanish border is another fifty miles along this road, over those mountains. I don't think we'll be going that far. Soult must have abandoned his wagons before going into that.' He pointed ahead towards the rising mountain range. 'What do you think, captain?'

Fabier was with them now, looking in the same direction. He spoke without turning to Keane and there was a tone in his voice which Keane thought might have been fear as much as it might have been anticipation.

'I think you are right, captain. I think we shall find your countrymen soon.'

# 11

The road to Montalegre, their destination and the spot at which they hoped to find the French, wound on and on, an interminable sequence of bends, climbing all the while, and the further they went, the more rugged the landscape became. All of them were weary, but it was Morris who spoke. 'Surely, James, there is no way that Soult could have brought his wagons up this road? By God, just look at the place.'

Keane shook his head. 'It could be done, Tom. You know that as an artilleryman. Think about where you can take your cannon. And look at the evidence.' He pointed to the shakos and helmets discarded by the roadside. 'The army has been through here, and with it the wagons. Look at those ruts carved into the road, Tom, and you'll see that something passed this way, and not so long ago.'

It was true. They looked down as they rode on and through all the litter of the retreating army they could see that the road surface was pitted and split with grooves that could only have been made by iron-shod cartwheels. And the depth to which they had sunk into the earth attested to the fact that they had been carrying a heavy load.

Morris shook his head. 'I still think we should treat his story with caution. We might be going nowhere. Or straight into a French trap.'

'Don't be absurd, Tom. Why would the French want to trap us? Five men?'

Morris's eyes widened. 'Don't you see, James? We are intelligencing officers now. We are privy to Wellesley's plans. Fabier knows that. He can see what we are doing in this country. Why we are here? Ask yourself that. Don't you think that he might have had a notion to lead us towards his countrymen with the idea that we should be captured in turn? You heard from his own lips how fanatically devoted he is to Boney. Such a coup might further his own career and get him closer to his beloved emperor.'

Keane froze for a moment. How, he wondered, could he have been so stupid? The idea of taking all that silver, real or not, had run away with him and he had lost his senses. It was true. For once Morris had seen the obvious. Fabier might well have made a plan to betray them to the French. They were certainly of some use to them, and he could guess what methods the French might use to get information. Not as bad as the guerrillas, of course, but they were all of them in danger and he had put them there.

He turned to Fabier. 'Captain, where do you suppose Marshal Soult will have abandoned his train?'

'These hills are bad, captain. I do not think he can have taken the wagons much further. Look.'

They had just rounded a bend in the road, and as if to bear the Frenchman out, a panorama had opened up before them. There, stretching away into the distance, lay mountain after mountain. Keane knew that any French driver coming to this spot must surely have sighed in desperation and that any general worth his salt would have recognized that there was from here on no possibility of continuing with the baggage they were carrying. He wondered how far the train might have gone on without giving up and then realized that once again he had bought into Fabier's story.

Fabier was talking. 'He is making for Montalegre. Down in the plain on the other side of these mountains. He knows that once he gets there it is possible he will reach the Spanish border and save his army. If he can get the wagons across the mountains he will save them too and what they are carrying.' He smiled. 'But I have been here before, Captain Keane. I have carried dispatches across these mountains, from the emperor. I know this country. He will not make it. The men, yes, and the horses too. But nothing else. Believe me.'

Keane listened and nodded but his mind was elsewhere. He was trying to decide what might now be the best course of action. Should they go on with Fabier and test out the truth of his story, potentially risking themselves and the integrity of Wellesley's plans? Or should he turn around and head back to Braga? But to do that would be to pass up the prospect of gaining the treasure, and he reminded himself just what it meant to the army, and not least to himself.

He looked out across the sierra and wondered, and tried to find in his mind some means of testing the hussar.

But there was none. At length he turned to Morris. 'Tom, we're going to go on. Captain Fabier is right. Marshal Soult is desperate to save what he can of his army and will do everything he can to get them into Spain and across the mountains. We have every chance of taking the wagons.'

Morris nodded. 'Whatever you say, James. I have spoken my mind. It's your decision.'

At Keane's signal they began to trot on. He yelled at them all to put more into it and digging in their heels they moved more quickly along the top of the mountain plateau. They were higher now than Keane could remember having been ever before. Small bright mountain flowers grew by the road-side amid the discarded weapons and uniforms, and the bodies of the scattered dead lay incongruously in the meadows.

To their right lay a huge basin, enclosed by the mountains, and within it a lake that Keane had not noticed on his map. As they rode he managed to extricate it from his valise and drew it in place. Martin saw him. 'You'll have sketched the whole of the Peninsula, sir, before you're done.'

'You may not be far from the truth, Martin. This map is hardly worth the paper.'

Morris interjected. 'The engineers do what they can, James. Remember some of them are friends of mine. I was at Woolwich with them.'

'They are engineers, Tom. They build bridges and storm fortresses. And they attempt to draw maps. There should be a quite separate department for that.'

'Perhaps you are the man to found it.'

'Perhaps, one day,' said Keane, strapping the map back into his valise and giving his mount a pat on the neck. 'At present I have one or two other things on my mind.'

An hour passed. Keane was growing worried. Perhaps after all Morris was right. Perhaps Fabier was lying and around the next bend they would stumble into the rearguard of Soult's army. Perhaps any number of things. He had almost given up hope when at the bottom of a slight dip in the road they found a wagon. It had lost a wheel and half fallen on its side. The traces had been cut and the horses were long gone. Keane dismounted and was followed by Fabier and Morris. He walked across to the cart and saw that it still contained three wooden chests, all of them fastened with a lock. Two others similar lay with their lids open, the locks blown off, while another, he noticed, was lying smashed on the ground beside the useless cart.

Keane climbed up on the cart and yelled to the men. 'Silver, come here. And bring your carbine.'

Silver handed the gun to Keane, who took the weapon and loaded it. Then, standing a little way off from the chest, he fired at the lock. The bullet struck between the metal and the wood and spliced the mechanism away from the chest. Keane put down the gun and knelt beside it. He opened the lid and looking inside saw a dozen or more green canvas bags, tied and labelled with the letter 'N' and an eagle. Grabbing one, he felt its weight, then opening it up he pushed in his hand and drew it out. In his fingers he held a shining silver crown. They gazed at it.

Morris spoke. 'Well, I'll be blowed.'

Fabier whistled. 'I told you. He cannot take it. The road is too bad. This is only the first wagon. But look. Others have taken some already.'

The smashed chests told their own story but Keane did not care. His decision had been proved right and Fabier, it seemed, was no liar.

Silver, standing over Keane, stared wide-eyed. 'Christ, there must be thousands in there.'

'Yes,' said Keane, 'there must be. And if we do this right then you'll get your share. You all will. You too, Captain Fabier.'

The Frenchman nodded. 'Thank you, captain. I did not expect.'

'You led us here. You deserve a share. Right. We need to hide this lot and then get on after the rest.'

'Rest?' queried Silver. 'You mean there's more of it, sir?'

'Yes. Much more. If we're quick and if we're lucky.'

They carried the chests, one between two men, out of the wreck of the cart and into the thick bushes that grew beneath the conifers at the side of the road. Keane looked about them and spotted a small area of rough rocky ground in a clearing some fifty yards away. 'Over there,' he said, and after he had unstrapped his valise from his saddle and slung it over his shoulder, they carried the chests across and found that the rocks formed a sort of semicircular shelter. It was natural but it might have been man-made, and it was the perfect hiding place for the strongboxes. They hoisted the chests inside the stones and before they left Keane opened one of the bags and pulled out a handful of the coins and then another. He motioned to Silver to open the valise across his shoulder and emptied his hands into it, filling it with the silver crowns. 'There,' he smiled. 'Now we're equipped for anything.'

Remounting, they rode on and passed further evidence of the gradual breakdown of Soult's retreating column. Cannon lay in the ditches where they had lost a wheel; limbers too and ammunition caissons, still packed with roundshot.

Morris shook his head. 'If only I had a team up here. We'd have this lot back in the lines before you could whistle.'

There were no more wagons of treasure, though. But as they reached the top of an incline Keane held up his hand and made a sign to be silent. They could hear voices. Quite distant, but nevertheless distinct.

They sat motionless in the saddle and then Keane signalled
for them all to dismount. They did so as quietly as they could,
and leaving the horses with Garland, Keane went forward with
Silver close behind him. Nearing the edge of the road, where
it bent left to hug the cliff face, Keane dropped to his stomach
and edged forward, followed by Silver. The road gave way to a
steep slope which ran down for three hundred yards to a plateau
beneath them, and there where the road turned back in on
itself further down the mountain they saw a troop of French
cavalry, hussars like Fabier, although from a different regiment, clothed in gaudy red with blue facings. They had pitched
camp at the roadside, their horses tethered in an orderly line
in the trees, and their leader, a stocky sergeant with a huge
moustache, was drinking wine from a bottle, clapped on by a
dozen of the men. What caught Keane's eye, however, was that
in the centre of the camp, just off the road, where it had
toppled on its side, lay a wagon. And inside sat three large
wooden chests.

He turned and was about to make his way back to the others
when Silver spoke.

'It's the Frenchie, sir. The captain, sir. I don't like it. It's not
right. He shouldn't be with us, sir.'

Keane looked at him. 'Thank you, Silver. I plan to keep Captain
Fabier alive. It is my duty as an officer.'

Silver shook his head. Then, crouching, they made their way
back to the others.

'French hussars. Not your lot, captain. Scarlet uniform. Sky-
blue facings.'

Fabier nodded. 'The 9th. Yes, I know some of them. My father
is their Colonel.'

Keane raised his eyebrows. 'Indeed? I pray that he is safe.

They seem to be without an officer. Deserters, most like. They're a way off from the main body of the army, I'd guess, and they don't much look like a rearguard. And they've found a wagon of the silver.'

'How many of them?' asked Morris.

'A squadron, near as dammit. Eighty men at least, I'd say. Maybe more.'

Martin spoke up. 'We could attack them, sir. Surprise and all that.'

'No, even with surprise we'd be at too much of a disadvantage. It's almost dark. We'd best wait up here overnight.'

They rode back to where they had left the silver and slept fitfully, conscious of the hussars' presence such a short distance up ahead. Keane in particular had a poor night's sleep. He was too conscious of Fabier, aware that, for all that the man had said, he must retain an allegiance of some sort to the cavalrymen on the plateau. He woke it seemed every hour and stole a look at the Frenchman, who all the while appeared to be asleep. The morning came cold and bright high in the sierra and they tried as best they could to rouse themselves and come to order. During the night Keane's mind had wandered across the events of the day and what they might do next. He was in no doubt but that they must do something about the hussars. He toyed with the idea of having Fabier lead him and the others into their camp as his prisoners but dismissed it as being too perilous. There still existed in his mind the faint possibility that Morris might have been right about the man after all, and now he could hear Silver's words ringing in his ears.

But the problem remained. How could five or at best six of them take on twelve times their number?

He decided that the only way to find out would be to return to the plateau. Something would become evident. And if it did not, then they would have to abort the operation and return to Wellesley. At least they had the contents of the hidden chests – whatever of it they were able to transport in their saddle-bags.

He led the party along the road, walking this time and leading their horses to make as little noise as possible. On reaching the spot, he and Silver repeated their movements of the previous evening, crawling forward to the lip of the drop. Cautiously, Keane peered over the edge and saw nothing. The wagon was still there but the chests and the hussars had gone. It was as good as he might have hoped for. Standing up, he walked back to the others. 'They've gone.'

Fabier raised an eyebrow. 'Gone?'

'Well, I doubt that they went to rejoin the army. But they've gone, anyway. Which means we can go on too.'

Now Silver spoke. 'Sir, I don't mean to be disrespectful. But where are we going?'

'We're going to find the rest of that treasure. According to Captain Fabier, Marshal Soult is abandoning the whole lot. And I intend to claim it.'

'Can I ask how much it is, sir?'

'Fifty thousand silver crowns, so the captain says.'

Silver whistled. 'Fifty thousand, sir. Blimey.'

Keane went on, 'Yes. That must mean ten or a dozen chests at the very least. I don't believe for a moment that we can get the lot. But I intend to take whatever we can, for the army. Mount up. I don't want those hussars getting their hands on that silver before we do.'

They rode on down the road and onto the mountain plateau,

and after another eight miles Keane stopped. 'Did you hear
that, Garland?

'Sir?'

'Up ahead. A noise. Like gunfire.'

'No, sir.'

'You, Martin?'

'I heard something, sir. Couldn't swear what it was.'

'Silver?'

'Yes. It sounds like muskets, sir.'

Keane thought for a moment. 'No, not muskets, it's . . . '

Fabier interrupted. 'Carbines. That's French carbine fire. I'd
know it anywhere. It's the hussars.'

On Keane's word they rode on quickly, anxious to find out
what was happening. It must be the guerrillas, thought Keane.
Cuevillas has caught up with them. He turned to Morris. 'It's
Cuevillas. He's attacked the hussars. He must have got wind
of the silver. Damn him.'

Clattering along the road, all need for caution now gone,
they headed towards the sound of the guns and found them
in a clearing. Below them, just off the road, the squadron of
hussars were engaged in a running battle. But it was not guerrillas who were their opponents. Standing in a ragged square
was a group of perhaps fifty French infantrymen. They were
dressed in a variety of uniforms, white and blue, some of which
were infantry, some artillery, while others wore a light-blue
coat with top boots which suggested they must be wagon
drivers. The hussars, fired up by their new wealth, had attacked
the wagon train. The French were fighting one another, killing
their own. As one the party stopped and stared down at the
carnage. Keane watched as a hussar charged at the square,
only to be shot from the saddle. Another followed him and

careered into his friend's killer, knocking him off his feet, and then raising his glinting sabre, brought it down on the man's head, slicing through the black shako and deep into his skull.

All around the square the story was the same. Men were locked in fierce hand-to-hand fighting, the hussars desperate to get to the booty, the infantry just as desperate to save their lives from the evil hiss of the slicing, razor-edged sabres. Every few minutes the hussars would wheel away from the square and retire behind a line of their comrades who sat on their horses by the treeline. These would then fire their carbines at the square and when they did, several men would fall among the defenders. It was clear to all of them which side was winning and that soon, give or take a few more dead or wounded hussars, the infantry must be annihilated.

Fabier stared in disbelief. 'Oh my God, my God. What are they doing? Why do they kill each other? You fools.'

It was all that Keane could do to stop him from rushing off down the slope to tell them so. He grabbed at Fabier's bridle. 'Stay here, captain. There really is nothing you can do. They would simply kill you in turn, hussar or not. It's hopeless. You can see for yourself, we can't do anything. Even if we helped the infantry, how do we know they wouldn't turn on us?'

'How can you think that? They are soldiers. Honourable soldiers of the emperor.'

Keane shook his head. 'Like those hussars, captain. Look at them. Are they honourable?'

Fabier paused. Then he spoke, gravely. 'They have lost their honour. They have thrown it away. They soil the uniform of the hussar.' He swore and went to draw his carbine, forgetting that it had been removed by the guerrillas. 'My God, Keane, stop them. We must do something.'

Silver spoke. 'Why bother, they're all Frenchies, aren't they? Just leave them to kill each other. Save us the trouble.'

Keane ignored him. 'I don't see how we can do anything to help. All we can do is wait till the end and hope the hussars lose more men, then attack them when they are weakened and hope that we have a better chance.'

'That's a coward's way.'

Keane bristled, but did not take up the insult. 'No, captain, it's a reasoned way and one that will not unduly endanger the lives of my men.'

Fabier looked him in the eyes. 'Captain, I respect you and since we met, I have always thought that for you, like me, something is more important than the fact that we fight on different sides. That there is something about humanity that matters more. That is why I know that you do not believe what you are saying. I know that you know what is the right thing to do here, just as well as I do.'

Keane knew. The Frenchman had given voice to the very thoughts that were in his own mind. He knew what must be done. Keane turned to the others.

'Garland, stay here with the prisoner. Captain Fabier, I'm sorry. You cannot come with us. But I have your word not to attempt anything. Garland will shoot you should you try.' Fabier nodded. 'The rest of you, come with me. Draw swords.'

Silver shook his head. 'No, sir. It's not right. I'm not dying for some bastard Frenchmen. This was done deliberate. It's a trap. We'll all be killed.'

Keane stared at him. 'Silver, that's an order.'

'We should kill him now, sir. Be done with it.'

Heredia spoke. 'No. That's not the way. We are human,

thinking men. Honourable men. We do not kill each other like dogs.'

Keane stood close to Silver. 'No, you're right. We don't.' He turned to Silver. 'Private, will you obey an order?'

Silver stared at Heredia and cursed, then looked at Morris and at Keane. He nodded. 'Sorry, sir. Not my place to say that.'

Then, on Keane's command, they drew their weapons. Most were the standard pattern, curved light cavalry sabres with which they had been issued by Scovell. Morris, of course, had his own fine hand-crafted blade and Keane his Egyptian scimitar. Together they shuffled into line as Keane and Heredia the cavalryman had taught them and then, with Keane in the lead, trotted as fast as they could towards the mass of fighting men. Although there were only five of them, they took the hussars by surprise, and, slashing as they went in, managed to dispatch three of the cavalry before they knew what had hit them. Four other French horsemen had disengaged from the fight and were turning to make their escape when they found Keane and the others blocking their way.

The sergeant was among them. His gaze met Keane's and Keane knew instantly the eyes of the deserter. Contempt for authority and hatred, coupled with fear and the desperation of hopelessness. The man made for Keane and raised his sabre. But Keane parried and pushed the blade aside, so that it slid down off his own, which he then brought back to cut at the sergeant's head. But the big Frenchman was quick and intercepted Keane's sword, sweeping it up and away from his body. For an instant Keane was exposed, and seeing this the man to the right of the sergeant pulled his horse across and lunged. But that left him open to attack and hardly had he made the move, his blade inches from Keane's body, than Morris pushed into him and with a deft move thrust forward with the point of his weapon and skewered the Frenchman beneath his raised arm. The man screamed and dropped his sword so that it dangled from the knot around his wrist. Grabbing at his arm he stared at Morris in horror, just as the artilleryman raised his weapon again and brought it down in a cross-stroke across the man's face, blinding him and sending him from the saddle.

Meanwhile Keane had recovered his posture and, turning in the saddle, made a back cut at the sergeant. It caught the man off guard and Keane felt his blade slice into the man's back. The sergeant grinned with confidence and pulled back before making a mad cut at Keane. But it was ill timed and again Keane's blade hit, this time slicing into the golden frogging across the sky-blue tunic, cutting it open and making a deep slash that ran from the sergeant's left collarbone to his waist. The man yelled and grabbed at his stomach. Keane cut again and it was over. He looked around and saw that Heredia and Martin were locked in combat with another two of the hussars. Silver, though, had made it through the cavalry and was fending off a bayonet attack from two infantrymen. Keane spurred across to him and caught one of his attackers a clean blow on the head that bisected his shako and killed him. Silver parried the other bayonet but the Frenchman was fast and caught him with it on the arm, tearing open his coat and drawing blood. Silver cursed then moved his blade fast, circling the bayonet and slashing with a savage uppercut that sent it through the man's jawbone to bisect his face. Then, seeing Keane, he rode over to join him.

Keane spurred on into the melee and in front of him saw one of the hussars, a tall man, rise high in the stirrups and raise his carbine one-handed to take aim at one of the infantrymen. And then, just as the man's finger seemed to be on the trigger, he fell, a black hole in his temple. But the shot had not come from the square. It came from the right, and looking across to that direction Keane saw the killer. He was a civilian, dressed in a tall hat, and Keane recognized him instantly as Cuevillas's chief of staff.

At that moment the trees to his right erupted in a sea of musketry as the guerrillas poured fire into the mass of the French with no care as to whether they might be killing infantrymen or hussars.

Keane yelled, 'Get back. Pull back,' and turned his horse away from the melee, followed by Silver.

They watched as the hussars, realizing what was happening, tried to break off from the infantry. There were fewer of them left now; barely a score forming what was left of the square. The hussars too had lost heavily and a good dozen of the sky-blue-clad figures lay motionless on the ground, with the same number again wounded, dead and dying, horses among them.

The guerrillas loosed off another volley into the melee and four men fell, and then they were upon them. Screaming, they came out of the woods, swords of all types waving above their heads. Some, still with their guns, knelt to take a final shot. The rest whooped like so many savages as they crashed into the confused mass of the French.

All around them the guerrillas were fighting hard, and dying where they stood. But from what Keane could see they seemed to be taking more of the French with them. He saw a party of the hussars making off on the other side of what was left of the square, in the direction of Spain. Back to Soult's army, he thought. You'll find no solace there.

But to his surprise, a few moments later the hussars re-emerged from the trees into which they had retreated, accompanied by more horsemen. The newcomers wore bright gold helmets and green tunics and their swords were drawn.

'Dragoons,' cried Keane. 'Look to your left. Dragoons in the trees.'

His men had seen them, and having won their individual fights, reined around to join him. But the guerrillas at the rear of what had been the square stood no chance. The big men in green coats were upon them in a moment and their world dissolved in a welter of blood and flashing steel as the dragoons' huge bay horses reared and kicked, their hooves dealing as much death as the long, straight, razor-sharp swords of their riders.

More deserters, thought Keane. There looked to be a dozen of them and obviously they had been waiting to see the outcome of the fight between the hussars and the infantry. He looked to his right, at the direction from which the guerrillas had come, and saw only a few more of their number in the trees, and among them Cuevillas himself. The leader could see as well as Keane that the fight was not going according to plan. At that moment Cuevillas saw him, and, followed by a handful of his men, ran towards him from the cover of the trees. He was raving.

'What are you doing? You don't bring any more men. Don't you fight them? Look. Dragoons.'

Keane yelled back. 'You should retreat. You can't win. We'll come with you. Disengage.'

The Spaniard stared at him. 'Fight them. We must fight them.' He turned towards the melee and waved his men on just as the dragoons, having dispatched the last of the guerrillas at the rear, began to pick off the few remaining infantrymen.

Keane was about to order his own men to pull back when for a second time there was a commotion in the trees to the rear of the dragoons and through the undergrowth appeared more guerrillas. But there was a difference to these men. They wore the same ragged part-military costume as Cuevillas's bandits, but these men were mounted and armed with lances. They fell upon the Frenchmen from the rear, pig-sticking them on their lance points. The dragoons turned and tried to hack their way through the newcomers, but there were too many of them. Keane could make out twenty or thirty of the mounted lancers now. The dragoons, realizing that they were outnumbered, began to panic, and he knew that this was the end. A green-clad cavalryman came riding towards him across the bodies of the infantry and instinctively Keane raised his sword to parry the attack. But he saw that the man's uniform had a new feature. A flower of red had spread across the yellow plastron of his green coat and at its centre there protruded the point of a lance and a foot of its wooden staff. The dragoon screamed past Keane, trailing the lance behind him, and looking back he saw the others trying to beat off the newcomers. The remnants of the hussars were also in trouble now. Unable to escape through the lancers and harried by the newly invigorated guerrillas to their front, they died between the two and fell on the bodies of their erstwhile comrades. It was quickly over. Keane watched as the last half-dozen of the French, standing back to back, raised their hands in surrender. He pitied them, for he knew it was of no use. The lancers advanced upon them, sword-armed now, and the sabres whistled and sang as they came down and the woods rang with the cries of the dying.

Cuevillas and his men stood and watched the carnage. He turned to Keane. 'You brought them here?'

Keane shook his head. 'Not me. Aren't they your men?'

Cuevillas shook his head. 'No. Not mine. His.'

He pointed to the trees and Keane saw a man emerge on a grey horse. He looked familiar, and as he grew closer to them, moving towards the lancers, he saw that it was Morillo.

The Spaniard shouted a word of command and the lancers, who had been holding back from the surviving French, went in again and cut down the men, even as they held up their arms. Keane looked away and heard Cuevillas swear.

He turned back to him. 'You knew about the silver?'

'Of course. Do you think I'm an idiot, Captain Keane? We trailed you here.'

'You were watching?'

Cuevillas shrugged. 'Yes, we were waiting.'

'Waiting for my men to die. So you could take the booty.'

'We saved you, didn't we?'

'You waited until we were in the fighting. You might just as easily have killed us.'

'Yes, I suppose so. But we still saved you. Tell that to your general.'

Morillo rode up to them. 'Captain Keane. Ignacio. I see that we arrived just in time. You might have lost.'

Cuevillas snarled. 'I don't think so. I was about to lead my men.'

'Too bad you waited so long, Ignacio. If I didn't know you better I would say it was deliberate.'

'What are you saying, Morillo? That I am a coward?'

Morillo held up his hand and smiled. 'No, no. How could I say that? I merely wondered why you allowed Captain Keane here to attack before letting him know of your presence.'

'What does it matter? We're all alive, aren't we?'

'Some of your men are dead.'

'You take losses. We've done what we came to do. Haven't we?'

'I don't know, Ignacio. What did you come to do?'

Cuevillas said nothing. Keane spoke. 'You know, colonel, why we are here. Why, I suspect, we are all here. The answer is over there.'

He pointed across to where beyond the carpet of dead and dying men and horses, two wagons stood where the square had been.

'That is why we are here. Is it not?'

Morillo nodded. 'You knew about the silver. Me too. But how will you get it away, with just five men?'

'I'll think of something.'

Cuevillas spoke. 'Once we have divided it between the three of us, it won't be a big problem, will it?'

Keane shook his head. 'I don't think you understand, captain. I am claiming this treasure in the name of King George and General Wellesley and the British army.'

Cuevillas laughed. 'How can you do that? With five men? Look at my men. Even with those we have lost we still outnumber you ten to one. Be sensible, Captain Keane.'

Morillo spoke. 'Gentlemen, neither of you appears to have noticed that if we are talking about force of numbers, my men outnumber either of yours. Besides, this is not a question of who has more men. It's a question of principle. I am a colonel in the army of Spain and I reserve the right to claim this silver for my country.'

Cuevillas held up his hands. 'My men died for this silver. Look. There they are. We need it, Morillo. And I intend to take my share.'

Morillo shook his head. 'Calm yourself, Ignacio. Did I say that you were not entitled to a share? Perhaps you too, Captain Keane, will have a share. But for the most part this is Spain's treasure.'

Cuevillas spoke quietly. 'How much? How much do you say we can take?'

'Shall we say a thousand crowns?'

'A thousand crowns? But there must be over thirty thousand in the wagons.'

'I think that's generous. Take nothing, if you will.'

Cuevillas said nothing. Keane too held his tongue. His men had gathered together a short distance away and the silence was broken by the sound of horses neighing and the moans of the wounded, but a third sound was that of gunshots as the guerrillas walked among the fallen French, dispatching each of them in turn. And gradually the moaning became less.

At length Cuevillas spoke. 'Very well. I'll take my thousand and go. But I don't like it, colonel. And don't think you have heard the last of this. I intend to speak to General Cuesta and he will be made aware of exactly what you have taken.'

'Yes, Ignacio, that he will. But by me.'

Cuevillas walked away and directed his men towards the carts. And as he did so Morillo whispered a command to his own chief of staff, who set off after Cuevillas to ensure that he did not exceed his quota.

Morillo turned back to Keane. 'So, Captain Keane. What are you to do?'

'Colonel?'

'I presume that part of your mission was to secure the treasure for General Wellesley. I am right?'

'Yes, of course.'

'And what will you do now?'

'I shall take my share of the silver. Half, I presume.'

'You presume too much, captain. What makes you think that I might give you some of what is rightfully Spain's?'

'The fact perhaps that we are fighting and dying on Spanish soil to save your country from the French.'

'We did not ask you to come.'

'No, but we have come.'

'Is that worth 25,000 crowns?'

'You tell me. All I know is that there is an army of British soldiers now near Braga, waiting for their pay. Pay earned in the liberation of your country. This is rightfully theirs.'

'Can I help it if your general forgets to make provision to pay his own men?'

Keane was losing his patience but refused to be drawn. 'You gave a thousand to Cuevillas.'

Morillo shrugged. 'What else could I do? I don't want to start another war. We have one already.'

'So why not reward us? If I return to General Wellesley empty-handed, don't you think that he might draw the wrong conclusions about your loyalty? Conclusions I myself have drawn from our conversation. I would not want to suggest that you will not support him. Unless, of course, that is what you wish me to convey.'

Morillo's eyes narrowed as he looked at Keane. 'You are a clever man, Captain Keane. You might not have realized that my men were following you, but you do appear to know my thoughts. Yes, I do intend to help General Wellesley. It is in the interest of Spain.'

And not least in your own interest, thought Keane. Morillo was no fool. Keane knew he was aware that whenever this war ended, when they had finally pushed Boney from Spain there would be rich pickings for the victors. Cuevillas couldn't see past the nose on his face. He was only in it for the short term. But Morillo was playing the long game. He smiled, as a plan began to form in his mind.

'That is very good to hear, colonel. Very good news. So you will hold off Marshal Ney while we push on after Soult?'

'If that is what is required now, then I will do it.' He paused.

Keane spoke. 'And what of the money? I cannot return empty-handed.' And then, almost as an afterthought, he added, 'You seem like a sporting man, colonel. What would you say to a game of cards?'

# 12

They did not linger long on the battlefield. The guerrillas had buried their own dead and had thrown the French into a gravel pit by the side of the road, which they covered with bushes.

'There's no point in trying to bury them. And they don't deserve it. The animals will get them anyway,' said Morillo. 'We have wolves in these parts. In just a few days they will be nothing more than a heap of stripped bones and tatters of cloth.'

Keane looked for Fabier but luckily the hussar captain was out of earshot.

They camped with the Spaniards that night beyond the Tamega on the outskirts of the little town of Montalegre. Approaching it, Keane had been struck by a sense of foreboding. High above the houses rose the huge mass of the old town's ruined medieval keep. It must have been over eighty feet tall and for all its crumbling condition it still appeared threatening. It stood like something from a Romantic novella, the sort he had mentioned to Ross. And it was perhaps because he shared Keane's sense of its sinister presence that Morillo had chosen not to make his headquarters in the keep, but here, away from the town, on the plateau. Morris and Keane messed with Morillo, the others on their own, making sure that they kept the guerrillas as far away as possible from Captain Fabier, who had been as good as his word.

The guerrillas stood guard over the silver, which they had carried here by pack mule, and as they ate Keane thought of the promised game of cards. Morillo, he thought, seemed less on his guard, and Keane wondered whether he really did mean that he was now an ally of the British. He thought back to the savagery of their first encounter. He had been appalled too by the callous way in which the colonel had instructed his men to give no quarter to the French wounded. But he was not surprised. Up here in the mountains it was easy to forget for a moment the atrocities that Boney's armies had committed, were committing even now down in the towns, valleys and plains of Portugal and Spain.

Morillo laughed and talked of Spain and his love for its people, its culture and its food, and Keane saw a different man. Perhaps the man he had been before the French had come. They dined like kings on local hams and sausages, cheeses, pork and strong red wine.

He wondered in fact if Morillo might be trying to get him drunk before their card game and to begin with merely sipped at his glass. But he soon gave in and drank with the others. Keane had a name in the mess for his hard head and tonight was surely no different.

From the direction of where his men were seated around their own fire he could hear music. Silver was singing. The man had an ear for music, born of his days at sea, perhaps, and as melodious a voice as any that Keane had heard in twenty years of soldiering. The tune he sang now was one of his favourites, 'The Girl I Left Behind Me'. It seemed a little strange to hear it up here in the hills, away from the rest of the army, particularly as at the same time in another part of the camp one of Morillo's men was playing a guitar. The lilting strains of some Spanish tune mixed now with Silver's offering. It was curious, thought Keane, how both seemed to mesh together. It might almost be, he thought, a metaphor for the alliance of the two nations against Boney. Yet at the same time there was something not quite right about the sound, for beneath each of the tunes lay its own distinct character, and the more he listened, the more he seemed to notice the discord. Perhaps, he thought, that is what is wrong with the alliance. Perhaps we simply don't understand one another's characters. Perhaps we are just too different.

Morillo brought him back to the present and he took another gulp of wine. 'So, Captain Keane, are we going to play cards for this silver? Are you prepared to lose?'

Keane smiled. 'I rather think that it will be the reverse, colonel.'

'You seem very confident. Do you have a reputation?'

Keane turned to Morris. 'Do I, Tom? Would you say that I had a "reputation"?'

'James. You are quite aware that you do. Colonel, I may as well admit to you that Captain Keane here is well known as not only the best but indeed the luckiest card player in the British army.'

Morillo laughed. 'Well, this time he has met his match. What is your game, captain? You choose. Like a duel, eh? What shall we play? Bassett? Hombre?'

Keane shook his head. 'You mean quadrille, I think, colonel. No, neither of those. Bassett is far too polite for this company.'

Morillo laughed. Keane went on. 'What then, shall we play?'
He smiled. 'I have it. Pharo.'

'Pharo?'

'Do you refuse my choice, colonel?'

Morillo looked nonplussed. 'But for Pharo we need a banker
and a box and I'm afraid that you would not trust my men,
nor I yours.'

'But we have Captain Fabier. He has no side.'

Morillo thought for a moment. 'Very well, captain. As you
wish. We shall play Pharo.'

It took half an hour to assemble the gaming table, which
Morillo's men fashioned from five planks salvaged from the
carts set on trestles made from the axles. This, with a fine
sense of irony, they had draped with a French tricolour they
had found among the wreckage.

The betting shoe they had made from a split ammunition
case and it sat at one side of the table, guarded by Fabier who
had been persuaded to act as banker. Keane smiled to himself
as he thought again of how in Morillo's mind the captain must
be unbiased. Only he had been privy to the hussar's true
thoughts and concerns about the fate of the money. In Fabier's
mind the worst thing that could happen to the silver would
be that it should pass to Morillo, and Keane rested in the knowledge that the Frenchman would do everything in his power
to assist him in winning the game.

Besides, Keane had a few tricks of his own learned in the
mess. He remembered something that an old colonel had once
told him when, still an ensign, he had taken up the older
man's invitation to a hand of piquet. 'Only a fool trusts to luck

when playing cards, my boy. You must learn to cheat grace-
fully.'

Morillo interrupted his thoughts. 'You're a brave man,
Captain Keane.'

'Not brave, colonel. Just confident.'

'As long as you don't feel lucky. Luck is no friend of the card
player, captain. You should surely know that.'

Momentarily dumbfounded by the fact that the man seemed
to have read his mind, Keane recovered. 'I never trust to luck,
colonel.'

Morillo leered. 'Still sure that you want to play?'

Keane nodded. 'Of course. More than ever.'

Fabier intervened. 'Very well, gentlemen.' He sprang a new
pack of cards and spoke in the tone of a true Paris croupier.
'Bank, gentlemen!'

On the table lay two piles of coins. Not the silver crowns
but pennies, acting as tokens, each of them representing 200
crowns. To the right of both Keane and Morillo sat a dummy
player, in Keane's case Morris, each with their own pile. Fabier
prepared to deal.

The cards flew from his hands and Keane turned his. He
looked at it and moved three pennies into the centre of the
table. The others drew their cards and each placed a stake,
Morillo last. He turned his card as they all did and Keane
groaned inside, beaten in the first hand by the colonel.

They played again and again until Keane had lost four times.

Morris looked at him in alarm. Keane reckoned his losses
and called on the next card: 'Four thousand crowns.'

Morillo's eyes widened. 'You are indeed a brave man, captain.'

Keane said nothing, although he saw Fabier look at him and
make a sign with his eyebrow, lowering it. It was the subtlest

of all movements but it was enough for Keane to know that Morillo had low cards in his hand. That this was the time to bet. He called again. 'No, in fact I'll double that lest you doubt my bravery. Eight thousand.'

There was a gasp from around the table. Morris said, 'James?'

Morillo smiled at him. 'Very well. Captain Fabier, cards.'

Keane gazed at the backs of Morillo's tanned and weather-beaten hands as they held his cards and looked across at those of Fabier, holding the rest of the pack in the shoe.

He wondered for a moment whether he was mad. He had just bet a greater sum of money than he had had in his possession for years, money that would have bought back the family farm and kept them all together and healthy for decades. And he was playing cards for it with a man who was undoubtedly one of the biggest rogues in the Peninsula. Gambling more than a sixth of the treasure on the turn of a single card.

For an instant reason took hold and had him ask himself how he had come to this. And he wondered too how, should he lose, he would explain his predicament to Wellesley and the others. But reason was the enemy of the gambler.

He watched Fabier's hands and waited. Had time to observe the thick dark hair that grew on their backs and the old scar, a duelling cut perhaps, that adorned the left. Then the hands shot out and dealt the cards left and right. Morillo's man looked at his hand and threw it down before standing up and walking away from the table. Morris looked sanguine and said nothing. Morillo shrugged and laid down his cards. 'I don't think you'll beat that, captain.'

It was a low hand, and just low enough. Fabier had indeed been signalling. Keane laid down his own cards.

'I win, I think, colonel.'

Morillo gasped. 'You win once. Once only when you play with me, captain. Bank.'

He took a sip of wine. 'I have no idea how you managed that, captain. Luck is fickle. Of course I would never accuse you, although I do hear that sharp practice is not unknown in the British army. I advise you to be careful.'

Keane reddened. 'And I would advise you the same, colonel.'

Fabier stopped them. 'Gentlemen, come now. We are men of honour. We would not indulge in such practices. Colonel, captain, I thank you. Enough. Now, another hand.'

'Deal then,' said Morillo, through gritted teeth.

'Yes, deal if you will, captain,' said Keane, wanting to appear equally furious.

Morillo looked at the pack, eyeing up the cards suspiciously as if he knew the card that was at the top. Keane watched him.

The Spaniard spoke. 'Damn. Damn that card.'

'Don't worry,' said Keane. 'I'm sure you have another chance. You were not trusting in luck, surely, were you, colonel?'

'Damn luck. You have the devil on your side, Captain Keane,' said Morillo, knowing that he had lost again. And once again Fabier began to deal.

It surprised Keane that it took as long as an hour for the other two players at the table to lose all interest in their own chances. All eyes now were on Keane and Morillo. Men had come from throughout the camp to gather around the table, jostling for a view, with Keane's men to the front.

Beside both of the men lay a slip of parchment, on the reverse of which had been written the orders given to the dead French commander of the wagon train.

Now each of them bore a list of figures, written in pencil.

Where before there had been five hundred, two thousand and four thousand crowns, now the figures lay in their tens of thousands and while Keane's stopped at ten, Morillo's was touching forty.

Morillo looked like a man possessed. His eyes were staring wildly and the sweat hung heavy on his forehead. On the table beside the cards stood two glasses and two bottles of wine. Fabier, cool as ever, held the cards in his tanned, hairy hands and dealt them fast.

'Gentlemen, bank and deal.'

They declared. Morillo screamed, 'The knave.' He paused then. 'All right. Double or quits . . . No!'

Keane picked up his cards and handed them to Fabier and as he did so he saw Morillo stare at him as if he was trying to read his mind again. It was almost over.

He thought to himself, he knows now that he's lost. That he cannot make me lose it all now. Why doesn't he just give up? Is it to save face?

And Morillo sat opposite him, hating him more with every moment and wondering quite how the Irishman had done this to him. Gone was the coolness of the early evening. Gone the bragging and bravado. He had seldom been beaten in cards. Not once in ten years, and now this. Keane must be cheating. Surely it was the only explanation. But to call him a cheat would be to challenge his honour and incur a duel, and he had seen enough of Keane in battle to know that a duel was something he did not want with this tall redcoat. And so it must be, he thought, that I shall lose the silver. He felt the sweat beading on his forehead and realized that he must look terrible. Like a man about to lose. He tried to regain his composure, determined that his men must not see him like this. That even if he did lose the silver, he must still retain his dignity. If he did not have that then he would surely lose their respect. In a game of cards fortune was your mistress. He must show that he was beyond this great loss, that he was the greater man.

After all, he still had the 150,000 francs he had taken at Vigo. And he had his men and his freedom and his kingdom in the mountains. And what did Keane have? He'd be lucky if he got away from Spain with his life. He smiled and Keane saw it and in his turn wondered what might be going through Morillo's mind.

Fabier spoke. 'It would seem, colonel, that the score against you is now a little in excess of 50,000 crowns. Have you the means by which to pay Captain Keane?'

Morillo glared at the Frenchman and for a moment Keane wondered whether he might order one of his men to kill the hussar and whether in the heat of the moment they might not all be at risk. But he reasoned that Morillo was an intelligent man, more intelligent then Cuevillas certainly, although equally callous.

'It would seem that you have won, Captain Keane, though how, I do not know. You may take the money. Whatever of it you can find here in the camp. I do not think by any means that we have the full amount.'

Keane thought of the boxes they had hidden on the road above the skirmish. 'No, I dare say some must have got away. But thank you, colonel. You are most sporting.'

He stood, as if to leave, and paused. 'Perhaps I have a proposition for you. What if I suggested that you keep half the silver?'

Morillo looked puzzled. 'Why?'

'In return, I would need you to make a solemn promise to

me that you will mobilize all the men you have in this area, Cuevillas's men too and any others, and prevent Marshal Ney from coming across to aid Soult. Can you do that?'

Morillo stared at him. 'You are an extraordinary man, Captain Keane. First you beat me at cards, by what means I do not know. And now you offer me back the silver to become your ally.'

Keane thought that he might have gone too far. Might he have offended Morillo's honour? 'I'm sorry. I did not mean to cause you offence. It was merely a gesture of goodwill. Between allies.'

There was a pause. And then slowly, Morillo's moustachioed face broke into a grin. 'Of course I am not offended. I am flattered that you would consider such a thing. Besides, I would be a fool to refuse. I will accept your offer. I will undertake the task and Marshal Ney will see that his master has made a grave mistake in thinking he can defeat the Spanish people. And in the morning we will pack your treasure on mules and send you back to your general. Now, though, come. Have a drink. We are allies, after all, are we not?'

Morillo was as good as his word. Early the following morning, a short while after the sun had broken over the sierra with the promise of a long, hot day, Keane led his men out of the guerrilla camp and back towards the south. They rode in single file and behind each man, tethered to the back of his saddle, walked a pack mule, hung with panniers into which Morillo's men had loaded half of the French silver.

The mountains seemed less forbidding now and the prospect of rejoining the army gave them the drive to move quickly as they climbed towards the clearing where they had hidden the two remaining boxes. They dismounted and, moving quickly lest they might be observed, uncovered the boxes. Keane knew that the only way to carry the extra silver was to distribute it among the panniers, but as the men prepared to carry the bags from the broken boxes, he stopped them.

'Wait a moment. How many bags are there here, Tom? What would you say?'

'There must be ten bags in each of the boxes.'

'Yes. And in each bag how much?'

'Four hundred, perhaps five hundred crowns.'

'And if each of us should carry one of those bags in our own baggage? That would leave?'

'Fifteen bags, of course. James, what are you talking about?'

'Didn't I promise you all a share of the treasure? Well, each of you should take two bags.'

Martin spoke. 'Sir, should we not declare any booty?'

'Martin, I swear you'll make a general yet. Yes, of course we should declare it all. But who is to say how much we recovered, and how much we gave to pay off Morillo? Do it now, and we need not declare it and thus lose whatever portion the army might choose to take. Silver, you and Martin will take four bags each. Two for yourselves and two for each of the others. Now, look sharp about it.'

They were not slow to respond, and as they transferred the bags to the panniers on the mules, Keane walked across to Morris.

'Tom, I think that, as officers, it might be appropriate for you and me to take four bags each. Do you not agree?'

'James, you do realize that this is strictly illegal, that we really should do it as directed by the book.'

'Tom, when have I ever done things by the book? Unless, of course, you no longer want a part of it.'

Morris thought for a moment. 'I may be cautious, but I'm not stupid.'

And then, with his head aching from too much wine, and his spirits as high as they had ever been, carrying more money in his saddlebag than he had seen in his life, Keane led his men away and over the hills, back towards Braga and the army.

Major General Sir Arthur Wellesley stood at a window of the loggia of the castle of Abrantes and looked out across the Tagus. He toyed with the cuff of his coat, hesitated for a moment and then turned to face the two men who stood behind him. His face was alive with interest.

'How much did you say?'

'Originally there were 50,000 crowns in the wagon train, sir. But the French managed to get away with a portion and we had to pay off Colonel Morillo.'

Wellesley smiled. 'Still, 25,000 crowns is not to be sniffed at. The commissariat is deficient in transport, the soldiers have no shoes and are without pay. Our hospitals are bursting and we need at the least £200,000 a month. We have a loan from Oporto. Yes, 25,000 crowns will do. You did well, Keane. And now you say that Morillo will do as we ask?'

'He's a good man, sir, if you tackle him the right way.'

'Which in your opinion included giving him half of the silver?'

'Yes, sir. It's the sort of argument that he understands. He will fight for his country but with such an incentive he is inclined to believe that we will keep our word and that in turn is sufficient to encourage him to keep his.'

'You are clever, Keane, damned clever. Would you say so, Grant?'

'Damned clever, Sir Arthur.'

It had taken much longer than Keane had anticipated to regain contact with the army, for shortly after reaching Braga Wellesley had turned and headed south.

He had decided not to pursue Soult any further. The men were exhausted and to do so would have drawn him uncomfortably far from his own supply chain. And so the army had withdrawn down the Cavado river to Braga and back to Oporto, and Keane had trailed them, arriving every time a day or two after they had left, finding nothing more than the evidence of the redcoats' presence and a population wondering why the British had come to their towns only to retreat back to the south. And Keane had been unable to offer them an explanation. Oporto still reeked of the battle and the earth of the burial mounds lay fresh in the shadow of the seminary. To leave the city had seemed absurd, but the army had gone to Coimbra and there was no alternative. At length he had found them at Abrantes, almost where they had started, and he had begun to wonder whether Wellesley was really the master that many believed him to be. They were not far from Lisbon now, and as Wellesley spoke Keane was pondering whether he might petition for leave and call upon Kitty Blackwood. He wondered too where her brother might be now and how he might find out. There seemed to be every chance. For although he had found the general in poor spirits, his news and the booty had lightened that mood. He would choose his moment carefully. Wellesley spoke again. 'Yes, Keane. Clever of you. And now I've something more for you to consider. What do you know of General Cuesta?'

'I know that he commands the army of Spain and that he is our ally, sir.'

'Perhaps it might have been better had someone had the common sense to inform him of that fact.'

Grant sniggered. Keane said nothing. Wellesley continued. 'General Cuesta is a thorn in my side, Keane. Marshal Soult is licking his wounds and Marshal Ney pinned down by the Spanish in the north, for which assurance I must thank you, Keane. Marshal Victor, however, is a very present danger to us. He is here.'

He stabbed at the map which lay on the table before them, hitting it with his forefinger in the south of the country, to the west of Madrid.

'We have done all we are able for the moment in the north. Now here we have a very clear opportunity to attack Marshal Victor and to take Madrid. But to do that I must have the co-operation of General Cuesta.'

'And that you do not have, sir?'

'No, Keane, that I do not have. Tell him, Grant.'

Major Grant walked across to the map. 'You see, Keane, General Cuesta has a plan. It is undoubtedly a fine plan on account of the fact that it has been constructed by the general himself. And it will without doubt, should it succeed, confer on the good general all the honours of his country. There is a problem, however, Keane, and the problem is that his plan stinks.'

'Sir?'

Wellesley spoke. 'General Cuesta may parade the fact that he will liberate the nation but his chief motive in all things is to cover himself with glory. He has agreed that we should advance together in two columns along the Tagus, directly towards Madrid. He has promised supplies but to date nothing has been forthcoming. I have every reason to suppose that as we near Victor's army, Cuesta will attempt to defeat it single-handedly. I met with General Cuesta yesterday to discuss our plan. It is a compromise, Keane, no less, and both you and I are aware that on a battlefield compromise seldom wins the day. But we have agreed on the plan and we will stick to it. Tomorrow we advance into Spain.'

Keane's heart sank. Surely Wellesley did not intend for him to lead his men with the army? There was no alternative but to go straight to the heart of the matter. He would ask for leave. 'Sir, I was going to ask whether I might . . . '

Wellesley cut across him. 'We advance into Spain, Keane. You will take your men and march with the covering force on our left flank. Cuesta has placed them there to warn of any approach from the left. But they're a rum lot, Keane. Spanish and Portuguese only. Cuesta dictated their make-up. I doubt that they'll stand when it comes to a fight, and I have no faith in their ability to give the alarm. You must cover them, Keane. And, of course, General Cuesta will not know of your presence.'

'You want me to spy on our allies, sir?'

'If you like, Keane, yes. Oh, and Grant, I leave you to tell Captain Keane of other developments. Thank you, gentlemen.'

They left the room, but immediately they were outside Keane turned to Grant. 'Sir, can he mean it? We have just come in from the north. To send us out again so soon . . . '

'I may agree with you, but I cannot argue with the general, Keane. You know that. He wishes you to shadow Cuesta and that is what you must do. I am quite aware of your wishes and of your interest in a certain young lady in Lisbon.'

'Sir?'

'I have my sources. Let it be said that I do not approve at all of that liaison. Not at all, given your relationship with the young woman's brother, and so I am only too happy that you are ordered out.'

Keane, astonished that Grant should know, shook his head. Grant went on. 'Now, James, don't take on. It's for the best. Besides, you're all to be kitted out before you go.'

'Kitted out?'

'Haven't you heard? No, of course you haven't. That was the "development" to which the general referred. The good Captain Scovell has designed a new uniform for the corps of guides and you're all to wear it. It is splendid, quite splendid. I believe that your men may even now be in the process of making its acquaintance.'

# 13

It was an impressive spectacle. Keane and his men sat on the hillside overlooking the road to Madrid and watched as General Cuesta led his men to battle. With their drums beating, their bands playing, and beneath holy banners that bore the ragged red cross of Burgundy, the arms of the king and images of the Virgin Mary, the Spanish marched to meet Marshal Victor. They marched to drive the invader from their country. And Keane and his men were going with them. They had barely had time to gather their possessions together and the reunion between the two parties had been a hurried affair, very different from that which Keane had envisaged. Now at least, though, they were together, even if half of them were utterly exhausted.

There was, however, one member of their party missing. Gabriella and Silver had been reunited for a brief time, yet he had decided that she should not come with them, but instead remain at Abrantes with the majority of the camp followers, women and children. She had protested, of course, but Silver had won the day. Perhaps, thought Keane, it was because she had at last managed to get what she craved: a husband and

enough money to make them independent. Keane had half
expected her to cajole Silver into desertion, but he felt more
confident that the man felt some spark of loyalty to his bene-
factor. Besides, Keane had led them to riches and there was
surely the prospect that there might be more to come. It had
been a clever ploy, thought Keane, to divide it up so blatantly
and in so doing to bring himself into complicity with the men.
He hoped that it would have no repercussions; that none of
them would use it against him in some way, but he trusted,
as always, to his intuition.

The news of the money had astonished and delighted those
who had returned to Braga before them, and there was something of a carnival spirit among the eight men who rode out
together on the left flank of the left wing of Wellesley's force
on this fine June morning.

In truth, Keane was almost fully content. He was happy with
his command and with the eventual outcome, hard won as it
had been. Morillo had been persuaded to block Marshal Ney
in the north. At least he trusted the man to keep his word on
that promise. They were all richer; Fabier too, much to his
surprise, had been cut into the booty and had, more importantly, been rewarded for his duplicity at cards by being handed
over to an English jailer rather than the guerrillas. Best of all,
though, was the fact that, courtesy of Major Grant, they had
all been given new mounts.

His own, which he had found awaiting him at the camp,
was a pretty bay mare which he had instantly christened Rattler.
She stood just over fourteen hands high and carried a white
blaze on her nose and two white socks on her hind legs. Quite
how Grant had managed to procure him such a fine beast was
beyond him and he could only hope that he might keep her

from being requisitioned by the cavalry. He patted her neck
as they rode on, and mulled over their situation.

The army was paid, Wellesley was happy and Keane and his
men had pockets heavy with silver coins, food in their bellies
and a fresh pair of boots on their feet.

This last was through no work of his. The boots, which
somehow had been contrived to fit, had come with new
uniforms. That was Scovell's doing. The man clearly had time
on his hands, thought Keane. Time enough, at least, to design
what he thought must be at one and the same time one of
the most absurd and one of the drabbest uniforms ever to
adorn a British soldier.

Scovell himself had remained behind at Abrantes, training
other units of his new Corps of Guides in the skills of carrying
dispatches, which was to be their principal work.

Keane glanced round at Ross who rode on his left and
wondered what on earth the bluff Scotsman must think of his
new attire. The short brown dragoon jacket was trimmed with
red at the collar and cuffs and finished with a black lace trim
and black frogging. It sat atop a pair of white riding breeches
and black hessian boots, and was topped off by a Light Dragoon-
style helmet in polished black leather with a black horsehair
crest. It was, mused Keane, something of a tribute to the alliance
between Britain and Portugal. The helmet had been devised
by that maverick cavalryman Banastre Tarleton during the
American war and the brown jacket was almost exactly that
of the Portuguese cacadores, the light infantry, who were at
this moment part of the column marching down below them,
behind Cuesta.

How clever of Scovell, he thought, to have made a uniform
into a political tool. Not that the men, save Morris of course,

and perhaps Heredia, would have understood its symbolic signif-
icance.

He had found most of them grimacing at their new costume
on his return from the interview with Wellesley the previous
evening. There had been exclamations of disbelief and several
refusals even to try it on, which were roundly shouted down
by Ross. The only two of them actually to admire the new kit
were Heredia and Morris. For the Portuguese trooper it was
'almost like the uniform of my own country'. To Morris, who
already sported the Tarleton helmet of the Horse Artillery, it
was 'fine, very fine. Damn close to what I have on at present.'
It was true, thought Keane; it did have something of the horse
gunners about it. Perhaps they might all cut a dash in it, and
on closer inspection in a glass shortly before they left the
camp, he found himself to look not at all bad. There would
have to be modifications, of course. He decided that the red
would have to go and that he would adopt the yellow facings
of his home regiment, the Inniskilling Fusiliers. And he would
keep his own boots. Another good thing about it was that they
were now seen as a unit. He had been concerned that the
others had from necessity had to make camp on their return
among the rest of the army, and wondered that some had not
been discovered for the felons they were. Now, though, they
were men transformed. Men who, short of actually changing
their names, had become as anonymous as the army could
make them. In effect, they had disappeared.

Morris saw him looking at Ross. 'Really, James, you surely
must have got used to it now. It doesn't look at all bad. Quite
suits you, in point of fact.'

'You really think so? Well, I'll tell you one thing, Tom, I'm
not keeping this red. I shall be changing my facings to the

yellow of the Inniskillens as soon as I can. Better to be dressed in this now – for the business in hand.'

'Yes, tell me again, what exactly are we doing here?'

'Tom, although you are most entertaining company and I swear a genius when it comes to logistics and the timing of a fuse, and although I'm sure we shall have need of your talents ere long, it does sometimes seem to me that you might be better playing piquet at a table at Brooks's.'

Morris laughed and patted his horse's head as it whinnied. 'Such flattery. James, I know that I may seem vague, but that is only because I am so very intent upon being precise. I like to have everything in my mind just so. I need to know the finer details before I can address the whole.'

'Very well. We have been tasked with shadowing Cuesta's army. We ride on the left flank of the advance. In these uniforms we are even better placed to appear to be no more than a picket of cavalry. But you will realize that we are close enough to observe. That is, after all, our role.'

He thought for a moment and determined that this might be the time at which to ask a question which had been preying upon his mind and which up till now he had been in two minds whether to broach.

'One more thing, Tom. I don't know quite how to put this, but I can only be blunt. Are you perhaps playing the spy?'

'No more than you, James. What do you mean? What? With whom?'

Keane smiled and looked his old friend in the eye. 'Why, with me.'

Morris looked surprised and said nothing, then, 'How? How would that be?'

'Merely that Major Grant seemed to know that I was enamoured of Kitty Blackwood. Seemed to know it all. And as far as I can recollect you are the only person whom I have told.'

Morris shook his head. 'You are a fool, James Keane, a fool to think that I of all people would do such a thing and a fool not to realize that Grant must have been aware of your preoccupation with her that afternoon at Coimbra. How on earth could he not be? Indeed, how could she not be? She must be aware, James, of your feelings for her. You have not been in contact with her?'

Keane shook his head. 'No. But give me the chance, Tom.'

Morris sighed. 'I presume that Major Grant warned you off such a liaison?'

'Of course.'

'Well, there you are. It was plain to see. And you choose to ignore him?'

'Of course.'

Morris laughed. 'James, I think that must be why I like you so much. You are so very contrary.'

Keane was about to reply when he stopped himself, for up ahead the road was a mass of men. They had caught up with the rearguard of the Spanish army; directly ahead of them limped a body of blue-coated infantry. Keane gazed at them and thought that the Spanish were a ragged army indeed. Most of the regiments wore the white coats and bicorne hats of the old regime, but recent arrivals of coats from England had kitted out some of the units in blue of varying hues. These they finished with tall black-and-brown hats of a new civilian style.

Silver stared at them suspiciously. 'Blimey, sir, they look like Frenchies to me.'

'Yes, they do. An easy mistake to make and one that I dare say will cost them a few lives before this war is won. But I suspect that while they resemble the French, they may behave unlike our enemies in battle.'

'You mean they'll turn tail, sir? What's the use of us having them on our side at all, then?'

Keane shook his head. 'No, Silver, I am not suggesting that they are cowards. Far from it. Just look at Colonel Morillo's guerrillas. It is not the quality of the Spanish soldier that is in question, but that of his commanders. They're brave enough men all right. But what they need is to be trained to stand and fight. They go to it with a will, but will they stand in the face of cannon and musket? And who is to teach them? Not those wine-soused lard-bellies who lead them. That's for sure.'

They were standing now, allowing the Spanish infantry to get ahead again, and Keane was in mid flow when the clatter and jingle of the harness and sabre of the Spanish cavalry announced their presence on the flank. Tucked into the hillside, Keane and his men watched them pass below them on the road, the dust from the hooves obscuring them momentarily before they emerged in a panoply of colours, plumes and sashes. They were most like the French, he agreed with Silver. Certainly in one aspect. For while the British army dressed itself principally in red and dark blue, with the rifles of course in their green, the Spaniards and Portuguese seemed to have embraced the very sunshine of their countries. They were a riot of colours, as likely to blend into the landscape as a virgin in a brothel.

Garland whistled quietly so as not to be heard – not that he would have been, above the din. 'What a sight, sir. If they fight as good as they look the Frenchies should be running for Paris.'

'Let's pray that the French think so.'

'Sir?'

'It's show, Garland. Like Boney's men. Designed to strike fear into the heart of an enemy. But you could give me a platoon of redcoats for both those armies put together.'

Keane realized that they must be in danger of being observed themselves. He held up his hand to signal a halt and together they pulled up their mounts. They had become accomplished at reading the terrain, and although Keane would not have claimed they were even approaching the skills of the guerrillas, they all knew how to hug a contour and to attempt the impossible – making yourself invisible against the landscape. This they now set out to do, and were soon moving more cautiously, still able to observe the army below them.

They had been riding for perhaps two hours when he began to perceive that the force below them had become fragmented, strung out on the line of march. While the bulk of the Spanish infantry could be seen away to their right in a dust cloud, the regiment of cavalry they had been shadowing had ridden forward and in so doing lost contact with the bulk of the force. Too far, he reckoned, leaving the infantry's flank exposed and creating a dangerous gap between them and the following unit, a brigade of Portuguese infantry. He reined in, and taking his eyeglass from the valise, put it to his eye and scanned the road below them and to the rear. As he had suspected, there was the lead battalion of Portuguese, and he could see that they had become detached from the others, labouring to catch up with the Spaniards, who had taken a path wide of the designated route.

He turned to Morris and handed him the glass. 'Look at that. Whoever is commanding has no conception of how to conduct a route march. They're strung out. Quite broke up. If Marshal Victor's scouts are out there they'll have a field day, Tom.'

Morris kept the glass to his eye and looked at the white-coated column of Spanish marching across away from them. Then he brought it round and found the Portuguese. Finally he looked at the Spanish cavalry, trotting away to their left, and as he did so he saw something else. Something that made his heart stop.

'James, over there. Look.'

He handed the glass back to Keane, who raised it and focused on the Spanish dragoons. Then he turned it to where Morris had indicated. 'Oh, Christ. Where the deuce did they come from?'

There in the circular frame of the glass he could make out a score or more of green-coated French dragoons, their gold helmets flashing in the sun. And there were more on their heels. And they were making directly for the flank of the hapless Spanish cavalry.

'What can we do?'

'Nothing. We can do nothing. We're too far away to let them know in time. Besides, remember: we're not meant to be here.'

'Well, we can't just watch. It's as it was with the hussars, James. They'll cut the poor devils to ribbons.'

'And what can we do? Tom, we are eight men. What effect could we have?'

They watched, powerless to act, as the French dragoons neared the flank of the Spanish. Keane could almost feel the sabres slashing into flesh; see the horror in the faces of the Spanish cavalry as they realized what was happening and the blades began to rise and fall before they had a chance to react.

He was aware that in the distance, beyond where the Spanish

cavalry were being butchered, another unit, a white-coated battalion of Spanish infantry, was running hell for leather away from the fight. In any other circumstance, he thought, the commander of the dragoons would surely have ordered his men to take out this easier and more numerous prey. But it was too late for that now. The French dragoons were fixed on destroying the Spanish cavalry and nothing would stop them.

In an instant, he spun round in the saddle.

'Wait, it might just work. Well, it's worth a try, anyway.' He looked at Morris. 'Tom, we may not be able to help those poor Spanish buggers but we can do something here. Come on.'

Turning his horse, Keane spurred her forward and down the slope, breaking cover. Morris looked round at Ross and the others. 'I'm as nonplussed as you. God knows what he's doing, but we have to follow him. Come on.'

Morris dug his spurs into the flanks of his mount and she careered away after Keane, followed by the others. He could see Keane ahead of him and his friend seemed to be making for a unit of blue-coated Portuguese infantry who had halted up ahead. Morris thought that he saw his plan.

Keane was almost with the Portuguese now and the rear ranks had heard him and turned to see what was approaching. The brown-coated figure looked friendly enough. His sword was sheathed, but he was calling out to them in English, which none of them was able to understand. One of them called to an officer who came riding down the flank of the column. The man pointed and the officer stared at Keane in wonder. Keane was nearer now.

'Dragoons. French dragoons,' he shouted, first in English then in Spanish, but his words were lost on the wind. The officer tried in vain to read his lips. Finally the words reached his ears and he stared in alarm. Keane was pointing now towards the dragoons, and the man turned in the saddle. Where the Spanish cavalry had been was now a mass of billowing dust as the French horsemen collided with their prey. Both men looked on in horror as the air filled with the screams of wounded and dying men. The sun flashed on the falling blades and Keane's nightmare image became a ghastly reality.

Keane was the first to come out of the trance. 'French dragoons. The cavalry have no hope. You must form square.'

The Portuguese captain turned to him. 'You're English. I didn't recognize your uniform.'

'Captain Keane. I'm on the staff. Can't explain now. These are my men.' He pointed to his rear, knowing that the others would be close behind. 'Captain, you must form square. When the dragoons have done with the Spanish they'll come after you. Form square and we'll make them pay.'

The captain suddenly snapped into action and began to shout to his men. Sergeants and NCOs moved fast, pushing and dragging the men into line, although Keane was surprised and impressed by the way in which they moved.

'*Fazer quadrado.*'

The words rang out and within a few minutes the column was beginning to establish the only formation in which they would be able to withstand the onslaught of enemy cavalry. But this, Keane knew from his own experience, was the critical moment. If the French dragoons closed with them now, as they were engaged in the complex manoeuvre of forming a square, the Portuguese would have even less of a chance than if they had been caught in column or line. They were unformed, merely a mass of moving men, a crowd milling around and

attempting to form up. He signalled to the others and they
closed up with him. Then, moving away from the Portuguese,
he positioned himself and his small command directly between
the confused infantry and the massacre going on in the road
up ahead. There must be a full regiment of French dragoons
up there now, he thought. Close on five hundred men, perhaps,
and more than enough to make short work of both his own
men and the infantry. But if they could just buy the Portuguese
a few moments more then they would be well-nigh invincible.
It was these seconds and minutes now, as the dragoons grew
tired of their shattered prey and began to focus on another,
that were crucial. Elements of the French were sure to spy the
Portuguese infantry and to gallop across, hungry for further
blood. If he and the others could only hold them off until the
manoeuvre was complete . . .

Sure enough, as he looked on figures began to appear from
the cloud of dust and the heaving mass of bodies. Green-
coated and shining-helmeted, they paused for a moment at
the edge of the melee and then began to trot towards Keane
and his men. He called down the thin line of horsemen.
'Steady. Hold steady. We must hold here and see these fellows
off, before the others join them. Then get into the square.
Draw sabres.'

As one the men drew swords from their scabbards and
brought them to rest on their shoulders, as they had been
taught. Keane, more used to looking down a line of bayonet-
topped muskets, felt strangely proud now as he surveyed the
rank of his improvised cavalry. Behind them the Portuguese
were a mass of movement, desperately hurrying to complete
their formation change. Keane called again, watching the
Frenchmen as they increased their pace from trot through

canter to gallop. He could see their faces now, mouths open in shouts of attack, eyes mad with bloodlust. 'Ready, trot.'

He knew that they would have to be moving when the dragoons hit them and hoped there would be time. 'Gallop.' They moved quickly, changing pace, and he congratulated himself on their speed. He could make out the French uniforms now, the leopard skin on one of the saddles denoting an officer. There were eight of them, the first to break from the melee. Keane called out again and as he did so pushed Rattler on towards the enemy. 'Come on. With me.'

The dragoons had levelled their swords in the classic French attack but Keane and his men kept their sabres at the present, in the English fashion. At ten yards out the ground beneath him moved with the pounding of the hooves. At five yards he saw the horses' breath and smelt the sweat and fear of the dragoon who was making directly for him. And then the man was upon him. Keane struck at the point of the Frenchman's sabre and deflected it away with all his might. The man followed it and careered into him, almost sending him flying from the saddle. But Keane held on and with a swift single action retrieved his blade and brought it down on the left side of the dragoon's body, cutting him at the shoulder. The man screamed and looked in disbelief at the blood spurting out from his mangled limb. Keane struck again, cutting at the man's belly, and the dragoon toppled from his horse, one top-booted foot caught in the stirrup. Keane did not linger, but reined Rattler round to hit the flank of another dragoon who had raised his sword in a fight with Silver, whose counterstroke was nicely parried by the Frenchman. But he had not seen Keane and the force of the assault caught him off guard. Silver found his moment and the long, razor-sharp blade of his sword slipped quickly into the man's chest, penetrating his heart.

Silver smiled and Keane pulled away from the dead man, who slumped over the pommel of his saddle. He saw Morris take a cut to the lower arm and pull back and then, notwithstanding the wound, deliver an expert uppercut at the assailant's chin, cleaving it in two. Garland looked to be in trouble and was being attacked by two dragoons. Keane shouted to Silver, 'Help him,' and glanced at the melee. More shapes were appearing from the crowd now. Many more. Twenty, thirty at least. He looked back at the infantry and saw that the square was formed, then as Silver dispatched one of the dragoons he yelled, 'Inside the square. Get inside.'

The others turned and pushed through the parting ranks of Portuguese. Keeping his head, Keane rode up towards the rear of one of the two remaining dragoons, and raising his sword, brought it down heavily, half severing the man's neck. The other Frenchman cut and ran back towards his oncoming comrades. Watching him go, Keane called to Silver and Garland, whose forehead was bleeding and who was half hanging over his saddle, 'Get him inside the square. Come on.' Then, turning and suddenly aware that the advancing dragoons were gaining ground fast, he turned Rattler towards the square. The ranks were closed now, with muskets levelled and bayonets fixed, and knowing that there was no alternative he signalled to the Portuguese to get down. Then, pushing the mare with his stirrups, he quickened his pace and sitting well down drove her at the three ranks of infantry. Rattler responded beautifully to his request and, as she neared the front rank, who had ducked as best they could, leapt up and flew across to land in the middle of the square. Keane pulled up, hearing commands behind him and the shouts of the approaching dragoons. Before he had caught his breath there was a deafening volley of musketry.

He turned Rattler and peered into the cloud of white smoke produced by the volley. Through it he could see vague shapes of men and horses turning, rearing and collapsing. The smoke began to clear and Keane could see that four horses lay on the ground while another was sitting on its hindquarters. Among them lay a number of green-coated forms, motionless, while in the half distance another horse, minus its rider, was galloping back towards the continuing melee. Close beside it a body of dragoons stood where they had stopped, after having run from the musket fire. The melee was finished now, as were the Spanish cavalry. Looking at where the fight had taken place, all that Keane could see now were mounted dragoons riding slowly through lifeless mounds of men and horses. Occasionally a sword would rise and then fall, signalling another kill. No quarter, he thought. They had spared no one. Most of the French had reformed and clearly now their commander had spotted the Portuguese square.

Morris rode up, a piece of bloody muslin neckcloth wrapped around his forearm. 'By God, James. That was damned close. Look at them.'

'Yes. It's not a pretty sight. They gave no quarter. You're wounded, Tom.'

'It's nothing. Not much. Garland took him before he could deliver the second. All I can say is thank God we're in the square. They won't attack now.'

Keane shook his head. 'I don't know. Think about it. They've just massacred a troop of cavalry. Their blood is up. They don't give much for the Portuguese. We know that from Fabier. And if they think the square has a chance of breaking, I'm wiling to wager they'll do it.'

Morris frowned. 'Surely, James, the square won't break, though. They never do.'

'Were you there at Alexandria? Do you know how close we came to breaking then?'

'No, of course. You have the advantage of me, James. But I should be surprised if it broke. At any rate, it is the only chance we have.'

'True. And we shall find out soon enough. Look.'

The dragoons were on the move. The fugitives from the volley had regrouped and with the bulk of their comrades were forming up in several long lines facing towards the Portuguese. Morris spoke. 'D'you know, James, I believe you're right. They do intend to charge us.'

Keane yelled to his men.

'Dismount. Get down. Draw carbines.'

The men dismounted and, taking their guns from the saddle holsters, grouped around Keane. 'Better off horseback. Less of a target. We'll make a space in their ranks. Not in the front rank. The bayonet does the job there, and we've none of those. Take position in the second rank and use your shots well.'

Keane walked forward and, seeing a Portuguese officer, announced himself. 'May we join you, captain? You will need every gun.'

The man nodded and Keane led the men forward to join the second rank of the face of the square that stood opposite the dragoons. They stood together in line, with a rank of the Portuguese in front of them. They smelt of sweat and fear, every man's eyes focused on the green horror across the sandy landscape. They had planted the butts of their muskets in the

earth at a forty-five-degree angle, the bayonets pointing
skywards to impale any horse whose rider might persuade it
to attack the hedgehog of steel points.

They loaded their carbines and each made sure that they
had another ten cartridges ready to hand in their bags, as
Keane and Ross had taught them. Keane stood between Morris
on his right and Garland on his left. He bit the top of the
cartridge and poured the powder down the barrel of the carbine,
then spat down the ball. Then, taking the small ramrod from
its bracket, he pushed hard on the ball and felt it slip into
place.

The dragoons were advancing on them now, breaking into
a gallop, and for the second time that day he felt the ground
tremble under their hooves. He cocked the carbine and waited,
glancing down the line to make sure that the others were
doing the same.

The French were riding hard and from within their close-
set, boot-to-boot ranks he heard a bugle calling the charge.
Swords levelled at the horizontal they came on, and at three
hundred yards he heard a crash as one of the Portuguese pulled
the trigger in his terror. An officer shouted and he knew that
they had been trained well by their British superiors. The others
would hold their fire until it could have the maximum effect.

Still the men on the big brown horses came on. Two hundred
yards. One hundred and eighty. At around a hundred and fifty
yards Keane brought the carbine up to his cheek, its butt resting
against his shoulder, and was conscious of his men doing the
same. A moment later, the Portuguese officer gave the
command. 'Fuego.' The face of the square erupted in musket
fire and at that moment Keane's men loosed their own volley.
For a moment he was deafened. His world had become a mass

of powder smoke and ringing noise. And then it cleared. With a sudden rush, like running water, his ears cleared again and what he heard was awful. Screams of men and horses came from their front, together with the crash of hooves as the ranks behind the first, which had been brought down, continued their charge, reduced to a trot, over and into the bodies of their fallen comrades.

If the Portuguese are good enough, if our instructors have taught them well, he thought, they will fire again. He and the others were already, automatically, almost at the end of their reload. He brought the carbine up again and sure enough another Portuguese volley rent the air just as his own gun kicked back into his shoulder with the recoil of the shot.

Again the rush and again the same noise.

He wondered for an instant whether it would have been enough. Whether the dragoons would carry on and come crashing into the square and perhaps even break them. But they did not. There was nothing but screaming and whinnying and the intermittent fire of carbines as a few of the unhorsed enemy tried to shoot at their assailants through the dense white smoke.

Then it began to clear and there in front of them lay twoscore or more of dead and dying Frenchmen and their mounts. The others had turned tail and fled, officers at their heels attempting to turn them. But Keane could see there was no likelihood that any of those men were going to ride back into that murderous fire.

There was a hurrah and the Portuguese flung their shakos into the air. The captain turned to Keane and clasped his hand. 'Did you see them? We did it, senhor. We did it.'

'Well done,' said Keane for want of anything else, feeling

grateful to be alive, and then he looked to his flank to see if anyone had been hit. But he was met by nothing less than a line of grinning faces.

'Be careful, Tom,' he said to Morris. 'They might not have had enough.'

And sure enough the dragoons were turning back now, forming up. But he could not be sure whether it was their intention to attack once more or simply to quit the field. They stood still, as if weighing up the odds, and within seconds he was sure that it was the latter. He heard a bugle call retire and saw officers rallying their men, and just at that moment another sound made him turn his head to the rear of the square. A huzzahing and hallooing that might more likely have been heard on the hunting field. Cavalry. And it could only mean British cavalry, at that. Staring, he began to see forms on the track to their rear. Cavalry in parcels of five or six men, one or perhaps two troops in all, wearing the blue tunic and Tarleton helmet of the Light Dragoons.

They came galloping past the square, hollering and shouting, their curved sabres whipping the air high above their heads. And as they flew past it was clear where they were heading. The French dragoons had seen them too now and, still reforming, seemed for a moment frozen to the spot. Then almost as if by magic they began to ride away, trying desperately to outrun the British cavalry before they hit.

Keane watched as the British made good ground and saw the leading troop smash into the almost stationary French, scattering bodies and horses as they did so. But the bulk of the French dragoons were well on their way now, back over the hills to the left from which they had come, keen to put any distance they could between them and the English cavalry. Keane looked for a moment longer and then turned to Ross.

'Sarn't, I think we might stand down now. Well done, all of you.' He watched as the Portuguese did the same, the men drawing straw-covered bottles and canteens from their haversacks. He found Heredia. 'Ask the captain if he has any rum, will you? We could all do with something.'

Heredia found the Portuguese captain, who laughed and pointed him towards his sergeant major before walking over to Keane. 'I'm sorry, captain. Bad manners. Perhaps you would prefer some of this.'

He held out an engraved silver flask to Keane, who thanked him and took a long draught of what turned out to be a surprisingly fine port. He was about to thank the captain again when he was aware of a horseman having ridden into the square. The newcomer rode across to the two men and, leaning down from the saddle, reached out for the captain's flask, which Keane surrendered.

Taking it, the man spoke as Keane rose to meet his gaze. 'Thank you, captain. Gentlemen. May I toast your good fortune?'

And Keane found himself staring up into the grinning face of Charles Blackwood.

# 14

Sir Arthur Wellesley frowned and rubbed at his forehead in a way that he was sometimes accustomed to do when he was, as now, profoundly troubled. 'You say, Captain Keane, that you had beaten off the French dragoons before Captain Blackwood attacked them?'

'Yes, sir. They were unformed, demoralized and quite ready to quit the field.'

'And yet you say that Captain Blackwood led an attack on these men. Men who to all intents and purposes were already *hors de combat*?'

'Yes, sir.'

'Most interesting, Keane.'

Wellesley folded his hands behind his back and walked a few paces. 'You may know, Keane, that Captain Blackwood has already made his report to me of the affair.'

'Yes, sir, I was aware that might be the fact. He gained a day's march on us, in his hurry to rejoin the army.'

Grant, who all the while had been standing close to Wellesley, gave a snigger. They stood in the shade of a tree on the spot that the commander-in-chief had chosen for his headquarters that day. Wellesley glared at Grant and chose to ignore the slight. 'And what do you suppose that Captain Blackwood might have told me in his report?'

'I would suppose, sir, that it might have alluded to the fact that Captain Blackwood, on hearing the sound of gunfire on the army's left flank, and being in close proximity to that position for reasons of his own, had ridden to the aid of the beleaguered Portuguese and had found a square under attack from the French. It might also have suggested that the square might have been about to break had it not been for the timely intervention of Captain Blackwood's troop.'

Wellesley smiled , but his response was terse. 'Two troops, to be precise, Keane. Captain Blackwood, by virtue of a brevet rank, was in command of two troops at the time. Yes, clearly you do possess the spy's acuity for being able to anticipate prevarication and detect possible subterfuge.'

'Sir?'

'Keane, do you suppose that I should be more prepared to believe your story or that of Captain Blackwood?'

'I'm sure I don't know, sir.'

Wellesley smiled. 'Don't know, eh? Diplomacy, Keane, is most certainly one of your strong suits.'

He looked across at Grant and then back at Keane. 'I am fully aware, Keane, of your vendetta with Blackwood and everything involved in it. Everything. And I expressly forbid any further meetings with his sister. Is that quite clear?'

Keane reddened. 'Sir, I can hardly think that I need to be commanded not to engage in the pursuit of happiness.'

'I am not asking you to curtail your happiness, Keane. I am merely instructing you not to exacerbate a situation which is already far beyond any that I will tolerate in my army. I will not have officers engaging with one another in personal vendettas. Do you understand?'

Keane nodded. 'Yes, sir, of course.'

'You will comply with my orders, captain?'

'Of course, sir. I would not go against your orders.'

'Very well. That's settled, then. And as you will be aware, I am more inclined to favour your description of events than that of Captain Blackwood. You say the Spanish will not fight, but that the Portuguese will.'

'Yes, sir. Given British commanders, they will fight and die where they stand. They are good soldiers, sir. I am sure that the Spanish too are valiant. But they are poorly led. It is as you supposed, sir. They have no spirit for a fight in which they know that their own officers will quit the field first.'

'You swear that you saw them run?'

'I saw an entire battalion break and run on seeing their cavalry attacked and cut to pieces by the French. Yes, sir.'

'Strong stuff, captain, if you can prove it. And you really wish me to believe this?'

'I do, sir.'

'Then I shall take your word as an exploring officer in good faith, Keane. You have done well. And as to the other matter, let that be an end to it.'

Wellesley turned back to Grant. 'Major Grant, it would seem from Captain Keane's account that we are unable to rely upon General Cuesta's forces.'

'Indeed it would. But the captain is right, sir. The Spanish, like our Portuguese allies, are a valiant people. Even as we speak many of them are flocking to the colours. They do wish to fight the French. And we can rely upon the guerrillas, Sir Arthur.'

'Yes, Grant, I am aware of that. And we need men like Captain Keane here to keep them on our side, do we not?'

'Indeed, sir. He is invaluable.'

Keane made the most of the moment. 'Do you wish me to take my men out again, sir? On the same mission?'

'We will continue to advance, captain, and you will continue to monitor the progress of General Cuesta's force. Yes, if you will. Rejoin the column and this time it will not matter whether or not you are in evidence. General Cuesta, I fancy, will have heard about your exploits from his own sources.'

'I am certain of it, sir, but I hope very soon to hear more of him. I have a man at this moment in his camp.'

It was barely ten miles from Wellesley's tree to the private house which Cuesta had requisitioned as his own temporary headquarters. He had chosen the only fine dwelling in the district, presuming that with it might come the contents of a cellar. He was not wrong.

Charles Blackwood took another sip from the chilled glass of twenty-year-old white Rioja which the general had been pleased to offer him and smiled across the table. 'As I was telling you, general, it was then that I seized the moment and took my dragoon with a swift uppercut to the face. Felt the sabre slice straight through the man's teeth. Hiss. Something like that. God, it's a bloody affair, doing battle, don't you agree, general?'

General Cuesta called to the servant to pour more wine. The man, not his usual orderly but a swarthy-looking fellow in the uniform of a Spanish grenadier with a handkerchief tied about his head, poured with a flourish. Cuesta, white-faced at the captain's gory accounts of his recent skirmish, took a hasty gulp from his glass and smiled at Blackwood. 'Yes, captain, a bloody business indeed. But we are men of steel, are we not? More wine?'

Blackwood stretched out his arm and accepted as the steward poured. He drank and spoke again. 'You are aware that a British officer is putting the word around that it was not I who saved the battalion, but himself?'

'Yes, you mentioned the fact. What was his name?'

'Goes by the name of Keane. An Irishman. A very forward fellow. Full of self-importance and desperate to get on. No money, you see. Lost the lot gambling away the family estate. Dreadful thing to do. And now it would seem he's lying to get the general's ear.'

Cuesta shook his head. 'Some men know no honour, captain. I will speak of him with General Wellesley when next we meet.'

'You are kind, general. That will be a great service to the British army. And you may be as disparaging as you please. I would not as a rule be so very uncharitable to a brother officer. But you do see that his word would have it that I simply exploited his victory, when as you and I know it was I and my own brave boys who chased off those Frenchies, risking our lives to save the poor, hapless Portuguese. How they got themselves into that position in the first place is my wonder. I'm sure that none of your own Spanish officers would have mishandled the action so.'

Cuesta grinned at him. 'You are so right, captain. My officers are professionals. Not like these fools of Portugueses. They even need your officers to train them. Which I am sure is most helpful. But don't they have their own men to do such a thing?'

'Presumably not, or they would not need our help. They

might quite easily have broken, especially with Keane whooping around and terrifying them out of order.'

'Yes. It really was an appalling way for an officer to behave.'

Blackwood took another drink.

'Yes. As a matter of fact, I intend to bring charges against Captain Keane.'

'You do?'

'Yes. It is evident that the officer in question was reckless in the extreme. His action endangered the safety of the entire column. What was he thinking of? Riding on the flank and coming in unannounced? He was foolish in his handling of the situation and has been more so ever since. I do not treat lies lightly, general. It is a question of honour. The man must be cashiered. He is a rogue, sir. A scoundrel who should never have been given a commission in the British army. I shall have him out, sir, I tell you. He will leave in dishonour.'

'What puzzles me is that he should have been on the flank of the army at all. What was he doing there with his handful of men?'

'You don't know? He is a spy, sir.'

'A spy? Was he spying on my men?'

Cuesta called for more wine, but on looking up saw the bottle sitting on the campaign chest. Of the steward there was no sign.

In their small bivouac close to the lines, Keane stood in his tent with Morris and Ross and questioned Gilpin. 'And you heard all this, just as you can hear me now?'

'Just the same, sir. The Spanish general was sitting there plain as day and Captain Blackwood was spouting out such slander against you. It was all I could do to bear to hear it.'

'You say he claimed that it was his men who beat off the French.'

'Yes, sir.'

'And that he was going to bring charges?'

'Yes, sir.'

'You did well, Gilpin. You may go.'

Keane turned to Morris. 'This is bad, Tom. The man seems bent on ruining me.'

'Quite so, James, and I wonder what we can do to prevent him.'

'There may be nothing to be done. Unless he can come by some accident.'

Morris looked at him. 'James, don't be foolhardy. We will think of some means—'

Suddenly they heard shouting. It seemed to be coming from a good distance away from the bivouac. Both men moved to the tent entrance and listened.

'Sounds like trouble,' said Keane, and together they advanced towards the noise, but it was not until they drew closer that they were able to recognize the raised voices. They heard Heredia first.

'You are lying. My countrymen are brave soldiers. We do not need you here. We will send the French from our home.'

Another voice joined in. Silver. 'You're the liar. You dago. Your bloody Spanish general's a coward. The only reason your bloody infantry didn't run was 'cause they'd been told not to by one of our commanders. They'll only fight with an Englishman in charge. That's all you lot – Portos, Spanish, the lot. If it hadn't been for our officers teaching you the proper ways then you'd all be dead. You're nothing without us.'

'Nothing? Have you looked at where you have spent the last

few weeks? Have you seen my country? How do you call it nothing?'

''Cause that's what it is. Nothing. Can't even speak English, can you? But you're happy enough to have us die for you. And to screw our women in the camp. I know where you've been, Mister Heredia. Down the alley with our women, haven't you?'

Keane was hurrying now, trying to push through the crowd of soldiers and followers that had gathered around the argument, anticipating the coming fight. But it was too late. He heard the thud as someone's fist crashed into bone. And then another, and by the time he managed to get to the edge of the crowd they were hard at it, fists flying and arms flailing in a vicious bare-knuckled brawl.

Keane yelled at them. 'Stop! Stop that now. Both of you.'

But either he went unheard or they chose to ignore him. Heredia's fist smashed against the side of Silver's jaw, sending the man reeling backwards, but the Englishman managed to recover and charged towards the trooper, headbutting him in the diaphragm and sending him sprawling before landing on top of him. Silver smashed a fist into Heredia's nose and the blood spurted out. Silver was kneeling on him now, shouting, 'Get up, you dago dog. I'll bloody kill you.'

The Portuguese pushed Silver off and rose to his feet, fists flying, one of them catching Silver in the eye.

The crowd was cheering now and Keane pushed through and stood just a few paces away from the milling men. He was about to intervene when a huge hand landed on Silver's shoulder and dragged him off Heredia, throwing him to the floor. Another arm went up and the flat of his hand took the full force of one of Heredia's punches without flinching.

Behind him was Ross.

'You're both on a charge. You filthy soldiers. Get up. Both of you.'

He saw Keane. 'Sir, sorry, sir. They were at it before I knew.'

Keane nodded. 'Yes, sarn't. Get them both cleaned up and I'll see them in half an hour.' He looked behind Ross to where Heredia was rising from the ground and saw a knife in his hand. 'Look out, Silver. Watch him.'

Silver turned just as Heredia launched himself at him, but it was Gilpin who was there, pushing himself between the two men. He caught Heredia by the arm and twisted his wrist, making the knife fall to the ground.

Garland was on them too, now. But Keane pushed forward and pulled them apart.

Heredia, his eyes rolling with anger, was held back by Garland as Ross looked at him. 'You bloody fool. What the hell did you think you were doing?'

Heredia struggled against Garland's grip and Ross shook his head.

'No, laddie, that's not right. I can't have fighting among us. Not right, see. Not for Captain Keane.'

Heredia pushed one arm free from Garland and managed to take another step towards Silver, but before either man could do anything there was a piercing scream from behind them, followed by a woman's voice cursing in Portuguese.

Heredia shrugged and Silver turned to see his wife. 'Bloody hell. What are you doing here?'

She screamed again in Portuguese and Silver answered her. Then she shouted at Heredia, who had become calm now.

The crowd had dispersed, with the prospect of any more bloodshed now gone. Keane walked across to her. 'Gabriella? I thought you were to stay at Abrantes.'

'Yes, sir, but I had to come.'

'You came after your husband?'

'No, sir, I came to find you.'

Keane was taken aback. 'Me? What do you want from me?'

'A woman, sir, she came to the camp asking for you. A fine lady. Very beautiful, with black hair and lovely eyes. A yellow dress. She found me.'

Keane felt his heart pounding. Kitty? 'Where is she now, this lady?'

'She came to the army, sir. She said she would find Major Grant. I told her you would be close to him.'

'You did well, Gabriella. Now go to your husband and stay with him if you will. I might have need of you later.'

He turned to Heredia and Silver. 'Sarn't Ross. As I said, I'll see them both at my tent in half an hour.'

Keane walked back to his tent and, sitting at the low camp chair that stood beside the folding table, rubbed at his eyes and smoothed back his hair. Both men would have to be punished somehow, though how he would manage that when both were needed on campaign, the devil only knew. Suddenly their fate and the whole affair had been diminished by the news of Kitty, and now there was only one thing on his mind. He would have to find her. To do that, though, he knew that he must return to Grant. But how, he wondered, was he to do that without alerting Wellesley to their meeting? For almost half an hour he sat pondering the problem but he had still not found a solution when Ross entered the tent.

'Beggin' your pardon, sir, but I've got them here, sir.'

Keane looked up and stubbed out on the tent floor the slim cheroot he had been smoking. 'Bring them in, sarn't.'

Heredia and Silver walked into the tent and came to attention. They had scrubbed up, but although the traces of blood had been washed from their faces, Silver's swollen and blackened eye and Heredia's smashed nose still bore the evidence of their fight.

Keane stared at them for just long enough to unsettle them, and then spoke. 'You're a pair of bloody fools.' They stared at the floor. 'Why the devil get into a fight over something so stupid?'

Silver spoke. 'He started it, sir. Said that it was us as was saved by the Portos. Sorry, the Portuguese, sir.'

Keane cut him short. 'Whoever started it does not matter now. What matters is that we cannot have any discord between our two armies, certainly none involving brawling of that sort. I won't have it. Were we not on the march I would award you both a hundred lashes apiece, and I am not a flogging man. As it is, I cannot do so, so I will have to content myself with a lesser punishment. You will each donate ten silver crowns to the company funds forthwith. Give the money to Sarn't Ross. Dismissed.'

Heredia spoke. 'Sir, I am sorry for what we did. Truly. I meant nothing by it.'

'I'd like to believe you, Heredia, but I'm not sure that I do. And you, Silver. How can I trust you? Tell me that.'

'You can, sir. Of course you can. Please don't send me back to the jail, sir. Please. I won't do it again and nor will he. Will you?'

Heredia nodded. 'No, captain, I will not. We will not fight, sir. It is hard for us. The French take everything and it is hard for a proud people to ask for help. But I know the British are good, sir.'

'Very well, but the fine still stands. Sarn't Ross, see to it. Dismiss.'

Silver turned to go, but Heredia hung back. Keane looked up from the order book in which he had written a record of the punishments. 'Yes?'

'May I see you, sir? In private?'

Ross did not move.

Keane spoke. 'Has this anything to do with Private Silver? If it has, then you will merely dig yourself a deeper hole.'

'No, sir. Nothing at all. I have some information, sir, and I think the time has come to give it to you.'

Keane congratulated himself. He had, thanks to his impromptu interview with Heredia, managed to engineer a private meeting with Grant. And where Grant was, it was likely that Kitty Blackwood might also be. He walked the half-mile from their bivouac to Grant's, thinking as he went. Keane was confused. Why, he wondered, should Kitty Blackwood come to look for him? Surely it was too much to hope that she might be pursuing him. Wasn't it? His mind whirled. As he entered the staff lines he was challenged by a sentry, confused at his uniform, but he managed to talk his way through. Grant's tent lay a short distance away from that of the commander-in-chief, and he hoped that Wellesley would be too preoccupied to encounter him before he had found Kitty. In any case, he had the perfect reason for being here. Heredia had imparted some information that had to be passed on to Grant.

He entered the tent and found the major with a bottle of wine. 'Ah, Keane, a glass?' He nodded to his servant. 'Cornish, a glass for Captain Keane.' He motioned to Keane to take a seat and, as soon as he had, began to speak. 'Your message said that you had new information. What is it? More on the Spanish?'

Keane shook his head. 'No, sir. It is more serious. I am informed that we have a spy in our midst.'

Grant laughed. 'Of course we do. Yourself.'

The servant poured the wine and Keane drank a draught and spoke. 'No, sir. This is a grave matter. One of my men has reason to believe that he was incriminated and imprisoned to cover up the presence of a French spy within the general staff.'

Grant put down his glass and as he did so his smile disappeared. 'You're serious?'

'Quite.'

'Who is this man?'

'Heredia. I plucked him out of the military prison at Coimbra on the advice of Captain Scovell.'

'Can you trust him?'

'I believe I can.'

'If he's right, then that might explain the fact that Marshal Victor appears to know our movements. If he's wrong, then he will surely hang.'

'I think he knows that, sir. He is willing to swear that when he was taken for theft, he had just discovered secret French plans with the seal of the emperor in the valise of an officer on the staff.'

'And he knows this man by name?'

'Yes.' Keane paused. 'He swears that it was Colonel William Pritchard.'

Grant raised an eyebrow. 'Pritchard? Have we any proof?'

'None, sir, of which I am aware.'

'It's a grave charge, Keane. Will you stand by your man?'

'I will, sir. I have no reason to doubt him. Unless of course

he has some other cause for a vendetta with the colonel out-
with my knowing.'

'That of course is a possibility. Pritchard, eh? We must have
proof before we act.'

'The only proof I can present is that Heredia was falsely
accused.'

Grant was still thoughtful. 'It would confirm my worst fears.
I have wondered for some time about Pritchard. He seems
constantly nervous. On the alert. I had taken it for battle fatigue
– his being worn out. But this gives a new angle. You do know
that Captain Scovell was acting on my advice when he ordered
Heredia's release? Our problem, Keane, is how we ascertain
whether Pritchard is indeed the spy and how we force him to
reveal himself.'

'There must be a means of doing it, sir.' Keane thought for
a moment.

'I have it. If one of my men were to become attached to
Pritchard's staff, he might observe the colonel and expose him.'

Grant mused. 'It's possible. Who could do it?'

'Morris, sir. He's an officer and he has the right manner for
the staff. He would be our man. We could have him appointed
as an extraordinary exploring officer to General Beresford.'

Grant said nothing, then. 'Very well. That is what we'll do.
Inform your man of our intentions and bring him to see me.'

'Is there time, sir? We march tomorrow, do we not?'

'Indeed we do, James. And we must unmask this man, if he
exists, as soon as the coming fight allows us. Although, as you
say, I doubt it will be possible before we engage the enemy.
The damage is done for now. I shall take it upon myself to
watch the colonel in the coming engagement. Your man will
be in place in good time, God willing.'

He took another drink and then fixed Keane with an unflinching stare. 'I had thought that you might have come here for another reason.'

'Sir?'

Grant smiled at him. 'You are an extraordinary man, Keane.'

'Sir?'

'God knows how you achieved it.'

'I'm sorry, sir, you have me at a disadvantage.'

'Miss Blackwood, James. She appeared here this morning and is billeted close to the general. How the devil did you contrive to have her follow us here?'

'I did?'

'Don't play the innocent, Keane, it doesn't suit you. You know quite well to what I refer. You realize that this is against the general's orders?'

'Sir, I admit that I agreed to it, but in truth, major, how can one order the heart?'

'The heart, is it? I had thought that it was quite another area of sensibility in you to which Miss Blackwood appealed.'

Keane shook his head. 'Either way, sir, what harm is there in it?'

'You know damn well the harm in it, Keane. Take my advice and do not attempt to speak to her. Return to your bivouac.'

'You know that I cannot do that, sir.'

Grant shook his head and smiled. 'I know, but it was worth trying, don't you think? Good luck, Keane. Until tomorrow. And be careful.'

Keane left the tent. Grant had let slip that Kitty's tent was close to that of Wellesley, as he would have expected. He turned and began to walk towards the commander's bivouac, hoping that the general would not be about and wondering what on earth he would say to Kitty Blackwood if and when he did find her.

He had not gone more than ten yards, however, when he heard a voice calling his name. He looked in its direction and saw Cuevillas walking towards him.

'Captain Keane, I was sure it was you.'

'Cuevillas, what brings you here? I thought that you and your men were in the hills.'

Cuevillas shook his head and shrugged. 'Not any more. We have come to give our support to General Cuesta.'

'Cuesta's camp is ten miles distant. In the north. Our left flank.'

'Yes, I know. I wanted to come here first, though.'

'For what reason, I wonder?'

'I have a number of reasons, captain, but since you ask, I wanted to see you again.'

Keane smiled. 'Why on earth should you wish to see me?'

'To tell you that I have not forgotten about the silver, captain. And the fact that you stole from me what should rightly be mine.'

'I stole nothing, Cuevillas. We gained a bounty of war by fair means. It was not yours. It belongs to Spain and to the British army.'

Cuevillas spat on the ground and wiped his mouth with the back of his hand. 'It belongs to me, captain. Don't forget that. For I will not.'

'If that is a threat, then it is worthless. The money is already with General Wellesley.'

'Aside from what you took for yourself and your men, eh?'

Keane was losing his patience. 'I don't have to listen to this slander, sir. If you want to call me out you know where to find me.'

'But you do not know where to find me, Captain Keane. You think you know the ways of my people, but you do not. You never will. I will get my money, captain. One day, when you are not expecting it, you will find me there. I swear it.'

Keane laughed. 'You can make as many threats as you like, Cuevillas. You don't frighten me. You're nothing but a bandit and that's what you will always be. I had hoped we might be comrades. But it seems that you are too concerned with what you can get for yourself from this war and not with driving the French from your country.'

Cuevillas took a pace towards him and Keane's hand went to his sword hilt. The Spaniard spoke, growling out the words, 'How dare you? I have told you, Keane. I will come for you.'

One of the sentries at Grant's tent had been watching their exchange and, having seen Keane's hand slip onto his sword, advanced towards them. 'Everything all right, sir?'

Keane smiled at him. 'Fine, sarn't. Fine. Just saying goodnight to the captain here.' He turned to Cuevillas. 'Isn't that right, Cuevillas? You were just going, were you not?'

Cuevillas smirked. 'Yes, I was. Until we meet again, captain.'

He turned and walked away from them through the line of tents. Keane turned to the sergeant of the guard. 'Thank you, sarn't. But as you could see, we had no quarrel.'

'Right, sir, goodnight.'

'Goodnight to you, sarn't.'

As the man returned to his post, Keane continued towards Wellesley's tent, unsettled by his encounter with Cuevillas but now more determined than ever to attempt to find Kitty Blackwood.

He was stopped by hearing his name called. A woman's voice. 'Captain Keane?'

He turned and saw her. Kitty Blackwood stood framed against the white outline of Grant's tent. She was as pretty as he remembered her. Prettier, perhaps. He stopped, unable to move, and then, clumsily he thought, walked towards her.

'Miss Blackwood, isn't it? What on earth brings you here? This is no place for a lady.'

'I came to find my brother and I thought that, being his friend, you might know his whereabouts.'

'Surely you might have had that information from Major Grant?'

She smiled, aware that she had been found out, but far from annoyed at the fact. 'Major Grant is a friend of my father's, Captain Keane, as is General Wellesley, but I did not want to trouble either of them.'

'No, it is just as well that you did not. They have a war to fight.'

'Don't you all?'

Keane laughed. 'Why yes, of course. You must not stay here for long, though. Where will you sleep?'

'Major Grant has arranged that. I have a maid and two footmen with me.'

'I'm afraid that you have come in vain. Your brother, I believe, is with General Cuesta on the left flank.'

She smiled and in an instant he knew her reason to be a pretext. 'It is pleasant though to see you again, captain.'

'And you, Miss Blackwood.'

'You must call me Kitty.'

'And I am James.'

For a moment they said nothing. Then Keane laughed. 'If you would allow me to escort you back to your quarters, I would be most honoured.'

'Of course. That would be my pleasure.'

She extended her arm and Keane took it gently, trying not to grasp too tight, although that was what he wanted most to do.

Together they walked through the lines until they came to a tent, not far off, by the provosts, outside which stood two redcoats of the Foot Guards.

'This is my home tonight, James.'

Keane let go of her arm and she smiled at him. He spoke. 'When we return to Coimbra, I would be honoured if you would allow me to call upon you in Lisbon.'

She smiled again. 'Of course. I should like that very much.'

He was about to turn and go when, on an impulse, she pulled him to her and in an instant he had kissed her. It was over in a moment, and both of them drew away for a second. But then Keane put his arm around her and kissed her again. And this time neither of them was inclined to stop. And when eventually they did, they looked at each other, aware of what had happened. Keane could not think what to say and eventually it was Kitty who spoke. 'If you see my brother do remember me to him, will you? I am so glad that you are friends.'

'Yes,' said Keane. 'I will, of course. So am I. Till Lisbon, then.'

She smiled at him and placed her hand on his for a moment. Then she turned and entered her tent and Keane walked away, aware that once again he had done that which he had regretted so many times in his life and lied to the person he loved.

And at the same moment, unseen in the darkness, just a short distance away, Ignacio Alonzo, the man they called Cuevillas, thanked fate for having shown him the path to revenge and set off on the ten-mile ride to General Cuesta's camp.

# 15

The morning brought news. Keane was awakened in his tent by Ross. He had been dreaming of Kitty. He had been stroking her pale shoulders and running his fingers though her hair, and the sight of the ruddy-faced Scotsman at his bedside came as something of a shock.

'Sarn't Ross?'

'Sir.'

'What the devil's going on?'

'That's just it, sir. The very devil is going on. Our cavalry have found Marshal Victor, sir, and the advance guard of the First Division went in last night.'

'What on earth's the time, man?'

'Oh, it's not late, sir. It's just them lads in the First as was early. It's touching six o'clock.'

Keane climbed from the folding bed and pulled on his overalls, buttoning up the flies as he spoke. 'Get the men fell in, sarn't.'

'Have done, sir.'

'Very good, then get me a mug of tea, will you?'

Keane ran through the events in his mind. So, he thought,

the scouts had found the French. That was as had been hoped. As he had gone to bed the previous night, word had come from Grant that the plan had changed. There was no longer to be a general advance. Wellesley intended to attack Marshal Victor in the flank to the north-east, while Cuesta would take him in a frontal assault on the road to Madrid.

The attack would go in at dawn. About 4 a.m. That, then, was surely what had happened. Their own role had remained undefined, but Keane guessed that it would be to report back from the Spanish camp, and was fully expecting to be ordered across to Cuesta. The prospect did not wholly fill him with excitement, for there he would surely find both Cuevillas and Blackwood.

Restored by the tea, Keane found the men waiting outside the tent. Morris came across.

'Sounds bad, James. Apparently the Spaniards didn't move as directed in the night. Wellesley rode across to Cuesta at three o'clock and the man refused to move. He wouldn't attack, James. What of that?'

'It's no more than I would have expected. We knew that might be the case.'

'Now our advance guard has had to pull back. Wellesley's furious.'

As he finished speaking Major Grant appeared and beckoned to Keane. 'Keane, a word.'

They walked a few paces away from the others. 'You've heard about last night's fiasco?'

'Yes, sir. It was as we thought.'

'Yes, the general is obliged to you and I'm quite sure that he wishes he had acted more fully on your advice. Marshal Victor has gone.'

'Gone, sir?'

'Gone. He's pulled back towards Madrid.'

'So surely we must follow him and give battle?'

Grant shook his head. 'Wellesley would have done so, but now he will not. It is as you said. We cannot trust the Spanish to advance alongside us. They are wholly undependable.'

'So we have no alternative but to sit here?'

'For the present, yes. General Cuesta is in a flying rage. Having refused to advance this morning, he now believes that we can chase Victor all the way to Madrid.'

'That's not good, sir, as I understand it.'

'It's not good at all, Keane. And I shall tell you what's worse. I believe that Cuesta will want to carry it off himself. I'll wager that even now his army is striking camp and going after Victor. He wants all the glory, Keane, and damn the consequences.'

Keane grinned. 'I have a feeling, sir, that you are about to detail my instructions.'

Grant laughed. 'James, you read me like a book. Am I so very transparent?'

'Not at all, sir. I merely presume that my men and myself might have some special function in this operation.'

'Your presumption is well made, James. General Wellesley has a task for you. He wants nothing to do with Cuesta's folly. But he must know exactly what the man is doing.'

'So he wants us once again to be his shadow?'

'Well, yes, you might say that. A discreet reconnaissance is how we might put it. And you are to take a squadron of Portuguese horse with you. They're good men, tried and tested.'

'Yes, you perhaps forget, sir, I have one of them among my own. Heredia.'

'Ah, yes. And for the moment, James, we must delay the

matter of which we spoke yesterday. Lieutenant Morris's new appointment.'

'I presumed as much, sir. And when do we start on this mission?'

'Precisely now, I'm afraid, James. You have no time to lose. We believe that Cuesta is on the move and you must get across to him immediately.'

Blackwood had found Victor. And he would contrive to claim the glory for himself. Of course, he would not take in his own men until Cuesta's soldiers had done the job. Oh, there would be losses, but not among his squadron. They would charge in as the French lay prone and cut them to pieces.

And Keane knew that there was more than martial glory here for Blackwood.

He knew that by now Cuevillas would have told him of his feelings for Kitty, and Keane knew that his sister's honour was excuse enough to finish a business. Somehow, when their paths next crossed – and he knew it would be soon – one of them would die.

Keane had been watching General Cuesta's army for a while now. He had watched from the surrounding hills, above the marching columns, as the man had blundered boldly and blindly onwards until at last he had stumbled upon Marshal Victor.

As he watched, the Spanish army to his right began to move into assault formation. It always impressed him to see such a manoeuvre. How seamlessly the move could be made from column of march to column of attack and then, when the time came, to line. As he looked at the Spanish, however, he realized with a sinking feeling just how different they were from the redcoats. Even the Portuguese he had seen move better.

Keane watched as the first Spanish attack went in, only to be pushed back, and now a second was taking its place. The French gunners were cutting swathes through the white-coated ranks, but much to their credit the Spaniards were pushing forward. Perhaps, he thought, this would do it, and then Cuesta would unleash his own cavalry and he would lead his men in with them, cutting and slashing at the French foot until the fields ran with their blood.

Then, as he watched, a third Spanish column marched into the attack and he could see to his right a regiment of Cuesta's cuirassiers preparing to follow up.

Behind them he could make out what looked like a regiment of British Light Dragoons. He rubbed at his eyes and then raised the glass again. Sure enough, that was exactly what they were. He wondered whether they might be Blackwood's men.

The French had broken now, were fleeing back towards the rear. The Light Dragoons, though, did not stop, but went after them, bringing them down even as they ran.

Keane had seen the new French army that had cut across from the north and had sent two men, Martin and Silver, to identify it. Their news, on their breathless return, had been grim.

They had made out the insignia of two units, the 28th Infantry and a regiment of Polish lancers. Keane had checked with the written descriptions given him by Scovell. These were Sebastiani's men. The general had come to Victor's aid. The listed strength lay at 30,000 all arms. That made a total of more than 50,000 Frenchmen before them. And Cuesta had found them with no more than his own wing of barely 30,000.

But it was too late now. Much too late to retreat. The Spanish general had committed his men to the battle.

They had gone in in force, unaware of the threat to their flank. It had taken time, but it seemed to Keane for a moment that Cuesta might just have a chance against Victor before Sebastiani closed in. He even spotted a charge by a unit of blue-coated cavalry as they smashed their way though a French battalion. But then Jerome had begun to move and within minutes the field presented a very different prospect.

Morris caught the mood. 'What should we do, James? We can hardly hope to turn back that tide single-handed, can we?'

Keane shook his head. 'No. I do not intend to sacrifice these men. If there were something – anything – I could do, believe me, I would.'

As he spoke he saw a block of French horsemen slip down a hill on the army's left flank and charge into the turning flank of the Light Dragoons who had laid into the French with such gusto only a short time ago. Their fight seemed to be a little divorced from the main fight and it was clear that they were outnumbered by the French to the tune of three squadrons to one. Keane thought for a moment and then spoke again to Morris. 'You know, I do think there could be something we might do. We might save those poor brave devils down there from being cut to pieces by the French. We have a squadron. We could take them in the flank. Counter-attack and drive them off.'

He looked for Martin. 'You and Gilpin ride like the devil back to Wellesley. Tell him that Sebastiani has come across and Cuesta's in trouble.'

As the two men sped off, Keane turned his horse and rode back to the young officer in command of the squadron of

Portuguese cavalry. 'Lieutenant, I intend to support that unit down there against attack. Have your men follow me.' The young man looked terrified and merely nodded at Keane, who found Heredia and spoke low, pointing to the Portuguese officer. 'Take care of him, will you. He'll listen to you.'

He looked to Ross. 'Sarn't Ross, we are going into that melee. We are to stay just as long as it takes to give those French hussars a bloody nose and turn them away, and then we are to retire. Is that clear?'

'Clear enough, sir.'

'Right, draw sabres.'

The men drew their swords from their scabbards and Keane was gratified to hear the Portuguese do the same. He gave the command, 'Advance,' and began to trot forward down the slope. They followed him, all of them, and within a few seconds they had broken into a canter. Reaching the foot of the hill they sped up, and the French hussars barely had the chance to look before Keane and the Portuguese were upon them. And it was then that he saw him. There was no mistaking that aquiline, aristocratic nose. For a moment he was tempted to wonder whether there might not be some way in which, in the fog of battle, he might kill Blackwood. But then he remembered his promise to Kitty and knew that he could never face her again, let alone make love to her as he longed to, and still play the lie. So he spurred on and called to the others.

And then he was lost in the crush.

For a few minutes their world became a heaving mass of men on horses, all of them wearing blue coats, distinguishable only by the shape of their headgear. Arms rose and fell, and as they did so the dreadful sabres found their mark. The chop and slice of so many cleavers became a blur as Keane was aware of the tiredness in his arm and the smell of sweat and blood, and the look of fear and hatred in the eyes of his enemies.

And just when he thought that they might be giving way and that the day was lost, there was a sudden surge from the right and the French seemed to judder in their disorganized mass. He managed to look through the men and saw on the far side of the melee a new element in the crush. Scores, perhaps hundreds, of peasants, armed with all manner of guns and weapons, had run into the French cavalry and were bringing down men, hauling them from their mounts and driving staves and lances into the beasts themselves like some vision of a medieval battle. Guerrillas, he thought. These must be Cuevillas's men. And it occurred to him that here in this melee were the two men who in all the world had most cause to hate him.

And then quite suddenly it seemed that the hussars were pulling back. Keane found himself on the other side of the melee, facing no one but the Spanish army. And Cuesta's regiments too were on the move. Coming backwards, in as orderly a fashion as they could manage, most of them. But certainly also as fast as they could get away from the French.

Silver found him. 'You all right, sir? Look, they're bloody running away. After we tried to help them.'

'We didn't help them, Silver, but a squadron of our own men. And it is the guerrillas who have helped us.'

Keane pulled Rattler back towards the fight but he knew that the French had had enough. He rode on in search of his men and had just spotted Silver and Martin when he felt a sudden thump in his arm. Looking down, he saw that he had been shot. It was not bad: a pistol shot, not that of a carbine, but it was enough to make him drop his sword so that it hung useless from the knot around his wrist. Silver had seen it. 'Sir. You're hit.' He reached over and grabbed hold of Keane, and as he looked up towards where the bullet had come from saw not a Frenchman but a British dragoon. An officer. The man was reloading his pistol, as if he planned to take another shot at Keane. Silver, keeping his hand on Keane, pushed him away, trying to move him back towards where the Portuguese were reforming to see off the French. 'That was one of ours, sir, what took a shot at you. I swear it. One of our officers.'

Keane turned his head and saw Blackwood, red-faced and waving one hand in which he held a pistol, as he tried to push through the press of horsemen in the direction of Keane and Silver.

'I know. I know who it was.' Silver was still pulling at Rattler's harness, but Keane was having none of it. 'Let go, Silver. This is my fight.'

'Sir, I don't understand. That's one of our officers, ain't it?'

'Yes. One of ours. Now let me go, man.'

Blood streaming down his arm, Keane at last pulled Rattler free from Silver's grasp and turned her towards Blackwood. Using his left hand for a moment, he placed his sword hilt in his bloody right hand and grasped it as firmly as he could. He could see Blackwood aiming his pistol again, trying to focus on Keane through the melee of bodies. Keane was closing now through the sweaty, bloody crush, driving Rattler on with his spurs. There was a flash, and in front of him a French dragoon jolted in the saddle. He looked through the smoke and saw Blackwood beyond the dead dragoon, desperately reloading the pistol. Keane pushed on, screaming at the horse and digging in with his irons. His sword was held in a vice-like grip now although the blood had soaked his white glove and the sword knot. And then suddenly there was a space, just big enough for him and Rattler, directly in front of Blackwood. The man was still reloading, fumbling with the hammer. He looked up and Keane could see the one thing in his eyes he had never seen there before. Fear. Keane raised his sword arm with the last of his strength and brought the blade down upon Blackwood's shoulder, cutting through the bone and flesh and deep into his chest. Blackwood froze for an instant, his eyes still wide and staring at Keane. His expression seemed to change to one of bewilderment and then he dropped the gun. And as he did so the wound opened up, spurting blood across his tunic. One last look into Keane's eyes and he had fallen from the saddle, and then all that Keane knew was that he had a strong hand on his shoulder and someone was pulling him away. His mind, still alert, began to fill with awful thoughts of what he had just done, but then the pain from his wound kicked in and he became less clear.

And now they were among friends. The young Portuguese officer was still alive, although his tunic was bloody from a sabre cut. Heredia was with him and Morris. Morris turned to Keane and his eyes were wide with horror. 'I saw it, James. Saw Blackwood try to kill you. I'll testify. Self-defence, James.'

Keane tried to smile through the pain in his arm, which had kicked in after the shock. 'Do you suppose so? Let's get out of this place while we still can. We have too many enemies here.'

The guerrillas were in among the French wounded now, slitting throats and stabbing and cutting off fingers and ears to take the gold rings. The Light Dragoons were scattered, some still in the French lines where they had gone in pursuit of the infantry, some intermingled with the guerrillas and some – too many, even after Keane's intervention – lying dead and dying on the ground among their horses and their foes. And the guerrillas dispatched them too. Death made no distinction between friend and enemy, and British gold was worth just as much as that of the French.

Quickly, urged on by Morris and Ross, the men made a square of horses around Keane and, at the suggestion of the Portuguese officer, positioned themselves in the centre troop of the squadron. Then, in column of march, they started off on the road, away from the retreating Spanish and back to the British lines.

General Wellesley's camp lay less than a day's march away. Nevertheless, it was with great relief that Keane found himself, bandaged and refreshed, standing before the tent lines. His men stood before him as Sergeant Ross had lined them up. Silver, Gilpin, Martin, Garland, Heredia and Ross himself. Morris stood a little way off, and Gabriella close to one of the tents.

Keane cradled his bound arm. 'I wanted to thank you, all of you. We've come through a good deal in the last few months. We started as nothing, no more than two officers and a group of men on whom the army had given up. There were some who said that what we were doing was pointless. But some believed in us. I can tell you now that they are pleased with what we have achieved. And so am I. I'm proud to call you my company and I know that soon our numbers will swell. You were nothing, worse than nothing, in the army's eyes. Well, now you're something. You're my men. James Keane's company, and you should be proud of that.'

Martin spoke. 'We are, sir, damn proud.' There was a chorus

of ayes and as Keane acknowledged them he was conscious of someone riding up behind him. He turned to see Grant.

'Sir?'

'Keane. Don't let us disturb your parade. You have done well, men.'

Keane looked up at Grant and saw that his face was as grave as he had ever seen it.

Nevertheless, Keane met it with a smile. It was not returned. 'You need me, sir?'

'This is a bad business, Keane. A proper bad business.'

'I quite agree, sir.'

'A word, if you will.'

Grant dismounted and was followed by Scovell, who had ridden up behind.

'Lieutenant Morris. Will you join us?'

The four men, led by Grant, walked a little distance from where the men were standing. Keane called to Ross. 'Stand the men easy, sarn't.'

Grant turned on him. 'What have you to say of this matter? Sir Arthur is most distressed.'

'You know the facts, sir, as outlined in my report.'

'I have read the report. It does not read well. You say that Captain Blackwood attempted to shoot you?'

'He did, sir. Here, and then again.'

Grant said nothing. Then, 'And you are quite sure of this? Be honest, man.'

'As sure as I have ever been of anything, sir.'

'And you, Lieutenant Morris. You say that you saw Captain Blackwood shoot Captain Keane? You swear to it?'

Morris nodded, solemnly. 'I am afraid that I did, sir, and I do. I should not have reported it thus, otherwise.'

Grant stroked his chin. 'Well, it's a bad business. A bad business, that is what it is. Sir Arthur is, to say the least, surprised. He has known Blackwood's father these many years, since they were boys. He always found Captain Blackwood a most amiable young man. And his sister too, most charming.'

He suddenly fixed Keane with a stare so piercing and so deliberate that the latter blanched. But realizing that he was being tested, he did not flinch from returning it.

'You do know, Keane, that there are several witnesses who saw you kill Captain Blackwood?'

'I imagine there must be, sir. Do you suppose they will be called?'

Grant looked at him. 'Do you suppose they will, Captain Keane?' He shook his head. 'A bad business, gentlemen, but we have no time for it now. Nor for other matters. We know, Keane, thanks to you, that we have a spy in our own camp. And that too we shall deal with presently, along with the matter of Captain Blackwood. For the moment, however, I have more pressing work than either of these unpleasantnesses. We have a battle to fight and we must beat the French. And on that count, Keane, I have a task for you.'

'An order, sir?'

'Yes, Keane. I should be obliged once again if you would take your men out in advance of the army.'

'Sir?'

'A reconnaissance. I need intelligence.'

'Of whom, sir? The guerrillas? Or the Spanish?'

'Neither, Keane. We require fresh intelligence of the French forces up ahead. Sebastiani and Victor. Both of their armies. Sir Arthur intends to give battle tomorrow and to carry the field. We want numbers, Keane, dispositions, batteries, strengths and weaknesses. The ground we already know. It is about that town of which you told me. On the Tagus, near those two hills.'

Keane recalled instantly the place on the road to Madrid. A place where a valley ran east to west in the shadow of the sierra, and where olive groves covered the gentle slopes of a hill on ground covered with farms and orchards.

'Talavera, sir.'

'Talavera, yes. And after Talavera there will be much for you to do.'

Keane nodded. He knew too that when the time came, when Victor and Sebastiani and Jerome and Ney had been driven back beyond Madrid, there would be more to do, much more, before they would find the way forward.

And he knew too, only too well, that after they had fought this battle, and settled the business with Pritchard, he would take his men out again, would see the French and would give his reports. And then he would have done all that an exploring officer could do, and perhaps a good deal more. And then it would be the job of the general to finish the business.

# HISTORICAL NOTE

Wellesley's opening campaign on his return to Portugal was one of the most masterly of his career, culminating in the major victory over the French at the battle of Talavera.

Twenty days after being given command of the army in Portugal, on 22 April 1809 Wellesley disembarked at Lisbon. The Portuguese army was demoralized and disorganized and the French had a strong foothold in the country. In late March the French under Marshal Soult had seized Oporto (today named Porto) and sacked the city slaughtering thousands of the inhabitants. In fact by April Soult was ready to retire to Spain. He had almost lost contact with the army of Marshal Ney in Galicia and felt insecure and isolated.

Wellesley resolved to push Soult out and moved his force to Coimbra, sending Beresford and the Portuguese to block Soult's escape eastwards from Oporto.

The truth of the battle is not dissimilar to Keane's account.

On the morning of 12 May, a Colonel Waters was reconnoitring the river Douro at the east end of Oporto when he was approached by a Portuguese barber who led him to a hidden skiff. There he also found the prior of the Serra convent and a handful of peasants. Ordered by the prior, they took the British officer across the river, and returned with four wine barges.

Wellesley then ordered the army across. First over was a company of the 3rd Foot (the Buffs) who occupied a walled seminary to the east of the city. Soon they had been followed by the rest of the battalion.

Soult was unaware of any of this but General Foy, realizing what was happening, led three battalions of the 17th Light Infantry against the seminary at around 11:30 a.m. and was beaten back. The French attacked again in greater force. But the British too had been reinforced and beat them off.

Soult now withdrew his troops guarding the boats on the river to reinforce Foy's attack on the seminary and immediately the French left the riverside, the people of Porto began to ferry more British troops over further downstream. The French, who had planned to retreat in good order, were forced to flee.

The British lost 125 men. Wellesley's second-in-command, General Paget, lost his arm. The French suffered 1,800 casualties. Soult was forced to abandon all his equipment and retreat through the hills to the north. The British advanced to Braga, forcing Soult to retreat further north-east. During the disastrous retreat, Soult's corps lost 4,500 men, its entire military chest filled with thousands of silver crowns and all its guns and baggage.

Wellesley now considered his strategy. With his 20,000 men he advanced into Spain to join 33,000 Spanish under General Cuesta. Together they marched up the river Tagus to Talavera, 120 km to the south west of Madrid.

Here on the two days of 27 and 28 July 1809, Wellesley

confronted a third French army under Victor and Sebastiani
and Napoleon's brother Joseph and won the first great victory
of his peninsular career, as a consequence of which he was
created Viscount Wellington.

It is fair to say however, that things might have been very
different had it not been for the efforts of his intelligencers
and exploring officers.

In 1809 the army intelligence service, of which Keane's
command becomes a component, was in its infancy. With the
growing threat from France after 1805, General Brownrigg, the
Quartermaster-General of the British Army, had approached
the Commander in Chief, the Duke of York, with a proposal
for a Depot of Military Intelligence on the model of Napoleon's
notorious Bureau d'Intelligence.

Wellington, taking his cue from Brownrigg and realizing the
value of intelligence in the Peninsula, organized his own corps
of 'exploring officers', recruiting men who were fine horsemen,
linguists, and able to write and draw. They worked hand in
hand with George Scovell's Corps of Guides who performed
recce, courier and espionage duties.

Both Brownrigg and Wellington had a hard time however
recruiting competent officers who might win easier promotion on the battlefield. There were few willing 'James Bonds'
at the time. Almost every capable officer posted to the Depot
soon had himself posted elsewhere. It was thought beneath
the dignity of an officer to dabble in the business of spying,
which was tainted with the whiff of treachery and dishonour
and Keane, already perceived as a maverick, instantly finds
himself further shunned by many of his fellow officers.

Men like Keane, whom we would today see as heroes, were damned for shirking the 'real' fighting. And so he always does what he can to ensure that, apart from doing his best for Wellington and of course himself, he and his men are always seen to be somewhere in the thick of it in the major battles.

One of the duties of Wellington's exploring officers, when the fighting was scarce, was to map the Portuguese and Spanish countryside. Also, under the command of George Scovell, Colquhoun Grant and others, they liaised with the guerrillas to obtain information from French prisoners, and leaders such as the real characters of Morillo and Cuevillas were renowned for their ruthlessness and cruelty. Needless to say in the course of the war most of the 'exploring officers' were captured or killed. They have never been given the full credit they deserve in Wellington's victory.

The exploring officers built their own networks of spies and spymasters, armed with money from Wellington and Grant. The guerrillas made a point of intercepting French dispatch riders but the dispatches were in code. George Scovell was the most famous cryptologist in Wellington's army, helping to break the Great Paris Cipher, the Napoleonic equivalent of the WWII 'Enigma' story.

In the course of the war, most of the exploring officers were either captured or killed. It was without doubt one of the most dangerous jobs in Wellington's army and the time has come for these unsung heroes to at last enjoy their fair share of glory.

James Keane will advance through the bloodbath of Talavera and go on to explore again with his band of talented jailbirds in the service of the newly created Viscount Wellington.

*

There is a wealth of non-fiction writing on the war in English, Spanish and French.

Napier's six-volume masterwork has been the benchmark for British readers for almost two hundred years and its maps remain exceptional. For colour, Ian Fletchers's *Wellington's Battlefields Revisited* is as evocative as it gets. One of the best recent complete accounts is the history of the war by Charles Esdaile, whose *Fighting Napoleon* is also the most comprehensive narritive to date of the guerrilla war.

Julia Page's *Intelligence Officer in the Peninsula*, a life of Edward Charles Cocks, is invaluable on the exploring officers, and Jock Haswell's classic 1969 biography of Colquhoun Grant is a good read, if you can get it.

Mark Urban's peninsular scholarship is again in evidence in the searching biography of George Scovell: *The man who broke Napoleon's Code*.